A Frank Waters Reader

A Frank Waters Reader

A SOUTHWESTERN LIFE IN WRITING

edited by Thomas J. Lyon

Swallow Press/Ohio University Press

Athens

Swallow Press/Ohio University Press,
Athens, Ohio 45701
© 2000 by the Frank Waters Foundation
Printed in the United States of America
All rights reserved. Published 2000

Swallow Press/Ohio University Press books are printed on acid-free paper ⊗ ™

09 08 07 06 05 04 03 02 01 00   5 4 3 2 1

Excerpts from the writings of Frank Water are reprinted by permission of Barbara Waters and the Frank Waters Estate from the following sources:

The Wild Earth's Nobility (New York: Liveright, 1935), pp. 309–30.

Below Grass Roots (New York: Liveright, 1937), pp. 256–70.

Masked Gods: Navaho and Pueblo Ceremonialism, 2d ed. (Denver: Sage Books, Swallow Press, 1950), pp. 92–100.

The Colorado in The Rivers of America series, ed. Hervey Allen and Carl Carmer (New York: Rinehart, 1946), pp. 17–25.

The Dust within the Rock (New York: Liveright, 1940), pp. 320–34.

Fever Pitch (New York: Liveright, 1930), pp. 170–80.

The Yogi of Cockroach Court (New York: Rinehart, 1947), pp. 171–73, 235–39, 251–63.

People of the Valley (Denver: Sage Books, Swallow Press, 1941), pp. 160–207.

Of Time and Change: A Memoir (Denver: MacMurray and Beck, 1998), pp. 70–99.

The Man Who Killed the Deer (Athens: Swallow Press/Ohio University Press, 1942, 1970), pp. 120–41, 164–84.

The Woman at Otowi Crossing, rev. ed. (Athens: Swallow Press/Ohio University Press, 1987), vi–1, 3–30, 120–27, 168–74, 312–14.

Pumpkin Seed Point: Being within the Hopi (Chicago: Sage Books, Swallow Press, 1969), pp. xi–xii, 1–13, 43–54, 63–73.

Mountain Dialogues (Athens: Swallow Press/Ohio University Press, 1981, 1999), pp. 3–34, 49–55.

Flight from Fiesta (Athens: Swallow Press/Ohio University Press, 1987), 72–80.

Library of Congress Cataloging-in-Publication Data

Waters, Frank, 1902–
[Selections. 1999]
A Frank Waters reader : a Southwestern life in writing / edited by Thomas J. Lyon.
   p. cm.
Includes bibliographical references.
ISBN 0-8040-1025-0 (alk. paper) —ISBN 0-8040-1026-9 (pbk.: alk. paper)
   1. West (U.S.)—Fiction. 2. Southwest, New—Fiction. 3. Mysticism—Fiction.
4. West (U.S.)—Description and travel. 5. Southwest, New—Description and travel. I. Lyon, Thomas J. (Thomas Jefferson), 1937– II. Title.

PS3545.A82 A6 1999
818'.5209—dc2   00-024432

CONTENTS

ILLUSTRATIONS

Following page 184:

Cutler Hall, 1878

Frank Waters's parents on their wedding day, May 7, 1901

Frank Waters's house of birth, 435 E. Bijou St., Colorado Springs

Pikes Peak from E. Bijou St.

Gallegos Wash, northwestern New Mexico

Victor, Colorado

Pikes Peak, as seen from Victor, Colorado

Frank Waters's high school graduation photo, 1921

Frank Waters in southern California, about 1927

Mora Valley, New Mexico

Taos Mountain and Pueblo land

Doroteo "Frank" Zamora and Frank Waters, Arroyo Seco,
     New Mexico, 1969

Aspen gate at Arroyo Seco, 1952

Frank Waters at Nevada Test Site, 1953

Rio Grande at Otowi Crossing, New Mexico

Pumpkin Seed Point

The Waters house in Arroyo Seco

Frank Waters at the Manchester Gallery, El Prado, New Mexico

El Cuchillo del Medio

Pueblo Peak

ACKNOWLEDGMENTS

Frank Waters's publisher, Swallow Press, has been most generous in its support of this collection. In particular, Senior Editor Gillian Berchowitz has furthered the book each step of the way. Mary Ann Torrence, of Cloudcroft, New Mexico, supplied copies of the three *El Crepusculo* editorials included here. Karen V. Mitchell, of the Carlsbad, California, Public Library, used the magic of interlibrary loan on this book's behalf. To Barbara Waters, whose knowledge of Frank Waters and his work is of course without peer, goes credit for the conception of a Waters "portable," and profound thanks for many succeeding suggestions and kindnesses. Ida Murdock of Kikotsmovi, Arizona, whose brother Oswald White Bear Fredericks worked with Waters on *Book of the Hopi,* provided invaluable help. "Navajo Bob" of Carson's Trading Post in New Mexico aided in the search for "Shallow Water," as did Dave Simonds, Archeologist, in the Bureau of Land Management Field Office, Farmington, New Mexico. Mark Lyon, of Lyon & Associates, Encinitas, California; Tom Seawell, of Seawell Photography, San Francisco; and Stella Kalaw, of Kalaw Photography, San Francisco, deserve very great thanks for their work with this book's photographs. Ginny Kiefer, Curator of Special Collections in the Tutt Library, The Colorado College, provided the archive photograph of Cutler Hall. All of these fine people made this book possible, and my contribution as gatherer pleasant work indeed. Thank you.

Thomas J. Lyon
Carlsbad, California

INTRODUCTION

Over the course of a twenty-seven-book career, Frank Waters dealt with the most excruciating contradictions of the twentieth century: our heroic technology, concurrent with spiritual impoverishment; our racial and ethnic antagonisms, persisting while we knit the world together mechanically; our declining sense of nature, fading as we gain almost godlike knowledge of the workings of biology. And underneath all this dissonance lies the divided modern self—mostly egoist-accountant-technician, perhaps, but still some part poet. In the face of the general fragmentation, Waters quested lifelong for what heals and unifies.

Unearthing his themes in his own background and life, Frank Waters appears to have sensed early that the world had its correlative in the inward dimension, and that his own narrative, including family background, could be a legitimate point of entry. In a real sense, he wrote his life, but without the obsessive self-centeredness that characterizes so much modern "confessional" literature. More steadily than most writers of his century, he focused not so much on the separate individual as on the idea of the one big picture, the unity.

So it is that nature and the West he lived in—the spare lines of the landscape, the clouds blooming overhead, the scent of pines, the heat of the air on a July day in New Mexico, the companionableness of horses, the mysterious feeling of belonging to the pattern—are Waters's basic reference. The Southwest is where the wholeness touched him. Sense of place in his writing is palpable, and a conduit to all issues. The residue left upon the imagination by a Frank Waters book, above all, is a feeling of where it takes place. This effect is vastly deeper than some sort of local color; it is a sense of being located, and through a particular location, with its lines and shapes and ambient sounds, of having the feel of the totality.

This matter of actual footing is worth emphasizing, because Waters is known as a mystic, and in our culture mysticism usually connotes otherworldliness. Within our dualistic tradition, nature and "the body," as the phrase has it, are thought to be different from, lesser than, perhaps even antagonistic to, spiritual insight. In this tradition, where you are is only a setting, a kind of stage for your drama—you yourself are engaged with more important matters. Any number of spiritual seekers and groups, in the "New Age" as in past times, have dedicated themselves to enlightenment or salvation strictly as a matter of personal sensibility, personal grace. The focus is upon the individual's consciousness or soul, seen separate from trees, wind, and soil. In the dominant paradigm, these are only "the environment," and are, for all intents and purposes, spiritually blank.

Frank Waters was never indifferent to nature and place. Some of his earliest memories, as recorded in his autobiographical fiction, are of the looming presence of Pikes Peak—the landmark by which the way to and from school was navigated surely. The known world was structured on that mountain, a real, present mass of reddish granite rising abruptly and hugely into blue, cloud-decked sky. Just to the west of the Pikes Peak massif itself, at about the age of ten, young Frank Waters had a very strong, direction-setting experience, which he later described in *The Colorado* (see chapter 4.) As a young man, the autobiographical protagonist "March Cable," depicted in *The Dust within the Rock*, bathed in the pool of a hot spring originating on Pikes Peak, and while relishing there the sensations of a stormy spring afternoon, again experienced the core feeling of ego-transcendence and oneness with nature—"a brilliant and indestructible illumination," Waters wrote (see chapter 5). As it happened, March made a big decision that afternoon. Significantly, Waters's initial foray into the writing of fiction (in 1925, when he was twenty-three) began with a description of an intense, transcendental experience in a desert landscape. Dramatized in his writing over the years, instances of deeply felt experience of place are more than just numerous: they are the armature upon which the writing is built.

It is revealing of the nature of his mind that Waters's delineations of place show simultaneously the particular dimension and the abstract-philosophical. Nature is both close around the body and as big and totalizing as thought can conceive. On the one hand, the leathery leaves of cottonwoods, rustling and clicking in the breeze at Otowi Crossing; on the other, the "wholeness in which every part is interrelated in one vast body of universal Creation" (*Mountain Dialogues*). If there were only the leaves, you might have at best imagism, and the potential for a kind of poetry. If there were only the wholeness, you might have metaphysics, and the potential merely for philosophizing. But Waters's great movement as a writer is to reach toward a full, proportionate expression in which both aspects of any given duality take part.

The specific places which for Waters hold this simultaneous physical-spiritual intensity are in the dry quarter of the country, and it is his connected, reaching-toward-totality consciousness of place that has made him one of the archetypal southwestern writers. There is the sense that a described place is at once out there in the world and deep within ourselves. In his "Introduction" to W. Y. Evans-Wentz's *Cuchama and Sacred Mountains,* Waters indicated his direction succinctly: "We have yet to fully realize that the physical and psychical realms are two aspects of one transcendental unity."

The aura of the Southwest has always been both intensely colored and somewhat rarefied—this has been noted by just about every writer, painter, or historian who has become acquainted with the area. It is gritty and spiritual, both; as mundane as potshards on the ground and as portentous as the future. Waters registers the colorful paradox of "Indian Country" perfectly. Only Mary Austin among writers, or D. H. Lawrence, was as ready as Waters to grant this region universal importance and possible redemptive power. Lawrence averred that it was his experience of New Mexico, "Curious as it may sound . . . that liberated me from the present era of civilization, the great era of material and mechanical development." Austin went so far as to prophesy that the Southwest would generate, as she put it, the "next great and fructifying world culture." And it was not mere random choice, probably, that led Aldous Huxley to locate his "Brave New World's" savage reservation, the dystopic future's one saving remnant of spontaneity and wildness, in New Mexico. Into our consumer era, famously a time of mass media and falseness, when even the Southwest has become a boutique item, Frank Waters's portrayal of the region retains both its authentic detail and its mysterious, beyond-all-markets resonance.

Along with his scrupulously equal regard for the physical reality and spiritual import of landscape, Waters habitually insisted upon overcoming the dualism of rational thought versus intuition, within human psychology. His core idea is that both particle and wave, as it were, are necessary parts of the whole. Although he realized that his own culture was strongly tilted toward the "particle" side of things, mentally, and stood in need of corrective balance, he refused to elevate one aspect of consciousness over the other. In *Pumpkin Seed Point,* he describes a horseback descent to the bottom of the Barranca de Urique in Mexico, one of the deepest gorges on earth and thus a fine symbol for the depths of nonrational consciousness. We need to go down into that canyon—if we never make the journey, we remain superficial. But such a return to "the depths of his [mankind's] archaic past in the fathomless unconscious," as Waters put it, must be combined with the "upper" layers of consciousness to foster genuine growth and a more complete psychic life. Only the whole equals health. The Tarahumara Indians of the deep canyon seemed revealing to Waters: their dark eyes expressed the "wild remoteness of the Barranca itself, the withdrawn look of a people who had not yet emerged from their dark depths; a pleading look, like that of an animal which begs [for] the light of understanding." Clearly, he means to depict them as incomplete, rather than as a model of unspoiledness. Their softness has a certain attraction, but it is not enough.

The Pueblo Indians may offer a different story. According to Waters's portrayal in both *The Man Who Killed the Deer* (1942) and *Masked Gods* (1950), the Pueblo tribes may have recognized humanity's need to integrate the two main dimensions of the mind—a major insight. Thus they would be further along, evolutionarily speaking, than either the mild, intuitive natives of the barranca or the hard-surfaced Anglos of rationalist/mechanist notoriety. In the climactic Deer Dance of *The Man Who Killed the Deer,* there is a ritual involving the polarity of individualism versus unity. Waters's protagonist Martiniano watches the dance with a "hypnotic horror," because what he is seeing is his own story. Individual animals dance toward the outer edge of the circle, particles trying to break free of the center, that deep source of energy connecting all. They dance toward the outside, but always there is the insistent rhythm of the Deer Mothers, at the center, drawing them back into relational unity. This is the dance of life. In the dance, both centripetal and centrifugal forces are at play and, if they are in balance, can create a beautiful pattern.

In human consciousness, the sense of separate selfhood is cognate with what is called rational, or linear, thought. That is one pole of our character, founded in one corner of the mind. The other is the impersonal or nonegoistic sense of embeddedness, deriving from the ability to perceive relation, configuration, pattern. Waters depicts the Pueblo ceremonials as dramas of this polarity. The dance of unity is itself the state of health, the desired, harmonious end of the ritual, and Waters's implication is that a people who have developed such an art form must be well along in the true Emergence. Martiniano, in *The Man Who Killed the Deer,* is slowly and haltingly learning this path, slowly opening up to his birthright range of consciousness. What makes *The Man Who Killed the Deer* one of the great novels of the inner life, and *Masked Gods* one of the farthest-reaching anthropological texts, is that Frank Waters holds so faithfully to the ultimate vision of health. He looks down each attractive byroad, but in the end the inclusive, paradoxical unity of nature is the only satisfying reference and standard. We rational skeptics do not measure up, and the gentle people of the barranca also may not, but the bloom of completeness stands before us as a common human goal. The vision of it probably constitutes our most important element of shared humanity. More than any other characteristic of his writing, it is his concentration on the transcendence of duality, his presentation of such elevation of vision as our shared work in this life, that makes Frank Waters an important writer.

Waters implies that wherever there is duality of some kind, there is also identity, and some degree of conflict. Whites differentiate themselves from Indians; men from women; human beings from the other animals; aliveness (as in a primate, mammal body) from unaliveness (as in a rock or a mountain). There is of course an element of truth in these and similar distinctions: seen by the rationalist side of consciousness, the world simply looks to be divided in this fashion. But if only that limited side of consciousness is working, or if it is excessively dominant, we will not see the complementary part of the big picture. We won't feel the relational pattern, nor, ultimately, the unity within all polarities. Nor will we rightly see the literal place where we are standing; we just don't realize, fully, the nature all around and within. Unseeing in this manner, we are apt to become structurally indifferent to the living quality of nature, to say nothing of its sacredness. Within a dualistically conceived world, stuck in identities, we are compelled to live in conflicts of one kind or another, all the way up to the insanities of racism and nationalism.

Frank Waters's central fictional characters are depicted on this map of consciousness. March Cable, Martiniano, the Woman at Otowi Crossing, and Tai Ling, the Yogi of Cockroach Court, all have at least intimations of the greater view, the hypothetical release from suffering and incompleteness that an integrated consciousness would bring. The Woman at Otowi Crossing actually emerges from self-partiality into a weight-free perception unbound by issues of identity. But the others are struggling, learning. Like the rest of us, they live in a culture that prizes self and identity, thinks mountains are spiritually unalive, and believes as an article of faith that all problems can be solved rationally and pragmatically. They have not awakened to the suppressed dimensions of consciousness. These presently hidden, relation-seeing powers, in a state of atrophy from disuse, amount to a kind of shadow country within.

In his major fiction, Waters's plots at their essence are straightforward. There is a movement out of the whole long human background of self, family, tradition, and seeming cultural necessity, toward emergence into compassionate, full seeing. His stories are dramas of consciousness and character.

The protagonists are learners, and for the portrayal to be experienceable, democratically available, the author also must be in a state of passionate openness, must himself be a learner. We are not talking so much about knowledge here, on the part of these characters and their author, for that is a function of the "thought" side of consciousness, and could be conveyed in a lecture. What is required here, in the fullness of life, is humble, character-opening experience itself, marked by vulnerability. It is perhaps telling that Frank Waters, as late as 1950 and *Masked Gods,* referred to himself as "the boy," as if eschewing the temptations of authority. Apparently he regarded the nondual level of insight as something that needed to be earned, and continually re-earned. In a fashion comparable to the yearly rituals of the Pueblo and Hopi people, Waters seemed to reenact the search for the great harmony, the great unity, with each new book.

This focus on the theme of transcendence might appear intellectually simple or even programmatic, considered in isolation as an idea extracted from books, but it seems clear that such a concentration was Frank Waters's own real, life work. Far more complex than a mere idea, the search for integration is heart work, character work.

Following the forthright leads in Waters's autobiographical fiction, we can see some of the origins of this practice in his background and early years. His mother, whose maiden name was May Ione Dozier, came from a solid Colorado Springs family whose standing in the town derived from her father Joseph Dozier's success as a builder. Dozier was one of the early settlers of Colorado Springs and as a trusted contractor had built several public buildings, including the first on the campus of The Colorado College (Cutler Hall, still in use). He was a man whose success was founded on strong will and strong principles. As Joseph Rogier in *The Wild Earth's Nobility* (1935), *Below Grass Roots* (1937), *The Dust within the Rock* (1940), and the decades-later redaction of these works, *Pike's Peak* (1971), this grandfather figure came to epitomize an imposing, mechanically triumphant, rational culture in its early days of glory. But Rogier (and Dozier as well?) also had an "oriental" side, revealed in his reading of Hindu and Buddhist texts and perhaps also in his liking for nonrational intuitions about mountains and treasure. After resisting for years the gold and silver fevers that had animated the life of Colorado Springs, Joseph Rogier gave in to his hunch that gold could be found in unimaginable quantities if only one were to bypass the relatively easy pickings just "below grass roots" and sink a shaft deep into Pikes Peak itself. In the novels, Waters portrays this drive to dig as an obsession, a trope for the search into the unconscious. Rogier/Dozier was not a simple man.

Nevertheless, the Dozier family tradition chiefly embodied mainstream Euro-American mentality and values, and as a typical family in class-conscious Colorado Springs (known at the time as "Little London") the Doziers naturally prized outward appearance. Thus life became more than just economically difficult when Joseph Dozier sunk his fortune into an unprofitable mine called the "Sylvanite," or "our family folly," as Frank Waters later termed it. The mine may have been a deep shaft into the mystery of life, but practically, Waters depicts it as ruinous for the family. The Rogiers/Doziers struggled to maintain some sense of their former status. Ione, called "Ona" in the novels, kept her father's accounts and became increasingly important in holding the family together.

One of the boarders in the big house at 435 East Bijou Street was a dark-complected, quiet man from the midwestern plains of Iowa, a man of a certain mystery. Frank Jonathon Waters ("Jonathon Cable") and Ione Dozier ("Ona Rogier"), described in the novels by their son as psychic opposites, were powerfully attracted to each other. In the books, there are strong hints, and more than hints, that "Jonathon Cable" was at least part Cheyenne. I have not pursued his historical prototype's genealogy, believing that what is of consequence here is that Frank Waters ("March Cable") perceived and was affected by unmistakable differences and oppositions between his parents. With their inherited "White" practicality and rationalism (the hand and the brain, so to speak) and from the other side a "Red" softness of intuition (the heart), Waters's mother and father were the makers of the map of his life.

That the differences between his parents had strong emotional impact on their first-born is shown clearly in *Below Grass Roots,* where Ona and Jonathon compete vigorously with each other for young March's allegiance. Waters describes the boy as "wavering" between them (see the excerpt in chapter 2), and in numerous scenes of conflict, or simple lack of communication, there is no doubting the stress of an emotionally divided household. The division begins with the basic one of gender, of course, in this case presumably exacerbated by racial background, with added tension coming from a difficult economic situation. It could not have been an easy or straightforward childhood.

The death of Frank Jonathon Waters in 1914 meant that Ione, with twelve-year-old Frank and his little sister Naomi, had to move back into the Dozier household. Superficially at least, life would now be lived on "White" terms, with the declining and eccentric Grandfather Dozier as the family's central figure. The "Red," of course, would not be effaced entirely; it would become the shadow element, the always looked-for. Waters had already had that profound, consciousness-integrating experience at the age of ten, on the tailings pile at the family mine, and he retained its taste of mysterious fulfillment as a kind of hidden gauge by which to measure what people accepted at home and in town as normal life. That tailings-pile experience probably helped make him a lifelong learner, because it stood glowing in memory as an example of the unexpectable, a refutation of all pat answers and all authorities.

Through high school and in his three-year study at Colorado College in the engineering department, Frank Waters tried manfully to play the roles expected of him, but something quite apart from the views of genteel, progressive, material-mechanical society, and in fact from the entire habit of mind of the culture he lived within, was simmering inside.

Soon after he had dropped out of college and left the family house, chance or, more likely, internal gravitation took him southward. He worked on and off for eleven years in El Centro, California, an Imperial Valley location less than ten miles from Mexico. The border region with its mixed-blood population, and then the vast and intimidating desert regions to the south, fascinated Waters. His initial attempts at fiction were set there. But first, it should be noted that this young man, working for the Southern California Telephone Company as an engineer, had indeed become passionately interested in writing. Judging by the content of his earliest efforts, it seems safe to say that he practiced writing as an inner, psychological, perhaps therapeutic exercise. In any case, he began by dramatizing his inward life. *Fever Pitch,* which was finished in 1925 (though not published until 1930), is a short, highly dramatic adventure story, told in a Conrad-like frame, in which a young engineer and a woman friend cross an expanse of wild desert to a gold claim being guarded by an associate of the woman's. The plot itself is almost a throwaway, perhaps embarrassing to Waters in later years—he was opposed to a 1955 paperback reissue of the novel. What is significant is that, by his report, the first fictional scene he ever wrote described the young engineer at a peak of intense experience, in the midst of wild nature. "Lee Marston's" awareness of the rocks and mountains and immense desert playas around him soared beyond rational accounting; "standing there alone in that immensity of creation and alone in the presence of God, he bowed his will to an omnipotent power of nature." "It is at such times," Waters continued, "that a man in an uplift of spirit loses all conception of the present and has removed from him forever that recognition of time and space into which he has been born" (see the excerpt in chapter 6).

The language of this first novel tries hard to express the inexpressible, perhaps a little too hard. But whatever one may think of the book's artistry, it is clear that Waters began as a writer by sincerely trying to capture the mysterious. In a way, he was occupied with his own Grandfather Dozier–like digging. As further evidence of this kind of motivation, he took up at this time a study of the Buddhist approach to enlightenment, incorporating it into his next piece of writing. This new project would turn out to be a longer, much more complex novel. It described the intermeshed lives of four people in a squalid border town, having as its centerpiece the quest of one of them, a Chinese shopkeeper, for release from all internal contradictions and all entanglements in ego-based, ordinary life. This search is noble, solitary in its intentions, and, as Waters depicts it, oddly self-contradictory. The Chinese man, Tai Ling, has to learn that to seek enlightenment in this way is in effect to be deluded, by reason of having objectified that which cannot be separated from life itself. Tai Ling puts years into his striving, while the life-plots of those around him run their tangled courses. The significance of this ambitious book in Waters's life is shown by his finishing a first draft in 1927, continuing to work on the story for two decades (putting it through several further drafts), and finally publishing it only in 1947. It is unique in American fiction, I believe, in focusing on the paradoxical nature of meditation, or the search for enlightenment. It clearly shows Waters's sense that rationalistic, objectifying consciousness tends to create contradiction. Tai Ling is forced to learn that truth is only experienceable, only totalistic, not something separate arrived at by force of will or intellect. It takes him years to discover this.

Frank Waters was not a writer attracted by Europe—he never went there—nor the wilderness North, certainly not the urban East. His compass always seemed to point toward the magnetic pole of indigenous, Indian life, in the Southwest and Mexico. In 1931, he rode horseback on a solo trip of several hundred miles, down the Sierra Madre

Occidental into the heart of back-country Mexico, staying with campesino families, sleeping on the floors of their simple houses, eating the country food, always on the intent lookout, one might imagine, for any hints and clues toward an understanding of what was indigenous in himself. This was neither his first nor last earnest journey southward.

Much of the decade of the nineteen-thirties was occupied by the writing of the family saga-autobiographical trilogy, *The Wild Earth's Nobility* (1935), *Below Grass Roots* (1937), and *The Dust within the Rock* (1940). The project represented, obviously, a venture toward the understanding of self, and was accompanied by a series of significant geographical moves. The first volume was written after the Mexico journey, as if certain understandings had begun to jell down there, in close contact with native people. In 1936, quitting the telephone company, Waters moved to Victor, Colorado, for some months (very near the site of Grandfather Dozier's mine), then to Mora, New Mexico, a small village in the Hispanic hill country. He began writing full-time. In 1937 and 1938, he spent time in Taos, New Mexico, moved back to Mora, and then finally settled in Taos—all the while, during this circling, writing another draft of *The Yogi of Cockroach Court*, a concluding volume of the trilogy, and finally, his first novel really to make a mark, *People of the Valley* (1941). His growing concentration, in the writing, on the theme of integration and transcendence of duality appeared to occur in synergy with his step-by-step zeroing in on the Taos area as his home of choice. The thirties and first couple of years of the forties saw Frank Waters gradually establish both his métier and literal home base as a writer.

Between *The Dust within the Rock* and *People of the Valley*, the narrative voice and locus of perception in Waters's writing shifted from young-white-progressive to ancient-indigenous-mature. This development seemed to be more in the nature of an emergence, to use one of Waters's favorite terms, than a sudden or reactive change. It had much to do, apparently, with coming to emplacement in Taos and with enjoying several friendships among Taoseños, including especially the Taos Pueblo Indian Tony Luhan and his wife Mabel Dodge Luhan, and the trader Ralph Meyers. Waters absorbed Taos intently, in both its community aspect and its spiritual-topographic aura.

People of the Valley represents deepening of Waters's capacities in two main areas: his main character is a woman, and the culture in which the story takes place is long-rooted, folkloric, Hispanic/New Mexican. Remarkable transpositions of consciousness are dramatized with confidence, almost as if from the inside. We believe instantly and completely in brown, fey Maria of the valley and her people, because we see, in detail and particularity, the way the world looks to them, and because their language patterns, smoothly lived into by Waters, give us their mind's rhythms. In the following year, Waters's evocation of the tribal voice in *The Man Who Killed the Deer* has similar authority. The italicized passages, in which the collective, traditional wisdom of the pueblo speaks, ring with a recognizable, sharable inwardness. It seems clear that Waters had "been there," seen enough of the psychological and philosophical territory of the elders to see, at the very least, how their nondualistic approach differed from the mental terrain he had grown up in. That he also intuited the divided and tortured sensibility of the main character Martiniano, and the also divided but somewhat resigned outlook of the trader Rodolfo Byers, as well as the unified, spiritually quickened mind of Martiniano's friend Palemon, altogether demonstrates that he was coming into the identity-entering, compassionate powers of a superior novelist. At the same time, by giving expression to the archaic potency of the landscapes of northern New Mexico, Waters grew in recognition as a voice of his chosen place.

The Colorado (1946) and *Masked Gods* (1950) gave that voice greater range and helped to solidify Waters's position as not only a significant regional writer but a cross-cultural student of humanity at large. In *The Colorado,* a volume in Rinehart's "Rivers of America" series, he gave expression to a powerful landscape notion, depicting the watershed of the Colorado River as an immense and alive pyramid with real connections to the nerves and spirits of all life forms dwelling on it. The land in this book is not merely a setting, it is coparticipant in a living, organismic system. But of course there have been people, even whole cultures, who did not realize this electric oneness, and so the history that has taken place in the watershed is marked by varying and conflicting mentalities. The great measure here is the ability to sense and to see—to have consciousness that ranges beyond the simply rational-mechanical, finally to apperceive the unity we all, land and people together, belong to. Failure to emerge into the greater consciousness would be a genuine human tragedy, a falling-short of global implications. Waters concludes "The Long View," *The Colorado*'s next-to-last chapter, with a concise summary:

> For all our technological achievements, our very lives
> tremble upon the delicate scales of nature. We are as ulti-
> mately dependent upon the ancient verities of land and
> sky as were the prehistoric cliff dwellers. Man has not yet
> completed the full circle toward a realization that his own
> laws of life must conform in the long view with those
> greater laws to which he still and forever owes allegiance.
> (370)

In Waters's conception of the "full circle," we moderns begin by following our bent toward rational and mechanistic thought as far as it can reach. We go as far as we can in seeing things one at a time. Eventually we begin to see that there must be something beyond the limits of such a procedure, and finally some of us see that what lies outside our favored powers seems in fact to have been intuited millennia ago—by people we commonly regard as less developed than ourselves. According to the outline set forth in *Masked Gods,* this arc toward realization is what many modern physicists traced. Searching with particle-seeing eyes for the ultimately tiny building blocks of matter, they discovered (in one of the great findings of modern science) that particle-seeing is a way of perception with a definite limit. A wider, softer perception would seem to be required for awareness of the shape-shifting between particle and energy-wave, and finally for awareness of the totally relational, unified nature of existence. When the twentieth-century physicists (some of whom, as it happened, worked on the atomic bomb at Los Alamos) came to the end of the road of one-thing-at-a-time thought, they stood in new wonder at the edge of the relativistic universe the Pueblo Indians, among other traditional peoples, had long contemplated. Full circle, indeed. (But it needs to be remembered that at Los Alamos these physicists were making bombs, hardly a holistic, unity-regarding activity. Realization isn't merely intellectual.) Waters finds it interesting that the canyons and plateaus of northern New Mexico should have been the setting in which the drive and power of the "White" rational approach sought security for its work, amid the color and mystic resonance of the "Red" culture's native landscape. But where, in real life on the ground, was the needed synthesis, the real completion of the circle?

Edith Warner, an unusual woman who in the 1930s and '40s ran a small café at the Otowi bridge over the Rio Grande, seemed to comprehend both elements of the needed integration. Poised exactly between the San Ildefonso Pueblo (where she had close friends) and the new, secret installation at Los Alamos, Warner seemed to be ideally placed for the illuminated view of life that in fact came to her. She became acquainted with many of the physicists from "the Hill" during the war, and at the same time maintained her ties with San Ildefonso; and in her inward life she apparently experienced a significant transcendence, so that her sense of place and nature became intense, and her mind—by the written evidence she left—open, still, and creative. She became locally well recognized, among both Indians and certain whites, as "one who knows."

Frank Waters began writing her story in fictional form, with the protagonist as "Helen Chalmers," as early as 1953. At this time he was working as an information specialist with the Atomic Energy

Commission, in the course of which assignment he had witnessed dozens of atomic-bomb tests, and had become intimately involved with the most advanced technical project of its time. His work with the AEC had given new scope to his innate rational-technical capacity, and perhaps also intensified the dissonance or discontinuity within the mind that Waters, as a child of the twentieth century, experienced with the rest of us. The same Frank Waters who had freighted his books of the 1930s with detailed exposition on mining now wrote technical reports and information releases for the most ingenious weapons makers on the planet. But he was also, still and ever, the same Frank Waters who like archaic man felt a profound, cellular, mystical connection with the earth.

Two views of existence. But Waters's writings from the 1940s and succeeding years reveal also the beginning of the projection of a third, much larger, in fact overarching, viewpoint. In terms of his contribution to the world, this ultimate or nondualistic view marks the essential Frank Waters. *The Woman at Otowi Crossing,* which after at least four drafts was finally published in 1966, conveys that higher understanding as clearly as any of his works. It tells the story of Helen Chalmers's coming into a timeless, intuitive, regardful view of existence, not dissimilar from that of some of her Indian friends. It also tells the stories of an atomic physicist who comes to the edge of the rational-empirical mentality; an academic careerist who works, sadly enough, to hide her heart; a respected member of the San Ildefonso Pueblo; and finally a bluff and folksy editor of a country weekly. Each has a close connection with Helen. All these characters' points of view are registered in a historically accurate plot involving humanity's development of atomic weapons. (As a race, we take a great and irrevocable step in this book.) Waters the novelist understands this tormented, mid-twentieth-century moment and also, at the individual level, empathizes with each person in the self-partiality of his or her consciousness, without condescension. This objectivity-with-sympathy suggests Waters's own profound, artistic integration.

The realized quality of Waters's viewpoint was apparent in his next two books to focus on issues of mind, *Pumpkin Seed Point* (1969) and *Mexico Mystique* (1975), and became evident as a comprehensive serenity in several of the essays in *Mountain Dialogues* (1981), particularly those dealing with his life in place in Arroyo Seco, New Mexico, just north of Taos. By the early 1980s, Frank Waters had become known (to a steady though comparatively small readership) as a writer with a large, evolutionary view on consciousness and a strongly felt, accessible sense of his home ground. In all three of the books just mentioned, he wrote familiarly from a philosophical synthesis entirely his own. Its elements seem not to have occurred to any other writer, in quite the Frank Waters fashion, yet in combination, in the end, they seem natural, even inevitable. There is, first, an Indian sense of existence, deeply attached to place and "soft," that is, intuitive, non-self-aggrandizing; second, an Eastern understanding of the mind, especially the point that its rational, ego-creating corner constitutes only a fraction of its range; and finally a Jungian approach to psychology and character, emphasizing the need to harmonize seeming opposites within (such as male and female dimensions), and also recognizing that we all share in collective, archetypal patterns at both conscious and unconscious levels. These are the three main influences on Frank Waters's thought, but his determinedly independent, even maverick, reliance on his own truth, and as a continuing influence his chosen southwestern emplacement, also need to be factored in. All of these elements, in a homemade combination, create the distinctive Waters voice.

There are any number of manners-and-morals novelists, and contemporary personal essayists, for whom enlightenment or apperception would perhaps be foreign territory. It took daring, or obsession perhaps, to write *The Yogi of Cockroach Court* at a young age, and to keep at it for two decades. Similarly, it took commitment, years later, to put together a long source study, a personal, Jungian understanding and a home-lover's sense of place and scene and make an anthropology out of these, in *Masked Gods* and *Book of the Hopi* (1963). But these leaps are, one can see, typical. In his long career, Frank Waters followed his intuition of unity faithfully, wherever it might lead and whatever words of rational caution various authorities might have laid down. His life and work represent a dedicated search for integration, and in this moral allegiance, "America's greatest unknown writer," as he is often called, may yet have something to say to our time.

A Frank Waters Reader

CHAPTER I

The Wild Earth's Nobility (1935)

In this passage from Frank Waters's autobiographical second novel, we see his East Bijou Street, Colorado Springs, household as he thought it would have appeared late in the 1890s, a few years before the author's birth. His parents ("Ona Rogier" and "Jonathon Cable") are just getting to know one another. Ona's grandmother, mother and father, sisters, and the absent Uncle Boné (who has musical talent, lives in the desert, in Indian country, and later will be something of an influence on the series' final protagonist, March Cable) are among the cast of characters. The head of the house is Joseph Rogier, who manifests his power with easy authority, but the real subject here is the compelling attraction, across worlds, between a young man and a young woman. This excerpt includes one of Waters's sharpest portraits of his father.

From *Book Three: Gold*

3

Late one afternoon Ona closed her ledgers and put away her papers. Feeling selfish for not hurrying home, she locked Rogier's office and strolled reluctantly down the steps. Mrs. Rogier had long forgotten that her work was supposed to be finished when she left the office and would be after her for a hundred trivial things. There was to be company for supper; everybody would be busy. And from last night on there would be no comforting solitude even at night. Sally Lee had rented her room and was going to share Ona's, the eight dollars a month to be halved between them for spending money. The new roomer had moved in late last night. It was he who was invited this evening for supper.

When Ona arrived home Mrs. Rogier, Sally Lee, and Mary Ann were out in the kitchen helping Lida Peck. Mrs. White with Nancy minding Big Joe were resting on the front porch. Ona sat down beside them. "Where's Daddy?" she asked.

"I reckon he ain't back from Denman's yet," Mrs. White drawled. "Akeepee's colt's been keepin' them all busy. He should sho' be a dandy, th' frisky little fella. Joe paid a heap to have his mammy bred."

"Well, I hope he turns out all right. Daddy was so cut up about Akeepee."

Mrs. White snorted, blinking her one eye furiously. "A lady to the bone, that hoss! It was the Judge that ruined her. Joe ought to of hosswhipped the skunk! Maybe he did—Colton has been layin' low evah since."

"Has the roomer come home yet?"

"Reckon not or Marthy and Sally would be buzzin' round him like flies ovah a sorghum barrel."

"Don't you like him?"

Mrs. White dug at the big wart on her finger. "I don't spare no feelin's foh any foreigner. Leastways a Jew or Indian. An' I allow this heah Cable is paht of 'em both. But Marthy'll be out heah to shake his hand soon enough," she ended contemptuously.

In a few minutes Mrs. Rogier came out and seated herself primly on a long bench, folding her hands in her lap. "I do hope Mr. Cable comes soon and that Daddy isn't late again. Baked ham gets so dry after it's soaked up all the cider."

"If y'all would leave Lida alone an' let her use some of that theah Christmas brandy we'd have somethin' wuth eatin'," complained Mrs. White.

Ona sat quietly resting on the top step. The sun had dropped behind the snowy cone of Pike's Peak at the end of Bijou Street, and already the sharp needles of the two pines in the front yard were beginning to blur against the graying sky. A vagrant breeze ruffled the scarf across her shoulders. As dusk thickened the lilac bush loomed up pale and full and fragrant at the corner of the house. Down along Shooks Run the crickets began a faint but strident chorus interrupted only by the sound of soft decisive footsteps coming down the walk.

"Here he comes," murmured Mrs. Rogier. "Mary, run in and tell Lida we'll wait only fifteen minutes for Daddy. He can't remember his own head when he's with those horses!"

Ona turned her head to see the figure of Jonathon Cable turning in the yard. What struck her immediately, before she could clearly distinguish his face in the dusk, was a sinuous litheness in his walk. An inch under six feet, his slender body gave out the conflicting impression of soft sensuousness and implacable hardness which was the man himself. Like a bundle of nerves wrapped together with wires of a stubborn will. Before she could move aside, his foot was on the steps beside her and she was looking up at a pair of abnormally large brown eyes and a big Roman nose set into a face swarthy as a walnut plank. Immediately he took off his hat and removing his pipe, knocked out the ashes against his heel.

For ten minutes Mrs. Rogier kept him on the porch. She had put on her Sunday afternoon dress of gray and black and was evidently taken up with Mr. Cable. He answered in a low deep voice and alternated his gaze between Ona and Mrs. White who did her best to ignore him by talking of horses to Mary Ann. To end her indelicate discourse on the subject of interbreeding for speed and stamina, Mrs. Rogier got up and led the way to supper.

In the revealing glare of the electric light—which had just been installed—Ona was impressed with the strange and foreign aspect of Jonathon Cable's face. His swarthiness was deeper than weather exposure. Even his wrists showed an even smooth sepia whenever his starched white cuffs crawled up his coat sleeves. With his big nose Ona admitted Mrs. White's implication of Jewish blood, yet his soft sensuous appeal, his quick emotional responses seemed more the Indian. Ona could not keep her glance from his hair. It alone was pure Indian to every strand. Straight and black without a sheen, it lay heavy and close, almost as coarse as a horse's mane or tail.

"I don't like this heah bran' new electric light shinin' in my eye," complained Mrs. White. "I don't see why them old lamps wasn't all right to keep on usin'."

Mrs. Rogier looked horrified that Mr. Cable should learn that the gloomy Rogier domicile had not always been illuminated like a Christmas tree. Before she could answer Rogier strode in the dining room and sat down.

"Hello, Cable," he said cheerfully. "How did the first night go in your new room?"

"Why, it's going to be fine, I'm sure," replied Cable.

"Well, I just wondered if the Kadles walkin' around all night kept you up." Rogier smiled around the table at the girls, avoiding Mrs. Rogier's set face.

"To be frank," said Jonathon Cable, "I did hear some one walking up and down the stairs until early this morning. I hope no one was sick." He looked from face to face as a restrained titter ran around the table.

"No indeed," went on Rogier, ignoring Mrs. Rogier's pinch under the table. "It was just a couple of white bearded old fellows who have been dead about fifteen years but who had to investigate the new occupant of your room. Any of the girls will tell you about them. They're old friends by now."

Cable's face had set darkly, as if he were suspicious of being made fun of. After Rogier's explanation he grinned humorously at Nancy who had the giggles, and turned to watch Mrs. Rogier cut into the ham.

"And how was 'Little Man,' Daddy?" asked Mrs. Rogier. "Do

you think he'll ever beat his mother's time of—wasn't it three minutes?"

"Three minutes!" Sally Lee ejaculated with a horrified look of amazement on her face. "Why Akeepee could pull that old lumber wagon of Daddy's around the track in less than three minutes! 2:16 for the mile is more like it."

Mrs. Rogier smiled apologetically at Cable. "We have so many lovely race-horses I just can't remember all the times they make." Sally Lee shut up with a look of disgust at Mrs. White and began upon her ham. Cable raised his head. "Maybe you can give me some information about Cripple Creek, Mr. Rogier. I heard you were a mine owner."

"I'm not," said Rogier curtly. "But if you come down to my office to-morrow I'll give you what information I can. Are you interested in mining?"

"I've got a third interest in a mine on Big Bull Mountain," said Cable.

Nancy, suddenly exploding another giggle into her napkin, ducked her head beneath the table.

"Nancy!—Get up from your chair! This minute!"

The girl, clutching her napkin to her red face, shoved back from the table and stood up with a small water spaniel rubbing against her leg.

"Whatever are you laughing at? The very idea!" demanded Mrs. Rogier.

Nancy, shamefacedly fronting the table, admitted the plausible cause of her guilt. "Yes, ma'am. Because Mr. Cable's name sounded so much like the Kadles. And then just when he said somethin' about a mine on Big Bull why 'Bull Hill' bit me on the leg. Everything comin' together-like, it was kind of funny."

"Well, you just take Bull Hill out of the room and leave him. And don't you come back until you can sit up in your chair quiet like a lady!" Turning to Cable as Nancy led out the pup, Mrs. Rogier explained with profuse apologies. "You see Daddy found that little puppy near Bull Hill and carried him all the way home. That's why we named him that. Once Daddy even brought the children down a little fawn. In those days everybody had a pet fawn playing in the yard—now they're all made of cement or bronze, especially up in the North End."

Rogier interrupted. "They're not the same hills at all. Big Bull Mountain is farther south—just east of Victor." Then turning to Cable he said gently, "I wasn't inquiring about your financial interests, Mr. Cable. I only asked if you were interested in mining."

The blunt remark was typical of Rogier. He might just as well have said, "I don't give a dom about your private business, Cable, and don't you be inquisitive about mine. I'm only interested in you." Ona turned around swiftly to Cable, seeing with relief that he did not take exception to the implication. His long dark face opened into a gentle smile. "When I was a child," he said, "I first heard about gold on Pike's Peak in a funny way and I never forgot it." Laying down his fork in his empty plate he related the incident.

His family had lived west of a small village on the Iowa-Missouri border on a quarter-section of land which merged into a block of uncleared forest where Jonathon took the cows for summer pasturage and from which his elder brothers hauled wood for winter. One evening, while a small boy, he had walked down the long lane from the barns on his way to the woods after the cows. Lounging against the fence at the edge of the forest a group of men were talking. Two strangers were describing a great snowy mountain out west that had just been discovered to be of solid gold. It stuck up into the sky almost two miles above the prairies, so steep that its discoverer, Zebulon Pike, had affirmed that only a bird could scale its lofty summit. A hundred miles out on the Great Plains you could see the sun glistening from its crest. And underneath the snow, imbedded in the rocks, were chunks of gold big as any farmer's knotted fist. Jonathon Cable crowded closer as one of the men emphatically slapped a journal with the back of his hand. Pike's Peak! It was all there in black and white, with directions across the Plains and a description of the region—no need to take a stranger's words!

With the snowy peak engraved like a picture in his childish mind, the boy had hurried across the creek and into the woods before it became too dark to find his cows in the thick hazel bushes. Letting down the hickory bars at the crossing an hour later, he saw a white shape fluttering against the fence in the wind. It was the same journal the men had been looking at.

How mysterious are men that the whistle of a train far off against the hills, a woman's smile in a crowd, can change their whole lives. That sheet of paper flapping against the fence and scaring the cows had determined Jonathon Cable's life.

There was little of it he could read at first. But day by day as he stole into the cowshed and lying in the hay spelled out the extravagant words, the high white mountain snow on gold flamed before him like a beacon. Long after he had hid the journal between the rafters the Peak reared in his mind. Milking steadily, his right temple resting against the warm flank of a cow in her stanchions, he stared wonderingly out at the red round disc of sun cutting into the softly curving hill in the west. Pike's Peak! It lay that way too. A hundred miles away it would look as high as a hickory tree. Some day he knew he must get there.

Rogier interrupted as Cable paused. "I know what you must have got hold of," he said nodding. "That journal raised a rumpus with more than one man."

Up until almost 1860, he related slowly, there was not a single settlement in Colorado to the barrier of the Rocky Mountains except Bent's Fort. The first American families in Colorado were a part of the Mormon battalion of 1846, forced out of Independence, Missouri, who resided for a time at El Pueblo until they joined the migration to Salt Lake. Later the emigrant wagon trains to the Pacific Coast passed northward up the Platte River Valley and taking the North Fork crossed the Rockies by the South Pass. The only other route was far to the south—the Santa Fé trail. Between them there was nothing but a hunting ground for the Plains Indians. Desolate as a tawny sea, the Great Plains stretched from the Gulf to the Dakotas and more than five hundred miles wide to the Missouri. Then a party of Cherokees in the gold rush to California taking by chance the Arkansas Valley route and a trail by the Squirrel Creek divide to the head of Cherry Creek, discovered signs of gold in the region. After returning from California the Cherokees organized a party to prospect in the vicinity of Pike's Peak. Rumors and exaggerations of the findings of the dozen whites and some thirty Indians spread rapidly through the Missouri River towns. In 1858 a company of fifty from Lawrence, Kansas, was organized and took the Arkansas Valley route to the foothills along the Rampart Range where they camped in the Garden of the Gods. After laying out a town at the site of Colorado Springs which they named El Paso from its location at the mouth of Ute Pass, the Lawrence party moved northward toward the Platte and Cherry Creek. News of a gold discovery in Bowlder Creek, and their two rival townsites of Auraria and Denver, further inflamed the Iowan and Missourian towns.

A man named D. C. Oakes, using a journal of W. Green Russell, published in Pacific City, Mills County, Iowa, a "Pike's Peak Guide and Journal" by which Pike's Peak was reputed to be a fabulously rich mining region. One had only to start a boulder rolling down the Peak. When it burst apart at the bottom one simply gathered up the chunks and nuggets of gold it contained and was rich for life. The lies spread. Thousands of covered wagons emblazoned with "Pike's Peak or Bust" set off for the Rockies. Within a year 160,000 persons were swarming over the plains. By summer more than a third of them were on their disconsolate way back, leaving their goods strewn beside the trail rather than to have their oxen drag it the hundreds of miles home to the Missouri River. The Pike's Peak rumor had been a factual "bust." The region at the foot of the peak was abandoned to the Indians; and northward, men stampeded down the Platte threatening to hang Oakes the minute they could lay their hands on him.

It was a copy of this journal of Oakes that Jonathon Cable had found and kept. "But go on," ended Rogier, "and light your pipe if you've a mind to. It won't hurt your dessert—it's probably tapioca. We always have it."

Mrs. Rogier flashed a sharp look at her husband, and left the table to tell Lida to be sure to put an extra helping of pineapple and whipped cream in Mr. Cable's tapioca.

Fumbling with his pipe which he had decided not to light after taking it from his pocket, Cable ended his story. He had finally got his chance to go out west when his step-father died. With a stubborn thoroughness he had made the most of his opportunities. Beginning as printer's devil on the town's weekly newspaper, he had learned to set type, to write up the simple accounts of the happenings for miles around. As combined editor, reporter, business manager, and a hand in the shop, he made that little newspaper give him an education which he could never have obtained in school. With an excellent handwriting, he had a good baritone voice and played the cornet in the town band. Thus equipped, he struck out toward the Rocky Mountains.

He got as far across the Great Plains as a small prairie town on the Kansas-Colorado line where he went partners in a small clothing and general merchandising store. For ten years he remained there, watching the wagons crawling westward into Colorado, and staring after them through the dusty sand storms that blew in from the vast prairies at the thin blue line of mountains barely discernible on the clearest day. And now, sold out, he owned a third share in a ten-foot hole dug in the rocky slope of Big Bull Mountain.

Dark and stern looking, a man who must have been almost thirty-five years old, Cable spread his hands and smiled. "I hope there's something in that hole," he said naïvely as a child, "or I'll be stone broke." His outspoken honesty, his childish candor nonplussed every Rogier around the table. Not one of them could have brought himself to speak as freely of a personal affair. Yet it was this in Cable that immediately drew them to him. Only Mrs. White, old, cantankerous, and unforgiving, glared back at him with her one eye while gnawing at her wart.

After a vain attempt to switch the conversation Mrs. Rogier excused herself with a loud "hem" in her throat and left the table with Sally and

Mary Ann. The sight of Rogier turned sideways, his left arm resting on the table where he had pushed back his dishes, calmly smoking his cigar and holding Cable like a fly in a web, made her so angry she dropped a dish in the kitchen. Peering around the corner of the china closet she saw that Cable had not even turned his head. The two men, with Ona listening silently beside them, went on talking. Mining was all very well when it came to bringing a gold mine into the family, but to hear it night and day, at every meal, was more than Mrs. Rogier could stand. She nearly ground her teeth because not one of the girls could move graciously into the parlor and sit down to perform at the piano like Lily Force. Ona, Sally Lee, and Mary Ann were disgusting chumps. Only Nancy showed any inclination at all. And then and there Mrs. Rogier made up her mind that Rogier should pay for his neglect. She would see that Nancy had the best music-teacher in town if it cost ten dollars a lesson!

In a few minutes Ona silently left the two men and went out on the porch. Cable's eyes followed her as she left the room, and after fidgeting about for awhile at the table, he got up and followed her. It was a warm summer night and in the darkness her white dress was a pale splotch on the front steps. The scratch of a match behind her and a swift yellow flare that illumined his face as he lit his pipe, roused Ona who turned around and said easily, "Oh, hello. Sit down if you want to."

Cable sprawled beside her and let down his long legs on the steps. "Do you want me to bring you a pillow from the bench?" Ona shook her head and Cable said again, "I guess I should have said 'fetch.' I notice all the family says that."

Ona laughed. "Well, go and fetch one then if that makes you feel better." Noticing the quick change in his face, she amended hastily, "I'm glad you thought of it. And pick up my scarf too. The minute the sun goes down it turns cold." How quickly responsive the man was. She couldn't get used to his quick sensitiveness, that soft sensuousness in a man who looked so sharp and stubborn. "What do you think of Colorado by now?" she asked.

Cable puffed at the straight briar pipe between his strong teeth. "Well," he said slowly, "I guess it's the difference in trees that first took my eye." He waved his hand at the two pines out in front that seemed black and metallic as if wrought of iron. "Back home we had big round oaks and hickories that seemed soft and fluffy especially in the moonlight. Nothing like those pines. They're funny things, those pines. They don't grow old and twisted before they die. They stand up straight and sound and then of a sudden one morning they fall headlong down into the cañon. I saw one do that. But say"—he spoke quickly, his voice rising, "I wish you'd tell me something."

Ona drew the shawl across her throat and waited.

"It's this," went on Cable. "Why do they call Colorado Springs 'Little London'? Especially when all the streets have Spanish names like Cucharras and Huerfano, or French like this one, Bijou, and Cache la Poudre. Ever since I've been here I've been wondering."

"It's simple enough," answered Ona. "The whole town was really built up by Englishmen. General Cameron—the manager of the Company that laid out Colorado Springs and whom they named Cameron's Cone for, General Palmer who built the railroad and bought all the land about Manitou, and Dr. Bell who helped survey the Kansas-Pacific Railroad, all sent circulars back to Great Britain. Why, half the money to build the railroad here was raised among Dr. Bell's English friends, and the rails were imported from Wales. Their advertising abroad brought so many Englishmen here that the town was called Little London. When I was a little girl—we came here in the early 80's—everybody who amounted to anything were all rich Englishmen. Miss Rose, the daughter of the English preacher Charles Kingsley, was one of the first school-teachers. And Mrs. General Palmer had a man named Blackmore send 200 books from England for the library. Daddy says that even with all the Indians it never was a real pioneering town no matter how the people liked to think it was. They played polo with Indian wigwams just over the hill, and had big greyhounds for coyote chases. That's why it's so snobbish. If you want to be anybody—a real North Ender—just call yourself an Englishman or a foreigner and everybody will fall all over you. We were French. Confederates from the South, too. That made it worse," she ended bitterly.

Cable turned to her with surprise. "I think you're wrong. You should hear what people say about Colonel Rogier. Like they were kind of afraid of him."

Ona laughed. "Don't ever let Daddy hear that 'Colonel'! He was never in the army—detests all crowds and organizations. Why, he never shot off a gun in his life. I don't know why they're beginning to call him that."

For a moment they were silent, staring at the two pines growing blacker in the night. A thin breeze filled with the fragrance of the lilac soft and pale at the corner of the house, and sweeping past them ruffled the leaves of Sister Molly's elm. Two pigeons moaned sleepily on the roof overhead as if disturbed by the crickets down at the creek.

"It's nice here, though," said Ona thoughtfully. "The fine climate and all the mineral waters are bringing the best people here. Musicians from Europe and college professors who never would have come if they hadn't had to for their health. If only all that mining in Cripple Creek doesn't drive them out.—You should see General Palmer's estate at the mouth of Queen's Cañon. Glen Eyrie. A real English castle right up against the mountains copied stone for stone from the ancestral home of the Marlboroughs in England. They say General Palmer brought every stone for the fireplace across the Atlantic."

"Yes," said Cable, and then nervously tapping his pipe on his heel, "I wonder—well, if I get a horse and buggy from the stable uptown will you ride out there with me sometime?"

Ona brushed back a wisp of hair from her forehead. "Some afternoon when I haven't much to do I will." In the darkness she smiled gently. With a stable full of horses out in back and more out at Denman's ranch, she was going in a rented rig. She wondered what Mrs. Rogier would think of that.

In the awkward silence Rogier came out upon the porch and took a chair. For a half-hour the two men talked, then with an unobtrusive "Good night" Ona rose and went inside. The moon came out and with the recrudescence of its luminosity the mountains stood out darkly outlined against the fragile moon-blue sky. Listening to the papery music of leaves in the elm, Cable filled his pipe and watched Rogier. How solid and resolute seemed the man, his arm flung out upon the banister as he sat gazing at the Peak's snowy cone pale silver against the blue.

"Those mountains sure make me feel what a prairie man I am." Cable said suddenly. "I was just telling Ona anybody can tell you were born and brought up in them until you're almost like them."

He stopped as Rogier put his cigar in his mouth and slowly turned his head to face him. An immobility of expression held firm his rugged face, but the gleam of his gray eyes went through Cable like unsheathed steel. An air of impenetrability enwrapped his heavy body in a silence Cable dared not attempt to break through. Confused, he wondered what he had said that so displeased Rogier. He broke a match lighting his pipe, and when he looked up Rogier had risen to his feet. With a curt statement about having to look at a horse he walked off toward the stables behind the house, leaving Cable to wonder what a queer man he was.

Out in back Rogier puttered around the stalls. The sleepy sound of pigeons, the muffled stomping of hoofs in the darkness, helped to quiet his jangled nerves. Cable's surprising statement had cut so close to his secret thought that involuntarily he had closed up like a clam. Yet he could not banish it from his mind. He had been away from Cripple Creek too long. It was time he was getting back up into the mountains to see about his plans. How much money the thing would take—had taken already! Wandering out into the moonlit yard, the flocculent black shadows of stables and open sheds enveloping his quietly moving figure as he walked about, Rogier thought on. The deep peace of night brought out detail after detail of his plans, and the hens perched on the wagons, the rafters of the hay shed, sleepily chirped their soft assents. Coming to the back fence he stopped, resting his arms on the top rail, and stood looking off at the distant mountains.

Slowly his gaze traveled from the finny Devil's Horn northward along the sloping crest of the range to the upflung snowy summit of the Peak. Like a great amphibian upburst from the depths of the flat prairies the range stood as if momentarily arrested in its swift arc. The tail dwindling into the sea of prairies to the south, the rising slope of the curved body, and finally the massive upthrust head all beclouded as if in the white of spraying foam. Perfectly symbolized in the moon-lit night the figure rose before him like a great sea-monster entombing all the secrets of the depths. So too the land, in the eternal palingene-sis of crumbling stone and the uplifting of new masses to greater heights, gives up the secret of its depths in the mountains that rise from ancient ocean floors. Like a dumbfounded mariner, now was the time for him to strike deep the steel that he may know of the life that goes on unceasing far below his depths. To pierce that body of living rock into the warm flesh that hides its secret heart, to drain its veins of golden life, to learn at the last that even a stone may throb to an unseen pulse, may vibrate in unison with all eternal life. To this Rogier hardly set his puny human will. For like the sea the land flows and ebbs in rhythm to the moon and stars. Mountains crumble and wash away. Old sea floors subside under the weight of their conglomerate ooze. And then with isostatic equilibrium, obeying those same unknown universal laws that keep the sun in place, new mountain ranges arise aloft with sea shells on their summits. Always, unceasingly, the stones and the rocks live and breathe and crumble away only to be born again. Rogier bent his head. Somewhere behind him a hoof stirred the gravel of the yard and old blind Colonel thrust a nose along his arm. Gently stroking the warm muzzle beside him, Rogier raised his face to the wind. Like a blind man he sensed the futility of ever knowing what lay before him. Men live and die never knowing if they have seen aright or even if they have seen at all. But the land remains. And the mountains—that great blue structure before him faintly luminous in the moonlight—they alone would rear solidly aloft until the stars themselves were pulled from their sockets by the hand of Time.

4

A family is a peculiar entity. Its members are a group of islands in the same blood-stream. Sometimes the eternally changing, enveloping stream of life itself tears a new channel through the archipelago. Internal ruptures break away reefs. Old atolls sink unaccountably and new ones rise from the placid blue depths. The eternal palingenesis goes on, but the group of islands remain a whole. Far down in the impenetrable blood-stream they remain fixed together, adjusted to the same internal vibration, knowing one communion in the deep unseen currents that wash between them, passive alike to the ripples of life outside breaking against their separate shores.

So it was with Ona and Rogier. At home Rogier was her father, and the indecencies of mechanical "heart-to-heart" exposures were not vices of the Rogiers. Yet all the time, attuned to the same vibration, a vitalistic communion passed between them. Allowing her through his ledgers to learn him better than any one, Rogier day by day emerged from the pages. She grew to see him not only as her father but as a man—a man whom no one had ever known before. Only their superficial contacts and his familiar presence obstructed the vision she had built up. Then going back into the mountains for days or weeks at a time and leaving her alone in the office, Rogier loomed before her again the man whom she knew only through his work.

The job of looking after Rogier's office was the worst Ona had ever attempted. She would have preferred the Herculean task of cleaning up the barny third-floor at home to spending the day puzzling over Rogier's ledgers. There were a dozen of the big volumes crammed with old letters, estimates, and sheets of figures that tumbled out whenever she opened the dusty linen-backed covers. The pages inside were even more confusing. Haphazardly scrawled in her father's handwriting were complete records of every job he had figured on, copies of bids he had submitted with their detailed supporting data, and periodic records as the construction progressed, together with monthly bills for material used and notices of money deposited in the bank to his expense account. Rogier always wrote in his ledgers with ink but seldom bothered to use a blotter. Many pages looked as if his big hands had closed the book with a bang that had been imprisoned like a crushed fly. With his small analytic calligraphy, his failure to label each set of data when he was figuring on two or more jobs concurrently, the incomprehensible array of figures—which Ona abhorred—and her own lack of training, the ledgers were a mess it took her months to straighten out.

It seemed paradoxical to Ona that Rogier could be so methodical, so sure and accurate in his work, and so sloppy in his ledgers. It was the same with his time-sheets and payrolls. Mooney, the timekeeper on the job, sent in to him impeccable records each week, and Rogier was always spoiling the looks of his neat rows of figures with comments scrawled on every page. He had an uncanny knack for handling men and he knew every man who worked for him. Ona had often seen him on the job talking to a stone-mason, looking over a mule with a teamster, holding a plumb-line for two bricklayers, or waiting his turn with a group of laborers for a drink from the water-boy. He could take off his coat and square a timber with any carpenter on the job;—a carpenter who worked for him more than once had to be a jim-dandy at his trade. He was hardly ever in the shanty that served as field office. Going through the records of the finished jobs, Ona could see the results of his observations. Rogier had the habit of jotting down such queer and apparently irrelevant things. Any place in the time-sheets she would run into a random comment on a laborer, or after pages of complicated figuring she might turn over to a single scrawled statement that Mary Ann had fallen and scraped her shin badly or that Akeepee needed more grain.

But it was when she came to balance his books and bank accounts that Ona was stunned into a frightened silence. Rogier owned five lots on Bijou adjacent to their own ungainly big house, three houses up at the corner on Wahsatch, and two pieces of valuable property and store-buildings in the business district uptown. Receiving the evaluation on each that Rogier had requested, together with statements from the banks, and making an approximate conversion valuation of his construction machinery, cement mixers, drays and tools, Ona stared open-mouthed at the sum of Rogier's holdings. She could hardly believe her eyes. Rogier was rich as any big North-Ender! The thought stunned her completely. Through the long afternoon she wondered if Rogier realized what he was worth. And that night, after listening to her mother's repeated query of "I wonder when we'll be able to move away from Shooks Run," she crept wearily to bed like an accomplice to a shameful act of deception.

Within a week she settled down to earth. She realized that like all of the family she had never thought of Rogier other than a good provider. Naturally he had made money completing contracts that ran as high as eighty thousand dollars each. Also it was necessary to post big bonds and to expend a great deal before he was paid his first installment on each job. Moreover the money was not in cash. And if he didn't want to build a big house up in the North End right away—well, Rogier was Rogier and that was the end of it.

He was a peculiar man. She learned that there were many, many things he did not trust into her keeping. He might walk in and tell her of property he had owned for ten years that none of the family had ever heard of, or give her a check on an account for which she had never seen the pass book. Open and blunt as he was he seemed secretive at times, never letting his right hand know what his left was doing. Ona never questioned him and kept to herself whatever she learned. Once a man from Cripple Creek had walked in the office and told her that he had come for a hundred and twenty dollars. While they were talking Rogier came in.

"Why, of course. Ona, write out a check." The two men shook hands. "I hope you haven't been put out any," Rogier had told the man.

A few months later an old man named Reynolds had come in to see Rogier. For an hour they talked in the corner.

"I tell you, Governor, this here Silver Heels is goin' to pan out right. The assay says so."

Ona pricked up her ears at the name. She heard the rustle of Rogier's big map. After a time Rogier sent her down to the bank for a thousand dollars in currency which he gave to Reynolds. "Now remember what I told you about going down the gulch. Down not up. On the left side. And mind you, keep my name out of it if you have to sign any papers. Use your own."

When Reynolds had gone Ona turned around. "Silver Heels—isn't that nice to remember her! Have you got a gold mine, Daddy?"

"I wouldn't call it that," said Rogier, abruptly turning on his heel to go back to his desk.

It was all the information she received. But when pressed a few nights later at the dinner table by Mrs. Rogier, he finally admitted that he was "interested" in a prospect named Silver Heels. It was enough for Mrs. Rogier and the children. Daddy had a gold mine. There was now no reason why she shouldn't have her mansion in the North End among the divine gentility of Little London. She was all for moving into a great house set deep in a lawn which contained a cement fountain and a bronze deer and which was appropriately enclosed from envious eyes with a high iron fence. Rogier put her off until they should see what would happen in Cripple Creek. Ona remained silent and went on eating. But she kept wondering if the prospect Silver Heels alone justified—or received—all the time and money that Rogier was spending in Cripple Creek.

One morning while at the office Ona received a letter from Boné. The begrimed envelope and single sheet of ruled paper, the post-mark even, held the curious power of a talisman to evoke with magic suggestiveness a world she could never quite forget. Shadows of clouds in the sunshine, distant abrupt mesas flaming red at dawn, faces dark and voices dim, passions cloaked like knives in the somber folds of dusk. Evoking those memories of a time when the world stood still and life eddied about her ceaseless and unhurried, the letter lay in her lap as she sat thinking of that remote and inconsequential Indian agency maintained in austere dignity by two old maids drinking tea in front of the fire which was their only symbol of home.

Rooted in the passionless stability of the big ungainly house down on Shooks Run and the irritating confusion of Rogier's office, Ona often looked back with amazement to those months on the Reservation. Not only the sea holds in its boundless solitude the illusion of life's mirage. That high western plateau, the sweep of desert uplifted to the glitter of stars and exposed to the merciless shimmer of the noonday sun, holds too a mystery profound and enigmatic as the sea. Against its somber background she seemed to see Lockhardt, Bruce and the Vrain Girls as figures more dwarfed but more distinct, more futile but also more heroic. Only in Boné she saw a man consecrated to a forlorn search for something in those hills that might not exist at all. A man attuned to the beat of Indian drums and stumbling after a mirage.

Again and again during the day she read through his letter. Lockhardt had died and Boné was leaving for San Francisco. She thought of Lockhardt impeccably dressed in his white shirt and dark worsted suit, the yellow flamelight striking white fire from the big diamond on his finger. Pounding the piano keys so harshly that it set atremble a tumbler of whisky and soda water above his head. A memory subtly denying forever the fact of his death. And Boné! What would he do so far away with nothing but a note to one of Lockhardt's friends? The metallic glint of moonlight upon a distant cliff, the shimmering thread of the San Juan unrolling in the lonely night, was for him the only silver; his gold no more than sun on sand. Some day he would have to return. For in the end we reject everything that we are temperamentally unsuited to assimilate, however much we admire it. She could hardly believe the scrawled lines.

Then suddenly, late that afternoon, the undeniable truth of the simple message struck home. Lockhardt had died, and Boné had left them forever. An irremediable sense of loss swept over her. Worried sick with the suspicion that the boy would be needing money, she addressed an envelope to the address given her and put in it the five dollar bill she had been saving for weeks. Slumping down in her chair she buried her face in her arms and wept.

It was thus that Jonathon Cable found her when he stopped in the office to walk home with her. Only for a moment he stood quietly beside her, then leaned forward. Not until she felt the light pressure of his hand on her shoulder did she know he was there. Startled, she jumped to her feet. Something in his eyes checked the words on her lips. Nor did Cable speak. His sudden involuntary gesture of sympathetic intimacy arrested, the emotion yet seemed to flow from him with an uncontrollable intensity. With it she felt the disturbing sensuousness always given her by his presence. Afterwards she was to remember the look that passed between them. A look perhaps no different than many others, yet symbolic of one of those rare moments in all our lives when we realize that we have crossed without thought a gap which can never be bridged again. She suddenly smiled, wiped the tears from her cheeks. "I've ruined my envelope. Look. The ink's run all over."

Cable, dark and unsmiling, replied gravely, "Here. I've got one in my pocket. You can post it on the way home."

During the long fall months when each evening they walked together, Ona was to marvel more at the contradictory expressions of Jonathon Cable's strange nature. Never in her life had she known a man so softly appealing and tender as he and who strangely enough showed it so little. A calm natural dignity of which he was unaware lent him a manner that went far to offset a faint suggestion of effeminacy to a stranger. Yet how different was he than a Rogier with all his seeming unexpressiveness. His every movement spoke. She had only to see him rising from a chair and coming toward her to feel instantly the strong sensuous flow given out by his graceful quick-moving body. With his dark face, his large brown eyes and coarse black hair, he seemed a somnolent volcano of a man perpetually seething with an inward fire of which he himself was unaware.

During their walks he came to tell her something of his early life. Besides the fact that his step-father was a "good man," Cable said little of his mother and three older brothers. His reticence about his own father whom he hardly remembered cloaked the derivation of his own swarthy foreign appearance. He portrayed a boyhood that had been singularly commonplace, and a family which had endured poverty dully and without spontaneity—that one charm which will lift an affair of squalor into the higher spheres of imagination and beauty, of sorrow and joy. Never in his words as he told of rubbing his boots with tallow for Sunday Church, of awakening Christmas morning to find his only gift, an apple in his stocking, was there a trace of homesickness, of gently remembered charm. Never—as with Rogier whenever he spoke of his own South—the poignant deep-rooted sense of affinity to the homeland of his birth. His big nose sharply outlined against his dark face, Cable spoke softly, but they were facts presented tersely and unadorned.

Watching him reflectively smoothing his bony brown hands as he talked, she sensed sympathetically that here was a man who did not warrant her mother's suspicion that he might be a future North-Ender, but only a man complex because so simple and hard through lack of sophistication. As if she cared! She listened carefully with that unconscious but possessive air of a woman who seeks always to fathom the mystery of a man's hold upon her.

CHAPTER 2

Below Grass Roots (1937)

By 1911, Jonathon Cable, first encountered in *The Wild Earth's Nobility* (1935), had begun working for his father-in-law, part-time at first, at Rogier's mine near Cripple Creek. The decision to do so would prove, ultimately, to have fatal consequences, for Cable's constitution, used to the open plains, couldn't handle the damp and stagnant air of a mineshaft. But tragedy was still in the future, at the time of the following selection from *Below Grass Roots.* Here Cable has taken his son March to Buffalo Bill's Wild West Show, sharing with him afterward some profoundly affecting silent moments. He will temporarily escape an atmosphere of conflict and distrust at home by escorting the boy to the Navajo Reservation for the summer. There Cable works in a trading post, while March absorbs, as perhaps only a nine-year-old could, the wild, spacious, colorful, mysteriously meaningful scene.

From *Book 2: Adobe*

5

"Ooh, Mama! And we saw Buffalo Bill. He's got long hair, long as yours, and he hits every time he shoots and a big pretty white horse. And one of the bandits got shot what held up the stage. You oughta seen the Indians. Hun'erds of 'em, Mama. You oughta heard 'em yell.

But the wagon train got away or they'd of burned 'em at a stake" . . . .

"Yes, yes, March. I'll bet it was nice. But you look awfully tired. You jump into bed and tell me all about it in the morning."

When he had gone, Ona turned to Cable. "It's ten o'clock. And you've been gone since ten this morning. That's awfully hard on a boy his age. I still think you might have taken us all. We could have walked up to see the parade this morning and taken a nap afterward. Then we could have gone to the afternoon performance and been home for supper. My goodness, Jonathon, what have you done all day long?"

"Seen and eaten everything from first to last," he answered cheerfully, unfolding the Gazette in his lap. "Mostly hung around the Indian camp. You know a boy likes such things. Good for him. And it wasn't any place for a woman."

"Well, I'm glad he had a good time. And I do hope you didn't give him anything to turn his stomach. Daddy, by the way, was a little put out at you."

Cable did not answer; he was busy reading the paper.

Walking home from the train he had met Rogier on the street. "What's the trouble? Or is it a new strike?" Rogier had asked, excitedly grabbing him by the arm.

"Not a thing," answered Cable easily.

"What are you doing down here from Cripple Creek then? Thought you were going to stay and see about that drifting."

"Told you I was coming down to take the boy to Buffalo Bill's Wild West Show."

"Buffalo Bill!" shouted Rogier. "Dom me, man! You didn't walk off and leave Abe and Jake up there all alone. They can't do that all alone. And for Buffalo Bill"—

"Exactly. You must have forgotten I promised the boy. I didn't."

Rogier had snorted and walked off without another word. And Cable, true to his word, had left the house at ten o'clock with March.

All the next day the boy prattled noisily to his mother about their marvelous time. They had watched from an uptown corner the long parade, with Buffalo Bill shooting clay balls from his wagon, and followed it down to the encampment. For two hours they had wandered among the stables and the big tents, eaten at the mess hall with all the soldiers and cowboys, and before the show Cable had taken him over to the camp to see the old chief Buckskin Charlie. The tepees and the Indians—these especially had held the boy raptly attentive. And after the show they had gone back to sit around the fire.

Ona had no need to ask questions of the boy. There was no stopping his excited ejaculations. He had a retentive mind and a sharp eye for inconsequential details—how an eagle's feather was tied with leather into a head band so that its quill would not snap in the wind; the pattern of an Indian pony's spots, "like Florida, mama, reaching right down his leg"; the way a gun-holster was looped to the leg with twine. "So it won't flap around and hold when you draw it out. That's what he said. The big soldier. I asked him. I want to fix mine that way, Mother. You fix it!"

Worn out, he was finally sent to bed and lay there, living over again the evening before. The Wild West Show in the afternoon had been exciting. But this, the deep darkness stung by tiny fires along the creek, held something more awesome than yells and shouts. His throat was raw from dust; he had wanted a drink of water. "The creek's right down there behind the willows. I'll wait here for you," his father told him, but he did not move. He was sure he wasn't afraid. But somehow, seeing the shadowy forms of fat Indian squaws brushing by on their way to the camp and braves lurking along the trail, he guessed he wouldn't go—not quite yet. The tall conical tepees began to loom up in the darkness. Holding to his father's hand, he walked slowly up the long lane. Dark, taciturn faces leapt at him in the glow of fires, their blanketed bodies huddled together in somber groups. Tepee flaps yawned open into the appalling blackness within. A shoulder of meat was lashed in the tree above; wondering for an instant if it were a body, he grasped his father's hand more closely.

Cable did not pause. He proceeded up the lane, threading his way among moccasined feet that did not move to let them pass. March looked up into his face: it seemed to he searching among all those indistinguishable groups a familiar face. They stopped in front of a big circle. For an instant no one moved. Then one of the men looked up and grunted. The boy wondered if he were the one who had been with Buckskin Charlie; the high cheek-boned faces looked all alike.

Cable nodded and squatted down. He tossed a half-dollar on a blanket and without hesitation reached for a hunk of bread which he laid in March's lap. Then getting out his pocket knife with the six-inch blade, always kept sharp as a razor, he leaned forward and began slicing off a piece from the meat spitted over the coals.

It was a memory of his father that was impressed forever upon the boy's mind: the red glowing coals, the circle of dark faces, and among them Cable squatting on his haunches, cutting meat. It was his father. His suit was neatly pressed, his collar was white and shiny in the flamelight. He was so clean and tidy as he deftly laid back the flap of thick fat and cut two slabs of lean meat from underneath. And yet, for the first time in his life, the boy sensed in his father something he had never felt before. The Indians did not seem to even notice him, but neither did Cable look at them. He made himself completely at home, as if he might have been alone. His face tonight seemed so dark, his hair so black and straight. And the way he crouched, so subtly drawn into himself: that too reflected a strange solidarity that forbade idle questioning. March accepted his piece of meat and bread in silence, and with Cable's handkerchief spread in his lap began to eat.

It was so dry! He could hardly gulp it down, and yet he dared not say a word. Cable looked down at him and turned away without a word. Then, a minute later, he casually reached out for an empty cup lying on the ground. "Here, son. Go get me a drink of water. Through those willows there at the creek." The boy stood up trembling, looking from the darkness back to his father's face. It was turned away, the big nose and high boned cheek silhouetted in the flame-light. He bit his lip, stood holding the cup in both hands. At last he crept away, turned back once to the fire, and plunged through the thicket to the creek. Cable did not watch him go, and when the boy returned, took the water at a gulp without turning around. The boy, still trembling, but with his own thirst quenched, sank back down beside him.

For an hour they sat there. Again and again March tried to ape his father's squat. His legs in the unaccustomed posture grew stiff and tired; he had to spread out and finally rest his weight against Cable who sat contentedly without moving, smoking his pipe. He had passed his pouch to the man on his other side who rolled a cigarette. They were now talking casually about the show, to which the boy paid no attention. He sat there, eyes sleepy and smarting from gusts of smoke, staring at the dark hairless faces, the long strings of braided hair tied with strips of red flannel, the greasy store-pants and neatly laced moccasins. They were without war-paint and feathers; they were silent, immovable, like effigies of carven wood. Not in two hours did any of them make a move to recommend them as the wild leaping savages of the afternoon—and long after the show had begun to fade in his mind, it was this memory of them that persisted.

If Buffalo Bill's Wild West Show had been the cause of a decided coolness between Cable and Rogier, it also led to a more serious breach between him and Ona.

March gave it voice not two days afterward. "I like Daddy, Mother!" he said that night cuddling on her lap, waiting for his father to come to supper. She had been talking of his growing up into a big boy, going to school—maybe to college, and being a great man like his Uncle Boné. "Yes, sir, I sure like my Daddy!" he repeated. "He takes me everywhere and he never watches me and tells me 'don't do this' and 'don't do that'. But a funny thing, mama, you know he knows what you're doing. Just like an Indian, huh? You never see him lookin' at you but you feel it. Anyway, school's goin' to be over soon. Then you know what he's goin' to do? Guess! He's goin' to take me up with him to Cripple Creek. To stay with him and Granddad, and learn all about the mine in the ground. Whatcha think of that!"

He felt her quick intake of breath, the sudden clutch of her arms around him. Slowly she relaxed and sat staring silently out the window. Then she put him down and led him into the kitchen, her face strangely grave and stern. "Here, March. I'll give you your supper now so you can go to bed. And get that idea out of your head. Your father knows you're too small yet to go up to the mine. You'd be hurt and you'd get lonesome. You're going to stay down here and have a nice time helping Mother. Of course. Now ssh! No talking back, mind."

Disappointed, the boy soon crept off to bed. Ona kissed him, turned up the covers, and went back to her seat at the window to stare silently into the darkness.

At the first sound of Cable's steps, she rose and slowly opened the door. Something in her tall, big-boned body confronting him betrayed the temper of her mind. Cable gave her a quick glance as he came in; her face was pale and set.

"What's the trouble?" he asked softly. "Either of the kids sick?"

"No," she answered him shortly. "I want to talk with you. But come have your supper first."

He ate silently but deliberately. Finished, he put down his napkin and filled his pipe with steady unhurried hands. "A good supper, Ona. Now do you want to go in the other room?"

She ignored the remark, pushing aside his plate and leaning forward with a tense, drawn face.

"March tells me you are planning to take him up to Cripple Creek when school is over. To stay at the Sylvanite with you!"

Cable looked up. "Yes. We're great chums. It'll be good for him."

"Jonathon, you know I'd never stand for that. Never. If it were the last thing in my life."

He leaned back without replying, his face grown dark and expressionless.

"No!" Ona went on, her voice thick and tremulous. "I've done what I could with Mother to keep Daddy back, and now I know nobody can help him. For years I've been trying to help you. I've tried to encourage you. I've borne up under your stubborn refusals. And what's happened? You gave up your shop—lost your business. You let your big chance in real estate slip through your fingers. You're making a mess of this insurance business. You, the business man! For what? To get into a miserable mine in Cripple Creek. Oh, yes! I know we've been playing it's just a temporary thing, but it's all you've been doing. But now I'm done!"

She saw him, elbows on table, drawn tight into himself, and continued.

"I remember Tom. I've seen Daddy. I see you now. All alike. All cursed by that damned mine. And now you want to take March up there. Do you hear me?" She was shouting now. "You want to take a small boy up there and get the thing started in his blood too. To make it seem so natural to him that when he grows up he won't know he's accursed like all the rest. Jonathon, you're a fool if you think I'll let my boy go like that!" She grasped the small table, drew a deep breath. Her voice grew quieter, more resolute. "He's my boy, a Rogier to the marrow of his bones, and he's going to have his chance. He's going to get an education, do something, be something, a credit to his breeding. He's never going to see a mine. My foot's down now to stay, Jonathon. I'm not fooling. My boy stays with me if I have to take in washing. You can do what you please, but you leave him alone. Understand?"

It was the climax of that quarrel which for two years had been beating them apart as with ceaseless, repetitive blows of waves upon the shore. Under the successive shocks it no longer had a meaning. They fought over trifles, quarreled over trivialities that once had been dismissed with a smile and bickered constantly, aware of the subtle differences of temperament that now cut each other's sensibilities as with a jagged edge. And it resolved, at last, into an open quarrel for the possession of a boy who still saw them undivided.

For a while they maintained in his presence a commendable behavior. Cable was quiet, taciturn. Ona was quiet, reserved. Then gradually they broke out into sudden eruptions at any cause. Cable no longer took March uptown for his weekly dish of ice-cream.

"I don't see why you should!" Ona had broken out one afternoon. "If you want to be so good why don't you take me and Leona. She likes ice-cream, too."

And Cable, coming in one evening to find Ona talking of Boné to the boy on her lap, was unaccountably furious. "Boné. Boné. That's all we hear around this house. What do you think he is, a little tin Jesus? March's grandfather and his own father aren't plaster saints, but his uncle's not perfect either. You let the boy alone. He can live his own life and form his own ideas without so much harping on the subject by you."

The last few weeks of school dragged by. Twice March was spanked by his mother for innocently asking when his father was going to take him up to the mine. To make up for the unjust chastising, she began to coddle him like a child. Her maternal poses, arms around the boy at every opportunity, aroused in Cable a sullen resentment. He began to embarrass the boy by treating him like a grown man who preferred sentimental and effeminate caresses to tumbling on the lawn and shooting imaginary bear. It was a subtle fight for his possession that left him shy and reserved, hermaphroditically wavering between both desires.

On the day school let out, Rogier came up to the house.

"Are you comin' up to help us with the Sylvanite or not, this summer?" he inquired of Cable without prelude. It was the first time since the Buffalo Bill incident that he had forgotten his huff enough to demand Cable's help.

"I might," said Cable quietly. "Been thinking of bringing up March for company. Then again I might not. I like to see my family too, you know."

"Why don't you move up to Cripple Creek? You can get you all a place in Victor."

The suggestion aroused Ona to justifiable fury.

"Dom it!" growled Rogier. "Minin's, minin'. It ain't a picnic. But there's no call for you to get so riled up." And mystified by the unbearable tension in the room, he strode out without an answer.

The quarrel, now that a decision was at hand, came to a head. It lasted two days during which Cable never left the house with March. Ona, on her knees with her arms around the boy, was like a she-animal defying danger. The quarrel, like the posture, was silly and melodramatic. But worn out and sleepless, nerve-wracked and upset, they both were serious.

On the last evening, Ona walked home with March from the corner grocery to find Cable sitting in his chair staring at the blank wall. She sat down opposite him and drew March on her lap.

"Jonathon," she said in a quiet, resolute voice, "this can't go on any longer. We both know that. This morning I settled it for good. I sent a telegram to Boné that I was sending March down to the Reservation to spend the summer. He will be quite all right. He will live at Bruce's trading post—Bert is lame and never gets out. Boné is there most of the time. And Lew is down the cañon a few miles in her old place. She will get up often, so it won't be like he won't have a woman to look after him too."

She bent down, carefully brushing the boy's hair from his forehead, and kissed him tenderly. "You'll like it, won't you, Sonny? And you'll remember your mother lived down there once. Remember the story of the rug beside your bed? And there'll be lots of Indians, like your father tells you about, only nice and kind. And a long ride on a train. Won't that be nice?"

"Ooh yes," the boy murmured, too excited to talk.

"Now get to bed and go right to sleep. When you wake up I'll have your suitcase all packed. And we'll take you to the train first thing after breakfast."

When he had gone, she turned a white stern face to Cable. "I'm sorry if you don't approve, Jonathon, or if I've hurt your feelings. But it's the only thing I can do. I'll say nothing if you insist on going up to the Sylvanite. And I'll miss you both and pray for the time we can all be together again for good."

"So you'd send the boy away among strangers rather than have him with Joe and me, eh?" Cable asked quietly.

"No! To keep him away from the Sylvanite."

"And you'd let him go down there all alone—ninety miles by wagon after he leaves the train," he continued thoughtfully, rising to his feet and standing before her.

"I have decided it's best."

Cable, without answer, walked out of the room.

The next morning they rose early. Ona had packed March's suitcase the night before. Now, while he ate breakfast, she sewed a ten-dollar bill in his pantaloons with his name and address, giving him minute instructions on what to do should anything happen. Meanwhile she kept calling Cable for breakfast; he was still puttering around in the bedroom.

After a time he came out with a suitcase and a dufflebag which he set down beside March's in the hall.

Ona stood and stared.

"Where—where you going? Not Cripple Creek so soon? I thought—"

Cable poured himself a cup of coffee and, ignoring the plate of bacon and eggs, stood munching a single piece of toast. "You probably love your boy very much, in theory. But the trip is too much for him alone. I'm going to take him down myself."

Ona's face paled and set. She stood biting her lip, her hands clenched together on her breast. Neither seemed aware of the boy's excited chatter over having his father for company. There was an awkward silence, then the neighbor girl came in to mind Leona.

They walked in silence to the station, stood tense and nervous, waiting for the train. There seemed nothing either could put in words. The train pulled in. Cable boosted up boy and bags and stood silently beside Ona until the whistle sounded. They kissed.

"Take good care of yourself," he said calmly.

"And you, Jonathon," she answered, too proud to confess her fears and longings.

He swung aboard and without a backward glance strode through the vestibule into the coach.

Ona stood watching the train until it had vanished around the bend. Then, the tears beginning at last to fall, she plunged sobbing up the tracks to home.

6

The queer retentiveness of the human mind that funks the important and fastens to the trivial! One remembers so little of the significant. And of that which lingers, like the smell of father's pipe, one never ventures an inadequate word. Sunlight on water, shadows of clouds upon the plains, the smell of sage and cedar, the glint of a man's greasy braided hair—of such things as these, evanescent and enduring, may be woven a boy's memory.

He sits so small and still on the faded blanket thrown over the seat of the stage, watching beyond the team the steadily receding horizon. Pine and spruce dwindle to piñon and cedar; gaunt grey cliffs to sand hills along the river. The lofty illimitable desert spreads out, cut by red arroyos and dry washes. The sky grows grey, then black, orange and brass again. He eats, sleeps and rides still farther into a land that is a vast emptiness without a frame, a monotone that is never monotonous. And thus without perspective he remembers only the odd jutting fragments as of a dream of time.

He remembers the great brown river at the ford, lit redly by the setting sun, the streaming horses and the water clutching at his knees. He sees forever and without meaning two braids of greasy black hair before him and the pattern of the blanket they hang upon. He remembers the smell of sage, the grey ghostly wash of the Gallegos under the rising moon. He awakes to the sight of the post, a long, low adobe squatting in the draw. There is a fire outside. About it group figures dark-faced and somber, springless wagons and a dozen horses. Stiff and sleepy, he is carried inside the barny, littered store-room to a smaller room. In ten minutes he is asleep in his shoes. He has seen nothing remarkable in three days of riding, nothing pertinent of the trading post. And yet these odd fragments—the wagon, the river, the post, its smoke-stained cedar vigas and the hawk-like face of Bruce glimpsed in the lamp-light, all these remain forever burned into his mind, the wordless fragments of an experience lived and felt so fully that it is inseparate from his inner self.

"Tell Mama," his first note reads, "that it is a big country a long ways off. I got cold and wet when the wagon swum the river. There are lots of Indians. They ride horses and mostly wagons. They wear bracelets like girls and ain't the scalping kind. They don't even look at me. They ain't no post-office or even a town so maybe you won't get this. But we're here anyway with love."

Yet in the slow slip of summer days it was a life that grew into a thousand pictures which in turn grew into the one. It was a wheel, a flat circular desert floor studded with sage, this world whose protruding hub was Bert Bruce's trading post—Hon-Not-Klee, Shallow Water. Not in twenty years had it changed a bit, said Boné.

Over fifty miles west across the sandy Gallegos lay the Reservation and the Lukuchukai Mountains. South and east stretched the same sage-studded desert, broken only by the Cañon Blanco, cut deep like an intaglio of shimmering color. To the north along the curve of the San Juan lay the little town, the posts at Shiprock, the Navajo Indian Mission, and the hospital where Lew went. But even these seemed far away, unreal as the railroad junction seventy miles farther north across the Territorial Line in Colorado. The world was like a sea; and March, watching from the post, could see rising from the swells and drifting in with their strange cargoes the squeaking, springless wagons filled with Navajos.

The trading post, for them as him, seemed the one substantial center of all life. For hours, day on day, there was little for the boy to do except to watch them. He would see a wagon come in, the man bareheaded, with a crimson band across his hair or boasting a tall round-topped felt hat, the woman fat and resplendent in a velveteen blouse of green, purple, or red, her fingers and arms laden with silver and turquoise jewelry. He would follow them into the barny room and slump down on a stack of rugs.

The place was like a dusty warehouse, ill-lit by the windows barred with iron strips. Huge cribs of onions and potatoes flanked the long wooden counter against which were piled goat hides and sheep pelts. The shelves were stacked with cans. Bolts of cloth littered the place. Clothing hung from the cedar vigas, and on one side stood a high glass case of hand-beaten silver bracelets and rings.

Behind the counter lay Bert Bruce on his couch, his left leg partially paralyzed; he seldom got up. Cable stood beside him to do the work.

How still they were! No one talked much and never tried to sell or buy. Somehow, pretty soon, it just happened. The Indian would come in, ask and receive enough tobacco for a cigarette, and stand around the stove to smoke with his fellows. The woman would lug in her burlap sack and squat on it beside the wall. In an hour she might get up, draw out of the sack a goat hide or sheep pelt and lay it gently on the counter. Almost before Cable could fling it on the scale or on the stack in the corner, Bruce would say something, close his eyes and seem asleep again. Cable would take out the money from the drawer and lay it on the counter for the woman to scrape up stealthily in a long dirty hand.

How March loved to watch her then, sliding up to the candy case, hands, nose and body pressed against the glass. Beneath her full, fifteen yards of skirt, her soft brown moccasins scraped lightly on the planks. Her knot of hair, twisted and tied with a white cord in back, moved lightly as she slid along the case. And Cable in time would give her some peppermint candy in a little paper sack.

But sometimes they would bring a blanket. Man and wife would be very much alive. Bruce raised on an elbow to inspect weave, weight and color. A can of tomatoes would be opened, and in an hour the trade would commence for flour, baking powder, six yards more of amber velveteen and a sack of Bull Durham tobacco.

All afternoon the boy would watch them inside the post and out, the women picking lice from their hair and the men methodically pulling out their whiskers a hair at a time. And at nightfall they would ride away—the men tall, slim-waisted and arrogant, driving their scrubby teams, and the women, passive and enduring, humped beside them in their brilliant velveteen blouses.

Were these Indians, the boy wondered, thinking of Buffalo Bill's painted braves, these arrogant, dignified men who appeared in haughty silence from out of that vast sea of sage and disappeared again so swiftly and completely?

An Indian—what was an Indian, really?

Out one day with Cable, he had stopped at a water hole. The Government at Washin'don had put up a windmill and a long galvanized trough. Two white men were just getting ready to leave. They had sloshed water over their arms and faces, drunk deeply from a bucket and thrown the remainder on the ground when a Navajo and his wife now drove up in their wagon. The man unhitched his team, removed their bits and led the horses up to drink. When they had finished, he led them back and carefully harnessed up again. The woman now got down with a tin cup. She drank, then trickled the rest of the water over her hands a bit at a time, bathing hands and face. When she had finished, the man did the same. Two cups of water had been used and not a drop had been spilled. These, surely, were Indians.

He watched, early one morning, a Navajo woman drive up to the post in her wagon with a boy some six years old. She left him sitting in the wagon-bed, leaning against the seat, while she went inside. The boy sat there, unmoving, for two hours. The sun rose, swung south, and glared down into his eyes. He did not move or turn away his face. The woman did not come out. Still the boy sat there. He did not play with the harness straps in the bed of the wagon nor with the silver conchos on the seat. He simply sat there as if carved of wood until mid-afternoon when the woman came out and climbed up into the seat. Then the boy got up and clambered beside her as she drove off. He too was an Indian.

It was a simple, subtle thing that made them what they were. The boy could see and feel it, yet he never knew beyond the mystery and the arrogance that marked their unsung lives. He was content to absorb with sunshine the countless daily incidents that marked the time at Shallow Water.

CHAPTER 3

Masked Gods: Navaho and Pueblo Ceremonialism (1950)

Young Frank Waters also absorbed an immense amount of social and even architectural detail on his first visit to the Reservation. This cell-knowledge, later backed up with names and dates by historical research, was formative. At Shallow Water, he saw for the first time the marginal or middle man, the trader who chose to live outside self-described civilization, in touch with the archaic. With full membership in neither realm, this figure nonetheless became heroic and tutelary to Waters. The trader bridged worlds, and suggested a citizenship of place that was beyond culture or ethnic identity.

From *The Trading Posts*

THE TRADERS

The usual trading post was a utility building rather than a country home. It was built to trade in and to live in, miles from any town or human habitation. It was necessarily built crudely with Indian help and from native material, and it was built strongly to withstand driving sand and wind and rain, heavy snows, and possible trouble. There was no set pattern. But with all their variations they conformed to a general type. The post at Shallow Water, remembered from boyhood, differed little from those found almost anywhere in the Four Corners.

Smaller or larger, they were all solitary oases in the desert; sturdy little forts on the frontier.

The walls were of sun-baked adobe bricks, from two and a half to four feet thick. No bullet could pierce them; they retained the heat in winter and the coolness of night in summer. The roof beams or vigas were huge logs of pine or spruce, hauled down from the mountains. Stripped of their bark, well seasoned, and cured like hams from the fireplace smoke of many years, they gleamed dark and smooth as honey. The roof itself was a layer of cross boards heaped with earth. The floor was of hard, pressed adobe until flooring could be freighted in, covered with innumerable Navaho blankets grown into rugs with the coming of the traders, and so durable that they out-lasted the floors. There was a fireplace in every room.

The main room was at best a huge hall. The walls were flanked with shelves of trade goods—bridles and spurs, bolts of flowered ginghams and solid-color velveteen, canned goods, staples, Stetson hats, knick-knacks, articles of clothing. Down one side and across the back stretched the long counter and showcases. The floor was littered with bushel baskets of onions and pinto beans, bags of flour, salt, and sugar put away from mice each night. Strings of dried chiles and coils of rope hung from the rafters. In the center of the room sat a squat-bellied stove surrounded by boxes of sand to spit in.

Adjoining this was the rug room, often serving as a general store-room. Its windows, if not every window in the post, were stripped with iron bars. Here were piled stack on stack of rugs, perhaps two hundred averaging $50 in value apiece and representing $10,000 in all. There was an iron safe full of silver currency and valuable pieces of pawn silver, a few loaded rifles.

Behind the big room and built at right angles to it were the living quarters of the trader, one room to a half dozen, depending on the size of his family and the help he required. In one of these might be a woman working on a loom or a man pounding silver if the trader was trying to improve the design and color of the wares in his district.

At sunrise the doors were opened. All day The People straggled in from the vast empty plain. Riding their shaggy ponies. Bumping along in their springless wagons, the man slimly erect in front, the woman slumped in her blanket beside him, the box full of children. In the post they stood spitting around the stove and sitting on the floor picking lice from each other's hair. The children knelt at the candy case rubbing dirty noses against the glass, silently staring at the peppermint sticks inside. A woman would inspect ten bolts of velveteen, dicker for a piece of calico.

Outside, the horses and wagons multiplied. People stood or squatted against the sunny walls, rolling cigarettes. Talking. Saying nothing. Everything was relaxed and easy. But pervaded too with a lurking tenseness, a sharp awareness. The trading post was a country store, but it was also the verbal newspaper of the region, a common meeting ground, and the focal point of perhaps a thousand square miles.

The undeniable master of all this was the trader. He supplied all the staples necessary for a people's changing existence, and was the only outlet for their wool, blankets, and silverwork. Loaning money on goods or articles given him for pawn, he tided them through drought and famine. He was their only contact with an alien, encroaching civilization. He interpreted this to them and them to it, excusing the ignorant foibles of greedy government Indian agents and missionaries, and protecting The People from the hasty anger of local sheriffs. He acted as law-maker, a judge and jury, a schoolteacher. At any hour of the night he might be awakened to set a bone or break a fever. He was often called upon to bury the dead, as Navahos would not approach a dead body. He contributed to all "sings" or ceremonials held in his area . . . All this required courage, absolute self-reliance, a quick wit, and a diplomacy as subtle as ever existed.

This writer could never subscribe to the obsession held by Oliver La Farge and other extreme romanticists that the traders were invented by Satan expressly to plague and cheat the Navahos. Among them, as among other groups, there were some who did cheat and contrive trouble of all kinds. They were few and they did not last. If they were not killed outright, they suffered peculiar accidents, became bankrupt, or disappeared. The traders were the first group of Anglos not expressly bent on obliterating the Navahos. Individually each became, to all purposes, the Great White Father in his wide domain. For during the first thirty years after the Navahos moved back from Bosque Redondo to what was now a reservation, twenty successive men held the post as government agent—a comedy of Indian administration.

What would have happened had the traders suddenly been expelled from the country? An interesting parallel is the case of a group of rural Chinese storekeepers, who established themselves among the Yaquis in the remote slopes of the Sierra Madres of Mexico. Parsimonious and scrupulously honest, they built their humble stores into the only banking structure of Sonora. Then late in the 1920's, while I was down there, Mexico decreed that all Chinese should be expelled. Hill-traders with thousands of pesos in beans and corn and beef in their ledgers, the Chinese storekeepers were suddenly driven out. The result was predictable. With no one to supply goods or credit, the abandoned stores were pillaged, groups of bandits formed and ran riot through the tiny villages, and another Yaqui uprising followed.

But in the Four Corners the traders were unmolested by the government, and it was they who enabled the Navahos to come through the difficult period following Bosque Redondo.

Probably the first trading post devoted primarily to the Navaho trade was established at Lee's Ferry, the principal articles exchanged being Mormon horses and Navaho blankets. "Al" Lee, grandson of its famous Mormon founder, John D. Lee, started the post at beautiful Tselani which his son, "Art" Lee, now runs. His other son, Hugh Lee, operates the post at Ganado and is currently president of the United Indian Traders Association.

A man named Leonard, about 1875, opened the first post at Ganado. In 1876, J. Lorenzo Hubbell opened a post three miles upstream from Leonard, on the Pueblo Colorado wash—near the site of the former

Fort Canby and the ancient Pueblo Colorado. Three years later he moved down to Ganado, bought out Leonard, and took C. N. Cotton as partner. Later he moved to Gallup, founding the oldest and largest Indian trading firm in the Southwest. Hubbell was, by all odds, the most famous trader in the area. For half a century his post was a mecca, his hospitality a legend.

In 1876, there was but one licensed trader on the reservation proper, Thomas V. Keam, a former government interpreter. In 1882, he took up a homestead and established a post in the canyon now named for him. It was in Hopi territory, just ten miles east of First Mesa, but drew Navahos as well. He later sold out and retired to his old home in Cornwall, England.

A man named Brown opened the first post at Manuelito, named for one of the two signers of the treaty at Bosque Redondo. In 1882, J. W. Bennett and S. E. Aldrich also located there, soon branching out with another in Washington Pass, in charge of Elias S. Clark and Charles Hubbell. Aldrich, in 1890, then established a post at Round Rock on Lukachukai Creek. For a new partner he took Henry Chee Dodge, destined to be the last great spokesman of the Navahos.

The first store at the important trading center of Chin Lee, at the mouth of Cañon de Chelly, was opened by Hubbell and Cotton. It was later replaced by one built by William Stag. The Lynch brothers, in 1881, started a post at Navaho, the farthest west; George W. Sampson, in 1883, located at Sanders; "Billy" Weidemeyer, in 1885, at La Cienega, later settled by the Franciscans and now called St. Michaels; "Joe" Wilkins, a freighter, the old post at Crystal, in 1890; and Charlie Fredericks opened a successful post at Navaho Church, the towering red cliff eight miles east of Gallup.

By 1890, there were nine traders on the reservation and some thirty traders surrounding it. The main article of trade was Navaho blankets—the best obtainable. Apaches, Utes, and Paiutes preferred them to the blankets issued by the government. Spanish-Americans still used them for serapes and ponchos. Anglo-American cowpokes and settlers used them for bed blankets and lap robes. For the first time an estimate was made of the yearly output—a total of $40,000, of which $25,000 worth were sold to the traders and $15,000 worth kept for tribal use.

Fifty years later the business had grown to enormous proportions. There were 146 trading posts, most of them licensed and bonded under government control, paying, in 1940, some $1,865,000 for Navaho products, selling $3,640,000 worth of goods, advancing $190,670 on pawned articles.

The first quarter of the century was the "golden age" of the trading posts, when, for a brief span, the integrity of Indian work and Indian thought achieved its only recognition. It was the traders who made this possible, and it is these old-timers I remember with a boy's love and respect for their high traditions.

Sam Drolet and Bruce Barnard, at Shiprock. Walter Beck and Dick Simpson, at Fruitland and Farmington. The Kirks, of Manuelito and Gallup . . . So many more, too numerous to record. Primarily and paradoxically they were not just "business" men. Like the Wetherills, at Kayenta, they made among the most important archaeological discoveries in the Southwest. Like the Newcombs, they recorded some of the first sand paintings. Like Ralph Meyers, of Taos, they were accepted by ethnologists as authorities on Indian life as well as Indian handicraft. Their remote posts were oases in the desert, landmarks in an unmarked wilderness. They were bankers, doctors, interpreters, school teachers, art agents, representatives of an encroaching White civilization to the Indians, and champions of Indian tribes against an inimical government. Scarcely 150 men in an area of over 25,000 square miles for a period of fifty years, the Indian traders were the media through which were exchanged the values of two ways of life.

THE TRADING CAPITAL

Midway between Fort Wingate and Fort Defiance there was built, in 1880, a general store and saloon called the Blue Goose. The site was ideal for a trading center. The Navaho reservation lay to the north, the pueblo of Zuñi and its reservation to the south. Past it streamed the tide of westward expansion following the 35th parallel route to California. To provide safer accommodations for travellers and to speed the delivery of mail, the Overland Stage was established and the Blue Goose was made a way station.

Next year surveyors came laying out the line of the new transcontinental Atlantic and Pacific Railway, followed by grading and bridge crews camping in tents around it. The following year, a locomotive engineer, named John Gallup, galloped the first iron horse into the tent city, the smoke billowing from its funnel stack and the whistle shrieking. A new town had been born and named . . . That's the story, although by prosaic coincidence the comptroller of the Frisco Railroad which was associated with the Atlantic and Pacific was also named Gallup.

There was nothing prosaic about Gallup's growth.

Coal, to fuel the locomotives, was discovered in the hogback near the new town. It became a mining center of Slavs and Italians, a division point on what is now the Santa Fe Railroad.

East of town, near Grants and Bluewater, were wide open grasslands for grazing cattle and sheep. Settlers came in, American ranchers and Spanish-American shepherds. Gallup became a frontier town in the noisiest tradition, with cowpokes riding in every Saturday night to shoot up its row of saloons and gambling halls.

From up in San Luis Valley of Colorado, John Wood came driving an ox cart filled with potatoes and bringing his wife to be delivered of the first white child in the new town. From the Navaho reservation came the traders in wagons piled high with wool and pulled by ten spans of horses. Other traders moved in from remote trading posts to establish large trading companies. Gallup became the trading and shipping center of the whole area.

Always there came Indians—a continuous straggle of Zuñis on foot and Navahos on spooky, quick-stepping ponies, to gawk and trade.

This was Gallup. The trading capital. The Indian capital. The metropolis of the Four Corners.

And this is Gallup today. Saloons and trading posts, bars and stores catering to the Indian trade. The Blue Goose infinitely and repetitiously multiplied. A frontier town with a backdrop of majestic red sandstone cliffs. Elevation 6,500 feet, population seven thousand. Still the largest, busiest town in the wilderness of the Four Corners. Still running high, wide open, and handsome.

It seems impossible that it can be so little changed since I first rode into it in a squeaking wagon. There are the tracks, the same grimy smell of smoke always so redolent of the far off, romantic, and unreal. The squat black buildings of the trading companies, each with their wooden loading platforms. And there—by all that is holy and ironic!—stands in one of their high facades the same wooden Indian, an unbelievable Hiawatha with the paint peeling from his feathers. Isolate in its cinder patch bulks the Fred Harvey hotel, a traditional haven of clean white sheets, famous coffee, and stacks of golden brown pancakes fortified by eggs and strips of bacon. Alongside it runs Railroad Avenue, with its row of ghastly bars, greasy little lunch rooms, pool rooms, and tawdry stores. Upstairs are the four-bit flop-houses, the dollar throws, and the privately public bedrooms.

The stubby block-short side streets run uphill to another street which has succeeded only in being more dull. One sees boarding houses, rooming houses, and little hotels, whose dreary parlors are impregnated with the odor of cheap cigars and the talk of railroad men whiling away time between runs. And these dwindle away into the wooden shacks and squat adobe huts of the Spanish-American half of the population, to the edges of town with its cheap dance halls.

No. It seems impossible that such an insubstantial bit of flotsam could have endured so persistently on this vast and naked earth with its heaving undulations of brown short-grass plains, the great bulks of the vivid red cliffs and the distant flat-topped buttes and mesas spreading out eternally under the strange, dark wings that hover about it—the spirit of endless time and illimitable space which is at once poignantly and forcefully evoked by no more than the haunting whistle of a train at night, the fresh smell of sage after rain, and the slight and almost imperceptible movement of the grass under the constant wind.

Yet Gallup endures. An ugly town. As tough as any that one might find. It seems to belong to no one and no one belongs to it. Neither the casual tourists, the alien Slavs and Italians, the weekend cowpokes, nor the passing railroaders. Groups of dark-faced Spanish-Americans, with black, sad eyes and thin, bitter mouths, stand idly on the corners waiting to take quick offense if they are called Mexicans. Everywhere wander Indians in cheap, faded, cotton blankets bought from Montgomery Ward. They slither aimlessly along the walks in fawn-pink moccasins with upturned toes and twinkling silver buttons. They squat along the walls, nursing babies, interminably picking lice. They reel drunkenly into the gutters with wild, red-rimmed eyes. The Whites step by them sprightly in white collars and shined shoes as if dreading to see fall upon them the inevitable hand of the law or the club of order. And in all their faces, the white, the brown, the red, there is evident the same quality of alien remoteness, the same fear and shame and horror that lies equally heavy on each.

Gallup, as the Capital of the Four Corners, expresses on every street corner the outer conflict of its two major races, the deep inner conflict inherent in its mestizos and the psychological conflict first evident in the early Mountain Men and now in us all.

Upon it impartially, too, descends the weather. Gallup has more kinds of weather per hour and square foot than any place you can find. You can be stuck there by snow in May, by rain in October, by driving sand in March. The heat is scorching. The cold is freezing. And the wind keeps blowing through the cracks of all seasons.

Yet we all—all we Wops and Dagoes, Greasers, Gringos and Indians—seem bound together here as nowhere else by some strange enchantment that dismisses all this misery, poverty, and shabby sinfulness as a transient chronicle of human error; a phantasmal spell that seems to substitute a hidden reality for an obvious illusion, and which again and again and again sets it down at the end of all trails and all roads as a gleaming image of all our unspent hopes.

CHAPTER 4

The Colorado (1946)

"The boy" learned much indeed, that time on the Reservation, including a hint or two about death during a sudden, destructive flood of the San Juan River. Then he returned home and continued his education, where the exciting new world was the high Cripple Creek District and the even higher land above timberline, the talus slopes where the Sylvanite lay. The mine proved, in the end, calamitous for the Dozier and Waters families, but when you're ten or twelve, you're on the upcurve; you're ready and open and learning, so imprintable that when you think back to that time from the vantage point of middle age, you become fired again, and your words, describing the place where the opening happened, take on a certain edge, have discovery in them.

From *Part One: Its Background*

HIGH COUNTRY

Next time, by hook or crook, make sure you're born with a mountain in the front yard. It comes in mighty handy all the way around.

When you're no bigger than that you can hang on to the grimy window curtains and watch it hour after hour. Then you know it best with all its moods and mutations, its sternness, dignity and immeasurable depth. It is like the face of an old medicine man, which only a child can understand. Other times it's just a grand spectacle of a thing—a whole show in itself. In the evening when the sun snags on the rimrock and the hollows fill up with red and lilac, damson blue and purple; when the summer storms explode against its shoulder like soap bubbles filled with father's pipe smoke, and the deer-horn lightning sprouts from the crags; or even in winter when its slopes turn slick and green as Blue Ribbon bottle glass.

But from the day you start to school it begins to be useful. The mountain has drawn back out of your yard, receded across the railroad tracks, even a mite farther. But like you it's got bigger too; you can see it even from behind the schoolhouse privy, so there's no need to worry about losing your way home. Just keep it on the right, on the side where you carry your back-pocket handkerchief. That's the rule to follow when you start camping out in the lower cañons; climb a tree if you can't see it. But besides being a compass the peak is a timekeeper and weather prophet too. A peek out the kitchen window to see what kind of clouds hang over the summit is the way folks always start the day. Later on, when you fancy yourself getting along a bit better than your neighbors, it's something to measure your success by; the peak is pretty chesty itself. Toward the last, of course, it's the best of all. When everything else seems gone and you're just another old fellow sitting alone on the stoop with your pipe, its big cone helps to fill up the heart's emptiness and you know it's one thing that won't pass.

A mountain peak, all in all, is about the handiest thing to have around and strike up friends with. Our mountain was a whopper, a beaut of a peak. We got along fine.

It poured gold into our laps, tons of it. In fact it built the town, both Millionaires' Row and the shanties of Poverty Row across the railroad tracks. It lent a dignity to all our lives, brought into them an enduring sense of mystery, and whetted our appetites with the sharp winds blowing down the Pass—which was no blessing to be sneezed at either, considering the hundreds of poor, sick, half-starved rich people who came to it for just that purpose.

Another thing, you didn't have to travel with the mountain so close. It was the whole world heaped up in layers.

There was the sandy, flat mesa, the first stairstep from the plains, with its garden of queerly eroded red rocks and its dust storms. Halfway up the peak at almost eleven thousand feet was timberline, drawn straight across it as if by a ruler. It separated two more distinct worlds.

Below it to the mesa was a dark and blue world: the forest world of leaf and needle with its silent shadows and singing streams, its chattering squirrels and gossiping magpies, its timid deer and shy brown bear. But like obedient citizens of that still lower world below tide level, none of them ventured upward. No stout exploring fir or spruce, not a single wind-stunted pine, scarcely a blade of grass. Only a mountain sheep sometimes stood poised on a crag, but for no longer than a seal rests on a rock before plunging back down into the green.

Above was a barren world of pink-gray stone—and man, that unbelievable creature to whom no domain is forbidden, even that of the spirit. This was the upper half of the peak that gave life and color to our town.

To reach it one rode the little Short Line that crawled a mile up and eighteen miles around the south slope of the peak. You knew you were getting close when a tourist's nose started bleeding and the ladies drew back dizzy from the windows. Suddenly there it was, unbelievable world: a half dozen little sprawling camps, small clumps of shacks and cabins that seemed to have been dropped out of the sky into the gulches, and everywhere, crowding the streets and littering the hillsides between them, the vast gray dumps and stark gallows frames of the mines. All hanging to an immense slope of rock seamed with great gulches.

Nothing could have been livelier, more entrancing and more pregnant with anticipation. Hills and gulches swarmed with men, burros and machinery. The birth of a monstrous mystery seemed imminent at every moment. Yet one famous and hasty visitor reported it a scene of appalling desolation, adding casually that no cat could live so high.

It was a challenging indictment. Timberline became Catline overnight, and every indignant miner's wife made haste to disprove it. Henceforth our lives were overrun with cats. By dozens they were sent up on the daily train. They roamed the streets and dumps like burros, made the nights hideous with noise, and finally went wild in the lower gulches. Unfortunately the visitor who had instigated the deluge had tarried only long enough to interview a certain Madam on the busiest street. To get even with him, the Town Council promptly renamed this, our local lane of prostitution, in his honor: "Julian Street."

It is a pity that Mr. Street did not remain longer. For the high country above timberline is like no other, and this was its boundary. In the absence of trees and foliage he would have seen here for the first time how everything stood out lucid and stark naked in new perspective. Like the weathered houses, the peeling log cabins, people's lives were stripped of decoration and verbiage by wind and weather. He would have noticed how everything tended to reduce down to stone. The faces of the men coming off shift were gray and colorless. The precious baubles in the parlor were heavy lead-gray samples, not needing roasting to bring out their hidden colors to the appreciative eye. Even the graves were blasted out of the hard granite with dynamite, that man could return not to dust but to stone.

A world, a life which even then seemed in the process of petrification. But still containing inside a hidden warmth. So watching on a winter's dawn the long queue of men plodding up the trail to the portal of a mine, a hasty stranger would be impressed only by the dominant drabness. He will not wait to see, a few minutes later, the window geraniums in their tin cans glowing like tiny fires lighted by the sun. He will not smell the yeasty buckwheat batter in the buckets set out after breakfast on every back stoop down the row of shanties. Nor see inside of an evening the walls livid pink in lamplight with the front sheets of the Denver Post papering the walls against cold. The tall peak itself is the core of an extinct volcano, and the running fire congealed in its veins still reflected the heat of desire which drew men here.

Everything, it seemed then, came from these high wastes of barren stone. I remember being taken by Jake to an impressive evening's entertainment. We sat next to the plank runway built down the center aisle from the stage, so that Jake in high humor and with boastful familiarity could snap the garters of the beautiful dancing ladies who tripped past. One garter I remember well—and also my unfulfilled ambition to grow big and bold and rich enough to snap it myself. It was a flower that came from no mere vegetable garden, a constellation that had never shone in any midnight sky. It was a beribboned rosette as big as Jake's fist and full of rhinestones and rubies and sapphires and diamonds. It was the most beautiful and vulgar, the most exquisite bad taste, the—"But, Jake, where did it come from? I never seen—"

The huge black-stockinged leg raised and pivoted over our heads, graceful as the steel arm of a crane. There was the close flash of light, color, ribbon and lace, the lusty wink of a dimpled knee, a raucous laugh. Jake made an ineffectual grab, and sank surlily back; it was a man behind him who was allowed to be successful. Girl and garter swept past.

"From the fourth level of the Sylvanite! Where the hell do you think it came from?" But Jake's habitual good temper was curiously out of whack; he might have spoken wildly. For certainly neither the fifth nor the sixth level of our mine ever produced anything to compare with it.

But all this, camp and people, still straddled timberline. It was still linked to the lower forested cañons, to the town below.

Our family folly lay even higher. Grandfather called it a mine though he had developed too many good ones to thus misname it. You could see it from the high saddle above the camp, a mere black speck far up the gulch. A bird could wing there in ten minutes. It took a boy on a burro an hour and a half. But if he waited at the station and rode up in the wagon with the supplies it was three hours up.

The speck had grown by the time he got there. There was the great gallows frame bestriding the shaft, a stout log cabin, and a small lean-to and corral of weathered aspen poles. And every great squared timber, every seasoned log and green pole, every stick of firewood, every nail—to say nothing of winch, steel cable and tools for the mine—had been snaked up here by mule and burro. One felt, upon looking downward upon camp and the dark slopes dropping from it, like a swallow resting on the side of a cliff.

Looking upward was worse. You were confronted with a steep terrain of bare frost-shattered granite that rose upward over two thousand feet. Nothing could convince the boy that this was the majestic, familiar peak he had seen from below since childhood. It lacked shape, outline and character. He simply felt imprisoned between sky and earth in a waste of stone. The feeling grew more oppressive daily.

There was no sound of rushing water, nor the sough of wind through pines. There was no smell of living green. No color relieved the surrounding monotone of rock. Only occasionally from deep underground rose a muffled roar, and at night there were new samples to assay. Here in this solitary little world of Grandfather, Abe and Jake, one lived a life of stone.

One blasted it, worked it, dug its dust out of ears and eyes. One cursed it, blessed it, prayed for it. It crawled into the blankets and into the dreams of night. It was at once the bane of your life and a resplendent future that at any crosscut might come to pass. For all that it was merely dead stone.

Then suddenly it happened, the boy did not know how. All this dead stone became intensely, vibrantly alive. Playing on the dump one morning after he had washed the breakfast dishes, he happened to pick up a pinch. In the bright sunlight he saw with microscopic clarity the infinitesimal shapes and colors, the monstrous and miraculous complexity of that single thimbleful of sand. In that instant the world about him took on a new, great and terrifying meaning. Every stone, every enormous boulder fitted into a close-knit unity similar to the one in his sweaty palm. For the first time he saw their own queer and individual shapes, their subtle colors, knew their textures, felt their weight, their strain and stress. It was as if in one instant the whole mountain had become alive and known.

No longer did the nightly assays seem meaningless chores carried out by a perpetually disappointed, white-haired old man and two gaunt, patient helpers. They took on the mystery of rituals that constantly attempted to evoke some deep hidden life within the stone. Each sample brought up from below, the boy eagerly rushed to examine. How did it differ from those on top—these cold, wet pieces wrenched from deep in the bowels of the peak?

"By cracky, the boy's got the makin' of a hard-rock miner!" grinned Jake.

"Dom fool!" snorted Grandfather. "What's he expect—nuggets as big as marbles?"

Late at night, tossing sleeplessly in his bunk, the boy kept wondering. The mountain was not one great big solid rock as it appeared from below. It was a million, trillion pieces all held together without cement: some hard, some soft, in all shapes and patterns, burned brown on the outside and gray inside, some with a purplish streak, but all with a preponderant delicate pink tinge against the snow. But it had lost its benign personality. It reflected a monstrous, impersonal force that pressed him from all sides. He was suddenly, mightily afraid.

"What keeps the Peak from fallin' down on us?" he blurted out in darkness. "I mean—"

From Abe's bunk came the usual silence. Jake let out another snore. But suddenly from across the room came two testy words in answer. "Isostatic equilibrium!" And then a moment later, "God Almighty, this time of night!"

Isostatic equilibrium:[1] it haunted him for years, both the phrase and

---

[1]*Isostatic equilibrium*

A high area, such as a mountain chain, is kept balanced on the earth's crust against a low area, such as a low plain or ocean basin, by "isostasy" (from the Greek meaning "equal standing").

its ultimate meaning. And not until long afterward did he realize that each of us has his own vocabulary for even Him who made the Word.

Thus he came to know that high realm of rock, the peak itself. Week after week the snowcap steadily receded. By day the drifts melted and trickled down into the cracks and crevices. By night the water froze and wedged the rocks apart. One heard, if only in his imagination, an eternity of sharp reports and booming explosions when the boulders finally split asunder. But to all this expansion and contraction, the rhythmic pulse of constant change, the peak remained immutable, bigger than the sum of its parts.

There came the day when the boy stood on its summit. For only a few moments the foothills, mesas, and the vast flat plains spread out 7,000 feet below to orient him to faraway Kansas and the Universe. Then mists swept up to cloak the forested cañons on all sides; it began to rain. He was standing—isostatic equilibrium to the contrary—on an island of rock floating in the sky. Far off toward Utah was another, and still another like a steppingstone into Wyoming. It was as it might have been at the Emergence. Or perhaps as it will be at the end of another paragraph in their geological biography when they will be the last to disappear. The feeling was indefinable. He did not know it, but it expressed at best the timelessness which is the core of that we know as time.

According to the principles of isostasy, eroded surface material from the mountain is constantly being moved to the ocean basin. In time this loaded part of the crust sinks, forcing solid rock, which behaves as a plastic substance under great pressure, to flow horizontally back underneath the eroded mountain. Thus the two blocks, or the high area of erosion and the low area of sedimentation, are kept in proper balance or in isostatic equilibrium. The comparatively level plains area between them remains unaltered.

CHAPTER 5

The Dust within the Rock (1940)

March Cable studied engineering at The Colorado College, continuing rather dutifully the lead of his mother's side of the family. The college (some of whose buildings had been erected by his grandfather) stood in the fashionable North End neighborhood of Colorado Springs, adjacent to fine mansions. The path to respectability and wealth was clearly implied. March moved closer to graduation, further along, that is, in the scientific and technical view of life, caught up in what he later saw as an imbalance of consciousness. He was deeply, structurally, unhappy.

From *Book Two: Tailings*

Late that spring, March came to the end of his rope. The sense of decay about the house roused him to fury: it was like a cancer: he was afraid lest it fasten on him and eat into his flesh.

Little London he had grown to abhor. Its stifling conservatism, its cheap pretense and sentimental vulgarity seemed to throttle him more and more. He knew now that it had never had the integrity to live its life openly, vigorously and unabashed. Indeed, it did not acknowledge and assert a life unified and all her own. There were the few rich who like the tourists fled at the first snow and while here lived the boredom of those who have no roots. And there were the few poor who without industry eked out an existence through nine months from their rapacious fleecing of visitors in three. And with them, it had a clique of town bell-ringers who spent their lives in feathering their nests at the expense of both: the little imitators tolerated and used by the rich, and abhorred and laughed at by the poor; the musty old families still living in the past and on the trust funds left over from Cripple Creek gold; the self-important custodians of the scenic concessions, the vast estates. Their high board fences were built around the carven and balanced rocks; their gates of admission blocked every waterfall and cañon; the springs were covered with their bath houses and bottling works. Everything of beauty had come to bear their price-mark until the region was little better than a fair-ground, and Pike's Peak's chief distinction now was that someone's nose had pushed a peanut up to its summit. These were the men who had prostituted Little London. The small minority of hypocrites, the sanctimonious conservatives who choked the town knowing that its first lusty breath of life would throttle them. Their highest boast was that they had made the town what it was. And the truth of that assertion would always be the indictment against them.

For if Little London is to the stranger a vast multi-cellular hotel closed up from September to June, they were but its obsequious proprietors with hands outstretched to the summer trade. They were not its life, and in their protests that there was no other of consequence the note of falsity crept in to sound the discord of the town itself.

March knew that the hidden life of his town went on silently and surely as always. With its roots sunk deep to draw forth the inherent strength from its own soil without dependence from outside, it was a life ever-growing in summer as in winter, and its flower would be of a pattern older than any yet superimposed upon Little London.

He sensed it because he loved it. For he was but one of its children: children in whom all this beauty roused inquietude and unrest as it had all the children who bore them; children tinged with the bitterness of the wealth which the hills had poured forth, and touched by its splendor too; children of that soil who hated it and yet were bound to it forever; who loved it and were driven from it by the same blind fury that brought their fathers.

But now March wanted no more of it. He felt like every boy who has ever lived: an arrow unspent in its quiver.

It was the Country Club which focused his misery. He had long withdrawn from the superficial, indolent life of the campus. The measure of success in a college, he saw, is not the measure of success in the world outside. The athletic heroes, the social-leaders, the pride of the faculty—these were the men who from the campus drifted gracefully and affably into oblivion. March looked around him at a bitter and sarcastic West End student, at a myopic hunchback, a queer outcast studying economics. It was of one of such unknowns as these that the school would hear later, scratching heads to remember what he looked like.

March had plunged into his work and now it too was unbearable. For months he had been taking nothing but science and mathematics. He felt himself turning to stone, his life being reduced to an algebraic equation.

Even during his lectures, Dr. Thomason insisted that his students sit with engineer slide-rules in hands. He would stop talking abruptly, scribble on the blackboard and wait for them to finish the long, evolved computation "within one-tenth of one percent—the accuracy of your rules!"

He had another irritating idiosyncrasy. He would whip around at any time, point his long bony finger at a boy and demand, "What causes the Aurora Borealis? The rainbow?"—"Jameson, what is thunder?"—"Lightning?"

Oh, it is the red forked tongue of the great serpent when the white-bellied clouds drift over the hills beyond Cochiti, over the parched desert of the Navajos, over the shrivelled little corn patches below the cliffs of Oraibi. The drums beat louder; the rattles shake; the dancing feet pound harder on the earth, and the horribly painted faces turn upward, ecstatically, to the darkening sky. It is the red forked tongue of the great serpent, the serpent whose image lies wrapped around the mouth of the huge water jars, the serpent with many names. It is one of the two great animalistic symbols of all America. It is the Great Snake of Picuris, and it is Quetzalcoatl, the feathered serpent of the Aztecs. It is the tall rain majestically striding the sky, walking over the desert bringing life to shrivelled corn and shrivelled people. Oh, look at the rain! Listen to the drum thunder in the sky. Watch the serpent stick out his red forked tongue. The old serpent-god of earth-fertility with his "moccasins of dark cloud," with his "leggings of dark cloud," with his "head-dress of dark cloud."

"Lightning, sir, is an electrical discharge caused by an electrical potential set up as a result of the rising air currents blowing the edges off the larger water drops in the cloud, and carrying away the smaller drops of spray which remain. Thunder, following the flash, is caused by the vibrations set up by the sudden heating and expansion of air along the path of lightning."

Who will ever find now the pot of gold at the end of the rainbow which only results from rays of light bent and reflected by passing into and out of drops of water?

Cold clear October, when the sun gleams through a haze of autumnal gold with the rich ripeness of Indian Summer! Ah, it too is simply a "figment of a poet's fancy. Indian Summer as a meteorological entity does not exist. The haze when it does appear is simply composed of collected and suspended smoke and minute particles of vegetation, and is caused by a stagnated high pressure area."

"Correct.—Cable!" The professor rapped the desk. "What is this? This table, the chair you're sitting on, wood—everything that exists?"

"All matter, sir, is nothing but an elemental charge of electricity, you might say. The molecules of all substances are broken down into atoms, and these atoms are composed of electrons with their satellite protons—positive and negative charges of electricity whose numbers and arrangement determine the outward form of matter which we call by different names. Scientists are now trying to break down the electron. By accomplishing this they will release the boundless locked-up power of the universe and harness it for the industrial uses of man."

"It will do. It will do. What I am trying to get you to do, all of you, is to regard even simple phenomena in terms of your calling. Clear your minds of old beliefs. Think freely. Life, nature, everything that exists is nothing in itself and has no meaning. We have reduced all to its simple expression in scientific laws. Now, by learning to apply them, we will at last be masters of the universe, of life itself."

This was his meaning of life, the mysterious and immense flow through interstellar space, the blade of grass, ourselves; the mysterious flow around us and through us, rising and ebbing like a tide through the breathing mountains, the rutting deer, the passions and sympathy of man. It was clear, mathematically precise, but it denied the mystery of creation, of the secret unknown gods who whisper in all men.

Some of the students were amazed and amused, like children robbed of a Santa Claus.

"Murder—social subtraction, eh?" they joked. And on seeing a length of silk leg hanging over the balustrade outside, they would mutter with a grin, "Tut, tut, my boy. Merely a biological necessity!"

But March sat through these lectures as if Dr. Thomason had him by the throat. He was inarticulate, unable to voice his misery. It was not as if he did not understand. His mind and imagination worked well enough, but something within him passionately rebelled.

Prof. Thomason did not encourage his perplexing questions—it was a sign of weakness to doubt. So week after week the boy felt himself hardening, damning in his secret soul the science that the Professor represented. He wanted life, the rich and secret flow. Not the frozen form.

He was not altogether unjust to the Professor. Thomason was a brilliant man, but he lacked what he denied—the warm flow of life itself in all its mysterious profundity. He was a mechanical mind, an excellent machine. Rogier, with his monomania, had had at least the vision of life with all its torment and beauty before him. Thomason, never.

So March worried. He began to refute the vision of life that science held out to him. He had no way of knowing that just as chemistry is nothing but a deeper physics, so all science with art, religion and sociology is nothing but a facet of the many-sided but eternal truth. Nor did he know that just as there are but few true artists, there are also pitifully few real scientists. He simply saw in them all what most of them really are: industrial engineers.

They did not know that science is merely the frame and not the content of life. Their consciousness did not gain with their deepening perception of nature and her laws; they were mastered by their own machines. They believed themselves geniuses, forgetting that genius is the power of evoking life, not throttling it. It is the love of truth, the love of life, that leads to pure science. But all these men, like Thomason, were really interested only in the application of science to commercial ends. They were industrialists.

March felt this clearly, but without being able to express it even to himself. He only knew that he could never give up life for industry, that he was on the wrong trail. He began to slump, neglecting his lessons. He was coming to a crisis.

During these few weeks he saw Valeria seldom, except in chapel. They were like stars, each in its separate orbit, which had touched in a moment of truth and passed. It was enough. Neither would forget the other. But there was nothing that bound them together.

March, instead, fled to the mountains alone. One afternoon in May it happened. He had sneaked through the vast and beautiful estate at the mouth of Queen's Cañon, past the great, grey stone Tudor castle of Glen Eyrie long abandoned but still protected against visitors by wary watchmen and landscape gardeners. The narrow cañon, behind, rose steeply between the somber cliffs on each side. There was only an old foot trail winding along the foaming stream. Several miles back he came to its end. For fifty feet above him was a series of huge bowls dug in the rock by the falling water—the Devil's Punch Bowls. He made his way up carefully, reached the top. Soon the stream felt warm. He remembered the old belief of a hot spring somewhere up in the cliffs above.

It took him nearly an hour to clamber up the mountainside and find it. He could have given a shout of joy. It lay on a narrow shelf of rock overlooking the deep forested cañon like the mouth of a cave. There was a huge bowl in the rock nearly fifteen feet across and filled with hot water. There was no sign of the spring itself: it seeped slowly, without a bubble, up through the white sand floor.

Wet with sweat, he flung off his clothes and stepped in. The water was up to his waist.

It was now almost four o'clock. The sky was black. A chill wind whistled through the pines. A few cold drops of rain stung his bare shoulders like thrown pebbles. In a moment the quick and passionate spring storm broke. And with it something burst inside him.

He could never remember clearly what happened, but the sensation remained with him always. He was aware of the lash of rain, the clouds snagging on the mountain rim around him, the swaying of the pine branches. The thunder, with a savage violence possible only in this vast high hinterland, broke forth in bolts likely to split the mountain any moment. There was suddenly a flash of lightning, a great jagged flame that raced out from the sky and along the cliff top like a monstrous snake's tongue.

The boy ducked to his shoulders, went cold as ice in the hot water, trembled violently. At that moment it happened. It was as if that flash of lightning had gone through him. He felt like a flame, as if lit up from within. And all about him remained this brilliant and indestructible illumination. In a moment it passed. He heaved up from the pool, flung himself upon the rock, weeping.

He was not sad nor frightened. He was cleansed, fused, made whole, happy and joyously alive. It was as though he had passed, in one moment, through a resurrection of the spirit.

Now he climbed back to stand in the pool. How naked and alone he was—gloriously alone, sublimely naked to the lashing of the storm. But a part of it, an inalienable part of the moaning pines reeking water, the sturdy mountains, the foaming stream far below him, the profundity of the aroused heavens.

And so he stood there high above the world of men, in pride and humility, and with a compassionate love for all that moved and breathed; he did not know how long.

When he got out, he was weak from the hot water; his clothes were wet. The trail back was long and difficult. He reached home, went to bed without supper, and yet in a wordless happiness of which he could not bear to speak.

In the next two weeks at school March did practically nothing. Four cuts from chapel were allowed each semester. He took them all in a row, lying outside on the grass under a tree watching the clouds, listening to the pipe organ wheezing inside. The Professors passed him with angry looks. He did not notice them, but lay drawn tight within himself, impenetrable. Through the daily class lectures he sat quietly but uninterested. His afternoon laboratory work he did lackadaisically and left for home early to read.

The queer sensation he had experienced in the mountains had passed. He was no longer bitter and worried, but wondered vaguely what had come upon him. Spring-fever, he thought, but without being able to overcome his lassitude. In a mindless calm, he seemed caught up like a leaf in the ghostly flow of time.

Early one Friday morning he walked up to school for an important examination. Only the six major students of Dr. Thomason were taking it. The end of the school year was almost a month away; yet, if each student passed this test, he was practically promised immunity from the final examination.

The Professor was in his office and did not come out. He merely handed a notebook to each student as he passed into the laboratory.

"Bring your slide-rules, of course," he had told them the day before, "and all the notes, text books and so on you want. It won't be necessary to write anything on your cuffs. You can refer to anything you want and you will need it all. Only don't talk among yourselves."

March strolled into the laboratory and sat down in a chair against a window. The other five students were there before him, scattered around the room. The short, solid pillars of brick covered with immense slabs of slate had been cleared of apparatus. On them lay text-books and lecture-notes, engineering hand-books and logarithm tables.

What were the questions?

There were none. But the blackboard on two sides of the room was covered with a drawing of one vast compound electrical circuit. It began with a generator plant, ran to a main switchboard with several circuit-breakers, and thence to an amazing network which seemed on first glance to contain every problem he had encountered in his three years' work. Some of the resistances only were labelled, the E.M.F. for some legs of the circuit were given, but not for others, the voltage had been stepped down through transformers but to what result was not then given—a devil of a mess.

One of the men turned around to March. "Professor Thomason said we were simply to solve the whole circuit beginning wherever it was necessary."

It was the only word spoken.

March leaned back against the window. He was in no hurry; they had four hours. He was not sure, but he believed that he could work it out. Still, he did not begin.

He looked up at the generator-drawing, remembering the old steam plant east of town he had visited, the whirling drums cutting the lines of magnetic force in the magnetized rims to generate the power drawn off from the plant to supply the town. Was this the source of power? No, because the drums had to be set whirling by steam from the old boiler. What made it go? Coal. What was the nature of coal, the inherent power of fuel itself, that derived from the enormous pressures of earth and time? The coal beds were simply the great forests of geologic time washed out upon the plains and covered with sediment from the crumbled, vanished mountains. And the life of these forests . . . . It all went back to a beginning no one knew. This was merely an industrial application of the power of life itself.

E.M.F.—electromotive force. Merely a scientific, modern name for the never-old, never-new, and indestructible flow of life through everything that lived and breathed, the stone, the blade of grass, the flesh and spirit of man.

It was the Great Spirit. It was Manitou. It was the Sun of the Incas, the red-forked tongue of the great serpent of America. It was Thor hurling his thunderbolts, it was Zeus and Jupiter of the Greeks and Romans, the god of the Persians, the Babylonians, and all the ancient peoples that ever lived and have vanished from the memory of mankind.

Mythology is the only true history of man and his gropings for the truth of his existence. And our science today will be the mythology of the long tomorrow. It is not new; only its names and its mechanical applications. For from the old anthropomorphic gods we have successively worshipped matter and form, light and darkness, and now force and mass. Each has been the thought-religion of a culture and a civilization which has risen, crumbled and died. And today science is but the speech of our own transient culture. Only the names have changed. It is not Manitou nor God to which we bend in obeisance, but to the all-pervading power we rename electricity, and its disciples molecules and atomic numbers.

But where now is our humility of spirit? In our immense and lofty pride, with our new, impressive terminology, we believe we have in our hands the key to the secret of all life. We are the masters of the universe. Our heads swell, our foreheads bulge. But our shanks wither, our bodies constrict and harden into stone. We deny the secret unknown gods that cry in our blood, the mysterious soft flow of life itself.

"Everything that exists is nothing in itself and has no meaning."

"No!" he thought. "A mountain peak, a drop of water, a blade of grass—each is a single smile on the face of truth, and a world within itself. I will not be denied, nor will I deny each particle of the unseen whole."

And remembering something his father had once told him, he thought:

"Let me always wear a feather and so be conscious always of that for which it stands, forgetting the personal me and remembering only the grace and power lent me to uphold it—a single upright feather to wear, not defiantly as men flaunt the faded cockades of their decadent heritage, but proudly, like the everlasting insignia of the wild earth's nobility."

An hour had passed. March turned and stared out of the window. The sun was bright and warm, the trees were leafing, the mountains stood up dark blue in the cloudless sky. He rose quietly, wrote his name in the empty notebook and laid it on the table. Without stopping at Dr. Thomason's office, he walked out and crossed the campus to the Administration Building.

At the cashier's window he collected twenty-two dollars due him for work as a laboratory assistant. He was supposed to turn it in at the next window as payment on his tuition. Instead, he jammed the money in his pocket and walked slowly home.

The two girls were in school. Ona was over at the grocery store. Rogier was lying down on the sofa, and Mrs. Rogier was dusting.

Without speaking, March climbed the stairs to his room and packed his leather-rimmed canvas duffle bag. Before long his mother came hurriedly up the stairs.

"What's the matter, son? I heard you had come home. This time of day! Are you sick?"

She suddenly saw the duffle bag. Her glance swept the bare top of his dresser and the empty hooks inside the open closet, flew back wildly to his face.

"Don't get upset, Mother," he said quietly, standing before her. "I've quit school, and I'm leaving home. Sit down, Mother."

He pushed her down gently on the bed, sat beside her and put his arm over her shoulders.

"You're mad, son. Mad!" she gasped. And yet there was something in his quiet tone, his assurance and unusual gentleness, that sent a chill up her spine. In him now, if only for the moment, she saw Cable. It stunned her completely. In him there was nothing to answer.

March explained patiently as best he might. "And so you see, Mother, it's no place for me. I've got all that I can. I had it a year ago, but I never knew till now. . . . Don't look so! Wouldn't I be leaving soon anyway to go to work? And we're poorer than ever now with Grandad the way he is. You'll be needing the money I can send you. So will the girls. You know there's no jobs in town. A few days' work at the station on the extra board. What is that? It would be years before I got on the regular list."

"But where? God in Heaven, boy! Where are you going?"

"The Salt Creek, Wyoming oil fields, Mother. You've read of the oil boom there. Men are pouring in from all over the country. There's work for everyone."

"What kind? What can a boy do? Son, it's a wild goose chase. Be sensible. Don't leave yet."

She knew it was futile talk. The moment had come that she had dreaded all her life, the moment that she had waited for, day by day, ever since that first night he had gone to Cripple Creek. How could she repeat now the pain and anguish, her protestations of love and affirmation of faith, go through that scene of parting in which she had participated nights on end for years? It was like a play she had rehearsed for years, and now at the rise of the curtain she found herself tongue-tied and frozen. Only the pain stabbing her heart was real.

Then suddenly there flashed upon her the vision of Tom's departure up the Pass to Leadville, of Rogier's departure for Cripple Creek—that one long departure endlessly repeated through twenty years, of Cable's final leave-taking. And now her son, her only son! Ah, the mysterious souls of men! Would none of them ever guess what went on in the hearts of the women they left?

She stood up and wiped away a tear as if ashamed of that single priceless pearl formed within her, years before, by the tiny grit of her first fear.

"Well, son!" She grasped him sturdily by the shoulders, her big heavy body hard as stone, her square jaws clenched. "So you're really goin'. Well!"

If she had only wept or argued or something! Anything but this slow fusing of despair and strength, a tear and a smile—this Rogier undemonstrativeness! It was more than the boy could bear. He flung his arms around her, stroked back her greying hair, kissed her beautifully white, girlish smooth face.

"I'll be comin' back. Hell! Sure, I will."

"I'll be fixin' up a few things for you," she answered simply and fled into her room.

March told Leona and Pauline good-bye when they came home that noon for lunch, answered their joshing with quiet grins. Mrs. Rogier was perplexed but loyal. "Well, sir, things happen. They do. But I count on my boys every time. Just remember you're a Rogier, March!"

Rogier, whose rupture had bothered him that morning, rose weak and ashamed. "Boy, I hate to see you leavin' like this without a dom cent. If things had panned out different—I—Dom, it's best though! Let a man stand on his own feet. It isn't minin', but you're diggin' in. Yes, sir. I" . . .

This one and only reference which Rogier ever made to his failure to wrest from the hills that fortune which would have put the family on Easy Street, cut the boy to the quick.

"Don't be funny!" he cried awkwardly and embarrassed. "Lord, Grandad! Everything I know about mining, real mining and construction, I got from you. Remember all the lectures you used to give me on geology and all? I won't forget, Grandad. I won't, ever!"

At one o'clock he left the house, alone, dressed in his one worn suit and lugging his duffle bag. He did not look back. This namby-pamby good-bye stuff made him feel like a fool. He would have liked to grab his bag and flee down the alley without a word. But walking swiftly to the station, he felt the regret and sadness lifted from him. He was alone and free at last! The world stood out immense and naked before him.

CHAPTER 6

Fever Pitch (1930)

Having written a scene that represented something burning brightly within him, Frank Waters the twenty-three-year-old telephone company engineer settled down to the task of giving that scene a plausible context. He worked up a more or less believable plot for a novel, and then, getting a bit more adventuresome perhaps, created a story-within-a-story structure for it. Then, having something in hand, he began to think about getting it published. He scanned the shelves of the El Centro, California, public library, looking for handsomely done books. Those of Horace Liveright appealed, and he sent the manuscript off to Mr. Liveright. In due time, Liveright sent back an advance, a contract that included an option on Waters's next two books, and a letter praising this first effort. This was probably Waters's quickest, easiest, and most straightforward initial deal-making, ever, with the world of publishers. Liveright regarded Waters's title, *The Lizard Woman,* as "ghastly and I think cheap," and called the book, over the author's protest, *Fever Pitch.*

From *The White Heart: I*

At that early hour the rocks and lava seemed drawn into folds and wrinkled by the heat. Even the air seemed to have been drawn away as if by an invisible syphon and slowly was being pumped into its place a heavy, odorless, tasteless substance which surrounded them, pressed against their bodies, and seeped like a gas under the folds of their garments. Like a dry steam it gathered about their nostrils and mouths and at each gulp drew sluggishly away, refusing to be drawn into their lungs.

Behind him Marston heard the feet of the burro scrape on the slippery rock and the thump of his belly flattening against the hill, his front feet doubled under him like the arms of an old bald monk at prayer and his back legs outstretched like a rabbit's. As he turned, he saw the burro's eyes rolling up at him. Like bowls of milk with a floating piece of toast and with strawberry stains about the edges, they looked. But, as I say, they reached the top.

Lee Marston reached it first, for Arvilla behind him had been hanging to the tail of the burro. On his belly he crawled over the last crust of that black volcanic deposit. He hadn't sweat a drop, you must remember, not the least bit of greasy moisture on any part of his body for two days. He seemed burning with heat. He imagined—he knew— that it was the radiating intenseness of his desire to reach the top rather than the reflected heat of the rocks which burned his breast and face. And between the jagged edge of an outcropping of ash and a three-inch cactus growth, Marston peered over and into what Arvilla had so often described as their last day's journey.

There can be no attempt to give you Marston's words. To give you his impressions is to give you himself, and you can see only through his eyes. To you as to me, truly as a confession, are given those few minutes in which a man conceived of life and baptized in human endeavors stood with God and received a soul; and gave it back again to that infinite power of all life and nature for which only God himself has name.

Let us go back to the beginning of the last four days across the desert. At that time all distance had shrunk to a flat ribbon edged with a heat-haze of white flecked with blue. The only tear in that beribboned blue string of heat-mountains, Arvilla had told him, was the wedge-shaped shadow of some prehistoric outpouring of lava which made the only accessible pass. This, then, was the steep ascent they had accomplished during the night. On each side now, in a curling somnolent haze, continued the rope of mountains around him. Like a rope of coral beads, to use his words, flung down in a broken heap because they had changed in color to a lifeless, rusty brown flaked as the skin of a rock lizard; and each bead a broken splotch of rocky boils, a sandy rash, and pimply lava crust.

Before him—and at the sight Marston felt as though he were squatting in the position of an ancient sun-worshiper, arms outstretched and fingers spread—before him and below him, perhaps two thousand feet, lay a round sea scintillating with untold waves of borax crystals and infinitesimal particles of mica, and sands of æonage forever unmoved by so much as a hair's breadth. Like two pebbles of agate, he felt his eyes were, at the very hour of creation, and he told me he drew back until he could barely see over the edge. Like a fly-speck on a teacup rim he knelt, with the mountains curving round in two outflung sweeps and interlocking with fingers of shimmering heat as indistinguishable as their own outlines. And all inside this great cup of creation was the drifted, crumbled, baked potpourri of nature, whose thick sugary crust lay miles deep. All the shimmering, incandescent softness and sterile whiteness of a sea within a sea, deeper than the level of the desert floor without.

There are times in a few men's lives when the very manifestation of all Nature seeps into their souls and fills the void to completeness. And in its ebb it takes but the inconsequential pride of being, and leaves in its wreckage bits of the very core of a man's birth. Then a man cries out in a very agony of comprehension and prays for relief from his burden. So it was with Lee Marston. He rose to his feet and felt every vestige and semblance of life stripped from him. He felt the knowledge and heritage of all mankind seep and fuse itself into his soul and transmit itself to his understanding.

He could have cried aloud and his words would have followed too closely to be recognized, and their context would have at once defied and admitted all religions. He threw out his arms and felt that should a brush have been placed in his fingers he could have painted the form of that transient heart of all beauty for which men have sought in vain. He was in accord with the music of the Infinite. And with that unlocking of all boundaries, all limitations, all the empty forms of that beauty which is known to man, he saw it as it was, the bare, untouched depth of all humility. And standing there alone in that immensity of creation and alone in the presence of God, he bowed his will to an omnipotent power of nature. He felt that it was as though that spot had never known the presence of a Creator. As though the very mountains seemed like a signet ring of God himself flung on that spot and preserving forever the enclosed space from creation.

It is at such times that a man in an uplift of spirit loses all conception of the present and has removed from him forever that recognition of time and space into which he has been born. Lee Marston, then, was on the very threshold of that realm of thought in which lies stark madness. For when a man has reached that peak at which he is cognizant of nothing but himself and his god, there is no return. Marston was at that point, but held to the sanity of the present by a single thread all the more strong for its imperceptibility—the thought of Arvilla. At that crisis of his soul when God had taken him by the hand and led him to the last barrier of His handiwork beyond which he must not pass, Arvilla had sustained him by his unconscious acceptance of her being, almost as part of himself.

He closed his eyes to shut out the dazzling brightness of that white floor, and heard Arvilla behind him. She was pulling herself up over the rocks by aid of the straps round the burro. There was no imagining her presence; always with her there was something—the life of her perhaps—something always missing. She had piled several layers of the limp panama matting on her head and had them bound turban-fashion with wide strips of blue burlap, the affair on the whole, seeming to edge over the rocks like an enormous hat. The alkaline water she had poured on her head had run down her cheeks and dried, leaving deep furrows of brine and mud. Over her shoulders was pinned the old black shawl which flopped open at each step, revealing a brown shirt devoid of buttons, and an inexpressibly dirty pink camisole covering her breasts. Her eyes, always glowing, looked as if a tobacco chewer had spit twice on a brown rock.

Arvilla had seen that deep circular depression before, yet she stood silent beside him as if appalled at its sight. After a time, however, Marston became aware that her gaze was fixedly anchored across the valley, if one could so flatter that pit of white hell.

"Ah, Le' Marston, por la Madre de Dios, she is yet there, the Lizard Woman! Do I not speak the truth?"

The words were hoarse, wrung from cracked and bleeding lips, and they came as though from afar to Lee Marston's ears like the wash of ancient waves upon the rocks, bitter as their salt deposits. She was fingering the bracelet now slung from her neck. At her words there came back to him the story she had told him of gold, of hardship—the tale of the land of the Lizard Woman. His own cracked lips split open and he laughed. A dry, gasping laugh of a fool, laughed at the woman he loved, whose words to her were almost a whispered sacrament; laughed because they were so true! He had smiled at the tale; it was all a part of the beckoning finger of desire and romance. He laughed again, and in that sobbing laugh of his was all the immeasurable gulf of a man's utmost imagination spanned completely. Why, every word of that tale was so true it seemed coexistent with his very conception of God.

Why, she was there too plain to see for a moment. Clear across the sea of belching heat and brightness, she rested on the topmost rim of that hazy horizon of fluttering heat and gasping mountains. A protruding hip, a scaled body, and out-flung arms reaching round to the very tips of their burned shoes . . . the Lizard Woman who at the recession of the waters of Infinity had created the world for God at His command. And then in the very throes of conception, she had flung herself down and begged Him to leave her this spot of untouched chaos she hugged to her breast.

And Lee Marston knew that God had forever turned His back upon the one spot at which He had put to rest the embodied spirit of that power conceived of all Nature to do His bidding. And he felt flood his mind an instant recognition of the fact that to descend but one foot into that immense inclosure was to remove themselves beyond the reach of prayer.

Why Lee Marston went on when every mind-muscle revolted against commanding his body, there was no doubt. It was beyond all question of fear. That had been drained from him wholly. Nor did he continue because of the simple fact that the day would see the end of his journey, for the long approach to the valley, he knew, would be as nothing compared to its short crossing. He continued, in short, for his love of Arvilla—and this could not be explained, for to analyze a man's love for a woman is to know at once the beginning and end of all things.

The facts are these: Arvilla, whose very nature allowed no backward step, had submerged his own indecision, had led him inevitably to the last barrier, and now in a fierce eagerness of desire, was berating the beast upon the ground. His love for her, in the intenseness of this desire which he began to recognize as a recurring lust for gold, counted for nothing. It was she who had won him to the start and who now, almost without thought, was spurring him toward its end.

CHAPTER 7

The Yogi of Cockroach Court (1947)

This book may be Frank Waters's least-read work of fiction—an ironic circumstance, if the supposition is true, because he certainly poured himself into it. It was what he wrote next, after *Fever Pitch,* and it commanded his devotion for twenty years, through several rejections (including Horace Liveright's), and obviously a number of event-filled years, including the Great Depression and World War II. Waters carried this novel into his middle life, finally to see a late draft brought out by Rinehart, publishers of *The Colorado. Yogi* is a candid work for its time of composition, including even-handed treatment of prostitution and lesbianism, but what sets it apart in American fiction, and may eventually get this book noticed more, is its sophisticated evocation of the practice of meditation. The complexities of spiritual seeking may not have been a hot subject for many readers, but for Waters they were apparently quite close to the bone.

From *Chapter Eight*

3

By day, by year, The Lamp Awake never changed. The boxes and bales, the sacks and cans, the matting, hardware and sundries forever cluttered the place in a hopeless confusion that never improved. New canaries came, sang their songs and were replaced by others whose voices seemed quite as sweet—just like poets who as unknowingly take up the one song of all the others who have gone before. So too its fish shimmered in the morning sun, faded and died, like rainbows that come and come again.

Yet subtly Tai Ling's cluttered shop did mark the passing seasons. With fresh hearts of mezcal and a stack of sugar cane; with strings of green, yellow or red chile—chile colorado, pasilla, sol seco, pequeno, poblano; fresh corn husks for wrapping tamales; a single poinsettia, la Flor de Noche Buena—the Flower of Christmas Night; and then a bowl of water lily bulbs blooming in the window; by such successive signs did The Lamp Awake mark time.

But now Chugoku had stopped sending him fish either for sale or pleasure. Reluctantly the old man emptied his last dead specimen in the alley. Likewise he stopped ordering fruits and vegetables; no customers came in to buy them. And for the first time in years Chan Foo had not sent him a poinsettia for Christmas, and Chewlee Singkee a lily bulb for New Year.

With this disappearance of variable matter, the phenomena of time vanished also. Day and night the yogi of Cockroach Court sat in his dusky shop unaware of the difference. The lamp on his counter was always lit. By its feeble glow he polished more assiduously that lamp of self-knowledge flickering deep within him.

That was his way, as opposed to the man of action.

For both, the road of evolutionary progress was an ascending spiral stairway. But each saw it from a different angle.

Seen by the worldly active from his horizontal plane it was always a broad and level highway that obscured the spirals above and below. So slight was its incline he never saw it lift. So long was it he measured it by time, which he could subdivide, rather than eternity.

Hence he restricted his attention to the relation between the individual and the society of fellow travelers around him. His life was concerned with action that bore directly on purely social ends. He had achieved an ascendancy of reason over spirit, matter over mind.

Tai Ling heard the yowling in Cockroach Court and knew it was repeated everywhere on man's horizontal plane. He saw in his mind's eye the jungles of vast cities; watched the beasts of nations creep upon others with the soft padded feet of diplomacy; heard the doctors of science wreaking death on the battlefields with the tools they had conceived to cure man of his ills; saw the tyranny of the Church give way to the divine right of kings, and it to the almighty power of the sacred dollar. All in the name of evolutionary progress. While mankind crept round and round, bound as if to a wheel, without knowing where it was going.

No! The horizontal was too limited a view.

But for the passive yogi on his vertical plane the illusion of this broad level highway was dispelled. He could see the spiral staircase for what it was—slowly ascending from the first spark of life in primeval muck, up through plant and animal kingdoms to man, and thence upward to the higher consciousness that finally knows itself a part of the one macrocosmic mind of all.

This was the Path. All else was an illusion. But each man had to tread it alone. And his progress depended, not on the ease, the pleasant companions or material encumbrances with which he traveled, but solely on self-realization.

Hence the yogi fixed his attention on the relation between the individual and the universe. He shunned society, ignored power, abhorred violent action. His life was concerned with mind, time, space and causality. He sought by meditation to achieve ascendancy of mind over matter, and to combine reason and spirit in light of the transcendental true knowledge.

So Tai Ling tightened his belt and meditated alone in his empty shop. Life was his teacher, intuition his guide, his own self his textbook, and obliteration of this self his goal. What a wonderful winter!

From *Chapter Ten*

5

An hour later, still sober, he returned to The Lamp Awake. The yogi of Cockroach Court was deep in meditation, sitting, hands in lap, in front of the turned down lamp. Barby stopped. For the first time in a year—perhaps the only time in his life—he saw the old man clearly.

His figure had shrunken in its greasy, black sateen jacket and patched trousers. The hair on his round, yellow, bony head was sparse and thin. The empty fingers of his hands, palm up, were long, thin and slightly curved. He looked exactly like a failing, inept, old shopkeeper who had dozed off into another nap.

A dim resentment arose in the boy against his benefactor. The old fool! Sending a girl upstairs. Letting his business go to pot, starving himself, being made a fool of! Barby was about to step forward and speak when he noticed that the old man's eyes were open. Sudden fear gripped him: Tai Ling was dead. Then the fingers moved slightly and were still.

Barby could not move. Like everything else in the room, objects, insects, everything that moved and did not move, he seemed held at the edge of that circle whose fixed center was Tai Ling's tranquil face. It was at once relaxed and strangely set, like yellowish wax pliable enough to accommodate the slightest change in its mass of wrinkles. Only the big domed forehead reflecting the glow of the lamp stood out hard and smooth. Occasionally his lips parted for his slow rhythmical breathing; and this, a miracle of life in a face so dead, only enhanced still more the greater mystery of the face itself.

Still Barby could not stir. That strange, tranquil face, so terrifying in its unconscious repose! Never before had it seemed so enigmatic, so subtle of expression. The unmoving features assumed their natural pattern, and thus composed lost all their individual meanings. This was Tai Ling as he was—voiceless, devoid of smile or frown, without the warmth or coldness of a look. And what was that? Mesmerized, Barby stared as if at something he had never seen before.

Suddenly the old man's narrow eyes gave a brief flicker. It was just a flutter of his eyelids, like dry leaves stirred by the wind; yet in that instant the windows to his soul seemed opened. The boy jerked back, then stood still again as if terrified by what he saw within.

All that he had known of Tai Ling was there: the intangible peace and mystery of The Lamp Awake, his generosity, his humor and forbearance —yes, all the poetry and the beauty of his life was there in the momentary gleam of his open black eyes. But something else showed there too. A vast profundity, a monstrous impersonality, an overwhelming empty wilderness. And this, whatever it was, was something Barby could not stand.

He backed away and retreated softly upstairs.

He could not sleep. Was the old man drunk, drugged or crazy? Whatever it was, all contact between them seemed forever broken. He could no longer recall Guadalupe clearly, no longer curse Sal. Something had happened to him; he had reached an end. Clutched by a nameless foreboding, he lay stiffly in bed.

6

Tai Ling, as Barby watched him, was peeling an onion and weeping. The onion he was unwrapping was his own ego. The tears were shame and humility at what he found—just another wrapping.

He had turned down the lamp to a tiny glow. Concentrating steadily upon it in the darkness, he knew it to be not only the one distinguishable spot in the room. In the universal darkness of mankind it became the one infinitesimal reflection of that clear, boundless and eternal light of the infinite mind.

As he quieted it focused upon himself: his outward shell.

And seated at the core of silence within the shop, within that

quintessential silence he had now achieved, Tai Ling heard a faint ringing in his ears. Gradually in turn he heard his regular and rhythmical
breathing, the beating of his heart, the circulation of blood through
his veins, the functioning of his bodily organs. It was as if he sat in the
engine room of a perfectly controlled plant. But knowing himself
completely detached from it.

Immediately it fell away from his consciousness.

There lay his mind. As an organ of his body also, its shape and
color and material substance were likewise immaterial and meaningless. Its physical aspect vanished immediately.

But as a cognizing faculty it still remained, ceaselessly spinning
thoughts. With every change of breath there came a change of thought.
Inhalation, retention, exhalation; he could not retain a single thought
longer than this normal duration.

Tai Ling wavered in his concentration; his breathing increased
slightly; he felt balked.

Was he then—this mortal onion in a dreary shop—no more than
an ever-multiplying layer of helpless thoughts? What lay beneath the
thoughts?

He tried cutting through them by stopping each thought as it
arose. And still they kept arising, one after another, so numerous as
to seem interminable and inexhaustible. Till he knew that thought-
forming was as natural as breathing, and could no more be stopped
than any other biological process of his mortal body.

Once he realized this, he was free of their hold upon him. It was as
if he sat on a mountain top indifferently watching the clouds roll by.
Tranquil and unperturbed, he let them stem forth, take shape, vanish
and be replaced by others, with utter detachment.

He had reached the realm of non-thought; attained mental quies-
cence. Like a weary traveler he rested for awhile, allowing his mind to
remain in its passive, tranquil state. How wonderful it was! The pervading calm, the deep peace and utter freedom.

The darkness held, and the silence; his mind continued to watch with indifferent detachment the formation of his thoughts. But slowly he became aware of their warning: this was not his goal. It was not the core of the onion.

He took up the search again; began to be conscious of the cognizing faculty of his mind itself. That mind at first capable of external analysis, and now equal to introspective analysis.

What was it? He had perceived that it was not a visible, substantial thing. Nor was it a complex of various sensations, feelings, reasonings, memories; these were but the thoughts it created, from which he could detach himself.

And yet it existed. It was able to examine itself.

Almost instantly he was intuitively conscious that it was not his mind which was thus observing itself. The observer had now become the observed. There was something behind the mind.

From this sudden, blinding glimpse of reality, the yogi plunged into darkness and silence. They eddied slowly about him like familiar waves rippling on his consciousness. Like an arctic explorer lost in the perpetual darkness of an unmarked waste, he floundered back to the known.

Immediately the darkness lessened; a tiny light appeared. The silence vanished, broken by the sound of his rhythmical breathing. He saw the lamp burning before him, heard Barby tossing restlessly on his bed upstairs. His meditation for the night was over.

From *Chapter Eleven (Section 3)*

The pounding and splintering went on above Tai Ling. The thin flooring creaked and groaned, the trap door began to sag. Suddenly he heard a shattering crash; something sideswiped him on the head; his whole being, with excruciating, crying pain, focussed on his left leg. One of the timbers supporting the stairway had collapsed with the flimsy wall and broken through the rotted flooring, crushing his leg.

Chino Juan did not see what had happened; there was not even time to toss a match in the cluttered back room. The rurales had reached The Lamp Awake.

Tai Ling, in a paroxysm of pain, heard shots, screams, a scuffle, without knowing what they meant. A few minutes later a rurale called down the small open gap. "Hóla! We want you, Tai Ling! Are you coming peacefully?"

The old man could not distinguish his words. Weakly he fumbled around, set off another firecracker. Then there was darkness and silence and aloneness at last.

<h1 style="text-align:center">4</h1>

Some time later the yogi of Cockroach Court awoke. His leg was numb, his head was clear. There was no sound overhead. He lit the candle stub on the wooden case at his side. Save that he was in the cellar and pinioned by a timber across his leg, he might have been sitting peacefully in his shop as on any afternoon. But he felt oppressed by a curious sense of guilt.

Little wonder! To be caught up so precipitately in a maelstrom of worldly action. To let his physical self give way to the sensory stimuli of fear, horror and repugnance. He was shamed at the hold the gross physical world still had upon him. Where did the root of his fault lie? Of just what was he guilty?

Chronologically and dispassionately he recalled the incidents of the past twenty hours without shirking the details. At least ten men had been killed. Their deaths had been horrible, none of them isolate, accidental, causeless. But who could say what had really killed them? They were anticlimactic effects whose causal genesis lay deeply imbedded in the victims' own karmic lives and in the society to which they subscribed.

Tai Ling imagined saying this to the jury of society. Well, they were facts. Barby, Tony Wong, three helpless aliens and Cheon's helper had died nominally accidental deaths; Chino Juan's two boys and barkeep had been murdered by Cheon and Chewlee Singkee, who doubtlessly had been murdered in turn with several more. The score was evened, the feud was over. He himself was innocent.

But no! Society demanded retribution. Fuming at the mouth it would rant of motives, accomplices, accessories to the crime. And it would clamor to hang him by the neck till he was dead too.

What? Did murder then consist, not only of the factual action, but of the evil cause, the motive, the contributory accomplices and accessories? Then society straightway indicted its own malignant functions— its international restrictions against the natural passage of free human beings across an imaginary line, its national and political chicanery, the economic slavery of the poor, its racial prejudices, its lawful greed, unrestricted disease, legalized immorality, and the hypocrisy of its churches.

Never! society would howl again. Stick to specific facts, not irrelevant generalities.

By the facts, the isolate circumstantial facts, Tai Ling was innocent. He had been ignorant of Barby's activities, had been forced to accompany Cheon and Chewlee Singkee, had not fired a gun.

But still the sense of guilt persisted in Tai Ling.

And he knew it would persist in society despite the factual proofs of his legal innocence. For society is not composed of members united for the express purpose of enforcing their ever changing laws of horizontal, social behavior. Society is also humanity. And humanity is the great forward life-thrust of millenniums which are dimly perceived only by man's vertical thinking in terms of spiritual abstractions. By these laws humanity knew itself guilty of every crime and every neglect suffered by one of its constituent parts.

This then was the one perpetual conflict of man: whether he give his allegiance to society or to humanity.

That Tai Ling gave his to humanity was alone enough for society to convict him. For society classes as outcasts not only the criminal and ignorant beneath comprehension of its laws, but also those who have advanced to the laws far above its own. To society the yogi is as far beyond its pale as the savage.

"I might just as well be hanged for a saint as a sinner," thought Tai Ling complacently.

But still he felt a sense of guilt more specifically than just as a part of humanity.

5

After a short nap he awoke again, not knowing whether it was day or night. His worries were gone. He felt peaceful and relaxed.

Barby had been killed, setting off a chain of events in the world outside. Two groups of rival thugs, thieves and line-runners had started a street war in a little town on the American-Mexican border. It might just as well have been any place in the world.

Mendoza was apprehended, then a group of wealthy American-Chinese backers. Mendoza implicated the corrupt Mexican officials; These Gentlemen, the American. Rich American ranchers controlled by powerful monopolies of land and water rights in Mexico became involved. Rival corporations and the public press in Mexico appealed to their government also. Old racial prejudices between American Yanquis and Mexican Greasers were stirred up. The Chinese began to clamor against the Yellow Peril restrictions of the Asiatic Exclusion Act. There was a split between Protestant America and Catholic Mexico. Notes between governments. An overt act. War was declared. Latin America south of the Rio Grande versus Anglo-America north to the Arctic Rim. Then Europe and Asia taking opposite sides. A shooting war, a racial war, a religious war, a world war—total war. Oh, the possibilities were unlimited! A street war of national thugs and thieves on a universal scale.

Tai Ling sighed. A perfect one-dimensional American movie.

But suppose Barby had not been killed. Suppose, instead, that he had prospered in his scheme. His little group of cronies grew on both sides of the Line to a large and powerful band. Defying authorities it soon became authority itself. State and big business, using Barby for its ends, became used themselves.

What of Mendoza and These Gentlemen? They had been assassinated as obstructing nuisances. For Barby had grown with power. He fed on power. A bastard half-breed, an ignorant cholo who had groveled in the gutters, he knew the secret of success—the promise of the wealth, ease, respect, authority and power denied all those as he had been denied. So now, a monomaniacal leader distorted by a chronic self-inferiority and the failure to hold as mistress a cheap cafe entertainer, he could not stop. Millions flocked to his call. Who could resist the hope of more power? Even nations applauded—until their own power was threatened.

And then over the five continents and seven seas spread another debacle. A new world-master, a modern Alexander, fell, dragging down with him another civilization. And once more humanity took up its weary march.

No; not until there were no conditions anywhere that would make possible another Barby, would the world ever be secure. Win or lose, thought Tai Ling, humanity was the perpetual loser. What had he to do with such a monstrous illusion? His only concern was with the eternally groping spirit of mankind, not its social behavior.

6

But unknown to him the world outside had reached another conclusion. The newspapers he had always ignored with a smile of contempt for their distortion of truth were screaming it in bold black headlines:

TONG WAR BREAKS OUT
Border Town Scene of Street Fighting

TWELVE DEAD IN CHINESE BORDER RIOT
Rival Factions Menace Lives of Citizens
Repercussions Feared in Los Angeles and San Francisco Chinatowns

News from the scene reliably reported that:

The initial killing of two men in front of the Casino Chino and one inside the Chinesca was instigated by the leader of a secret Chinese tong engaged in transporting aliens across the International Line.

This was confirmed by "Chino Juan," owner of the two business houses, arrested for participation in the ensuing street war. Chewlee Singkee, a butcher, seriously wounded, confessed to the slaying, admitting he had been forced to accompany the mysterious leader.

This "mystery man" is believed to be one Tai Ling. Little is known about him. An aged Chinaman posing as a retired shopkeeper, he was a virtual recluse. It is known, however, that he controlled El Sol de Mayo, a notorious bar in the quarter, and had previously engaged in the sale of opium. Police are working on the theory that he burned it last night, together with one of his own henchmen, to avoid detection by officers.

The quarter is one of the most lawless districts along the whole American-Mexican Border. Largely populated by Chinese, it is a refuge for petty criminals of both countries as well. Immediate steps to clear up conditions once and for all are indicated. The resourceful detection of the Tong's activities by the Border Patrol, resulting in the slaying of two of the leader's accomplices, precipitated the outbreak.

Later dispatches revealed:

BORDER DISTRICT UNDER CONTROL
International Line Closed

Promptly following this morning's outbreak, a troop
of soldiers were rushed out of the military garrison to
assist local police. The quarter is now under martial
law. All cantinas and casinos are closed. The streets are
effectively patrolled. Members of both rival factions are
being ruthlessly hunted.

The International Line has been closed until further
notice as a precaution against fleeing tong slayers. The
forces of the U. S. Immigration Authorities have been
doubled and are standing by.

Governors of both neighboring states, American
and Mexican, have expressed their willingness to meet
for a discussion of joint precautions to be taken against
any future outbreaks of kind.

Flash:

TONG LEADER TRAPPED

MYSTERY MAN BARRICADED IN OPIUM DEN

The aged Chinese "mystery man," Tai Ling, instiga-
tor of the current tong war, has been trapped. Armed
with a machine gun, he is defying capture in his pseu-
do shop long used as an opium den. Little hope is held
that he will be taken alive. He is known to be a desperate man.

Chugoku, a fish dealer on the gulf coast, and
Mendoza, a line-runner, have been apprehended by

authorities. Both were in Tai Ling's employ. They positively identify him as the sponsor of Tony Wong and the mestizo Barby killed Saturday night. The latter, they say, was his chief lieutenant and lived with him.

His shop is located near the junction of Callejon de los Chinos (Chinese Alley) and Plaza de las Cucarachas (Cockroach Court), in the heart of the quarter. It is entirely surrounded by heavily armed guards and under constant watch. The aged, wily Tai Ling has no chance to avoid paying for his many years of undetected crime and recent ruthless slayings.

Col. Maria Trinidad de Eluria y Policarpio, director of the assaulting party, was reached by telephone in his spacious suite at the Governor's Palace. He stated: "Tai Ling will be taken by the troops under my orders by noon tomorrow (Monday). National honor demands it. No mercy will be shown him. This arch criminal has plied too long his evil crimes of an outmoded century in this resplendent decade of glorious civilized achievement."

7

Tai Ling was roused again near morning by the weight of an intolerable sadness.

Spasms of pain contracted his whole leg. He was cramped, stiff and sore. Only by the greatest effort could he twist his body enough to relieve his swollen kidneys. He craved water, hot tea. Days seemed to have passed; he could not imagine what was happening outside that he should be so ignored even by his enemies. None of this mattered. He could overcome it. But the heavy sadness overwhelmed him.

A half inch of candle remained. In its flicker he tried to compose his thoughts. They no longer speculated on effects. They explored causes. Doggedly they trudged back from Barby's betrayal of him to the boy's greed and lust for power; to his obsession for Guadalupe and his bitterness and cowardice as a child; to his bastard birth and drunken father.

Fully now Tai Ling exonerated society for all blame. And more surely than ever before he knew that the effects of the boy's actions were largely predetermined by causes far beyond his conception and birth. For just as all mankind is the forward life-thrust of milleniums of evolution, so is each man the individual summation of his own extended past—his own individual karma.

But being the slave of his past, he is also the master of his future. At the choice of his free will he can at once expiate all his previous misdoings and so escape from his bondage by achieving complete realization of his at-one-ment with the infinite whole.

Progress, then, must be made only by each man's efforts toward that perfection which lies within himself. Separate and alone, he must be his own leader, his own judge, his own priest and savior—a lamp unto himself. Society, civilizations crumbled away. Man remained. A vast humanity forever groping toward the truth of its existence. A conglomeration of divergent life-principles slowly but inexorably tending to a fusion.

And suddenly his own sense of guilt and his intolerable sadness were made plain. How could he have separated life from the principles which guided it; ignored the fusion that already existed if one could only see it?

He forgot himself entirely, and all the precepts which had engrossed him: the Ten Things to Forget, the Ten Things to be Done, the Ten Things to be Avoided and the Ten Things Not to be Avoided, the Ten Errors and Thirteen Grievous Failures, the Fifteen Weaknesses and Twelve Indispensible Things, the Ten Signs of a Superior Man, the Eight Worldly Ambitions, the Three Fires of Desire, the Ten Grievous Mistakes and the Ten Necessary Things.

He only remembered the tragic, human loneliness of Barby and Guadalupe, the crying fear of the white woman who had come to him and had been frightened away, the pathetic hungering of Cheon and Chewlee Singkee for help, the haunting insecurity of Chino Juan. He thought of all the poor little fish and human cucarachas, the blind beggar at the corner, all the men betrayed, the mothers who had lost their sons, all the misery and sadness, ignorance and loneliness throughout the world.

The old man wept. He wept because he no longer felt separate; because he too was a part of all the misery that ever had existed.

Strangely enough the realization brought joyful relief. Tai Ling no longer had friends to forgive him, or enemies to forgive. Cockroach Court no longer was a geographical reality, not even a vast grey brain. All seemed to have been created for this one purpose of teaching him, in this brief incarnate existence, the falsity of his human ego. He could have fallen to his knees and thanked these circumstantial manifestations for the excessive trouble to which a mere old shopkeeper had put them.

Yet at the same time the yogi was more preternaturally aware than ever of that lurking consciousness which still separated him from Tai Ling's contrite mind and humbled heart. If he had only been more pure and courageous, if he had been granted but a bit more time! Perhaps even now . . .

The candle stub was almost gone. He pulled himself upright and gazed steadily at it. What was it made him feel and know what he felt, and offered him the path of freedom if he were only strong enough to climb?

8

Upstairs in early morning the time had come.

"The street blocked off, Corporal, the alley clear and the plaza also?"

"Yes, Captain."

"Select your men. Recall your sentries from the doors and come with me!"

"Yes, Captain."

In shiny boots and buttons, and with a drawn revolver, the Captain peeked in the cluttered area of Tai Ling's back room. Covered by the Corporal's rifle, he stepped closer to the small crack underneath the crashed timber.

"You down there! Tai Ling! Are you coming out peacefully? We will give you exactly one minute," he shouted, without wondering how Tai Ling could get through the narrow crack.

There was no answer.

"Corporal, is the charge ready?"

"Yes, Captain."

"Light the fuse. Withdraw your men from the field of explosion." He shouted again.

Still there was no sound, not even a signal.

The yogi of Cockroach Court was deep in meditation.

9

There had been the cellar and the tiny glow of the guttering candle, and that which came to know itself freed from the illusion of this space that cramped it and this time that flickered around it.

This knowledge, knowing itself composed so largely of physical sensations and stimuli, then knew itself a knowledge which detached itself from all this sensory phenomena; knew now neither the darkness nor the silence into which it retreated.

Yet again this knowledge began to know itself known. It knew itself known as another complex compound of perceptions, cognitions, reasonings, memory, reflections.

And gradually the knower separated from the known with another curious certainty of detachment. In a boundless, timeless void, the knower observed the known give birth to the knowledge. The knowledge that included, impenetrated and connected the known and the knower. All in a vast and aching void.

But now the observer began to be observed. The knower itself became another known. And no sooner did the new knower know the known, than it too became observed by a new observer.

So through the immeasurable, timeless void the observer pursued the observed, and becoming the observed was itself pursued by the observer.

And now suddenly in the unfathomable darkness, the quintessential silence of the illimitable void, there exploded light. An explosion of silent, radiant light. An explosion of transcendental bliss.

There was no longer separation of observer and observed. The knower, the known and the knowledge merged together and knew itself one.

There was but one consciousness that in radiant light, in transcendental bliss, became identical with the immeasurable and timeless void. As it was identical with every microcosmic reflection of the void in its illusionary boundaries of space and time and matter.

So that this consciousness being aware of its nature of the void, was also aware of its nature in the illusion of space, of time, of matter. It was aware again of the cellar cluttered with debris and falling earth, of the pale morning light flooding it, and of the figures bent over it.

10

"That him, Corporal?"
"Yes, Captain."
"Is he dead?"

For answer the Corporal spread his fingers, smote his palms together with a loud clap, then looked up and grinned.

CHAPTER 8

People of the Valley (1941)

This novel comes out of profound absorption into a place, the Mora Valley of northern New Mexico, a study worthy of a folklorist of the culture once inhabiting that mountain vale, and perhaps most important, a realization of the thoroughness of that people's life-tie to their land. To write *People of the Valley* Waters had to go back, as it were, to a time before the "Maquina of progress overrode them all," and reimagine the landscape vibrant with meaning, life full of mystery and possibility, and virtue tied close to simple ways, simple faith and endurance. The story he tells covers a hugely eventful century, at the end of which the old life will be tested as never before. The dam that the engineers and *politicos* propose will change everything. Among its victims, only a near-blind, illiterate old woman recognizes that fact. All that she can bring to bear against progress is the mysterious sum total of the way the people have always lived—an elusive quality in the air, in the heart, in a book.

From *Chapter 6*

For months a somber gray had overhung the valley, blotting the beauty and obscuring the blue. Fall it was and still raining—an incessantly dripping mist, a sparse quick splatter or the lash of a heavy storm.

The earth was soggy. Adobe walls kept crumbling. Anemic, water-logged corn straddled puddles. Beasts and birds of the field dragged hoof and claw as if too discouraged to shake off the clinging mud. When the sky appeared to be clearing, the river bloated with more debris; there had been another heavy rain up one of the tributary cañons.

"Mother of God!" a man would exclaim, tramping in from the fields. "I have not seen it so wet in thirty years. For all I feel it might be that long since I have seen the peaks against the sky, the clouds lie so low and heavy."

Weeks ago when the crops were given up, Maria had put away her goat skulls and marked willow twigs, had discontinued watching for dry stars. She was a woman vigilant of the future, not unaware of the past, but wise enough to give herself to the present.

So she sat quietly in her hut, head down and listening to the orchestration of the day's storm. She was cooking beans. The fire rubbed long red hairs against the pot. Its reflection lay like thin straw on the floor. Outside, the apple trees shivered; fruit thudded on the ground like lazy thumps of a drum. The rain on the roof was a pizzicato, the rumble of the creek a sustained adagio.

At mid-afternoon came a violent crescendo. A bit of roof dirt trickled down between the rafters, followed by a steady drip of water. Maria set a pot under it. Soon there were seven pots filling on the floor. "Diablo! A seven pot rain! One more than the worst!"

When the hard mud floor became sticky, Maria grew uneasy. She opened the door. It was scarce five o'clock but dark. The creek roared beyond the little orchard. A sour smell tainted the air. The rain was coming down, as it is said, in buckets. In the corral Maria saw lanterns.

"Teodosio!" she called. "What is the matter with you? It is a seven pot rain, and more, for I have none left. Come! Move my things into the house."

"What is the matter with you?" he shouted back. "We are carrying chickens into the house. We have lost two already. Are you blind? The corral is ankle-deep in water from the creek."

Maria grabbed up her rebozo, and went out. The little stream coming down the cañon was a torrent. At its junction with the creek, the water had banked up against the cliffs and was creeping through the orchard. Above, the wall of stones which protected the corral from the creek was hidden by water.

Hurriedly she lugged out armfuls of things from her hut. The house was already full of chickens, goats and a calf, Niña and her daughter, Gertrudes and Teodosio. The chickens picked at her seed corn, the calf nibbled at her precious herbs. The goats stared disconsolately at the heaped skulls of their predecessors. Gertrudes and Niña's girl examined her old clothes. Teodosio grumbled at the half-cooked pot of beans, and Niña at the weather. The rain clawed at the walls, trying to get at them all.

"These beans!" muttered Teodosio. "Not only are they half-cooked but full of water. Now I would not say you failed to put the lid on as you carried them through the rain. Carajo! You could make me believe it rained through the pot itself, so strongly it drives!"

Maria sat still, head cocked; there had sounded outside a queer splintering. "The hut," she said, rising, "it—" Even as she spoke came the crash.

They ran outside; the path was shin deep under water. Maria's hut had fallen down. Water had dissolved the lower bricks.

"Well!" shouted Teodosio. "Now you will be glad to go back to your beans, in warmth and comfort, be they half-cooked and cold! Our Lady! You moved out but in time!"

They trudged back. But not before Maria had looked long and anxiously up the cañon. It was raining harder than ever.

The roof of the house was the usual: large hand-hewn vigas laid across the tops of the walls, a cross-hatching of small aspens, on these a few planks, and covering all, two feet of dirt. By eight o'clock water had soaked through. Everyone and everything was wet.

"We are on a rise. The walls rest on stones. We are safe but miserable," observed Teodosio, with water running down his back.

"But Madre mia! It is like trying to escape fate to dodge these trickles. Even my cigarette papers are wet. I do not have a dry pocket."

"Let us go down the road toward the village," pleaded Niña. "We shall come to a dry house. The beasts here will be safe. But I can stand no more."

Teodosio opened the door and stuck down a foot. He drew back a leg, wet to the knee. "Mother of God! Go? How? We should need a boat! But not this one. Why should he go outside to get wet? There is plenty of water in here."

Maria stood beside him, holding up the lantern. She was smelling the air.

"Come! I have a certain foreboding. But leave the doors open for the beasts." With this she plunged out into the night.

The others waded after her flickering lantern. Near the road they heard the splash of horses, saw the light of a torch. It shone on a bedraggled family down from the opposite side of the valley.

"Teodosio! And Doña Maria!" exclaimed the man when they met. "Thank God for such good neighbors. You look upon ruined friends. Our house has fallen in. And here you stand in water to meet us, and lead us to spend the night in your own warm house. In this storm we might never have found the way."

"Jesú Cristo!" answered Teodosio. "You mean to tell us that water floods the north as it does the south? Us, who are washed out like rats, even as yourselves? Cristo, Cristo!"

All straggled on in wet and darkness. "Maldito!" cursed Teodosio. "Is this road or river? I can tell only what it once was by the fence posts."

They came to the house of Santiago Jacquez; it was dark and crumbling. They came to the house of Mechor Sandoval; it was deserted, the chairs were floating out. They reached the house where Quiteria Pacheco lived with her three sons, the ranchito of Fidencio Romaldo y Trujillo, the long adobe wherein lived the three poor families of Santistevan, Espinoza and Donaciano Romero. They were all abandoned and besieged by water. It was midnight and still raining when they saw a light.

"Ójala! I know it now!" exclaimed Teodosio. "It is that old stable of gray stone near the bridge. Across from the mill of Don Fulgencio. We have come not more than a kilómetro! Imagine! Pues. Are we ducks, are we fish? Come! I smell coffee and tortillas, a warm fire."

But inside were only Santiago, Mechor and Quiteria with their wives and sons, Don Fidencio and the families of Santistevan, Espinoza and Romeros. There was no coffee, no tortillas. There was not even a fire; there was no dry wood. There was hardly room to squat down. "So this is what a man gets, swimming like a fish a kilómetro that seems ten leagues!" grumbled Teodosio. "Not even a dry cigarette."

One by one more groups splashed in to stand dripping in the light of torches. From Tramperos, Cañoncito, La Corriera.

"What! Is it raining there too? You brought no dry cigarettes? No?" Teodosio asked each.

No one answered. They were a people elaborately dumb under misery and misfortune. All watched Maria who kept opening the door to sniff the air. The light from her lantern flickered out to the watery fields. All the stock had been let loose. Horses, cows, burros, goats, pigs and sheep splashed round the building, whimpering.

An hour after daybreak Maria turned back from the door. "It is coming. What I feared and suspected. A new smell and fresh mud. The creek brings down not only wreckage and willows, but fresh pine tips. Come! We must go! To the village."

They straggled out again. The pallor of dawn was reflected in their muddy faces. Their features were set like cement against sleep and hunger, fear and misfortune. A child whimpered with cold, their only voice. Behind them splashed twenty head of loose stock. No one seemed to notice that the rain had ceased. For at the bridge the creek was still swelling.

They looked back. The valley was no longer beautiful and blue. It was gray and slimy. It smelled sour. They looked ahead, and it was the same: soggy fields crossed by rivers that had been roads, and sodden adobes from which no smoke rose. But there stood the church tower of Santa Gertrudes. Down to it from the southern slope of El Alto del Talco, from the northern slope of El Alto de los Herreras, plodded more people across the fields. And down the little mountain pass from La Cuesta, Ledoux and El Oro, from the Cebollita valley, trudged a steady line of people and stock.

But Maria was staring back up the crescent valley, at the tall cliffs near the curve and the shrouded mountains toward the north. A man had stuck a stick down in the creek bank. He came running back with it.

"Mira! Doña Maria, look! The water was here when I placed it. Now it is here. A good two inches. The rain has ceased, but the creek yet swells. And swiftly. Look!"

Maria did not answer. Neither did she turn around. She stood staring at the swirling water. Fence posts came down, broken planks, dead chickens, willow branches and brush—pine tips. Then a drowned goat which lodged against the bridge piling. Maria waded down to it, and remained.

"Señora! What do you see? . . . Doña Maria! It is dead!"

"Of course, fool!" she replied, coming back, wet to the waist. "But I saw on it the burnt three bars of Filadelfio Eluria. He lives up the steep cañon beyond Los Alamitos . . . Burro! Are you yet blind to its meaning? How do you suppose this goat came here? There has been a cloudburst on the pine ridge between the high cañons of Luna and Lujan. The first rise of the river is coming. Get the people to the village. Sound the church bells. God knows what to expect."

The people fled on—save Maria, Teodosio and two other men. "For why?" chattered Teodosio. "Why do we remain? Look! Mother of God! What fury! In ten minutes the water will be over the bridge."

"It will be enough!" answered Maria curtly. "I have business across the bridge. Are you unaware that that is Don Fulgencio's old mill?"

One of the men stepped up. "Doña Maria. A thousand pardons. I am not unaware that he is your husband in name, and that you feel a certain anxiety about him now that the old blind crone, his sister, is dead. But look. The flood will sweep round the cliffs directly upon the mill. Not only that but the bridge will go out. Besides, he is probably not there."

"He is a fool, and you. Look!" She pointed across the river. Below the mill and under a great chestnut tree stood a tiny old man waving a stick. "Will one fool listen to another? I must talk to him myself." Maria shook off his arm and hurried across the bridge.

Above the roar of the water, as she approached, she could hear Fulgencio's screams. His sombrero had fallen off. His thin white hair stuck to his bony head like wet silk. He was soaking. "Away, cursed woman, who has laid a spell upon me!" he screamed, dancing about with his uplifted stick. "I saw you. I saw all the people you brought to gaze at me. You sent them away to hide behind the bushes. You come alone. But I see you and them. Away!"

The great chestnut stood on a small rise. The acequia had burst, the empty sluices were filling; from the mill above, water was streaming down upon the tree. But around it Fulgencio had been heaping up a tiny barricade of mud.

Maria rushed upon him. "Fool! Will you be drowned with your gold? Here, give me that shovel! We shall carry it into the mill where the walls are strong."

The old man let out a shriek of rage. "She told you! That magpie with no eyes and a loose tongue. She guessed and told you!" With a stick he beat down her upraised arms. They fought, sliding in the mud. But it was the old man's insane strength which secured the shovel. With a mighty swipe meant to take off her head, he leapt forward. Maria slipped; her feet went forward, her head back. The blade of the shovel caught her a glancing blow on the jaw. Teeth flew out, blood spurted. Her cleft chin opened like another but vertical mouth. Maria dropped like a log.

But now the men came running across the bridge. The old man leapt for the lower branches of the tree, and scrambled up to perch shrieking above them.

"Blessed Mother!" shouted one of the men. "He would have killed her who would have saved him. But there is no time to lose. The water washes over the bridge. Come. Let us get her between us. She awakes. Jesus, the blood! It is a miracle that we waited not too long to save her."

Halfway to the village, Maria came to her senses. She was being pulled along between two men, her chin held together by a strip of torn rebozo. Teodosio, in front, kept turning around to throw handfuls of muddy water in her face. "Blood and mud! You look like a slaughtered pig. And yet you keep mumbling of the gold necessary to rebuild our house. Mother of God! That day will never come. The valley is ruined forever. It is the day of judgment."

They reached Santa Gertrudes. The stub streets were filling with refugees from all directions, even from the pine slopes above. Among them milled horses, burros, cows, pigs and goats. The plaza in front of the church was packed solid with people. From the tower above, the bells were ringing. On the steps stood a priest, praying. Inside, a hasty mass was being said.

Suddenly the priest stopped his prayer. The bells stopped. In the tower a man had begun to shout. The first rise was coming down.

A cloudburst had broken in the high mountains to the north. Down the V-shaped cañons of Luna and Lujan the water rushed to an apex, grew into a flood, and swept down the one narrow steep-walled cañon into the upper end of the valley.

Here, from the high Sangre de Cristo on the west, it was joined by the swollen Rio de la Casa. A mile farther, the flood separated to follow down the river to the east and the creek to the west, and thus spread into the already soaked valley from both sides.

As the water crept up to the village streets, Maria roused from her lethargy. She plucked Teodosio's sleeve, spit blood and another tooth. "These bells! This praying!" she said faintly. "I myself would trust high land to religion. Hoist me upon a loose burro. Let us go."

Again they plodded on. Up the steep little pass between the valley and Ledoux. Others followed. A long bedraggled line returning to the highlands whence they had come, if only to prove that while misfortune seeks company, danger calls them back to solitude. Here on the pine slope they looked down to see the second rise sweep down the valley.

Two hours later a strange thing happened on the opposite side. Just beyond the high cliffs at the curve of the crescent valley a white snake leaped forth. It was transparent. In it straws twisted and jammed and poked through the skin. The snake roared and flashed. It tore loose great boulders as it unrolled down the mountainside. Maria's apple trees lay down before it. Swiftly it uncoiled, stretched and dived into the creek. But still, unending, its body kept unrolling from behind the cliffs.

Maria discovered her voice. "It is as I feared! As I said, yet not as I said! It is worse! The flood comes down La Cañada also!"

The cloudburst had broken in the high mountains to the north drained by the Luna and Lujan which in turn empty into the valley from the northwest. But between these cañons and that of Guadalupita there is only a ridge of pines. The clouds had but shifted slightly. And now the water coming down La Cañada del Carro was sweeping into the valley from the northeast. Into mid-valley, at the center of its crescent beyond the jutting cliffs.

Maria saw her apple orchard sink, her barn float off in pieces, her house become an island. And now, six feet high, the snake rushed at Don Fulgencio's mill. The hewn stones held—a small gray pillar in a surging flood. Surprisingly, the old chestnut on its rise still stood, but half submerged in water. And now through the afternoon the clumps of people watched the water creep up into the village, a foot deep.

At dusk Teodosio found something to say. "They are having a wet mass down there in the church. . . . But Jesus! It cannot be so cold. . . . I shall try to light a fire. Did you bring matches? I have none. Not in that pocket, nor in this. . . ."

At dawn they crept down the mountainside, half-starved and stiff with cold. The water was receding, the sun coming out. It was unbelievable. It was ugly. It was revealing only an earth that was for them stricken and homeless, an earth that stank.

Bodies were being brought in, and reports of others. "Emeliano saw something sticking in the willows. . . . Myself and Abrán buried him, Señora. The head, you will realize. . . . It is best to be truthful in misfortune, Señora. He will not return. My sympathy, Señora. . . . There where the crows and buzzards are already gathering. But yet the water is too high. Patience! And prayer!"

Maria listened. That night she heard of Don Fulgencio. His body had been found nearly a kilómetro downstream. He had evidently been swept from or fallen from the tree. "But the chestnut?" she asked. It still stood, but weakly, gouged out to its roots.

Maria sighed. Her sigh included, perhaps primarily, the lost box of gold pieces he had buried at the foot of the tree. Now there would be no money to rebuild and plant again.

In the morning she gathered together Niña and her daughter, Gertrudes and Teodosio. "Let us go back," she said stiffly, toothlessly.

"To what?" grumbled Teodosio. "Out of this you have a scar. A fine scar; nobody will recognize you. But nothing else. Mother of God! Not even a tooth! To say nothing of a place to sleep, a scrap of tortilla, a sip of water. Jesus! And I! I do not even have a cigarette. Not even a wet one. I tell you this has been a flood. Without doubt, a flood. Why—"

Chapter 7

At the age of seventy Maria was living alone in a small mountainside hut. It was the old one that lay in the little clearing just below the tall weathered cliffs which jut out to separate the crescent halves of the beautiful blue valley, and just above a steep corn milpa sloping up from the rutty cañon road. Thus unseeing eyes placed it. Maria, whose eyes saw it in time as well as in space, saw it as the point of a completed circle.

But Maria was a character. Such is regarded one who has outlived virtue and vice, having proved invulnerable to both and more powerful than either.

"She is strange and wise," people said of her.

The strangeness implied her uniqueness among their orthodoxy. The wisdom reflected her ability to see through their opinions.

"But I do not trust her fully," added some in a whisper.

Such a secret lack of faith do people below have in the truth that awaits above them.

Maria was content to wait. Seldom she allowed Teodosio to drive her down into the valley in his rattletrap buggy. She only saw to it that he came up often enough to weed the corn and to bring her salt, sugar and tobacco. What more was necessary? She milked her goats, split her own wood; was too toothless to eat meat, too contented to require conversation, too busy to relish interruptions. "Besides," she said, "I can watch from here the empty doings of you all."

So she thrived on loneliness, and proved that energy creates inert mass. This energy, this ununderstood vitality in one so old and wrinkled, she had sucked from her loves and labors, anxieties and follies, the illusions of her life. Its inert mass sat hour after hour day by day, on top of the cliffs.

Below her the valley grew, new houses rose from the earth. New roads crawled up the cañons where only foot trails had come down. Burros diminished, rattling tin automobiles appeared—to be pulled out of chuck holes by teams and wagons, the mean that held between these extremes of travel. She saw the valley green, yellow and whiten, the mountain peaks step forth and back again into mists, scant harvests and days of plenty. Gringo voices came back, greaseless wagon hubs squeaked on frosty mornings, the church bells tolled births and deaths.

It all went on outside her as it went on in memory inside, changing but changeless, and thus an illusion. What remained was their common core. It was the reality she pondered.

Wind and rain matted her straggly hair. Sun and frost made leather of her swart cheeks and cleft chin. Her black, bright little eyes took on a queer remoteness. At times her steady gaze seemed turned inward—as if it had rounded the earth only to return to the duplicate within her.

But occasionally her meditations were interrupted. She had gone long to the people of the valley; now they came to her.

"Doña Maria," a man would say, respectfully standing before her, hat in hand, "you will forgive this interruption, but something is wrong with my house. It is a new house. It is a well built house. I built it with these hands. Yet something is wrong. In it I have always a cold, my wife sniffles, the noses of my children drip. It was not like this in our old house, which is now a stable—where no doubt our beasts are better off than we with colds."

"This new house of yours. It has windows?"

"Of glass, Señora! And two doors."

"It breathes through the eaves?"

"An air space, as they say. It is the new way."

"Pues!" grunted Maria. "These new ways! These new windows of glass by which one would be outside and in, at once! That is your trouble. Hereafter take care to stuff the eaves and doors. Remember this:

> *"When a draft gets at you through a hole,*
> *Go make your will, and pray for your soul."*

Advice on all matters she gave, and new remedies for old ills. Especially she recommended for headaches pieces of blue paper or the blue government tax stamps taken off tobacco cans and pasted on the forehead and around the eyes.

So her power still grew, and her name. She was not only a character but an institution. The trail up through the steep corn and pines to it wore deeper.

The fat, red-cheeked priest from the village church took it yearly. He came up hopefully, went down discouraged. "Father in Heaven!

Give me strength! This miserable and faithless old woman is more powerful than a priest! Her fees are surely fatter!" Once he nearly swore.

It had happened on his autumnal visit to convert her to the faith, and so draw her power over the simple into the church, that he encountered her below the cliffs. She had driven down to her old home and orchard where Niña's family lived, Teodosio having moved with Gertrudes up the cañon. It had been a good apple year; there was a huge stack against the barn; Maria was in a tender humor.

"Let us have no empty words, Padre," she said kindly. "For twenty and more years I have heard your pleas, threats and arguments. They are all the same. I will listen no more. But of this heap of apples take plenty. Verdad! Fill your buggy. Take them to your church—wherever you will."

Niña's eyes popped. Teodosio's jaw dropped. But over the priest's red face crept a look of beatific triumph shadowed by a tiny irreconcilable doubt. Hastily, still smiling, he dropped to his knees, clasped his hands.

"God, O Father and His Blessed Son!" he prayed rapidly, before Maria could change her mind. "You have rewarded Your servant's toil of twenty years and more. To me it is to be given the baptising of this woman so long without faith and divine aid. Nor in my ecclesiastical joy am I unaware of those in this same church who preceded me in prayer for this admirable soul who gives this day in the name of the Father, the Son and Holy Ghost—"

"Momentito, Padre!" interrupted Maria harshly. "What is all this about? I said merely to take these apples to your church. The pigs will eat no more."

The story spread. Men in the cantinas roared, women tittered in the stores; the whole valley shook with laughter. The remark became a saying. "Take it! The pigs will eat no more!" Thus they joked when giving the unneeded to one another.

The priest's visit was followed by Pierre Fortier's. He was no longer merely a shopkeeper who sold clothes and canned goods, fresh meat, harness and tiny sewing machines; who bought wool, hides and grain by the car load. He was something of an art dealer. Agents from the cities came to him for arrowheads, for old tinwork, leather trunks and great carved chests, for precious old blankets and lacework, and for Santos of all kinds—the carved bultos, and the retablos or tablas painted on wood or tin.

Old Pierre had a nose for all these things. He had lived in the valley a lifetime. Every hut in all its cañons he knew, and if it contained an unknown treasure: an old carven chest from Mexico half sunk in the damp earth floor, a browned old Santo hanging above the rickety bed. Moreover he knew the idiosyncrasies of their owners.

"This dirty old chest!" he would say, giving it a kick. "The wood is rotting away! Bring it in some day when I am in a good humor. Perhaps I can find use for it as a wood box, and give your wife a new dress on credit. In such a tidy house it is a disgrace. But not today, compadre!"

Those places where the Santos were stubbornly clung to by the old, he merely noted. This old woman would die soon; her son liked whisky.

What he had long wanted from Maria was an old burnt-orange Chimayó blanket. One edge was tattered, it had holes. It was dirty, it was thin. But whenever Pierre saw it glowing in the sunlight, felt its weave and wonderful softness, his mouth watered. "Mon Dieu! It is a blanket too good for the top of a piano in a home of the rich. It is fit for a museum. An old woman who yet knows the old way, to patch the holes. Another to wash it in amole. Yes. Then for this blanket I could begin to ask seven hundred dollars!"

But also every time he saw it he groaned. Maria used it in Teodosio's buggy. When the blanket was thrown over the seat the protruding springs poked through the weave. When it lay over her lap she trod most of it underfoot. Always it was assaulted by sun and dust, by rain and hail and snow. And Teodosio used it to cover his horses.

Where this old blanket came from Maria did not remember. She had never been without it, even as a child. So she ignored first the gruff and then the polite preludes of Pierre to buy it.

On the day he came up to Maria's hut, Teodosio's old buggy was waiting at the foot of the trail. In its seat lay the blanket. Pierre's eyes gleamed. He rubbed his long black whiskers, and on his wooden leg stamped wheezing up the slope. Maria he hugged and kissed on both cheeks.

"By Jesus, old friend! I tramp up this cursed steep trail to commiserate with another old and poor, broken in health and miserable. To find you sound as mountain beef, glowing with health and bubbling joy through bright eyes! Are you in love, have you found the fountain of youth? For shame, having not told me, your oldest friend. Why do you never come down to see me?"

To Teodosio he even gave a cigarette.

His visit was brief; he was buying cattle, he said. And when Teodosio left, Pierre accompanied him down the trail. At their adjacent buggies he stopped. As if on a sudden impulse, he jerked out of his own a new, bright-colored Navajo blanket, and spread it carefully over Teodosio's seat.

"We have been compadres for uncounted years," he said, slapping Teodosio on the back. "As a present I give you this fine new blanket. May comfort and protection, pleasure and joy, it give you both. . . . But I shall just take away this forlorn old rag that you have been forced to use all these years. . . . Adiós, compadre!"

When a few days later Maria asked for her old blanket, she was presented with the new one. She inspected it silently, its color, its weave and design. She drove down to Pierre's store with Teodosio.

Pierre was out in the mountains. She sat down on a sack of pintos. She waited all morning. She waited half the afternoon.

"What is it, Señora? Is it important, as surely it must be, that which keeps you waiting?"

"Well, it is about that faded old red blanket that Señora Fortier took of me. . . . I forgot to tell him that it was full of bugs. Bugs of sickness." Maria fixed the clerk with a shrewd look. "I can trust you? Maria can trust a boy who seems so bright and helpful, who will keep his counsel? . . . Well then, listen. Those bugs of sickness were none other than the plague itself! Now! Do you see my anxiety, its importance? I shudder to think of the hands—whose hands, amiguito, have touched it?"

"But three, Doña Maria.—Thank God, not mine!—Those of Señor Fortier himself. Those of the old woman whom he gave it to mend, those of her who washes it now."

"Excellent! To them I shall go at once with herbs to relieve them of possible danger. Their names quickly! And to Señor Fortier when he returns, my thanks for his gift."

Maria obtained her blanket from her who had washed it. "Pierre Fortier will pay as agreed. Give him my thanks for washing it, amiga. It has never been so clean and soft."

To the woman who had mended it she went with a message. "Pierre Fortier will pay. But give him my thanks for mending it, amiga. It is as good as new."

Maria rode home content. It was an old blanket, though mended and washed; it was true it had once covered a child with the plague. Yet she liked it, and thenceforth slept under it.

Behind her she left Pierre Fortier cursing in French and stamping his wooden leg. Throughout the village and echoed up the cañons shouted the gossip. "My thanks, compadre. But Pierre Fortier will pay."

"Mother of God!" people laughed. "What a strange and wise old woman! She fears neither God nor man. She has a mind of her own, has Doña Maria. It knows everything."

It is true that those who laughed the loudest feared worst the priest and owed Pierre Fortier the most. It is the tribute of slaves to bondage, that they never learn to use their strength in freeing themselves, but only to applaud others.

Maria sitting in silence on her crags neither heard nor needed their approbation. It was sunset. The valley before her deepened in color from plum to blue; it was no less beautiful when blue-black. Behind her in the little clearing among the pines waited her little hut—no larger, no more changed than it had been, off and on when patched, for seventy years. It was the point of her completed circle. She too had endured unchanged.

She had withstood the ebb and flow of the seasons; the sullen hostility of commerce and misfortune; the anaesthesia of religion, wealth and acclaim—all the passions that warp the mind, flesh and spirit of man.

She was immune from all but the ultimate destruction of her inessential outer shell.

At eighty, she heard of the dam.

It is late afternoon. The whole day in the valley has churned like a fiesta. Wagons loaded with people rumble down the cañons. Double-mounted horses too have passed: the front rider with left foot in the stirrup and leaning sideways, the rider behind him with right foot in the stirrup and leaning to the opposite side,—the old way, when mounts are scarce and must carry double over the rocky trails. Men have left their fields, women their houses and wood piles. The roads are full. Santa Gertrudes and San Antonio both swarm. From each, continually, a battered tin automobile chugs up one cañon after another and returns with a load of people.

It is not a Diá de Fiesta. It is not a Saint's Day to be celebrated. It is Election Day in the beautiful blue valley.

Across from the courthouse in Santa Gertrudes stands a gaunt adobe. It is unfurnished save for a wooden platform at one end. Here each Saturday night, and all day during fiesta, sit the guitar players who pluck out music for dances. Today the floor is even more crowded. The walls are lined with tables partially screened by mosquito netting. Near the door sits a man at a table with two huge boxes. It is the place of voting.

The road in front is crowded. The sheriff and two deputies wear their guns outside their coats. The deputies are too drunk to use them. The sheriff cannot read the sign which says in English that no electioneering is permitted here.

When the crowded Ford sputters up and unloads, he makes way for driver and passengers and a político who meets them. The político smokes a cigar and wears a cloth vest.

"Ah, you brought them," he says to the driver. "Our good friends from up the cañon! Welcome. Welcome, amigos."

The passengers have no shoes. They are rudely dressed in dirty gingham and black rebozos, in denims and leather vests. Their eyes shine like polished obsidian.

"To you our devout thanks. We have never ridden in a máquina before. Our wits are turned by its swiftness. We were there and then here. A day's hard journey transformed into the flight of an hour. It is a miracle!" She stoops and kisses the político's hand.

"Por nada, por nada!" he answers gruffly. "Here are your papers."

They look at the sample ballots wonderingly. None can read.

"What is the name of him for whom we mark the cross this time, Señor? Is it a new Gobierno? Perhaps a new Presidente, himself? Strange. We have had no pictures of him for our windows. We have heard no talk."

"Bastante, compadre! It is not a great man you vote for this day, but a great thing. Your hand is put to the paper so that there will be no more floods to sweep cañon and valley with death and destruction, that there will be water for all in time of drought, that it will be measured, to each his proper share. The Government can do all this. But it wishes the sign of your will. . . . Here now! Each! See, I have marked on your paper the tiny crosses. Inside, Fidencio will give you others like this, but empty. Fill them with crosses as these, without mistake. Thus you will do your duty!"

Slowly the people file inside. Carefully, tenderly, they spread out the clean sheets on the little tables, lest they be soiled. Pencil stubs they lick with nervous lips, and hold awkwardly in calloused brown hands.

They talk through the mosquito netting. "See? I have made the crosses as instructed. Do they look right to you, primo? I would not have the Government consider me too ignorant though I cannot read."

At the center table they give their ballots to Fidencio. He looks them over casually, and stuffs them in a box.

Outside, the político gives each man a sack of tobacco and each woman a stick of candy. They are hurriedly stuffed back into the car.

"Have you got them all?" the político asks the driver in English. "Know anybody else? Anybody, anywhere! If they won't come get their names. Get the names of their horses, their cows and pigs and dogs. Where is that list of names you brought from the graveyard? We might need that too. . . . Now get on! For God's sake! Give her another twist."

And till dark the battered tin máquina chugs back and forth from the dark cañons.

Maria has watched it steadily, all day, from the top of her cliffs. She rises stiffly and walks down to her hut. In the dusky clearing she chops a few sticks. She boils tea, spoons some beans with pieces of a torn tortilla, puts up the tea leaves to use again with fresh.

It is eight thousand feet high, and already cold. Her mind is cold with foreboding, too. She huddles before the blaze without moving. An hour. Two. Her thoughts begin to boil. Her old, dark and impassive face thaws into wrinkles. Her loose lips draw back from her one tooth. Suddenly, savagely, she spits into the coals.

"Los Mofres! Those cursed Mofres!"

Many, many years ago when Maria was a goat girl, a stranger had wandered into the beautiful blue valley. He had blue eyes, fair skin and a sharp tongue which lurked behind a perpetual smile. On his broad back he wore a pack. His hands were clever at mending broken pots, and dexterous at warding off occasional knife thrusts with the staff he carried. He was an itinerant peddler, an Irishman from County Donegal, and his name was Thomas Murphy.

Respect gathered round him with the walls of the beautiful valley. Perhaps its own blue seemed green. He remained. Soon his brother came, bringing a wife for each. Shortly they had land at the mouth of one of the little cañons. And before long, Tomás had a house and a store, and Roberto a house and a tiny mill for grinding the grain both raised and which Tomás sold.

It was amazing how they prospered. Their land grew and was fruitful. The store enlarged, rivaled Pierre Fortier's. The little water mill duly supplanted the big one of the Garcias. Sons and daughters came in abundance, grandchildren. Finally, with all of these, came power.

The source of this power really lay in a hairline difference between them and the people of the valley. Outwardly they lived as all. Their Spanish was even better. The women could dish up costillas adobadas flavored to the exact heat with chile carribe and dance a varsoviana as gracefully as any neighbor. The men could rope and tie a wild steer as quick, and hold as much liquor. To their own innumerable Celtic superstitions they added those of the valley. Their first born sons they sent to the priest as altar boys for training. And by most they were accepted not as the only gringos to remain in the valley, but as proper vecinos. Their name was changed from "Murphy" to the more easily pronounced "Mofre," and the little cañon they controlled became known as "El Cañon de Mofre."

But inwardly they remained gringos and Irish. As gringos they held to a certain cold objectivity which enabled them to see themselves apart from the land and the people. As Irishmen they felt it incumbent to always get a shade the better of both. In trade, land and argument, they were still sharp peddlers.

The one trait they inherently possessed in common with their neighbors was a natural gravitation toward politics. Drunken rows, cold scheming and hot arguments over candidates for a school teacher, a county clerk, a new sheriff—these offered a pleasure surpassing that in a good trade. They became políticos.

Los Mofres then, through land, business and politics, became a power in the beautiful blue valley.

Maria did not trust them. Year by year she watched them fence in a piece of land, a field here, a few varas there, and still another pasture. Year by year she heard of another paisano falling into debt to store or mill. She began to smell a rat.

There is the power of the mind. It says, "There are no tribes, no races, no peoples separated by the color of their eyes, their hair and skin. There is only mankind. All men are brothers. Each has the same passions, thirsts and hungers. The greed for gold and the greed for land is common to all. The Murphys of the world have it, as do I. I will not unjustly condemn my brother."

But there is also the power of the blood which keeps beating, "There are many earths, and each has its own irreconcilable spirit of place. Now what is a man but his earth? It rises in walls to shelter him in life. It sinks to receive him at death. By eating its corn he builds his flesh into walls of this selfsame earth. He has its granitic hardness or its soft resiliency. He is different as each field even is different. Thus do I know my own earth; I can know no other. I am greedy for my land, and that is right. Does not a child cry for its mother's breasts? But when the Murphys desire my land, it is false. For they would not belong to it; they would only that it belonged to them. By this they refute their own mother, and would enslave another's for a ransom of gold. So I suspect them."

Maria listened, and remained silent. But watchful.

Into the valley came talk of a dam. There came strange gringos who answered to no names as men standing on their own feet, but whose mother was the same: "La Compañía de Agua y Tierra de Demora." With the Mofres they talked. Always.

A little longer, and the Mofres supplied beef and mutton for a fiesta down in the campo below the village. Many important men, they said, would be there to tell the good people of the valley, our neighbors, about the dam. The dam of which you have heard, no doubt. Has there not been talk?

So all the good people of the valley assembled on the campo. Maria went herself. And there were the important men who talked about the dam to all: men of the Government, of the State, the nameless men of the Company, officials, políticos. And beside them, looking more important than all, the Mofres.

Instantly, intuitively, Maria distrusted the dam. She rode home perplexed. She withheld judgment. But all the time she pondered the question up and down, back and forth.

The dam had its virtues, no doubt. There had always been floods, down one cañon, then another, and once from two—Madre mia! There had always been droughts which were equally bad. Now with a dam, as it was said, there would be no floods and no droughts bearing death and destruction in each. There would be water at all times, measured to each man his proper share.

But this dam is to be built only for the benefit of the good people of the valley, and the Mofres' eagerness for it, did not quite coincide in Maria's mind.

The Mofres loved the good people of the valley, their neighbors. They loved them, besought them with great credit in store and mill. "Just sign this paper, compadre, to show that it is not your will to forget." And then, very quickly, they took away their land for payment.

Mother of God! Can one believe a man who says he loves his family, when he allows one member to starve? Can a man love his country, and yet neglect his own field?

There is no patriotism beyond the few leagues we would really die for. There is no love of abstract humanity. There is only the love we show each man as an individual.

So Maria questioned the Mofres' intent to benefit the people by the dam while they robbed them individually. She wondered what they would derive from a dam that would control the cañon water for their mill instead of themselves. She wondered how they would exact payment for the beef and mutton eaten at the fiesta.

The election came. People waited to bear Maria's opinion. Some went to her. She was silent. So they listened to the busy Mofres and to the políticos who sputtered up the cañons, they accepted rides in the máquina to mark their crosses as instructed, candy and tobacco. The políticos came up for Maria.

"Just what is this election?" she asked quietly.

"Well," answered one man, with the ready formula. "It is for the people to express their will for a dam. That there may be no more floods, no more droughts, but water always, as needed. Is it not a wonderful thing?"

Said another who knew Maria's shrewdness, "Madre, it is the water district election, granted by our county commissioners whom we elected ourselves."

Maria rolled a cigarette. "Water District?" she asked slowly. "Is there not water in all districts?"

"It is like this, Madre. Allow me to explain fully. This valley is one water district of many in these parts. It is a judicial district. It is a County. Do you see? When one regards water, it is as a water district. When one regards justice and law, it is as a judicial district. When one regards government, it is as a County. And none of these districts, of which there are many of each, may be different and thus interfere with the others. Thus we are the United States! Now do you understand? We are no longer merely the valley."

"No, amigo," said Maria, puffing deliberately. "It is you who are dumfounded with words. We are still the valley. Water is our problem; our fights over a stream's flow have always been the fiercest; too much of it has killed us also. We have our Masters of the Ditch. Hence also our need for justice, for government. But with all of these, and more, Señor, we are still the valley. The mountains enclose us, the earth feeds us. It is a thing of itself. Do not talk of a district on paper!"

"But how—granting what you say—will this dam be built if it is the will of the people? Who will pay? We ourselves are too poor."

The político alternated between impatience to be off and the desire to show his great knowledge of these matters.

"Señora," he stated tersely. "You will not understand, nor is there reason to. The election for the dam will win. Its result will be an issue of papers worth money—bonds, the great men call them. These will be sold in the city by the officiales. This money will pay for half the dam. It will be given to the Government which will then supply the other half, and build the dam. The Government, Señora. For the people. For water conservation and safety."

"And what will the people in the city do with the paper they have bought? I cannot imagine . . ."

"It is clear, Doña Maria, that you have no mind for such matters, despite being the widow of Señor Garcia whose knowledge of these things—and money—was profound. He himself was of this Demora Water and Land Company, as are the Mofres—two of them. Besides being, one of them, a Water Commissioner. . . . I may add, however, that this illustrious Company will no doubt buy much of that paper. They will then collect money from the people they save from death and destruction. In taxes. So much for the water they use. No more than reasonable, of a certainty. Are they not our neighbors? . . . Bastante! We must be off. No one else has asked so many questions. . . . Come now, Doña Maria. We will help you mark your paper with a cross for this great thing."

"I shall not vote," replied Maria wearily. "As you see, I am old and weak. That swift máquina would break all my brittle bones. . . . Go with God, Señores—you do not have far to go."

For two days she sat alone, studying this new problem. She had the miraculous memory of those who do not read and write. Moreover her years with Don Fulgencio had already opened to her the new world of worldly matters. She was more shrewd than anyone—even Don Fulgencio—had suspected.

On the third day she had Teodosio drive her down to the village. The overwhelming results of the election had just been announced. She also nursed the new fact that Don Fulgencio had been a member of this water and land company. She went to the courthouse, puffed up the warped pine steps to the office of the recorder. He was an old man, this Sanchez, with puffed cheeks and small eyes. He had been a friend of Don Fulgencio.

For twenty minutes they battled with elaborate politeness.

"To the point!" directed Maria sharply. "I come in haste and in distress. I am old. I shall soon be dead. How much land do I own? Get out the papers. . . . We are going to have a dam. Advise me, as a trusted friend of your friend, my husband, about this dam and my land."

Sanchez tottered over his maps as if he did not know that she knew every tree, rock and ravine that marked the limits of her land.

"Your strip of land here, from the tall cliffs across the valley to the opposite mountains. . . . This piece, your share from one Onesimo. . . . These pieces of your children, Refugio Montes, Gertrudes Paiz and Antonio de la Vega, yet in your name, as that of Teodosio and Niña. All in the valley, Señora. That without, you have already sold."

Maria brushed back her thin gray hair. "Sold? Yes, of course. But my memory fails. What land did you say, amigo?"

Sanchez blinked his small eyes suspiciously. Maria drew out from her tattered rebozo a heavy, yellow coin. It was square in shape, and gold. Her old wrinkled hands turned it idly as she watched the greedy glitter come into his eyes. Then she slid the gold piece across the table. He clutched it; it was gone.

"Come, Sanchez!" Her voice was hard, metallic. "All what land? My memory weakens. Refresh it, Sanchez."

"Why surely you remember! All that land up in the mountains. Beyond the valley. The share which was yours equally with that in the valley, according to the old Grant," he went on complacently. "The original Spanish land grant to the first seventy-six settlers in the valley. It gave them not only the land within the valley which they developed and was all they could use or want. It gave them all the land outside, nearly the whole Condado, which they forgot.

"Now the time came when this grant was confirmed by the new gringo government. And the time came, as you remember, when all the descendants of these seventy-six were given titles to their land, and the Presidente caused these titles to be made Patent. Now a title to

every piece of land within the valley was also a title to a share without
—ten times the size. But who remembered? Nobody. Save Don
Fulgencio, Señora.

"Cómo no? He was simply shrewd and careful. It was business.
Like this. A poor farmer comes to him for a loan on his land, with land
to sell. My wise friend takes title to all his land—the piece within the
valley the man knows he owns, and the larger piece outside that he
knows nothing about. Pretty soon the man raises a litle money, he
wants his land back—it is the Devil the way they hang on to their
land! So my friend simply transfers back to him his valley land, and
retains title to the rest. No one is the wiser."

"Ah!" sighed Maria.

"Ah, indeed! What a head he had on those narrow shoulders of his,
Don Fulgencio, my friend, your husband! Most of this land was mountainous, fit only for grazing. But he smelled the new railroad approaching, which needed timber for ties. . . . But more important! This land
was on the watershed. With it water rights could be controlled when
eventually a dam was needed. There was even a Compañía forming.
And Don Fulgencio had the land. So he became one with the
Compañía. Only one piece more was needed. You remember? Title to
that long cañon draining into the valley past the tall cliffs. The perfect
site for a dam that must be built."

"My memory returns, Sanchez," said Maria soberly.

"As I thought!" he replied shrewdly. "A great price Don Fulgencio
must have got for it, too, from the Compañía. Why, for ten years I
myself watched pass the timber they cut from it to sell the railroad. To
say nothing of all the other land like it he got from these dull people,
our neighbors. I myself arranged the papers of title for him—at very
little profit to myself, for keeping a tongue in my cheek. Though he
promised more. But died too soon." He was eyeing Maria steadily
now. "Of course you are poor according to custom, Doña Maria. As
was he, being wise. But a little of that gold now. . . ."

Maria stood up. "Enough! Well do I recognize my husband's
shrewdness in being a político to maintain you in office. You who are

so cunning yourself. But I think not too poorly paid for what you have done. No doubt these new políticos, the Mofres, who have taken up the dead one's power, pay you less than he. Verdad?"

"A little but not enough. Cristo Rey! But when the dam is built, and they have the water to measure and sell, and theirs is the new electric plant, and taxes moreover—well, it is best to bet on the winning horse. . . . But now. About this land of yours. That in the valley. The piece by the tall cliffs. It is good with respect to the dam. Very good, I will say to you with the memory of Don Fulgencio between us. But, as you say, you are getting old. If you would sell, to the Mofres I myself—"

"No, amigo. No, my cunning friend. I have decided not to sell my land. Not a vara. Now I must go. To you I leave the memory of Don Fulgencio and a piece of his gold. I would not know what to do with either."

Sanchez looked at her curiously as she went out.

Winter crept down the mountains. The valley paled from a lake of blue to a lake of white. Cold clutched and throttled it. And then its white turned blue again with the shadowy reflection of the peaks upon its icy crust.

So do men, their deeds blanketed, still reflect the natural color of their lives.

Maria from her cliffs watched the mutations. She knew at last why Don Fulgencio had desired her in marriage. But so long ago! It meant nothing to her now. He was but one of many, his shape a shadow mirrored for an instant upon the one enduring earth.

For days, a week, she was snowbound. It gave her time to properly consider the dam. There was this about it: it was more than a dam: it was a step in progress. And progress men define as that step toward giving the greatest good to the greatest number of people. Now Maria believed neither in the majority nor in the minority. She believed in all men. Good for the strong at the expense of the weak she saw as a natural inevitability. But also she saw that intentional wrong dealt the few can never be paid for by the right derived from it by the many. Maria believed in fulfillment instead of progress. Fulfillment is individual evolution. It requires time and patience. Progress, in haste to move mass, admits neither.

So she pondered, beating her way up the snowy trail to her seat on the crags, and wrapping herself in the soft burnt-orange blanket.

The suspicion never entered her head that she was philosophizing. She thought that she was making up her mind about the dam. It merely shows how abstract are all things in perspective when seen from a height. In dimensional time and space nothing is only what it seems.

Over the icy fields below her raced a spot of black. It had length and breadth, form and movement. Yet deep ravines did not halt it, nor rocky slopes, nor fences. It was the shadow of a crow in swift flight overhead.

The dam too would cast a shadow. The misfortune of men who would lose their land would not stop it. It would flit across their lives with fear and suffering, anger and evil. All shadows of the shadow of the dam itself. But can you tell a man who starves that his hunger is unreal? Can you tell a man that his own life is but a shadow when he has no eyes to see the real?

Maria sighed. How long it had taken her to climb above it all, this valley of illusion with its pain and incomprehension! Yet to it she was still bound. There is no philosophy of value which would deny the earth below. For it is life with its injustice and cruelty, and its patience to suffer both, which gives us even the philosophy to lift ourselves above it.

The wind had come up again. It curled round the crags streamers of snow. It shrieked through the pines, whistled over the rocks. The leaden skies dropped and crushed its voice and action. The pandemonium became a pause.

Maria trudged back to her hut. Another snow was coming. She would need plenty of wood.

The snow came, a foot of it and more. Another came, and yet

another. A day of sun welded the layers together. The earth became solid as a frozen peach. And still the cold persisted. Twice a night she got up stiffly to replenish the fire. For water she had to chop up the stream. The pine outside split open with cold. In the clearing, gaunt, heavy-headed deer stood up to their bellies in snow. With them Maria shared her own corn.

Late in February winter broke. The earth began to soften like a spoiled peach. Its muddy juice ran down cañon and mountainside. The roads began to open. Soon came Teodosio. She could hear the squeak of his greaseless hubs a kilómetro away.

For an hour they sat talking in the hut. Then Maria got up and placed a bag of pesos in his hands.

"There are twenty pesos," she said sharply. "You will say there are not enough. But with them I want that old buggy fixed. A new tongue. Rims for three wheels. A bit of leather. Much grease. Perhaps a lantern to tie behind. No less! The last time I rode, the wheel broke; I would not fall again."

"Mother of God! Such expense. To say nothing of the work to me. Why, to fix it as you say would require a fortune. Do you think it has remained the same? Jesus, Madre! Now the top is gone. The seat is hard with chicken droppings. Its—"

"Enough! Let it be fixed with your work and my pesos."

"For why? By all the Saints—"

"Because," answered Maria slowly, "because I have remained up here alone too long. Spring comes. We ride down through the valley as before. There are things that need my attention. Especially this new dam. I do not approve of it."

CHAPTER 9

Of Time and Change: A Memoir (1998)

Settling on Taos in the late 1930s marked a significant turn in Frank Waters's life. This was one of the few places left in North America where the Indian way had managed to retain most of its coherence; to live here within the magnetism, and to become a student of Pueblo culture, shaped Waters's subsequent writing decisively. Noticing the differences between Indian and Euro-American psychology and society, and the common elements as well, he could be keyed into new insights about human life in general. He appeared to be in search of nothing less than a unified-field perception of culture and consciousness, and of course this would include himself. His friendships in Taos, particularly with Ralph Meyers the trader and with Tony Luhan and Mabel Dodge Luhan, helped him to the nexus, the points where two worlds touched. The following appreciation of Mabel, written late in Waters's life, attempts to cut through her notorious surface reputation and come to the place where she too lived with duality.

4: Something about Mabel

For years I've been plagued to write "something about Mabel." The apparent assumption was that I knew a bit more about her than those hundreds of others who have written about her. Mabel and Tony were intimate friends of mine for almost twenty-five years. I lived for a time in two of their houses in "Mabeltown," went with them on two trips to Mexico, and saw them in New York, Los Angeles, and Tucson, so there was ample opportunity to see Mabel in many of her various moods.

The thought of adding to the reams already written about her repelled me, perhaps because we seldom write about those we love and know intimately. This reluctance is not encountered when we write about one known only from published books, articles, letters, autobiographical writings, and opinions from interviewed friends. Such an objective study presents a full-figure character against his or her background. But it lacks eye-to-eye, intuitive, personal contact. Unconscious empathy or antagonism is replaced by a rational balancing of the subject's positive and negative qualities according to the biographer's own value judgments.

This is true of the two biographies and many commentaries written about Mabel. All the facts of her colorful and controversial life are well known. Emily Hahn's *Mabel* is a recital of her faults and foibles. *Mabel Dodge Luhan* by Lois Falken Rudnick, which may not be surpassed, was compiled from her exhaustive research into 1,500 pounds of papers Mabel left to the library of Yale University. It fully documents her childhood in Buffalo, her years in Italy, establishment of her salon in New York, relationships with three husbands, and her move to Taos.

This comprehensive account of Mabel's active years is judiciously impartial, analytical, and written from the viewpoint of Ms. Rudnick's own intellectual, metropolitan, and cultural background. Definitive as it is, I find too skimpy Ms. Rudnick's coverage of Mabel's last twenty-five years in Taos. As she told me during a pleasant evening we spent together in Mabel's reopened Big House, Rudnick had never been in the Southwest and knew nothing of Indian life until she made a brief visit to Taos. Here, she gained a fleeting and casual picture of that small town and nearby Indian pueblo whose reputation had spread worldwide. She did not experience the impact of the ancient, indigenous culture that was Mabel's obsessive concern during the last part of her life.

I didn't know Mabel during her active years when she was moti-
vated by what has been called her sexual drive, feminine wiles, and
mental will to dominate everyone she knew. I knew her only during
her later, more passive years when an aspect of her hidden inner self
revealed itself only to be obscured again by her individual ego. This is
what interests me more. Hence, these comments will contribute little
to the continuing squabbling about her. They simply reflect my gradual awareness of this neglected aspect of her complex character.

I met Mabel in Taos, where I was renting Spud Johnson's house in
Placita for the summer. I had been living in Mora, just over the mountains. Tony I had met at several pueblo dances downriver while I was
there. He had invited me to visit him, but I'd never gone. This I mentioned to Spud when he returned to town and wanted to reoccupy his
house. He promptly took me to Tony and Mabel's Big House, where
they were giving a big party that afternoon.

The Big House was swarming with guests. In the large tiled dining
room, an orchestra of Spanish musicians was playing. Food and drinks
were served in the crowded living and sun rooms. And outside on the
portal, Indians were dancing and singing to the beat of a belly-drum.
In this crowd, I met Mabel. She was a rather short and compactly built
woman with one of the loveliest voices I had ever heard. She dispelled
my uneasiness at being an uninvited stranger by her warm friendliness.
There was little for us to say among the swarming guests. I left without seeing Tony, who was singing outside.

Back in Placita, I gave up the house to Spud, packed my few
belongings, and drove back to Mora. Here, I moved in to stay a few
days with Fran and Ed Tinker in their small adobe outside town. A
week later, however, Tony and Mabel drove there to see me.

"Spud tells me you don't want to stay here in Mora and that you
haven't found another place to live in Taos," said Mabel. "Come on
back. I have a small empty house just back of Spud's you can have if
you fix it up a little."

Her surprising offer I couldn't refuse. On the day I arrived there,
Mabel invited me to lunch. For something to do, she got out a copy

of the ancient Chinese book of divination, the *I Ching*. This early translation by James Legge simply showed the six lines of the hexagrams not separated into their two trigrams. To represent the six lines someone had made for her six small sticks, three of which had been marked with a dividing line and three of which were unmarked. To obtain an oracular pronouncement, Mabel explained, one simply threw the sticks, observed the hexagram shown, then read its meaning in the text of the *I Ching*. This Mabel did after silently asking a question. Then I, in turn, threw the sticks and obtained the same hexagram. The *I Ching* was new to me, and the text was so full of archaic Chinese allusions, I could make no sense of it.

This was irrelevant. For as I read into the book, unbroken yang lines often changed into broken yin lines and yin lines changed into yang lines; it was possible for each hexagram to change into another for a total of 4,096 (64 x 64) transitional stages, representing every possible condition or relationship in the world.

What seemed significant was that I had thrown the same hexagram as Mabel against the odds of 4,096 to 1.

Today, I wish I knew which hexagram we both obtained, what image or relationship it represented, and the psychological meaning of this extraordinary coincidence. Oracularly, it may have foretold my long, close friendship with her. Or perhaps it may merely account for my recalling the incident here.

At the house in Placita, I repaired the loose window frames and installed a wood stove. The following spring, when Myron Brinig bought and modernized the house, Mabel let me have the huge studio room above the garage of the Tony House on the Pueblo reservation. Dorothy Brett lived in the one-room Studio House nearby, and we shared an outdoor privy.

Mabel's life in the Big House seemed simple and pleasant. She was served breakfast in her room at promptly six o'clock while Tony ate leisurely in the big kitchen before going out to his fields. Then she was up and about, seeing that things in Mabeltown ran smoothly. There was always a succession of cooks and maids in the house and two permanent Spanish men for work outside. José looked after all living things, the dogs and horses, vegetable garden, and orchard. Max made all the needed repairs in the various buildings, driving around in a big truck with a dog whose patient expression matched his own.

Every evening Mabel invited someone for dinner. Those who came most often were Spud Johnson, who kept her accounts and published the weekly *Horse Fly*, Rowena and Ralph Meyers, the grizzled Indian trader; Eve and John Young-Hunter, the English portrait painter; Myron Brinig, a popular New York novelist of the time; and various Taos artists taking turns at her table. Never invited were members of the business community and town officials. Their omission created in them a deep, repressed resentment, which in later years emerged in a movement to run a road through her property; this would have destroyed the Big House. Fortunately, it did not happen.

John Evans, her son from her first marriage, came infrequently with his wife, Claire, and their children. He was handsome and charming, and had held several important business and government positions, but had retired to their home in Maine. I enjoyed seeing him, though their visits were short. He and Mabel did not get along, perhaps because they were too much alike.

Mabel's gifts to the town included its first hospital and a bandstand in the plaza. To the Harwood Library she gave sets of rare first-edition books, a collection of Persian miniature paintings and Spanish *santos,* and yearly donations of popular books. Few people knew of the money, food, and personal help she gave to needy families. As Claire Morrill wrote, "Her reticence was somehow reserved for her virtues."

If Mabel was impervious to what people thought of her, Taos was always slightly in awe of her. This held true even during a time when she was receiving medical attention for a condition that might have embarrassed anyone else. Driving through the crowded plaza, she would suddenly stop the car, leave the motor running, and dash into the nearest shop or restaurant. Everyone hastily cleared the way for her. It was a distinctly understood imperative that Mabel had to go to the bathroom.

During one of the two trips I made to Mexico with her and Tony, she was surprisingly adaptable. Late one evening when we were walking in the upper plaza at Pátzcuaro, I was struck by the somber mystery of the huge church belltower looming high in the darkness. "I'd like to climb up inside it and see what it's like," I murmured.

"Why don't we? Let's go!" she said instantly.

So we fumbled our way through the dark church to a steep, narrow flight of stairs, and climbed steadily up into the lofty tower beset by bats and roosting pigeons. How eerie it was, but how beautiful the view when the lights of town and of Janitzio on its island far out in the lake finally spread out below. For a rather heavy woman, sixty-one years old and dressed in skirts and flimsy slippers, the climb must have been arduous.

A few years later, when Tony and I visited her in New York, I later drove her back to Taos, Tony having taken the train a week before. Throughout the South, she always chose to stay overnight in the "tourist homes" found in every small town and village. They were old family homes with rooms for rent, a common bathroom down the hall, and no coffee available in the morning. Had Tony been with us, he'd have insisted we drive on to a modern hotel in the next large town. Mabel, so used to having breakfast in bed, accepted these discomforts and inconveniences as a matter of course.

We arrived in New Orleans on the evening of the town's first showing of the lauded movie *Gone with the Wind.* The Old South had come alive to welcome it. Confederate flags hung from every balcony and rooftop. Crowds of costumed people swarmed through the squares and streets, ladies in lace and crinoline, gentlemen in frock coats and top hats, every woman a Scarlett O'Hara, every man a Rhett Butler. Every seat in the theater had been long sold, of course. This did not deter Mabel. She barged into the office of the manager and cajoled him into selling her two tickets. The seats were in a back row whose view of the screen was partially obstructed by a tall pillar. Mabel promptly moved us down to center seats. And now began a battle of wills.

The ticket holders for the seats arrived to claim them. When Mabel refused to budge, the head usher came to oust us. A small crowd gathered in the aisle; the picture was soon to start. The manager arrived to expostulate. "You sold me tickets to seats from which we couldn't see," Mabel said quietly. To his indignant protestations and threats to evacuate us by force, the angry muttering of the audience, and my own embarrassment, Mabel was deaf. She sat there silently, hands folded primly in her lap, exerting the will that had so enraged D. H. Lawrence.

Such displays of combative self-assertiveness were rare. At home she was generally relaxed, sure of herself and her place in the world. How different she seemed from the self-portrayed Mabel in the four volumes of her *Intimate Memories:* a woman of contradictory moods and desires, selfish, willful, contriving, and demanding. There was a great rift between them I couldn't understand. She had loaned me the books and followed my reading with a curious interest. From one volume to another, she told me additional details about incidents and persons recounted in her writing. They were most frank, for she didn't spare her own role. It was as if she wanted everything, good and bad, to be known about her eventually.

Mabel's openness is reflected in 183 letters she wrote me between 1939 and 1960. Some of them were short notes delivered by hand while I was living in Taos. Others were long letters mailed to me in New York, Washington, D.C., or Los Angeles. All were undated, handwritten in ink on white manuscript paper in a flowing, bold script as if dashed off impulsively and without reservations. She also gave me her complete medical history and a dozen or more unpublished articles she had written for Arthur Brisbane when he had suggested she do a syndicated newspaper column.

It was not enough for her to reveal everything about herself; she desired to be fully understood. Deep below her revealed surface, I sensed an unknown part of her that had always endeavored to emerge into upper consciousness. My intimation of this threw into focus all I had read of her past life. She became at once more intensely personal and vastly impersonal, as if she had been acting out the same universal role we all are blindly following.

Mabel's admission of being "nobody in myself" leaves no doubt that she became aware early of her incompleteness. Her primary approach toward discovering what she lacked came when she met Dr. A. A. Brill. Brill was a Freudian psychologist, the first to translate Freud's writings into English and the first to practice in America. Soon after his arrival in New York in 1921, Mabel consulted him. Off and on for the next twenty years she consulted him as an analyst and a friend. He came to visit her in Taos, and when I was in New York with Tony, Brill invited us to dinner at his home.

Almost coincident with Mabel's introduction into psychology was the beginning of her interest in the mystical teachings that Georges Ivanovitch Gurdjieff had brought from Central Asia. To propound them he established the Institute for the Harmonious Development of Man at the Chateau du Prieure, Fontainebleau, near Paris. Mabel was impressed by his teachings and by Gurdjieff himself when he came to lecture in New York in 1924. She introduced him to Tony; and, as she told me, he took one look at Tony in his Chief blanket and hairbraids and said to her, "What a clever woman you are! You have broken the mold!"

Unfortunately, Mabel became briefly infatuated with Jean Toomer, one of Gurdjieff's followers and loaned him $14,000 for use by the institute, which she later learned had been misspent. This cut short her contact with Gurdjieff. Still, she continued to correspond with Orage, another disciple, and to follow the gradual spread of the Gurdjieff movement. As late as 1949, when Gurdjieff was preparing to publish the first volume of his objective writings on the world and man—the mammoth *All and Everything*—Mabel received letters from Lord Pentland in England requesting that she share in the expense by buying one of the expensive copies of the first edition. Whether she did or not, I don't know. Nor when or from whom she received a typescript draft of Gurdjieff's first section, *Beelzebub's Tales to His Grandson, an Objectively Impartial Criticism of the Life of Man.* This rare manuscript she gave me with the terse comment, "Here, this will probably interest you!"

Forty years or more later, the Gurdjieff teachings are no longer regarded as a hodgepodge of Asian mysticism and occult practices put together by a master charlatan. They have established their philosophical and psychological values. Gurdjieff centers have been founded in all large cities. I myself find his imaginative view of mankind's evolution most instructive.

A few years ago I was privileged to visit Madam Olga de Hartmann in her home in New Mexico shortly before her death. Her late husband had composed the music for all of Gurdjieff's celebrated dance "Movements," and both of them had accompanied Gurdjieff on his flight from Russia, through Turkey to Europe. Soon after I met her, I watched these therapeutic Movements, derived from ancient ritual dances in Central Asia, performed in a private school in Arizona. The dancers were teenaged men and women charged with criminal acts and prostitution; they had been released to the school to reform or to be sent back to detention homes or face prosecution. Vigorously "dancing" without moving from their places in line, sweat dripping from their bodies and running down their faces, hoarsely chanting meanwhile, one of them sobbing incontrollably, they were giving release to long-repressed emotions and feelings of guilt. I have never experienced such a strong emotional impact. Such physical as well as mental exercises were required of Gurdjieff's pupils.

Mabel, of course, could never have submitted to such discipline. I doubt that she ever intellectually comprehended the systems of either

Freud or Gurdjieff for attaining realization of her inner self, nor the spiritual teachings of many world religions she had read. Her approach to any subject or situation was never mental but emotional or instinctive.

When Tony and I visited her in New York, she was reviving the famous evenings held in 1913 in her salon at 23 Fifth Avenue. To them came old friends, psychologists, anthropologists, artists, writers, publishers. I was impressed by seeing for the first time the world of wealth and power they represented. "Take a good look at it," Mabel told me. "It's falling to pieces. I know. I was part of it."

At home she had collected a great library of books on philosophy, psychology, and world religions, many of which she loaned me. "But don't believe any of them," she cautioned me. "You've got to discover your own truth within your inner self."

Yet if she had not assimilated their teachings, she must have gained from them an objective view of her outer world. She had become convinced that Western civilization had reached a dead end like other civilizations of the past. A decadent, dying world in which she had been trying to play a part, always feeling unrelated to it. "The world," she wrote, "is an alien place to nine-tenths of those who live in it or who appear to live in it but who merely go through the motions . . . as though they were alive throughout." How strange this sounds, coming from one pictured as a social butterfly flitting from one salon to another.

She had resolved, as she told me, to record its false values and superficial attitudes, its materialistic greed and corruption, as Proust had recorded his time and world in his voluminous *Remembrance of Things Past,* without sparing her own faults and foibles. This illuminating statement of purpose reveals her *Intimate Memories* to be more than the writings of an egotistical exhibitionist, as they often have been regarded.

Today, a half-century later, her belief that our materialistic Western civilization, threatened by a nuclear holocaust, faces collapse or a drastic change in values is a major theme widely expounded. We must give her credit. Although her measure of objectivity didn't draw her inward, it led her to reject the outer world of appearances. There kept growing within her the desperate need to break away, to find a place where she could start living at last.

The break began one winter evening in 1917 when she rode the stage into Taos. One quick look in the snowy twilight was enough. She surrendered immediately to the remote, almost primitive village that became her permanent home until she died forty-five years later. One event followed another. She fell in love, for the first time, with Tony Lujan, an Indian in the nearby Pueblo, divorced her third husband, Maurice Sterne, and married Tony. Together they built on the edge of the reservation the adobe Big House of seventeen rooms, which drew visitors from all the world. Mabel began to live at last.

From the first, she was entranced by the life in Tony's pueblo. "Little by little," she later wrote, "I found out that every interpretation of Indian life by a white person from the most ignorant villager up to the most learned archaeologist or anthropologist, was rationalized from a false premise, the standpoint of his own white psyche. . . . There has never been written any true version of the Indian spirit. These people, one race from North America down through Mexico, Yucatan and Peru in South America, have never been known by any of the white people."

She viewed their life, contrary to the materialistic life of white people, as geared to universal realities—the living earth, the fructifying sun, the invisible forces of all life. This intimate relationship of man to the universe enabled Indians to survive as tribal societies through centuries of genocide by the incoming whites.

Taos townspeople could hardly believe Mabel had actually married a blanketed Indian. Nor could they believe the marriage would last long. Each time she left on a trip to New York, they would wisely assert, "This time she won't come back." And every year the rumors spread that Mabel was finally going to get rid of him.

Another thing difficult for Anglos to swallow was Mabel's so-called mystical view of their Pueblo neighbors. Indian women were reliable maids who worked for a few dollars a day. The men were considered excellent gardeners. They straggled into town ridiculously wearing blankets in winter, white sheets in summer, and sloppy moccasins instead of shoes. A people dirt poor, generally illiterate, buying cheap scraps of meat from the butcher and cadging a pint of whiskey from their friends. That they were highly evolved spiritually was pure bosh! Especially Tony—that lazy Indian—driving around in a car and supported by a rich white wife. As for Mabel, if she believed so strongly in Indian life, why didn't she move out to the Pueblo, cut her own firewood, draw water from the stream, and cook her own meals in the fireplace?

Knowing herself incompetent to interpret Indian life, Mabel drew others to Taos. With them she hoped to instigate here a rebirth of the dying Western civilization from the body of Indian culture. Among them, of course, was D. H. Lawrence, in Mabel's view the greatest living writer. He and his wife, Frieda, lived for short periods on a mountain ranch that Mabel gave him. Lawrence savagely resented Mabel's will to dominate him and, ill with tuberculosis, fled to Mexico. Although he admitted that neither he nor any white man could identify himself with Indian consciousness, he predicted that the cosmic religion of the pueblos, although temporarily beaten down by Anglo materialism, would see a resurgence and "the genuine America, the America of New Mexico" would resume its course.

This is the theme of Lawrence's great novel *The Plumed Serpent*, published in 1926. It was laid in Mexico. In it the government of Mexico is overthrown, Roman Catholic churches are closed, American industries are expropriated, and the ancient Aztec religion of Quetzalcoatl, the Plumed Serpent, is resurrected. This is the book Mabel wanted him to write, springing from their condemnation of the materialistic Western civilization and their belief in the resurgence of Indian culture. Though the book was not laid in Taos, it transported

Taos Pueblo and everything Lawrence had learned about its Indians to Mexico. It is all there—their dress and customs, dances, songs, the very drumbeat.

Lawrence's novella *The Woman Who Rode Away,* published about the same time, repeats the same theme on a smaller scale. The wife of an American mining engineer in Mexico rides horseback into the Sierra Madre. She is captured by the Indians of a remote pueblo and sacrificed by their priests in a secret cave. Awaiting the knife, the woman silently assents to her death, a symbolic sacrifice of her white culture to that of the Indians. The pueblo was again Taos Pueblo. Even the sacrificial cave was that which lies in the cliffs behind my own back pasture. These are both wonderful, evocative stories. And in each of them, the leading white woman is clearly Mabel.

That same year, a friend of Mabel's induced the famous European psychologist C. G. Jung to visit Taos. Mabel was away when he arrived, but he met and talked with Mountain Lake (Antonio Mirabal), a religious leader in the Pueblo. As recorded in his autobiography and *Collected Works,* Jung found the Indians' life "cosmologically meaningful" in contrast to "our own self-justification, the meaning of our own lives as it is formulated by our reason." He believed the preservation of their secret beliefs gave "the pueblo Indian pride and power to resist the dominant whites. It gives him cohesion and unity, and I feel sure that the pueblos as an individual community will continue to exist as long as their mysteries are not desecrated."

Still another important man Mabel persuaded to visit Taos was John Collier, a social worker. He arrived in the mid-'20s. His talks with Mabel and his visits to other pueblos with Tony convinced him of the importance of preserving Indian life. He worked with them to help defeat the infamous Bursum Bill, just introduced into Congress, which threatened all Indian land holdings. His interest in Indian welfare continued. Becoming executive secretary of the Indian Defense Association, he finally succeeded in being appointed commissioner of Indian Affairs in 1933, when Franklin D. Roosevelt took office as one of the great presidents of the United States. Collier's first move was to put through Congress the Indian Reorganization Act, designed to grant cultural, religious, and economic freedom to all tribes. Controversial as it was, it gained him the reputation of being the best Indian commissioner in the nation's history.

In 1940 he organized the First Inter-American Conference on Indian Life. It was held at Pátzcuaro, Mexico, and attended by delegates from the United States, Tony being named as a delegate, and all the twenty countries of Latin America. A permanent Inter-American Indian Institute was established, with Collier as president. The United States then created by executive order its own National Indian Institute, but Congress refused to appropriate funds for its operation. It was quite clear that prosperous Anglo America was not going to be drawn into any movement to rejuvenate Indian life.

Mabel's activities evoked some of the most harsh and humorous criticism in her career. Her chief function, it was remembered, always had been that of a catalyst, bringing together disparate persons to see what happened and to attain goals she couldn't achieve herself. As Maurice Sterne, her third husband, stated, "Mabel had no vitality or creative power of her own. She was a dead battery; she needed constantly to recharge with the juice of some man, though she might leave him dead in the process." Yet her "compulsion to meddle" in other people's lives, as in the cases of Lawrence and Collier, resulted in some of their outstanding achievements. And she was aware of an underground current that broke surface fifty years later when Congress finally restored to Taos Pueblo, for religious purposes, clear title to the mountainous area surrounding its sacred Blue Lake. The Pueblo's poor tribal members, once derided, are now potentially the richest people in the valley. Countrywide, the racial antipathy between the red and the white is gradually breaking down. The Indians, now called Native Americans, are asserting their rights; and we are realizing the soundness of their religious beliefs.

Mabel's extravagant ambition to achieve a resurrection of Western civilization from the body of Indian culture was a failure. She realized she was not cut out to make wide political and social reforms in her outer world. She retreated into herself, still aware of the old feeling of being "nobody in myself."

Who was she, anyway? She began writing her *Intimate Memories*. It is amazing how quickly, in such a short time, the four long volumes emerged in her loose, flowing script—the first volume published in 1933, followed in quick succession by the others in 1935, 1936, and 1937.

There is a great break between the first three volumes and the fourth. *Edge of Taos Desert*, the last, is the fulcrum of the series. The writing is warm and personal as she recounts her life in Taos.

How different it is from the preceding three volumes, Mabel herself explains. "In the other volumes of these *Memories*, I have written more like an anthropologist than a human being. I wrote observantly and coldly like one recording his findings, having returned from an unknown island, telling about an undocumented race of beings. . . . Never mind the blame and the shame, the hurts and regrets, the burned fingers and angry looks. I know what it cost us all and I know what it has been worth. Particularly, I know that it was a preliminary exercise for an eventual self-realization."

How this finally came is recounted in the most revealing and moving chapters of *Edge of Taos Desert*.

During her years in Taos, Mabel learned much about surface pueblo life, but it had a subterranean depth she had never penetrated. What religious belief gave the Indians their "cosmologically meaningful" perspective, as Jung called it? The rituals in their underground kivas and their pilgrimages to the sacred Blue Lake were closed to all outsiders. Everything about their religious beliefs was a guarded secret. Even Tony refused to say anything about it. With her compelling curiosity to discover the secret that made Indians tick, Mabel found herself facing a locked door.

I can well believe that she was confronted with the equivalent of what Zen Buddhists call a *koan,* or insoluble riddle. The purpose of such a riddle, they tell us, is to make a seeker realize there is no intellectual solution to it. When the seeker finally reaches this impasse, a simple incident is enough to reveal its meaning. It can be triggered by a word, a touch, anything. But one must be ready for such an instant realization. So it must have been with Mabel's fruitless efforts to discover the hidden mystery of Indian belief.

Her awakening, self-realization, or whatever we choose to call it, happened during a trip to the mountains with Tony and a group of his Indian friends. One night she became ill. One of the Indians gave her a drink of "good medicine," which most likely contained the hallucinogen peyote. In *Edge of Taos Desert* Mabel recounts her feelings as she lay listening to the Indians singing outside her shelter.

> Beginning with the inmost central point in my own organism, the whole universe fell into place. . . . On and on into wider spaces farther than I could divine, where all the heavenly bodies were connected with the order of the plan, and system within system interlocked in grace. I was not separate and isolated any more. . . .

> The singing filled the night and I perceived its design which was written upon the darkness in color . . . and composed of a myriad of bright living cells. These cells were like minute flowers or crystals and they vibrated constantly in their rank and circumstance, not one of them falling out of place, for the order of the whole was held together by the interdependence of each infinitesimal spark. And I learned that there is no single equilibrium anywhere in existence, and that the meaning and essence of balance

depends upon neighboring organisms holding together, reinforcing the whole, creating form and
defeating chaos which is the hellish realm of unat-
tached and unassimilated atoms. . . . How this flash
of revelation worked out into fact and substance took
twenty years of living to be proved a reality.

These were pages of beautiful and meaningful writing. They echoed the insight of Eastern sages. To give words to the wordless has always been man's highest endeavor. And here was Mabel's attempt to record a transcendental glimpse of her ultimate completeness of being and the secret of Indian religion. This was the psychological climax of Mabel's life.

It was not strange that few of her book reviewers and critics mentioned this spiritual experience. A rational, practical people, we are inclined to ignore all such nonrealistic excursions as flights of fancy into the realm of the mystical or the occult, the dark and dangerous mysterious. We are committed to the reasoning, intellectual faculty of our dual nature, as other peoples throughout the world have been polarized to the intuitive.

Yet even in our Anglo culture there always have been aberrant individuals who have experienced totality, the Peak Experience, as it's called. Most of them hesitate to talk about it for fear they will be considered abnormal, having succumbed to an illusion, or will be made fun of. Also the experience does not last, for, as Zen Buddhists assert, it can be maintained during their daily lives only by those who dedicate themselves to strict religious discipline.

So it was with Mabel. The realization of completeness that replaced her long feeling of being "nobody in myself" must have lasted for a time. But the lifelong domination of her personal ego asserted itself, and her expanded awareness began to fade.

I was working in Washington, D.C., during the war years, and then in Los Angeles. When I returned to Taos late in 1949 to edit the weekly newspaper, I noticed the change in Mabel. It may have been accounted for by her advancing years; she was now nearly seventy. But she had lost much of her great vitality and sharp perceptiveness. Of the five guest houses in Mabeltown, the Pink House, Two-Story House, and the Studio had been sold or rented, and the Tony House had deteriorated too much for occupancy. Mabel had bought and modernized a small adobe, the River House, downriver at Embudo where she and Tony could spend quiet weekends.

It was well known that Tony had a mistress in Arroyo Seco or Arroyo Hondo. Mabel apparently ignored this, but now occurred something that worried her more. Millicent Rogers had arrived in Taos, buying and restoring an old hacienda south of town. Commonly known as the "Standard Oil Heiress," she had been left great wealth by two husbands and maintained other homes in Jamaica and Virginia. Furnishing the hacienda with excellent taste, she hung in it a notable collection of French Impressionist paintings. Meanwhile, she became romantically fascinated, as had Mabel, with the Indians at Taos Pueblo. Taking several of them along, she drove throughout the Southwest, buying Navajo blankets, Zuni and Hopi kachipas, pottery, artifacts, and handicrafts. Also she acquired Spanish colonial items of historical value. Her large collection is now displayed in the Millicent Rogers Museum, located on a beautiful estate just outside Taos.

To work on her house Millicent employed several Indians, including a young man who had returned from war dissolute, alcoholic, angry, and violent. She became infatuated with him, paid all his successive debts, and took him with Brett to Jamaica. Upon their return, and in late afternoons after work, all these Indians sat in the house drinking and cutting slices from the huge roast beef always available. How pleasant it was for Tony to join them! Not until late at night did he return home, well fed and smelling of scotch. Mabel ate a solitary dinner and went to bed seething with anger and jealousy.

She was still the grande dame of Taos. Millicent could not have challenged her prestige, nor did she wish to. Still, they had little to do with each other, and Millicent unwittingly had struck at Mabel's Achilles' heel—Tony.

One afternoon Millicent telephoned to ask me to call. I found her a beautiful, sensitive, and sensible woman. She came to the point immediately. "I want to talk to you, for I understand you're one of Mabel's and Tony's closest friends. She thinks I'm trying to steal Tony away from her. How preposterous! What do I want with an aging Indian when there are so many young and attractive men of every kind? He isn't invited here; he just comes, and I have nothing to do with him. Nor can I control the boys' eating and drinking; I have my dinner served in my own room. I don't want to hurt Mabel, nor offend Tony. What can I do about this dreadful situation?"

Mabel already had made up her own mind. "I can't stand this any longer," she said. "I'm going to get rid of him—this old man so infatuated with Millicent that he comes home drunk late every night! He's never here. Let Millicent have him for whatever he's worth to her. Judge Kiker will get me a divorce."

I looked at her drawn, pale face for a long time in silence. It was no use telling her of my talk with Millicent. Nor did I have the right to remonstrate with Tony. If Mabel did divorce him, he would simply go back to the Pueblo to live with his own people, perhaps depending more upon Millicent for daily amusement. No, I didn't worry about Tony. It was Mabel's distress that concerned me. Her confidence in me demanded all the honesty I could summon to reply haltingly, "That is the pattern you followed most of your life, Mabel. Years ago you broke it— 'broke the mold,' as Gurdjieff told you—by marrying Tony. It gave you a new life. You can't go back now to the old, outworn pattern after all you've achieved. I think, Mabel, you should stick it out, distressing as it is."

She gave me one long, searching look from comprehending eyes.

Then she turned away and went into her bedroom without a word.

Things straightened out somehow. Millicent died of tuberculosis. Mabel and Tony were still dependent upon one another, but their relationship no longer had the close intimacy of the past. And, more significantly, Mabel lost all interest in Indian life and religion.

How this change affected her had a parallel in what happened to the noted sinologist Richard Wilhelm, who had translated and interpreted the ancient Chinese *I Ching* and *The Secret of the Golden Flower.* Wilhelm, living and studying in China for many years, had submerged his intellectual European background and entered wholly, mind and heart, into the spirit of Chinese metaphysics. Psychically, wrote Jung, this resulted in an essential rearrangement of the component parts of his psyche. At the completion of his task, Wilhelm returned to Europe and reverted to his native German culture. Jung termed this *enantiodromia,* the process by which yang goes over to its opposite pole, the yin. Wilhelm's feeling for everything Chinese turned negative, resulting in his spiritual and physical illness, and death.

I seldom saw Mabel and Tony after that; I was working in Los Alamos and Nevada during the atomic test series. On the few occasions when I was in Taos, I visited them in the new two-story house Mabel had built on a nearby hillock. Completely modern, it was drastically different from her old Big House. The upper story was one huge room with picture windows on all four sides; but it had no access save an outside staircase, and no bathroom, and was thus unsuitable for living quarters. The downstairs lacked the charm and graciousness of all the other houses Mabel had built. The living room was large and comfortable, but the small alcove kitchen didn't have the hominess of the one in which Tony and his friends used to sit over coffee, joking with the cook and maids. Between it and the living room ran a narrow hall off which opened two bedrooms and opposite bathrooms. The house always gave me the uncomfortable feeling that it somehow repeated the pattern of the hotel suites and apartments she had occupied in the past. Here Mabel spent her last years.

My visits with her and Tony were saddening failures. Both were drinking too excessively to talk intelligently, and Mabel was becoming senile.

The end came when Mabel died on August 13, 1962, at the age of eighty-three. I was living on the Hopi Reservation, doing research for a book at the time, and was not present at her funeral.

There are many contradictory versions of how and where she was buried. This one I like best. Some years before, Mabel had invited me to dinner with the grizzled trader Ralph Meyers and his wife, Rowena. When Meyers walked in, he proudly announced that he had just bought a burial lot in the historic Kit Carson Cemetery. "You'd better buy one too, Mabel. There's not many left."

Rowena remembered this too when, upon Mabel's death she went to see Jack Boyer, who managed the cemetery for the Masonic Lodge. Mabel had neglected to buy a lot as Ralph had suggested, and there were no more available. "But Mabel has done so much for Taos; she must be buried there instead of in the newer cemetery across town!" pleaded Rowena. "Can't you please find a place for her?"

"Ralph was buried in the last empty lot," replied Boyer. It's in the corner, as you know. There may be room for Mabel between his grave and the fence, but it would be a tight squeeze."

"That's all right," said Rowena. "I know Ralph would be glad to move over a bit to make room for her."

So here Mabel was laid to rest. A woman who had focused all the social, radical, and art movements of her generation; who had helped to change the tenor of our time; a legend in her own life span.

To me this international role mirrored her egotistical outer persona, concerned with the material world of appearances. If my view of her here reflects any measure of objectivity, it is an attempt to show that she, like all of us, embodied two selves. Their conflict is the great theme of all philosophies and religions. "Who am I?" We each, consciously or unconsciously, ask ourselves this ultimate question.

And yet in long retrospect I see her more personally than abstractly.

I remember her lovely voice, the horseback rides, the fun we had with Tony on our trips to Mexico. And best, as an intimate friend whose private virtues have outlasted her public faults in the memory of those like myself who knew and loved her.

CHAPTER 10

The Man Who Killed the Deer (1942)

The carrier of "white" consciousness in this novel of Pueblo life is Rodolfo Byers, a western character whose curmudgeonliness can't quite hide his genuine feel for people. He's a bit irascible, but he has also been patient and curious, looking all his adult life for something that would explain why he so helplessly loves what he loves. Among his friends at the pueblo is a young man, Martiniano, who has recently returned from several years at a U.S. Government–run boarding school. The young Indian has missed out on his traditional Pueblo education, having been given in its stead some training as a carpenter and with it, among other seeming accomplishments, a "white" habit of looking at the world from the standpoint of separate selfhood. Out of harmony with his wife, the tribe, and indeed the world, he is literally self-contained—and unhappy. The travail Martiniano is going through dawns on Byers, and gradually he and the Indian become something like friends. Though they came to it from different angles, they share existence in a middle ground, a kind of no-man's land between cultures. Martiniano, for his part, is struggling with the greatest of human burdens, personal identity and personal desire. Slowly, from living next to the pueblo and being in contact, he begins to see himself in a tribal context; pride is still well ensconced, and contentiousness, but subtle differences are beginning to manifest themselves. "The deer he had killed and himself" occur now in the same sentence, the same thought, as paired objects of his anger.

Chapter 7

Easter came late. The heavens wept, the people wailed with grief; and then to the peal of bells, from the ecstatic murmurs of mankind, He rose triumphant from the dead—Nuestro Señor Jesu Cristo, Our Savior, the Blessed Son, Our Lord.

But Easter came late. The earth of which He was a symbol was already resurrected. Ice-locked avalanches plunged down the cañons. The river roared through the gorge with the spring thaw. Over the new-plowed fields crows flew low, cawing. Ai. Our Mother Earth was awake again and crying for new seed, the little pinto stallions were fierce with love, men were clutched by strange longings.

Even the strange white man, the trader.

Martiniano had gone to see him; he was stamping around in his tool shop behind the post, and cursing the rats which had been gnawing at one of his pelts. Martiniano opened his jackknife and squatted down to make a mousetrap: a narrow gangplank of two sticks meeting over the top of a bucket of water in a loose notch covered by a piece of cheese.

As he whittled, he said quietly, "We have not discussed for many months the money I owe you—the fine you paid when I killed the deer. It is about this I have come."

"Let it go—let it go," Byers replied gruffly. "Pay when you can."

"There was that one-hundred and fifty dollars," Martiniano continued. "There was forty-two before that, and sixteen dollars after. That was two hundred and eight. But this winter I brought wood, chopped in little pieces for stove and cut in big logs for fireplace. Fifty-six dollars' worth. There still remains one hundred and fifty-two owing. That is a great deal of money. Perhaps from my small field I will not harvest that much money, and still it will be owed. Yet I must pay, and quickly. I feel it so."

"God damn it! Don't bother me about business. Talk to my wife."

"That is what I thought this spring. And so I worked as I have never worked before. On that far slope rising toward the mountain, along the Acequia Madre. I dug out the sage with its obstinate roots until my hands bled. I cleared this new land. I plowed. I harrowed. It is ready. But I am not. I have no seed for planting. I have no money for seed. So I have come to you with the debt between us.

"This I mean. I have cleared new land to show you, not knowing whether it would be planted. Now buy seed and the first harvest will be yours in payment for both debt and seed. . . . It is peaceful there up the cañon and over the slope. There is an old sheepherder's hut there—of adobe. We will live there this summer; my wife, being Ute, likes the mountains. We are not well regarded in the pueblo, besides. And besides that, I have my old horse to ride down to my smaller field. Thus above I work for you and my debt, and below for ourselves. What do you say?"

"Lazy Indian! It will probably be a bad year besides!"

Martiniano stood up and threw back his pig-tails. "There. It is finished. This mousetrap. As my father used to make them."

"Mousetraps! God Almighty! On a day like this! I need a new room, not a mousetrap."

"Another room! Is it truly needed?"

"Hell, no! What more does a man need than one room with a stove to cook on and a bed to sleep in? I have too many already. It is this weather that makes me want to feel new walls rising, fresh adobe taking shape."

Martiniano drew up his blanket. "You will think about this seed? El Día de Santa Cruz approaches, the day for planting."

Byers turned around; he had been leaning against the doorway, listening to a meadow lark.

"No!" he said. "What I need is a little new dust on my shoes. A buying trip. Yes, by God! Look here. My wife and I are going down river; I have just decided. I will buy some new stuff. Pick up some clay at the bottom of those red cliffs for my new room. Get that seed too; it's cheaper down below. Three or four days, that's all. But I need someone along. I'll pay you for the work. You and your wife be ready at daybreak tomorrow. Bring along your own blankets."

So just past Easter at sun-up, in a muck-smeared automobile, they started out. Byers, unshaven, driving with Angelina in denim trousers beside him, and Martiniano and Flowers Playing squeezed by luggage and blankets behind. With them all, unseen, rode Spring.

It was not quite noon of the third day, and the drum was still beating as they knew it had been beating all morning—like an almost imperceptible echo of a pulse within the lifeless, lumpy mud hills.

The car ground through a sandy arroyo, lurched up a barren slope. "There," said Martiniano when they reached the crest. "That pueblo."

There on the sandy plain below, between the lumpy mud hills and curving brown river. A low mud town as if sliced out of a low mud hill. A few corn fields outside. A patch of ancient cottonwoods across the river. And beyond, the pale, cedar-splotched desert sloping up and away to a far blue rampart of mountains.

They could hear it clearer now. A deep, resonant beat that held against the wind.

Leaving the car near the little church within its low mud wall, they walked into the corona of filth and acrid odor of urine and ordure that edged the pueblo, past the lanes opening between rows of squat, flat-topped houses. Dust eddied in the empty streets. A dog sprawled in the sunlight, biting at his fleas. A pig ran squealing out of a blue doorway. Only the drum, full-toned now, betrayed the lifeless negation.

Abruptly they came upon the long, wide street that served for plaza. A stinging blast of sand swept up and lifted. It revealed not only the pulsing heart, but the voice, the will, the bloodstream and the ligaments—the hidden and working anatomy of the body of the desolate town. Its function was the Spring Corn Dance.

At the near end of the plaza stood a high, circular, adobe kiva whose smooth wall was broken by a flight of terraced steps. On these stood resting a file of dusty painted Indians. In front had been erected a little green shelter facing the plaza. And in this, on a rude altar, sat a wooden Santo bedecked in bright cloths and silver ornaments.

The four visitors squatted on the ground against a wall, and stared down the arid street. At the far end rose another kiva. Out of it, to the beat of a drum, was filing a long line of dancers.

In front, up one side of the street, came straggling four rows of old men in their brightest colored shirts, tail out over gaudy, flowered, full-legged pajama pants, and carrying in each hand a sprig of evergreen. In their midst one beat a small drum tied round his waist.

Beside them, up the middle of the plaza, walked a man beating powerfully a great belly drum. With him walked the flag carrier. The long smooth pole carried on top a narrow hand-woven kirtle and a fox-skin, and was adorned with parrot feathers, shells and beads.

Behind them, in two files, slouched the dancers—perhaps a hundred and fifty men, women and children.

Little by little as they straggled forward, colors screamed against the dun gray walls, a life emerged into the monotone of sand and sky.

The men, naked to the waist, were painted a golden copper. Their freshly washed hair, now gray with dust, fell to their wide shoulders and held entwined a few green and blue parrot feathers. Each wore a white ceremonial kirtle embroidered in red and green, and tied with a red and black wool sash, the long fringe dangling from right knee to ankle. At the back, swaying between their legs, hung the everpresent fox-skin. On their legs tinkled straps of little bells, sea shells and hollow deer hoof rattles. Their ankle-high, fawn-colored moccasins were trimmed with a band of black and white skunk fur. They carried in the right hand a gourd rattle, in the left a sprig of evergreen.

The women, alternating with the men, shuffled along bare-footed in the eddying dust. Their squat, heavy figures were covered by loose, black wool Mother Hubbards beautifully embroidered around the hem in red, leaving one shoulder free, and belted round the waist with a green and scarlet Hopi sash. Their waist-long hair, like that of the men, rippled free in the wind. Each carried on her head a turquoise-blue tablita held by a string passing under the chin—a thin wooden tiara, perhaps a foot high, shaped like a doorway, painted with cloud symbols and tipped with tufts of eagle-down. They wore heavy silver bracelets and rings, silver squash-blossom necklaces and strings of turquoise and coral, and carried in each hand a sprig of evergreen.

Everywhere evergreen, the symbol of everlasting life. It was as if they had chopped down a spruce forest and brought it down to the mud flats.

The two files stopped, facing each other, the children on one end. Between them the flag carrier dipped his long pole over their heads, the drummer began to beat the great drum.

The outside ends of the four rows of old men halted, curving round and inward to form a four-deep semi-circle facing the two lines of waiting dancers, the small drum in the center.

Now in wind and dust the thing resumed.

The great belly drum throbbed hoarsely. The gaze of the forty old men turned inward, became fixed. They began to chant—a powerful soughing like wind among the pines. The pole dipped and rose. The sprigs of evergreen lifted and fell. Then came a tinkle of bells, the clatter of deer hoofs, a rattle of gourds. The lackadaisical dancers drew together like the segments of a chopped up snake.

They were dancing.

In two long rows, the stable, stolid women alternating with the leaping men. Then in four shorter rows as the women stepped back to face the turning men. And now in a great, slow moving circle, each woman a shadow at the heels of her man.

A powerful, down-sinking stamp, insistent and heavy from the men. Then faster, double-time, stamping to one beat and to the next marking time with bending knees. But from the old gray-headed crones, from all the subtle, submissive women, the barely lifted flat feet and the whole body shaking with the rhythm.

Occasionally an instant's pause. Then a shrill yell, a quickening rattle of gourds. The thunder-throb, the blood-beat of the great belly drum. The old men's rapt voices soughing through the green sprigs. A spruce forest moved down to the mud flats to shake and toss in the acrid stinging dust, under the hard, alkaline sky.

The group danced for a half-hour or more, then filed back to its kiva. But as the Summer People left, the Winter People came out from the opposite kiva. Thus alternating as winter follows summer, and summer yet again winter, the two groups kept dancing.

None of the four visitors moved from the lee of a protruding wall. Angelina had wrapped a handkerchief around her face to breathe through; Martiniano was shrouded in his blanket. Byers squatted patiently, legs crossed. Only Flowers Playing's eyes, uncovered, gleamed as she watched.

Gleamed at the insistent, down-pressing stamp; the same insistent, lifting chant. The stamp that sinks down deep into the earth, as the throb of the drum sinks deep into the bloodstream; and the rising chant that lifts, lifts up into the shaking spruce twigs, up to the rain-feathers on the pole, to the clouds in the turquoise sky.

It was all one: a mesmeric beat of the blood that closed the mind to sight and sound, to wind and dust. The beat of the blood through the flesh of the earth and the earth of the flesh, through the growing corn and the earth-flesh of the people who would envelop the ripened corn again for the strength and power to perpetuate both.

Late in the afternoon the wind increased. Swirls of dust blew down into the plaza from the bare mud hills. A choking gray mist through which the little children, too, still kept dancing. The boys in little kirtles and doll moccasins, and the girls wearing on their heads diminutive blue tablitas painted with tiny sunflowers. Two straggling rows of fresh-hatched chickens caught in a sand blizzard.

Easter had come to the mountains above with rushing spring torrents, the smell of fresh plowed fields. In the hot river lowlands below, the earth had been longer awake; the fruit trees were already in blossom, the bottomlands planted with chile and melons; the sun glared white and hot. But here on this dreary sandy plain no sign of resurrection appeared. And so the people called forth, group after group, with rapt and unrelenting persistence. The people who were themselves the seeds of everlasting life planted between the mysterious depths and heights of the wide universe. They shook the earth awake to give forth the tiny shoots of new green corn in the scrubby patches. They stilled the serpentine clouds writhing overhead, they gathered the fat bellied clouds hovering there over the far buttes and mesas, above the desert. They called down rain, they called the tall walking rain out of the doorways of cloud with the fluttering tufts of eagle-down.

And all the while the Koshares pantomimed the insistent prayer as the people danced it, and as the old gray-haired chorus sang it. The eight loose Koshares, the most vigorous and alive of all.

Their ashy gray bodies, naked but for dark blue loin cloths, were splotched with white and black spots, their faces weird masks of zigzag lines. Their hair was gathered up into a knot on top of the head, plastered with white clay, and tied with a dirty blue rag. From the tuft stuck up a thick cluster of corn-husks, dry, brittle corn leaves. Fantastic figures. Blackened ghosts of old cornstalks.

But beautiful of movement as they weaved continually through the unheeding dancers like alert, spotted leopards. Head down, eyes lowered, they danced up and down, between and outside the lines. Their loose flexible arms with gentle motion drew up the deep power from the blackness of the earth with which they were painted, drew up the hidden juices into the roots, drew up the corn shoots. Then at a change of rhythm, their heads raised. They drew down the rain like threads, drew down from the sky its star-power and moon-glow, its pink-tipped arrows of fire, its waters.

But also they were very watchful to correct a child's step, to mark a change in timing, to hitch up a little boy's knee strap and tie on a girl's tablita blown off by the wind. For the dancers must not hesitate to the end. And when a tot squatted down exhausted, one picked her up, piggy-back, to carry off for rest.

And so it kept on all day. The tossing forest of spruce twigs and the deep soughing among it. The leaping, golden-copper bodies of the men amongst the forest. And the women, powerful and subtle, holding the green tablitas, the painted doorways, almost steady as they danced between the men. All in long lines, flexible as corn, straight as rain.

Till finally, towards sunset, the two groups merged. A hundred singing old men, three hundred dancers, two dipping poles, two great drums.

It was over.

Angelina looked suddenly a little sick. She held a hand against her belly.

"Here. Take this," said Martiniano, passing her a crust of bread. "It is that empty-sickness when the drums stop beating. I have seen it many times."

The dancers, spitting dust, were beginning to line up in front of the little shelter, each in turn to kneel and cross himself before the wooden Santo.

The visitors walked slowly past.

"I feel that I could fly!" said Flowers Playing simply.

Byers strode on without speaking.

They camped that night in the grove along the river. With dark the wind had died. Only the massive cottonwoods creaked above them like old, unstable pillars of an abandoned cathedral. They finished eating: thick steaks laid on the coals, potatoes charred in the ashes, coffee, bread, fruit. Martiniano threw on fresh wood. By its light he unloaded blankets from the car, and went down to wash the dishes at the river's edge.

Angelina and Flowers Playing sat talking, woman-like, of many things. It had been a good trip. Much had been bought: thick blankets from a Navajo trader, many pieces of silver and turquoise, a few old pieces of pottery. They had packed a bag of red clay for Byers to use as a wash for the walls of his new room, and had bought two bags of seed for Martiniano. And there had been this day-long, Easter, Green Corn Dance. There was something about it that made all these familiar trivialities seem very important, very precious. The day-long soughing of the old men's voices had swept the cobwebs from their cluttered winter minds. The dancing had shaken loose their own stiff ligaments. The continuous pound of the great drum had shattered the corpuscles of their blood into a new pulse pattern. It all had been a great purge, a resurrection, that made life new, quick, immediate.

Byers, his own chemical make-up rejuvenated, felt this keenly. He lay outspread before the fire, unheeding the light patter. This is the life, he thought. Foot-loose and fancy free, with women not too far away to worry about nor too close to bother one, and an Indian to do the work! Such trips were his one indulgence. They reminded him of the old days, his trading days.

Well, those were all over—and soon these would be too. He himself belonged to the vanishing past. But he was no sentimentalist, he reminded himself again sternly. No sickly nostalgia! There is no going back. There is no standing still. There is only that everpresent change which keeps life fresh and ever new.

But he wondered less about the changing form than the enduring substance. These pueblos all looked alike. The same church, kivas, mud floor adobes spread out or in tiers, a few head of stock, some scrubby corn patches. A mountain behind, the desert in front. Even the people seemed alike. The squat powerful men, the squat shapeless women, all with their proud, simple, rosebrown faces and quick, poetic hands. But still there was a difference.

Here in this pueblo was a passive inertia to change more formidable than any barrier, and an old rich ceremonialism that seemed at once sufficient and indestructible. A people, like the dough of their own bread, heavy and down-sinking, unassimilative. Wary, self-sufficient, remote in these dreary mud flats, they still resisted every advance.

Two years ago there had been a quarrel over the dancing between the white priest and the old men. The priest had left, the church was closed. No more Masses, marriages or baptisms for these ungrateful, sinning people. The Indians kept dancing. A year later the Church sent back another priest. The Pope, the Father, had relented and for- given, he said. The people accepted him calmly—and went on dancing.

"Good!" grinned Byers. "Let 'em stick to their guns."

But the pueblo at home was not so remote. It had always been a link between the mountain and pueblo Indians, and the Plains tribes. And so the people, as a dough with all the heavy, close-knit solidarity of the settled Pueblo stock, seemed leavened with the restless, arrogant individuality of the roving Plains tribes. Like this Martiniano, shell and kernel.

Was it this infiltration of new stock which had made it the only pueblo yet susceptible to peyote? Or was it because their racial faith itself was gradually disintegrating? Byers did not believe in peyote. No people, no sect in possession of the awareness of spiritual power within themselves requires an outside stimulus or depends wholly upon sacerdotal paraphernalia. And the majority of Indians still believed in life with only their own natural symbolism, ceremonials and great myth and dance dramas expressing their wordless faith.

That, he decided was the trouble in a nut-shell. These great forms, whose meanings to most whites were intelligible only by an imperfect translation of their values, were gradually being lost to the Indians themselves. In many already only the empty movement persisted. And soon they too would pass forgotten, inarticulate in any other form.

It was still the content that plagued him. The instinctive, intuitive, non-reasoning approach to life; the magnificent surrender of self to those unseen forces whose instruments we are, and the fulfillment of whose purposes gives us our only meaning. By infallible instinct and undivided consciousness the Indian had proved the validity of his approach. And because he couldn't or wouldn't express it articulately the whole shebang was passing with him.

Well, let it go. Byers had had his fling. Only . . . only there were one or two things he'd like to know first. Not that he ever would, of course.

Like that rattlesnake business.

Indefinable and remote as the sensations of a dream remaining after its outlines had faded, it had hung for years at the back of his mind. Now as the moon rose, and down the nave of cottonwoods he could see Martiniano's solid shape faintly outlined against the river—the great slow-curving river which coiled like a snake around the quiet pueblo and ran on, unending, with a rippling glitter of scales—it all returned to him with the force of something not forgotten but only sleeping within him.

It had begun when he was a young man first come to La Oreja. He lived any way, in any adobe hut. But every day he put on his faded pink shirt and walked out to the pueblo. Byers was a little romantic then, though shrewd and hard. He did not admit to himself why he went. He told himself the lesser truth. The life appealed to him. He listened to the drums, the songs. He watched the people. And then, having spoken to no one, he walked back home to cook his simple supper.

One afternoon a group of Indians came up and led him into an empty house. "My people. We watch you," one told him sternly. "Young white man she want one of our young girls mebbe. No? No good, Huh?"

Byers sputtered and cursed in denial. But he was frightened away. He became a forest ranger of sorts in the mountains above. Between times he shot and trapped beaver and muskrat, bear, mountain lions, skunk and deer. Passing Indians stopped at his camps, became his friends. After a time he returned to town and set up a little shop for trading.

He became friends with an old Indian who warned him to be careful. Some of the old men at the pueblo still disliked him, and had cast a spell upon him.

They were sitting one day in his little shop when a young Indian came in to sell him some apples. Byers refused. The seller offered him one free. The old Indian shook his head warningly. Later he said that a spell had been cast on those apples; there was a worm in one that would have grown into a snake and devoured him.

"The devil!" laughed Byers. "Where did you get that nonsense?"

Well, that spring the old man had been up in the mountains cutting wood when he heard voices around him in the empty clearing. Soon he could distinguish their meaning: the rattlesnakes had been invoked to harm his white friend, the strange young trader. Now, and always, he must be very careful of snakes. They were his bad medicine, perhaps his fate.

Two or three years later, when he had established his post and was beginning to be well known, Byers had driven a wealthy white woman down river here in his buckboard. His client had given him a hundred dollars to buy for her a great belt of old, hand-beaten silver conchos— the oldest, heaviest and the best he could find. Here in this pueblo Byers had once seen one hanging from a rafter. He located the house, and they entered with small gifts. The belt was still there, dangling from a viga.

It was a beautiful old room. The walls were nearly four feet thick and plastered smooth, cream-white inside. The dirt floor had been trodden hard and level as cement by generations of naked feet. The cedar door posts were gray as moss. The great vigas overhead gleamed dark brown as old honey. In the corner was a large, old-style Santo Domingo fireplace, now seldom seen. While the woman remained to study it, Byers walked with his host into the back room to dicker for the concho belt.

There were no windows. A thin light filtered through the breathing shaft and revealed seated about a little fire of twigs several old women. As he entered, flinging back the blanket that hung in the doorway, the oldest of the wrinkled crones suddenly jumped up on her bare, twisted feet. Blind, clutching her flabby breast with a withered hand, she began to spit and scream invective.

Byers stepped back a pace from the sudden assault. His host, a man of fifty, stepped forward. The old woman could not be hushed. The stranger, this white man, she kept crying vituperatively, carried about him the slimy stench, the poison and curse of rattlesnakes.

He had almost forgotten this strange occurrence some two years later when he was invited to go fishing up La Jara Creek. Benson had just got married and bought an automobile to celebrate—the first in town. Excited and voluble, he squawked the rubber bulb and brass tube horn, loaded the back with fishing paraphernalia, lunch basket, easel and water colors, and gallantly handed in his bride in a linen duster. Byers moodily climbed in the back. He hadn't wanted to go.

As the car rattled out of town his moroseness increased. Half-way up the rutty cañon road he had a sudden premonition of evil and danger, and begged to be let out to walk home.

Mrs. Benson giggled. Benson squawked his horn and roared with laughter. "That's a bachelor for you! Scared out by newlyweds! We're not going to make love in front of you, old boy. You can take her fishin' up the creek, and I'll make a couple of quick sketches. Then we'll eat. Peek in that basket! Fried chicken!"

Byers leaned back, frowning.

The cañon usually so beautiful, seemed darkly foreboding. Byers did not see the clear running brook, halting in deep still trout pools like pauses in music, the green open clearings, the fresh leaved aspens, the banks of tall, wild columbines. He only felt the tall somber cliffs increasingly closing in upon him.

The car had begun to boil against the steep climb. Benson stopped. "This is as good a spot as any," he chuckled. "Fish and pictures are where you catch 'em. We'll just leave the car here in the road. Nobody ever comes up here anyway."

Clambering out, he suddenly stooped, picked up a rock and threw it in a bush. "Look out! Saw a rattler!" he warned.

Byers had already got out. Halted at the side of the road, legs apart and breathing hoarsely, he stood staring in a hypnosis of horror into the brush. As if obeying some deep inward compulsion that he dared not question, he suddenly strode forward, bent and plunged his hand into the bush.

Mrs. Benson screamed.

Byers had brought up a rattlesnake writhing as he choked and cast it from him. Now he stood there, sweat running down his face, stupidly staring at a small red mark on the end of his right thumb.

Immediately they started back to town. The ride up the steeply rising cañon had taken scarcely an hour. Now, downhill, with Benson driving like a man wild with fear, their return trip seemed beset by every possible, improbable obstacle. The hot brake bands froze and had to be loosened. A tire blew out which none of them knew how to replace. And when they at last reached the main road, it was only to find a Mexican wood wagon stalled crosswise before them.

Throughout this excruciating fantasy of strangely interrupted haste, Byers maintained the calm, deathly acquiescence of a hypnotic. His weathered brown face had turned sallow. He sat head down, his hands dangling between his knees, without any feeling of pain or fright. But the prickling in his thumb was spreading up into his fingers.

The car sputtered into the plaza. Benson jumped out. There were two doctors in La Oreja. One, a capable Anglo, had taken a hospital case to the city, a day's ride away. The other was a Mexican who was gradually displacing with his forceps the horde of native midwives with their herbs—and had just ridden away on his horse to a hut up one of the mountain cañons. But there was a new young dentist in town. His office was locked. To his home ran Benson.

A crowd of bystanders dragged Byers out of the car. One slashed open his thumb with a knife blade cauterized in the flame of a candle. Two others, taking his arms, began walking him round and round the little square plaza.

People poured from shops, markets, corrals and alleys. An old Mexican woman ran up with a squawking chicken, slit it down the middle, and clamped the bloody mess on Byers' hand. With this dripping, feathered appendage, he kept going round and round. He was staggering now, and the prickling in his hand had spread up into his wrist.

"Here, by God! Who ever heard of curin' a snake bite with anything but whiskey? Hold on, boys!" A long, emaciated old gambler with pale, watery blue eyes and walrus mustaches stopped them and poured a pint of Bourbon down Byers' throat.

Benson came running up with the dentist, and together they dragged him up to a dusty, cluttered office. The young dentist, a mere boy, was plainly perplexed. He could draw out teeth but not poison. But he had a bottle of grain alcohol into which he was mixing water and lemon juice. "If whiskey's good, this ought to be better," he said in a timid, cheerful voice. Byers, in a daze, finished the bottle.

He was now ill. A terrible drowsiness was beginning to choke him, as if he had taken a powerful sedative. The impact of whiskey and grain alcohol for a moment shook him awake. He leapt to his feet, knocking over a tray of instruments, and flung up the window. Clutched behind by the coat tails, he leaned out bellowing with pain and screaming his inarticulate convictions that he had met his fate, and demanding to be left alone.

The plaza by now was crowded with teams, buckboards, wagons and horses; the news had gone round. Indians, Mexicans and whites stood below the window shouting encouragement and advice, laughing at the ludicrous spectacle bellowing above them, murmuring with patient pity, or maintaining the stolid silence of complete awareness. Among them crept Mrs. Benson weeping and nervously wringing her hands. Just as Byers was yanked back inside the room, his old Indian friend shuffled into the plaza in split moccasins and wearing a dirty, torn blanket. He listened patiently to the crowd, then unobtrusively shuffled up the stairs.

The door was ajar. Benson, the dentist and two companions had thrown Byers into the stuffed chair, let it down, and propped up his feet. Here he lay, stripped of coat, and sweating, with his throbbing hand laid across his chest. He was breathing hoarsely, eyes open but unseeing, his mind a maelstrom of fear and pain.

What he was first aware of, as he hazily recalled it later, was a sudden deathly silence and with it a peculiar sensation of extraordinary brightness which enveloped him. He turned his head. Benson, the dentist and their companions were gone, and the door was closed. The street window and blinds were drawn; but those on the south, opening upon a stunted apple orchard, had been opened to let the sun stream in. The old Indian was standing beside him. As if obeying a clear but unspoken command, Byers staggered to his feet. His companion swiftly and gently stripped off his clothes, led him into the immersing sunlight, and propped him up like a puppet against the wall. From somewhere under his blanket he brought out a small tuft of eagle feathers with which he began to stroke Byers' body while singing softly.

A great undulatory wave swept over Byers, caught him up and carried him away, gently rising and falling. He could feel its drowsy warmth, the wash of its ripples against his skin, the dim and far-off music of its flow. In it he felt at once reassured and helpless, and gave himself to it wholly. His knees buckled, he slid down. For a moment he was hazily conscious of the sunlight pouring in the open window, and the old Indian crouched beside him, singing, and gently stroking his body with the feathers. The old man's eyes were upon him—large, black, steady, like deep pools from which ripples spread, kept spreading, to enclose him. And again the wave carried him off.

When next Byers was conscious of his surroundings, he was at home, alone, in his own bed. He was neither asleep nor wholly awake, but cast up on that shore which lies between—that shore to which he had been carried and deposited by some strange wave. For only a moment was he conscious. But in that moment was the strange conviction of a man long ill who had awakened after his first rest to know he had made the turning to recovery; the peculiar consciousness of a man, terribly drunk, who awakens in a stupor, but yet knowing his realization of it is the first sign of later clarity.

He was ill for days; it was two months before he really recovered. The Anglo doctor had returned to attend him, and now muttered jovially of a strong constitution, the rarity of fatalities by mere snake bites, and of the psychological fear that once removed. . . .

"Get the hell out of here!" muttered Byers. "I want to sleep."

And so he had recovered, admitting the fear so slowly built up, unknown, which had suddenly leapt out at him from ambush. Perhaps the old Indian had given him some neutralizing herb he could not remember taking. But yet within the indistinct memory of that old man crouching beside him, singing and stroking his body with feathers, there lurked something invisible and unprobed, like the assurance of an indefinable faith, that had never left him.

Byers stirred and looked around. The two women had turned in. Angelina, close to the car, in a double sleeping bag laid on an air mattress, and Flowers Playing farther off in the brush on a pile of blankets. The moon had risen high above the great, still trees. He could see between them, on one side, a jaundiced vista of the desert sloping up and away past a far, flat-topped butte to the long line of mountains lying like the upturned edge of the horizon. On the other side, across the broad, flat river still flowing sluggishly as a snake with a tiny play of light on its scales where the current struck sand bar and snag, the pueblo rose black and solid. Mountains, mesa, mud hills and pueblo; they were all of a piece.

"Get me that bottle hidden in the side-pocket of the car," he said abruptly.

Martiniano, squatting silently across the fire, rose silently as he was bid. Returning, he handed the pint to Byers and squatted down again, drawing his pig-tails over his shoulders into his lap. The white man popped the cork out of the half-filled bottle and took a long swig.

"Here," he said, passing over the bottle. "Have a drink. There's just two apiece."

"Whiskey?" answered the Indian. "Here on pueblo land? It is against the law."

Byers could not restrain a flicker of astonishment across his face. This school-Indian, this Martiniano who had killed the deer, had been fined and beaten for wearing American clothes and refusing to dance—the most stubborn trouble-maker in the pueblo, now objecting to a drink of whiskey because it was against the law! He eyed him carefully.

Martiniano was sitting cross-legged, a thin blanket wrapped round his shirt and store pants, and slowly undoing his hair braids. The glow of the fire brought out the deep rose-red in his dark cheeks, chiselled sharper his clear-cut features. The hunch came to Byers as suddenly and clearly as if a voice had spoken in his ear: this school-Indian was going back to the blanket.

Martiniano finished unbraiding his hair, rolled up the colored cloth wrappings, and shook loose over his wide shoulders the long, coarse black hair. Then deliberately he picked up the bottle and took a long drink.

"Yes, there is a law. There are many laws," asserted Byers. "Little laws for little men, and big laws for big men. But the most difficult laws are a man's own. . . . So I have no fear of drinking when and where it suits me, taking care to make no trouble for any man." As if somewhat astounded by this platitudinous declaration of defiance, he added petulantly, "What the hell! Have I ever been known to sneak liquor into a reservation for sale or trouble? The devil take it! This is the time I like a drink!"

He leaned back against the bole of a tree, crossed his outflung legs, and stared upward at the stars tremulous and shiny hanging above them. He could not get that rattlesnake business out of his mind, nor something else which had long troubled him.

It was not in Byers to ask any Indian a direct question. What prevented him now was not only his own extreme sensitiveness to mood, his delicate tact and apperception of the truth that explanations are but poor substitutes for understanding—themselves qualities essentially

Indian, but the appearance of the man across the fire. Martiniano, long hair down, seemed no longer the obstinate, open rebel he had known. There was about him a soft, pliable, yet resistant secrecy, a deep impenetrability that forbade probing.

Without realizing the devious evasiveness of his own nature, Byers considered insinuations and suggestions, means and approaches.

"That deer skin," he said abruptly, "the one you left with me for pawn and came after that night . . ." He lashed at the fire with his boot, sending up a shower of sparks. The words had jumped out of him against his will and nature.

"The skin of the deer I killed," assented Martiniano softly, without looking up.

"Yes. I have never asked. But I have been troubled for my friend. I could keep it no longer."

The Indian kept combing the long, streaming black hair with his fingers. He combed time as well. The river flowed by, the moon sliced through the clouds.

"That deer I killed. It troubled me. I thought: I cannot escape it. It is best not to try. So from you I got the skin. On my wall it is."

There it was, simply asked, simply answered, without evasiveness and explanation. And suddenly for Byers that barrier he had fancied between them, all mystery, was gone. It was as if from the darkness a long-legged antlered shape had stepped forth, touching both their lives, and then dissolving into light. It was no longer a deer, but an evanescent glimmer of the truth which appears once to each man and then is gone, not yet completely understood, but revealing a shape dimly sensed within its own outward shape.

"Boy, I too have had my deer," muttered the white man deeply, staring into the fire. "Believe me, son, it will pass."

"I believe," Martiniano answered shortly, without raising his head.

A great weight seemed to have lifted from Byers. He gulped down all but two fingers, and passed the bottle to Martiniano to finish. "Ah! A little drink at night in front of a fire before bed! That is life. A good drum, a dance, that is life too. Anything that warms the heart, the blood, the mind, and makes one feel alive. Not to refuse it. That is life. That is my law. . . . But to avoid causing trouble to others, I would just take that empty bottle back to the car. We will not leave it here to be found on the reservation."

Martiniano did as he was told. He came back with a small drum. Squatting down with it across his lap, he began to beat it gently. In a moment he began to sing. His dark face relaxed with a peculiar womanly softness. His white teeth gleamed. Perhaps, with just two drinks, he was a little drunk. Liquor gets these people so quickly, thought Byers. But his eyes were clear, his voice steady.

So they sat, watching the embers cool. A song. A pause. And then another. Very low, but very intense, and sounding through the glade.

And suddenly as Martiniano began again, a rich clear voice from behind joined his. It was Flowers Playing singing from her blankets. At its end came a low, joyful laugh. "The one we sang in the car yesterday, all afternoon, as we crossed the desert," she cried. "Now let us try that Corn Dance Song. How I would love to dance it! Now! We will see if it comes in song."

So they sang in the chill, dark spring night, parted but yet together. Angelina stirred drowsily in her warm bag. Byers sat with bowed head. For him this had always been and would be always—a fire, darkness, the low beat of a drum, and a shape of something unseen yet dimly sensed within the shape of things visible.

Each man has his deer, he thought, and I have had mine. And for the first time he admitted to himself the secret desire that had lay coiled so long within him. How beautiful she had seemed then, so young when he was young and lonely and alone. The gentle moon face and the long, blue-black hair, the slow tantalizing movement of her hips, and the quick brown hands shucking corn. Who would ever recognize her now, so toothless, pock-marked, fat and shapeless, shaking with mirth as he cursed her goodnaturedly for messing up the kitchen—Buffalo Old Woman!

He looked over toward his wife waiting for him in the darkness. Loosening his boots, he stood up and jerked off hat and jacket.

"Up early tomorrow. Home at noon," he said gruffly, and strode away.

Flowers Playing had stopped singing. Martiniano sat thumping gently on the little drum. After a while he laid it away, secure from sparks and dew, and slipped away into the opposite darkness.

Chapter 9

So little by little the richness and the wonder and the mystery of life stole in upon him.

In the hush of high noon he flung himself down to rest. From the shadow of a pine he looked out upon his corn, their sturdy gold-green stalks marching down the slope like warriors to battle adversity for him, their tassels swaying like war feathers in the breeze. He smelled the water gurgling through his ditch, watched his wife raking out the hot ashes from the outdoor oven before putting in her bread to bake. In her and in his fields he had deposited his seed. There was another power which gave them life and made them both grow. He had partaken in the mystery of creation, yet he did not know what it was.

He lay beside Flowers Playing at night, already gently feeling her body to see if it had grown, and he wondered sleepily, is it my wife's thighs I feel, or the long rounded thighs of pine slope outflung upon this sage desert? Is this her breast, now flattened at the crest, really incurved like that old buffalo bow, or is it the outline of the mountain above? Whose heart do I hear beating faintly but steadily like a muffled drum? And he thought of the little blue lake of life hidden deep within them both. We are all images of one great shape, obeying its same laws.

Occasionally he slept alone outside. He could hardly go to sleep sometimes, so exquisite was the feeling that possessed him. The yellow moon low over the desert, the stars twinkling above the tips of the high ridge pines, the fireflies, the far-off throb of a drum, the silence, the tragic, soundless rushing of the great world through time—it caught at his breath, his heart.

His resentment against injustice left him, his bitterness, his sullen anger. Life was more than what he saw, heard and sensed. It extended beyond the visible, the audible, the sensory limits. Whenever he went down to the pueblo he was very careful—and cautioned Flowers Playing to be, likewise—of looking with scorn at an old woman's harelip or twisted feet, a man's odd eye or anyone's physical defect lest as prospective parents their own child be born that way. He advised her never to use a knife in water lest her own child be cut in its prenatal lake. The moon in eclipse eats a child and so retards its growth, so he gave her a stone arrowhead to carry for protection.

Early one morning Martiniano rode down the slope alone. As he entered the plaza he knew something was wrong. The ovens were still smoking. Women in their big snowy boots waddled spread-legged to and from the stream carrying water jars and pails on their heads. Young men were busy at the corrals, old men sat smoking against the sunny walls. It was the old, old form which nothing ever altered—the open secrecy of Pueblo life. But the substance within had changed. It was tense. A dangerous lull had becalmed the place over night. Whispers spread. A word here, a phrase there. The lifting of a hairless eyebrow, the flip of a blanket over the shoulder, and a man walking swiftly, but not too swiftly, away from another.

Martiniano went about his errands. First to Byers' post. "Our crop is doing well. Very well. You will be both comforted and pleased to hear this, no doubt."

The trader grumbled a curt reply. He wore a frown and seemed out of temper.

Martiniano rode on to La Oreja and tethered his horse to the rail. The plaza as usual in midsummer was full of visiting whites, Mexicans and Indians wearing their brightest shirts and cleanest sheets. But the Indians kept to themselves in wary groups about their wagons or did their trading and rode somberly away.

Martiniano did not delay. He rode back to the pueblo with a sack of flour laid across his mare and a little paper bag of ginger-snaps tied in his sheet for Flowers Playing.

All afternoon he worked in his small field outside the walls; he had neglected it a little lately for the big one above. At dusk he went to see Palemon and stayed for supper. There was a strange touch of formality about the hospitality: he and Palemon ate first and alone at the little kitchen table, then Estefana and Batista who had served them. While the women ate, the men sat silent in the other room. Palemon's face was relaxed and inscrutable, but Martiniano could see that he was worried. Martiniano let it pass. When the women came out he gave them each a ginger-snap and carefully tied up the little sack again. Batista had grown up; her hair was banged in front and tied behind. She stood in the open doorway looking down into the dark plaza.

"You will hear them soon," Martiniano chided her as he rose to leave. "These foolish young men who sing all night among the willows. Well, I would join them too and sing to my friend's new-grown daughter if it were not for that Ute girl who captured me—and now waits, doubtless, with a stick!"

Batista smiled shyly, then giggled.

Palemon answered slowly, "I think there will be little singing tonight. It draws white people from town to listen. We don't want them here any more. Perhaps we shall keep them out . . . Come, I shall walk with you to your horse."

It was as he said. As they walked across the plaza to the corrals the singing broke out, one voice after another to flood the night. But as Martiniano was saddling his mare, a car from town came down the road. The headlights shone down the lane between the corrals, across the plaza, and upon the white-sheeted singers grouped along the stream. The singers stopped. A shadowy figure stepped forth and halted the car. Martiniano could hear the conversation.

"What you do?"

"We just drove in to listen to the singing. We're not going to get out of the car. Just turn off the lights and sit awhile here."

"No good. You go."

"Why, we've always come down! We like your singing. You know us, Joe! We've always given you cigarettes for yourself and the singers."

"Governor she say no. She say this Indian land, this our pueblo. These our songs. That what *we* say. You go now."

"Why, of all things! You—"

"You go! You back up!"

The car backed out of the narrow lane, turned around reluctantly, then roared angrily away. The singing did not resume. Already pale splotches were walking across the bridge; there was a Council meeting that night.

When Martiniano mounted, Palemon took the bridle and led him up the trail away from all ears.

"Now I will tell you what you have wanted to ask," he said quietly. "About this grievous thing, this terrible book of paper." His voice lowered. "It tells all—all," he repeated tonelessly. "All about our pueblo, our customs, our beliefs. It gives our names!" He paused to let this dreadful fact sink in, and then in a voice that expressed the greatest horror and sadness possible, he said, "It has given, on paper, for all to read, even the names of our kivas!"

Martiniano saw him glance around in the darkness at the ears in the bushes, the eyes in the stones, at the desecrated earth on which he stood and at the stars reeling in their orbits above.

"I do not know what will happen," Palemon went on sadly. "Perhaps it is the end of our good life. I have heard how the snows laid four feet deep just outside the pueblo in the old days. Now there is scarcely enough to cover a man's foot. The great spring in the Big Pasture where our buffalo are kept no longer bubbles up with water. The grass is dry and brown since I was small. Why? Because we have not kept the faith. We have lost our medicine. So the life is going out of the earth. The skies are wrinkling dry as old skin. And now the last of all evils has overtaken us. Our secrets have been betrayed. . . . No, I do not know what is going to happen."

Without farewell he strode away into the darkness.

Martiniano rode on home.

Who knew how it came? These Indians did not read books, magazines, even newspapers. How could they have been aware of a thin, paper-backed booklet that appeared inconspicuously in a store or two in the city nearly two hundred miles away? No one in La Oreja, not even Benson or Byers, had heard of it. But there it was in the Governor's hands scarcely a week after it had been published.

The booklet, "A Preliminary Study of Pueblo Culture," contained a few photographs, a description of customs, and a short history with the usual discursive assumption that the American Indians were descendants of Mongolians who had migrated over the Bering Crossing.

But in it was something else. A sketch map of the pueblo showed the location of the kivas properly named, and the arrangement of communal fields and pastures. A long list of family names, both Indian and Mexican, was segregated into kiva groups, and reference was made to an extinct kiva. This Never-Covered-by-Flood kiva was described as being not only historically and culturally important, but dating back to mythical times. It had been established here at the mystical center of the world by the Old First Ones when they emerged to the surface of the earth—the writer ignoring the contradiction of her assumption that the Indians were of Mongolian descent. In it undoubtedly human sacrifice had been made, and Montezuma had been received when he was carried by litter to visit the northern tribes four hundred years ago—carrying the sacred flame still kept burning in its "unused" depths.

The Governor lifted his hand for the interpreter to stop. He could read no further. These things and conjectures of things looming suddenly before him from a printed book stiffened him into an attitude of unmitigated horror. His old face cracked. His composure would have suffered less had his seatless pants suddenly fallen down as he was receiving a group of tourist ladies come with a dollar apiece to take his photograph. He felt more naked and shamed. Resentment and anger came later, when he called the Council together.

All night for five nights they sat together wrapped to the eyes in their blankets. There was only one voice, that of the interpreter reading through the booklet, page by page. He was not interrupted. At dawn he stopped. The book was hidden away, and the old men filed out, without a word, to return again at dark.

On the fifth night, just after midnight, the interpreter came to the last chapter. "In August culminates the yearly ceremonial life of the pueblo," he translated slowly, "when the people in a great procession climb up the mountains to their sacred Dawn Lake." Tepees were pitched on the shore. Great fires shone upon the clear blue water and the leaping bodies of naked dancers. The throb of drums, the whine of singing voices echoed through the pines. The ceremonies were secret. No stranger had ever been allowed to witness them. The trails were carefully guarded. For even revealing what went on the penalty was death. Yet there were indications. Young unmarried men and women were forced to go, and virgin maidens who came back like wilted flowers. It seemed certain all participated in a monstrous sex orgy.

The interpreter laid down the booklet and took his seat in the corner. The old men uncovered their faces. The talk began and continued for more nights.

It was not a question of how much or little of the contents of the book approximated the truth. They were a people who so identified their lives with the one great flow of all life that they showed no sense of individuality, and seemed at once impersonal and anonymous. They had attained the faculty of so obliterating themselves when gathered together in a group that even their faces lost individual expression, and looked blankly out with the one face of the tribe. To them spoken words robbed a thought of power, and printed words destroyed it entirely. They never looked at or pointed to an object or person being discussed; never spoke another's name; and always referred to a man as "she" and a woman as "he" lest direct reference rob the one of his power.

And now this!—the unbelievable, the impossible, the unbearable. The fingers and the eyes of the world were pointed at them. Their names were spoken, they were printed. Their power was taken from them.

A cold fear beset them. A quiet fury possessed them. So cold, so quiet, that of all those nights of Council-talk only one pronouncement filtered out to waiting ears—the calm judgment of the oldest of the old:

"It would not be too much if a man would die for this."

Who had betrayed them? They began to probe about. This book of paper. It had been writen by one Mrs. Blackstone. Even her name denoted evil. She had stayed in La Oreja last fall, a friend of that picture man who had painted so many faces of Panchilo that now he had no face left. Drunken Panchilo was brought. All could see how his life, his power had been taken from him.

"Now what did you give of *our* lives, *our* power, to this white woman for a bottle of whiskey?" they demanded.

"I took whiskey, but I gave nothing. I lied!" quaked Panchilo in his rags. "He said, 'Panchilo, you are poor and unfortunate and not understood. Now come and talk to me every afternoon where we will be alone, and I will give you money for new shoes, a new shirt.' So I went. I talked. And I bought whiskey with what he gave me. Can I help it because I am poor and unfortunate and not understood—and am possessed by this strange craving? But even drunken Panchilo was more crafty than he. I lied and he did not know the difference, this ignorant white woman who thought I would betray my people."

His courage was returning; a smirk crawled into his dissolute face. He mimicked and pantomimed his patroness. They could see it all.

"Panchilo, I would hear today the story of creation. How the Indians began. How the Great Spirit gave life to his Red Children."

He had scratched himself and begun. "Now God she make world. She make trees, flowers, birds, animals, fish. She make sky and stars too. This good. No good 'nough. Dios say, 'I make people.' So she make big oven. She make big oven hot. Now she take clay and make fingers in like man and put in big hot oven. Pretty soon take out of oven first man: she alive but all black; Dios leave in oven too long and she burnt. 'Ai!' Dios say. 'You black man. You go odder place live.'

"Now Dios she try again. She take clay out too soon. This man alive but too pale. 'Ai!' Dios say. 'You pale face. You go odder place live.'

"Now Dios she try once more. She leave clay in oven just right time. Man come out cooked just enough. Nice red brown. 'Ai!' say Dios. 'You Indian. Good! You live here.'"

Panchilo's smirk grew into a lewd grin. "This white woman he say, Panchilo, that good story, but I would know where this clay come from.' So I say, 'From those clay pits up Arroyo Blanco. Is not the name true? Now that why Indian she paint her skin with this white clay when she dance.' Then I do this."

He drew apart his tattered shirt to reveal his dirty belly, and poked his exposed navel.

"I say, 'Indian she have this hole in belly. Why? Because when Indian in big hot oven, Dios she open door and poke finger in this clay to see if cooked, and leave this hole. See? Now you show Panchilo if white people have this hole in belly too!'"

He leaned back on his heels and finished laughing. Panchilo was a drunken reprobate but still a "good" Indian. They let him stalk out in the only sober dignity he had assumed in months.

More information came. They sent for Manuel Rena; he too had been seen talking with the white woman one day at the trading post.

The Peyote Chief did not look from under his eyelids. He answered in good voice. "We have quarreled about this Native American Church. I still uphold it. I still believe in Our Father Peyote. That is our business; we are all Indians together. But what man accuses me of betraying my people, my tribe, my pueblo to those outside?"

Next brought before them was Buffalo Old Woman. "You work for the trader, Señor Byers," they told her sternly. "One day this white woman came of whom we speak: that was how you knew her. One day after, she went down to the river to cook meat and coffee to listen to some of our boys beat the drum and sing songs. On a picnic. She paid you to go, to cook this meat and coffee, to wash those dishes afterwards in the river. Now! What did you give her of our lives for more money? Speak!"

Fat shook on the frightened woman. "I talked to her but I lied as is proper! What woman knows anything of the kiva, of solemn matters? Are we not all magpies who always talk—but of trivial things only? Listen! That was how it was. Of little things only I talked. And I lied.

"This white woman ask how the dead are buried, about the turkey feathers, about the Corn Mothers. He ask for our customs. For two silver dollars I give big Indian-woman secret! That when something is lost or stolen we burn on San Antonio Day a candle upside down so that the flame will point to the missing thing. Ai! It is but a Mexican custom, as you know! Such things only I tell him. So I lied, as is proper."

They were still unsatisfied; they would always be unsatisfied. Thirty years ago a fetish of white stone had vanished from one of the kivas. Several men since had been taken to Washington as delegates to see the Great Father, the Presidente. The first place each had asked to visit was the Indian museum. They were still hoping to find on display the missing figure and to trace who had stolen it.

So the probing went on, and over the face of the pueblo dropped the invisible and impenetrable mask of secrecy and aloofness. Old Mexican neighbors were avoided on road and trail. Thin threads of friendship between whites and Indians snapped. An Indian girl working for a family in town suddenly lost her tongue, became shy or sullen. A man in town approached by a tourist who desired a horse and guide merely hitched up his blanket and said quietly, "I have my work," and went back to sleep in the sunny plaza. Whenever a visitor came to the pueblo an Indian boy stepped out from the Governor's house and stuck at his heels like a shadow wherever he walked. All the faces seemed blank. No one seemed to understand English. Occasionally a horseback rider happened to get past the pueblo and upon a mountain trail. Immediately a thin line of smoke rose from a housetop. And soon an Indian stepped out from the brush, his arms outstretched to turn back the rider.

Even Byers became annoyed. He had bought tobacco leaves from Mexico for their Council meetings, and parrot feathers for their ceremonials—gifts whose acceptance showed how long and fully he had been trusted. Now this relationship seemed changed. They treated him respectfully but aloofly, like a shop-keeper.

He got hold of a copy of the booklet and read it through. Over parts he frowned, over pages he laughed. It was mostly all damned stuff and nonsense. But the reaction of the old men to it was not so simple.

They had begun to calm down. It was indeed much foolishness and many lies, this ignorant writing, though the sketch map showing the peculiar arrangement of their fields, and the list of names could have been taken from old Government records. But there in print, like letters of fire, like fingers pointing, like voices shouting, were the names of the kivas, their own names.

Lastly, there was the allusion to their secret Dawn Lake ceremonies. This was something that could not be ignored. Their Dawn Lake!

The District Superintendent had found out about the booklet. It was unfortunate—damned unfortunate!—it had come at such a time. He managed to have it withdrawn from sale in the State lest it provoke both Indians and whites still more, and wired the Commissioner.

Now he could put off a visit no longer, and came up to inquire why the old men had not sent a representative to the All-Pueblo-Council-Meeting.

"We have our lives, we have our own pueblo," he was answered coldly. "We see no need of talk, talk, talk when it brings us nothing.

We are still waiting to see what the Government is going to do about our land, our Dawn Lake."

So was Strophy—and the Government too.

The investigators had sent in their findings. A Land Board of three men was created to examine the claims—one member each representing the President, the Department of Justice and the Department of the Interior. They seemed agreed that where the Indian had lost land to a white or Mexican, the Indian should be compensated. And where the whites and the Mexicans had been in possession of the land and paid taxes for many years, though without title, they too should be compensated. But what they looked at made their head ache. To compensate the pueblo they would require over $84,000; and to compensate the white and Mexican claimants for land within the pueblo grant would require over $57,000. This was a total of over $141,000 for compensation on claims within the shrunken grant of some 18,000 acres.

But what about the whole town of La Oreja? That—the fantastic impossible—would require the proceeds of a Government mint!

While the deliberations went on, another telegram came from Strophy and the district Indian Office. All the pueblos had heard of the rumpus and were likewise demanding restitution of or compensation for their lands—their promised lands.

Strophy, called back to Washington, talked again with the stubborn Council. "I am going to see the Commissioner, the Great Father at Washington, the President himself—the great Government that rules all councils," he said. "I have come first to talk with you. To see what it is you wish. Do you want all your white friends, all your Mexican neighbors to move off their land and be homeless? Do you want all the people to leave La Oreja? Where then will you buy flour, salt, blankets, shoes—where then will you sell corn, trade a bag of wheat for groceries? Is that what you wish?" he asked wearily and ironically.

"We want our Dawn Lake!"

"Then let us talk about it, this Dawn Lake." he answered curtly.

"No. We will talk about it no more. Already we have talked about it. In three ways. Are there more?

"We talked about it when we talked about this peyote. We talked about it as a church. The Government said, 'We will give you this peyote church, this Native American Church.' And we said we do not want any other church. We already have a church—our Dawn Lake, from which comes all the good things we get. That is what *we* say.

"We talked about it when we talked about the compensation the Government promised for our lands. And we said, 'Give us back our land—the land in the mountains about our Dawn Lake. So that it will be our land. Not land full of American policemen and Mexicans with their sheep.' That is what *we* say.

"We talked about it another way. Side by side with this matter of the book of paper. White people come at night to visit our pueblo. They listen to our young men singing down by the willows. Now these young men do not sing to ignorant white people who do not understand their songs. They sing to their girls in the pueblo who stand in the darkness, hidden in their doorways. White people come all day to visit our pueblo. They poke noses in our doors like hungry dogs. They walk into our houses unasked. How is this? Does an Indian walk in a white man's house in town and say, 'Well! So this is how a white man lives! How funny!' Does he pick up a blanket, a pair of shoes, and ask, 'How much you want for this?' And still white people come all a time. They look at our dances. They picnic under our trees and leave paper bags to make the land unsightly. They dirty our streams. And then they write books of lies about us! So we say, 'Whose pueblo is this, whose dances and songs, whose houses, whose customs, whose lives?' And we say, 'It is not the Indian way to put out his belly before all people, to shout out his business, to empty his heart. We must have one place where we can go and sing and dance, live and worship as we will, free from the eyes of the world, without fingers pointing at us, where no voices shout out our names. Give us our Dawn Lake.' This *we* say.

"So we talked about it as a church, as land and business, as a matter of living with due modesty and not naked and ashamed before the world. We talked from the heart, the mind, the body. How now would you have us talk?

"We are all one together. We want our Dawn Lake. This is all we say."

The Corn Ripe Moon rose above the ridge pines. The nights began to sharpen. A thin blue haze smoked the days.

Martiniano was cutting wood. He had taken off his blanket and tied his pig-tails together in back so they would not whip about him as he worked. His dirty denim trousers were tightened about his narrow waist with his wide, brass-studded belt. His faded red cotton shirt stuck to his broad sweaty shoulders. He was stripping a felled pine. The blows of his axe were precise and rhythmical. The chips spurted out evenly, one after another, like leaves being torn from a book. The sound rang sharp and clean in the silent glade. When he was through, he wiped his dark face and moved on to another.

Flowers Playing followed behind him in a turquoise blue shawl and old shoes laced with greased string. She kneeled and laid out a piece of rope. Crosswise on this she stacked the faggots she gathered. When the stack was nearly waist high she drew up and knotted the rope around it, laboriously hoisted it upon her back, and staggered off toward the wagon. Within a few steps she straightened, and when she came back her breath was even.

It is not the force of a blow with an axe that matters, but its preciseness and rhythm. So too have Indian women learned the secret of carrying heavy loads, how to compensate for the gravitational pull.

When the sun was high they built a fire and cooked meat and coffee. "These lifeless sandwiches white people eat, they make my blood run cold," said Martiniano disdainfully. "A fire and something hot in the belly. That is the way to live like people, not dogs." He stretched out and rolled a cigarette.

Flowers Playing scrubbed off the sooty tin on which she had heated their corn cakes, and washed the dishes. A rabbit hopped across the pine-needled floor of the forest. The smoke had drawn blue-jays to squawk in the trees above. The stream below gushed musically over the stones. She lay back and stared at the clear blue sky, felt the sun eating through her clothes. Life was all one. How beautiful it was!

Only one thought marred her deep content. Last week they had driven down to the pueblo. Leaving team and wagon in the grove of cottonwoods, they cut across a field to the plaza. Like them all, this one was irregular in shape, conforming to natural contours and flanked by thickets of wild plum. Trudging noiselessly along the hedge they were suddenly arrested by sight of a strange figure crouched down before them in the thicket, her upraised hands parting the branches.

It was Palemon's wife, Estefana. The stealthy, secretive posture of her body, and a glimpse in profile of the hungry, agonized look on her face showed them a woman too raptly absorbed in something beyond her to have noticed their approach.

Before Flowers Playing could speak, Martiniano nudged her for silence and nodded toward an opening in the thicket. On the other side sauntered a small boy. Flowers Playing at the first glance did not recognize Napaita. His moccasins were coarse and ill-sewn. He had grown; and his blanket, discolored by smoke, flapped open to reveal a long thin body from which the outline of ribs protruded. It was the boy's face that held her attention. It was drawn and pale, and yet curiously enlivened. His mouth was open and gulping rapid lungfuls of air; his nostrils quivered with its wild, sharp scents; his gaze swung from side to side with less wariness of detection than delight in the open fields and hills before him. He walked with quick, springy steps, flexing his legs as if they had never before known freedom.

The woman kneeling in the thicket did not stir, and let him pass. Martiniano drew Flowers Playing back; they retraced their steps and crossed the field on the other side.

"Napaita. Her own son it was, and she . . . poor Estefana!" mumbled Flowers Playing. "Why did not—"

"He is still in the kiva according to custom, but just out for air. Would you have him speak to a woman, which is forbidden?" interrupted Martiniano curtly. "That much I know. But you understand less."

And now remembering the look on her face as she knelt hidden in the bushes, Flowers Playing was sad for her friend. Why, it might be Estefana and not herself waiting these months for a son to be born to her—a son secretly glimpsed striding in the sunlight, but one to whom she could not yet speak.

They quit early, not quite midafternoon, and drove down to the pueblo. The heavy, loaded wagon rumbled slowly past the clearings. In one a fat, husky woman got up from a log as they passed, pushed back her big brown breast inside her cerise dress, and handed the child she had been suckling to an old crone in rusty black beside her. Then taking up a double-bladed axe she resumed work. Two older children were gathering the branches she chopped, while a girl of four was picking up the chips. Farther along two men were felling pines and stripping off the shaggy bark. All winter the long, smooth yellow timbers would be left to season for vigas, and then snaked down to a new house. From down along the stream came the crackle and cackle of women picking chokecherries and wild plums. On the slope above crawled shadows of stooped old women patiently filling bags with piñones. The road was full of quick-footed, fastidious-stepping little burros heaped with faggots and being beaten onward by small boys. Bright, sweaty shirts and flowered shawls flashed in the dark green glades. Colored head-bands gleamed against the sunny hillsides. Bursts of song jetted from the somber, rocky cañons.

For as the voice still delayed announcing from the housetops that it was time to gather in the corn, the people, ever responsive to the change of weather, stirred through the smoky autumn haze about their new tasks.

"One more load to our little house down below," muttered Martiniano complacently, jogging on the seat. "Then I will feel we can face fall. It keeps a man busy when he has two houses, two fields to care for."

There was a strange new pride in his voice. Flowers Playing smiled to herself. Martiniano was preparing for a long, cold winter down below as if for a family of ten! This thing which had happened to them was giving him a new importance.

It showed in his eyes, his walk; and it remained for the little while they stayed in the pueblo before returning home. Suddenly, half-way back up the dusky slope, he gave it voice.

"Now I know what makes me feel so good! 'It would not be too much if a man died for this.' That was what they said, those foolish old men worrying about this book. Did you hear the quaver in Palemon's voice as he told me, see the fright in his eyes? Hah! Why not Martiniano? They have suspicioned me, punished me, fined and whipped me for everything else. But not this! Imagine that! This is the first trouble in the pueblo that has not been laid at my door! They are coming to their senses at last."

Martiniano went to bed unable to sleep for the satisfaction which possessed him. For the first time he had found peace. The crop from his new fields would pay off his debt; next year it would make him a rich man. By then he would have a family. And he had found a faith. All this accomplished by himself, alone! Triumph mounted within him.

He lay thinking, Never before have I really seen myself. Never before have I really seen the old stories truly. For one day these days will be in the dim past, and we who live now. Yes! And in them I shall be a legend!

Swiftly he built up the fantasy of his immense pride. One time long ago, the stories would tell, the pueblo was in trouble. The people's land, their Dawn Lake, was taken from them. White people and Mexicans intruded on their privacy. Then something happened. There was a poor young man whom nobody liked. Now this Martiniano killed a deer, was beaten and punished. But his act roused the old men about their Dawn Lake. A strange religion came. It was called the Peyote Road. This Martiniano ate this peyote, and was punished for it.

But he had learned it was no good, and his action turned his people back to the good simple life. Now something else happened. This Martiniano beat a Mexican sheepherder off his land, the mountain slope that rose to Dawn Lake. He was whipped. But he took his whipping like a man for he had roused all the people to desire back their land. Ai! For all these he was fined, he was punished, he was whipped. No one spoke to him. He was called Martiniano the Trouble-Maker.

Life shows as the still surface of a deep blue lake. But the impact of a thrown pebble causes ripples that beat upon all shores—that affect all men's lives, that travel from pueblo to pueblo, to Washington itself. And his was the hand which had cast the stone. This poor young man who in his wisdom and strength of will defied all men, suffered trouble, and so saved his people. And now he is no longer known as Martiniano the Trouble-Maker. He is a great man, a savior—he who in legend is known as the Man Who Killed the Deer. . . .

So dreamed his smug satisfaction in having for once escaped trouble, and his monstrous pride in having seen the first glimmer of faith.

It was interrupted from time to time by a certain faint rustle and crackle outside, and the queer sense of eyes peering in the open door. He thrust them from him and slept.

Next morning when he awoke and looked outside, he saw he had had a visitor. His corn, his beautiful new brave corn had been trampled. And there on the ground just outside the door, like a contemptuous refutation of his dreams, lay a few round balls of fresh spoor and the single imprint of a deer's split hoof.

A strange foreboding clutched him. His anger shook it off. He cleaned and oiled his gun, slept afternoon and kept vigil on his corn at night.

Carefully he selected his spot. On the pine slope above both the spring and corn milpa, and hidden behind a great boulder. Wrapped in his blanket he watched the moon rise, the shadows dissolve in a pale greenish effulgence that flowed unobstructed over mountain, sage slope and desert.

Rabbits played about him till frightened by the shapeless terror of a floating owl. Coyotes yapped far down the draw. Once he watched a small fox trot past. Aspens were turning in the high cañons; the small brown bears would soon be ambling down to frighten old women away from their berries. Night birds cried sleepily. At dawn he saw a turkey cock strut down to water in all its bronze, pristine wildness. . . .

Late the third night they came. Three deer gliding dream-like and noiseless out of the great trees to halt below him sniffing the breeze. A five-pronged buck and two small does standing behind.

Martiniano raised his gun, laid the barrel noiselessly in the hollow between thumb and forefinger of his left hand resting on the boulder, drew the butt up snugly against his shoulder.

Slowly the three moved forward—moved like shadows of clouds in the sunlight, having shape but no substance. Three ghostly gray dreams in moonlight. Aware of their wild pristine purity; self-possessive as masters of the earth they trod and which fell away, unbroken, down the sage slope and across the desert to the hazy blue horizon; and fastidious of every movement as patricians conscious of their heritage, they emerged into full moonlight. Martiniano drew a bead on the buck at the base of the brain.

He did not fire. His finger froze on the trigger; his mouth went dry; his knees trembled. Terror struck, he counted the five points of the horns, appraised the body of the deer. There was the same-toned gray though discolored by moonlight, the marking of black, and the little splotch of white under the left shoulder.

The deer had sauntered slowly across the strip of sage between the pines and the corn milpa. The buck was in the lead. He suddenly turned as if with a curt command. The two does stopped, the great petals of their ears thrust forward. Then suddenly—too swiftly to be remarked for mere motion—he was in the air clearing the fence around Martiniano's corn. It was as if he had been invisibly lifted and suspended in the air—as if his skin had been jerked off the wall of the hut and flung in the air to swell with life. His antlered head was up; his front legs curved gracefully under his chest, his hind legs thrust back; his white tail piece lifted. He lit lightly as a butterfly, bounded twice and disappeared in the corn.

The two does looked at each other, rubbed noses. Then like demure doves they too soared gracefully over the split aspens.

Martiniano gripped his gun with trembling fingers. Impossible! He had been betrayed by a foolish memory of the deer he had killed! He gritted his teeth; this time he would not lose his chance. Picking up a pebble, he tossed it into the dry stalks. Immediately, flushed like quail, the deer rose out of the corn. But lighting on the other side of the fence and standing quietly, gracefully and stupidly still, awaiting the message which had summoned them.

Again Martiniano had no power to deliver it.

He angrily kicked loose a stone. It rattled down the slope behind him, bumping dully against the protruding roots of a washed-out spruce and settling with a faint rustle upon a mat of needles. One of the big buck's ears twisted around in its socket to follow the noise. Then disdainfully lifting his nose above the horizon, and stepping high with his thin brittle legs, the deer walked coolly away, followed by his two meek attendants.

Martiniano stood up, banged the stock of his gun against the rock and began to shout. In a flash they were gone, as if erased with one sweep by the hand of night. Still he cursed them, the deer he had killed and himself, then curled up in his blanket for a sleepless night.

Twice later he saw them again, but did not shoot. Something about them from a distance, their untrammeled freedom and wild gentility, stayed his hand. Nor did he let them get close; he could not chance the possibility of being tricked again by a vision. So he settled down each night, shivering in his blanket, to frighten them away with mere noises and angry shouts.

He had not only lost the fleeting comfort of his immense pride, but knew himself a coward. He blamed the deer. And each morning after his vigil he rose stiffly and glowered at the dawn. "This deer I killed," he muttered sullenly. "I will be even with it yet!"

Cutler Hall, built by Joseph Dozier. This was the first structure on the campus of The Colorado College, as it appeared upon completion in 1878. Courtesy of Special Collections, Tutt Library, The Colorado College, Colorado Springs.

May Ione Dozier and Frank Jonathon Waters, parents of Frank Waters, on their wedding day, May 7, 1901. Courtesy of Barbara Waters and the Frank Waters Foundation.

The "ungainly house on Shooks Run" where Frank Waters was born. It is located at 435 E. Bijou Street, Colorado Springs, across from "Frank Waters Park." Courtesy of Thomas J. Lyon.

Pikes Peak in sunshine, during a summer thunderstorm in Colorado Springs. "Next time, by hook or crook, make sure you're born with a mountain in the front yard." Courtesy of Thomas J. Lyon.

Gallegos Wash, northwestern New Mexico, where the now-"ghost" trading post Waters always referred to as "Shallow Water on the Gallegos" was probably located. Courtesy of Thomas J. Lyon.

Victor, Colorado, in the Cripple Creek Mining District. As a boy, Waters stayed here occasionally with his father and grandfather, and returned to this town in 1936 to begin his career as a full-time writer. Courtesy of Thomas J. Lyon.

Pikes Peak, as seen from Victor, Colorado. This mountain compelled the attention and allegiance of both Joseph Dozier and his grandson Frank Waters. Courtesy of Thomas J. Lyon.

Frank Waters at the time of graduation from Colorado Springs High School, 1921. Courtesy of Barbara Waters and the Frank Waters Foundation.

Frank Waters in a rare Southern California photograph, about 1927. Courtesy of Barbara Waters and the Frank Waters Foundation.

Mora Valley, New Mexico ("the beautiful blue valley"), location of *People of the Valley* (1941). Courtesy of Thomas J. Lyon.

Taos Mountain and Pueblo land, seen from the "studio over Tony's garage" (Tony Luhan, that is) where most of *The Man Who Killed the Deer* (1942) was written. Courtesy of Thomas J. Lyon.

Doroteo "Frank" Zamora, a prototype for "the man who killed the deer," and Frank Waters, Arroyo Seco, April 1969. Courtesy of Barbara Waters and the Frank Waters Foundation.

Aspen gate (built by Frank Zamora) at the entrance to Frank Waters's Arroyo Seco property, May 1952. Courtesy of Barbara Waters and the Frank Waters Foundation.

Frank Waters being checked in at the security gate, Nevada Test Site, April 1953. At about this time, while working at Los Alamos for the AEC, Waters began writing *The Woman at Otowi Crossing*. Photo by Don English and Dave Lees, Desert Sea News Bureau, Las Vegas. Courtesy of Barbara Waters and the Frank Waters Foundation.

The Rio Grande at Otowi Crossing, New Mexico. "The rustle of branches in the breeze, the rattle of a stone rolling down the steep escarpment, the ripple of the river, the call of birds . . . ." Courtesy of Thomas J. Lyon.

Pumpkin Seed Point, seen from the house in Kikotsmovi on the Hopi Reservation where Frank Waters worked on Book of the Hopi, 1959–62. Permission to photograph granted by Ida Murdock. Courtesy of Thomas J. Lyon.

The Waters home in Arroyo Seco, New Mexico. Courtesy of Thomas J. Lyon.

Frank Waters at the Manchester Gallery, El Prado, New Mexico, 1976. Photograph by Robert Kostka. Courtesy of Robert Kostka.

El Cuchillo del Medio, seen from Waters's back pasture. "A malign, masculine mountain." Courtesy of Thomas J. Lyon.

Pueblo Peak, the Sacred Mountain of Taos Pueblo, seen from Waters's back pasture. "A benign, motherly mountain." Courtesy of Thomas J. Lyon.

CHAPTER II

El Crepusculo (1949–1951)

"*El Crepusculo* makes no pretension of being more than a small weekly serving a relatively isolated community," said an editorial note of October 20, 1949. But its editor, Frank Waters, who had been with the paper six weeks at that time, went on to state that since Taos was in the focal area of the development of atomic energy, which in turn made all men neighbors, its newspaper held a certain significance and could legitimately comment on larger matters. Waters penned just under three hundred editorials for *El Crepusculo,* some no more than brief notes on very local matters, some casual expressions of the editor's state of mind, some more ambitious essays. A sense of what the weekly's management and office atmosphere might have been like during Waters's tenure (which ended December 6, 1951) may be gleaned from the fictional portrait of *El Porvenir* in *The Woman at Otowi Crossing.* Here are three sample editorials.

Time for Staying Still (December 22, 1949)

Now being observed at Taos Pueblo is the Time for Staying Still. In accordance with tradition, all the people move back into the pueblo from their summer homes in the fields. The plaza is barred to iron-shod hoofs and wagon-wheels. There must be no noisy sweeping, no wood-chopping within the walls. It is the interregnum between the annual death and rebirth of Our Mother Earth, a period of quiet gestation.

We need not stretch our imaginations too much to conjure the benefits to the world at large if we too observed such a tradition. Not for forty days. But for only one hour.

What devilish havoc that hour might play with our illusion that we are controlling the stream of life! The competitive scramble for wealth and power stopped. Cars stalled on the highways. Trains dead on their tracks. Lights, radios, and power turned off; crowds immobile on street corners. Congressmen holding their tongues for once. [The Soviet leader] Vishinsky frozen in a tirade. The United Nations caught like a cold congregation in the middle of a preacher's prayer.

Yet for that hour the illusion of our egotistic self-importance would be dispelled. We might feel in the stillness the swish of our earth-planet rotating about its axis at the rate of 1,000 miles an hour, and revolving around the sun 20 miles per second. There might come to us the deeper rhythm of our solar system moving within the immensities of inter-stellar space. In the ghastly silence we might hear the crash of falling snowflakes, the roar of sap running through cold trees, the terrified shrieks of our imprisoned consciences. We might even become aware, in 1949, that mankind is still dependent for survival upon ancient verities not controlled by our technological sciences.

It always has been in such individual Times of Staying Still that there has come to all the creative personalities of history the intimations of the great religions, philosophies and world-movements which have benefitted mankind. It was at such a time, nearly 2,000 years ago, that there appeared to three lone wayfarers on a desolate December plain that star of faith which we have followed since.

Out of another Time for Staying Still as our neighbors observe here, there will appear again perhaps a new symbolic star, that renewed faith for which we all are seeking to lead us through the ever-noisier, ever-faster ensuing Atomic Age.

Blame It on Blossoms (*May 11, 1950*)

As often happens to the best of mice and men, our mind is not on our business today.

We feel immune to the worthy innovations that are making Taos a more Comfortable place to live in. We have no invectives to hurl at Labor, Big Business, or even the Chamber of Commerce. Nothing in the horrible state of world affairs could induce us to preach a tidy little sermon on the injustices of mankind to man.

In our distorted frame of mind, the world looks like the best possible abode for mortal man. Still we know that there comes a time in the Fat Forties when a man must resist the blandishments of nature, and look only at the facts of life seen through the myopic gaze of middle age. Not at the thickets of wild plum blossoms heaped like snowdrifts in the sagebrush . . . crossing the pastures like a file of white-blanketed Indians.

That is probably what threw us off balance this morning. The deplorable necessity of having to walk to work through a country pasture instead of taking a city subway. And being inflicted with the unavoidable sight of that beach of white blossoms flanking the blue pine mountains all the way to the pueblo.

It could be a touch of May fever. It could be us. But the safest bet is to blame it on those blossoms.

Work, Sex & Society (*October 25, 1951*)

In a talk at Los Alamos last week, Dr. Donald Powell Wilson called America the only neurotic nation. He traced the growth of our neurosis to such factors as "moral legislation" and resulting gangsterdom and crime, and the prevalence of "Horatio Alger" ideals that can be realized by only a few.

His advice was: "Life is work, sex and society; if you adjust properly in all three areas, you need never worry about insanity or neurosis."

From behind our obscure, battered, roll-top desk, we are a little worried about this rather glib formula. Somehow it seems to us that there must be a little more than plenty of work, sex and social contacts to give our lives direction, meaning and a sense of inner security.

Affluent gangsters often work quite hard in organizing and supervising their far-flung crime rings. From the photos of their glamorous mistresses, and their reception by respectable neighbors, they evidently also have made excellent adjustments in the areas of sex and society.

On the contrary, the late Mahatma Gandhi did very little work in the acceptable sense; he abstained from sex; and removed himself as far as possible from all society.

The difference between this great leader of mankind and any influential TV'd gangster is, of course, a factor that is not mentioned by Dr. Wilson. A spiritual factor that is simply a deeply felt or dimly perceived sense of relationship to something beyond the work-sex-society scope of our wordly existence.

It need not be scientifically defined. For it has been appreciatively felt by all primitive peoples since the beginning of time, and it has given rise to the profound truths of Navaho ceremonialism as well as to the great creative structures of Christianity.

Without it, although we are "properly adjusted" to the "areas" of work-sex-society, humanity as well as each individual, will be bound in a neurosis of frustration.

CHAPTER 12

The Woman at Otowi Crossing (1966, revised 1987)

In 1943, Waters published an article in *The Writer* entitled "Relationships and the Novel," an artist's credo describing the importance of long fiction. "The modern novel," he wrote, "is so generally bad that all forms of non-fiction far outweigh it." But it *could* do something significant indeed. "[T]he main function of the novel, whatever form it takes: to reveal the relationship between man and his surrounding universe. This is the only true business of art." Knowing of Waters's earnestness, we are not surprised that his last major novel was thirteen years in gestation. For materials, he had the story of a sensitive, prescient New Mexico woman, Edith Warner; the saga of the Manhattan Project at Los Alamos, and behind it the mad intensity of world war; the quiet, ancient, nearby presence of an entirely different way of being, focused at San Ildefonso Pueblo; several characters of widely varying philosophy and psychology, each of importance to the others; and finally, the mysteriously potent landscape of one of the world's instructive places. Waters found coherence for all of this, and thus the relation-showing, "true business of art," in his title character.

→►

Much has been published about the actual woman who lived at Otowi Crossing, including her recipe for chocolate cake corrected for every change in altitude.

Despite the homely facts known of her simple life, there gathered about her an air of mystery no one could dispel. Today her life story has grown into a myth compounded by her Indian, Spanish and Anglo neighbors. This novel is a narrative of the growth and meaning of that myth.

PROLOGUE

Excerpt from the *Secret Journal* of Helen Chalmers, now so widely known as the "Woman at Otowi Crossing."

There is no such thing as time as we know it. The entire contents of all space and time co-exist in every infinite and eternal moment. It is an illusion that we experience them in a chronological sequence of "time."

As you know, Jack, I didn't learn this gradually during all my lonely years running this obscure tea room at a remote river crossing. I was trying to escape a miserable past, suffering the makeshifts of the day, dreading the future. Then suddenly it all spun before me like a wheel turning full circle. Everything I had known and would ever know congealed into one rounded, complete whole. And it's been that way more or less ever since.

Perhaps none of us really ever learn anything by degrees. We just keep on absorbing things unconsciously without realizing what they mean. Till suddenly, for no apparent reason, it all comes into focus with a blinding flash. Civilizations like people must evolve the same way. Not continuously. But by steps. Sudden unfoldments and blossomings like the Renaissance and the Atomic Age, followed by another dormant period of darkness and ignorance. So too do planetary systems form and re-form in bursts of fiery nebulae, solely to conform with our own expanded realizations. For they are all within ourselves—the continents, worlds and stars. We contain the contents of all space as well as of time.

What determines when we are ready for these mysterious upsurges and Emergences? I don't know, Jack. I don't know why this happened to me when it did. All I know is that it started late that afternoon when we were waiting for the last run on the Chile Line. We heard her whistle as she came around the bend. I was thinking then in terms of time. That this was the last lonely screech from my darling little narrow-gauge and a life going from me forever—and with it my livelihood from a lunch room here. I didn't know that it was whistling in a new life, a whole new era. But these, I found, were illusions too. There are no beginnings, no ends, nothing new. Everything has always been within us, just waiting to be recognized.

It happened like this . . .

From *Part One*

I.

The woman at Otowi Crossing heard it now for the last time as she had heard it day after day for years on end: that long-drawn, half-screech, half-wail of No. 425 whistling round the bend—to her the most mysteriously exciting, excessively romantic, and poignantly haunting sound in the world. Sitting on a weathered bench in front of the narrow-gauge siding, she peered eagerly forward through the blood-reddening New Mexican dusk.

"Take it easy, Helen." The man beside her her laid his hand lightly but warningly on her shoulder. She reached up her own hand to grasp his without swerving her gaze from the jutting mountain slope ahead.

Even before the train rounded the bend, the woman could see the smoke rolling up the blackened face of the redrock cliff, hear the flanges of the wheels squealing on the curve, feel the earth trembling with a nervous and joyous expectancy. And now she was coming round the mountain as she had always come, impacted with all the mystery of the far off and unreal, of mountain, mesa and mushroom butte, the mournful beauty of the timeless river that kept its pace, and all the aching loneliness of the ancient and eternal earth it threaded; coming round the mountain with a last loud whistle from her quill echoing up the dark canyon like the scream of a cougar.

The locomotive snorted in, spitting steam. One of the little Mikado eight-wheelers, with a polished brass number plate, a big square head-light box, a straight stack spouting hot cinders, and a brass bell tinkling behind it. A squat tender. A mail-express car followed by a single coach.

Helen caught her breath. There were no fishing rods protruding from its bay windows, no childish faces glued to dirty panes. The proud red plush seats were empty; the car was dark. Where were the Spanish *paisanos* come from visiting *primos* forty miles upriver for the first time in their lives? An Indian sitting stiffly upright in his blanket, his enigmatic face turned a bilious green by the smoke, the jolting, and the dizzy fifteen miles an hour speed with which he was whirled around hairpin turns and over high trestles? The hunters standing in the vestibule with their rifles? No! There wasn't even a lady tourist and a city Anglo crowding the tiny observation platform in back.

It slid in slowly now. A locomotive and two cars. A ridiculously small train for all the noise and smoke it made, really. So ominously dark, so heartsickenly empty!

"Oh Jack!" She rose in disappointment as well as in welcome.

"You can't possibly expect her yet. Her letter didn't say when she was coming." The man's warm soothing voice lacked any trace of exasperation.

"It isn't that. It's—"

"But you knew the last passenger run was made a week ago."

"Yes, but to meet an empty train—"

The wheels screeched to a stop in front of the adobe squatting on the high bank of the Rio Grande, and the woman and man standing on the weeded siding before it. The warm, poignant smell of steam and coal smoke, cinders and clinkers—that cloying, irrepressible smell which for years had seeped into her tight adobe, her clothes closets and cooking pots, her very blood stream—choked Helen like a shawl. She threw it off to greet the crew.

The engineer was the first to climb down from the cab: a white-haired, portly Kewpie doll swaddled in starched, faded blue denim jumper and overalls, and wearing a red bandana around his throat.

"Uncle John!"

"Miss Chalmers, I do declare! Why, the minute we come round the bend and I seen the lamp in the window I knew you hadn't gone." Red-faced and grinning like a schoolboy, he shook hands formally, then permitted himself the paternal familiarity of patting her clumsily on the shoulder. "Howdy Jack."

"Did you hear that last whistle? It was just for you, Miss Chalmers. Strictly against regulations," added the scrawny fireman who had come up behind. Winter or summer, she had observed, Andy Hawkins was always wiping sweat from his narrow, bony forehead with a grimy blue rag.

"For that she'll probably give you a second piece of cake, Andy," said Turner.

The brakie's last name Helen could never remember. He always seemed to be hunting it for her with a lantern. She watched him amble up, a lanky, loose-jointed Tennessee hill-billy who as a boy had heard, miles away, his first train whistle, and had followed its echo ever since.

"Hello Bill."

"Howdy, Ma'am. Mighty nice to find you here, Ma'am. To pass by a dark station on our last run would of broke our hearts."

"And Mr. Jackson." She stuck out her hand toward the conductor, patiently, waiting for him to stow away his sheaf of onionskin orders in a worn leather case, and to remove his gold rimmed spectacles. You would have thought he carried in the pockets of his thin, black alpaca jacket all the operating responsibilities of the whole Denver and Rio Grande Railroad, to say nothing of this inconsequential branch Chile Line.

"Yes indeed, Miss Chalmers. The wrecking crews are behind us, tearing up the rails. It's a sad business."

"I've got a bite for you," she said resolutely. "It's on the table now. Come in, all of you."

The chocolate-mud adobe seemed dwarfed by the huge cotton-woods around it, the patches of alfalfa glimpsed across the swollen Rio Grande, and the blue Sangre de Cristos rising beyond.

"Ready, Maria? Let's go."

She walked through the tiny entrance room, turned left into the dining room, and pulled back the chairs from the table. In a moment they were all seated: herself at the head, Jack Turner at the foot, two members of the crew on each side.

"Miss Chalmers' posole," sniffed Uncle John bending down.

The Indian woman shuffled in with an earthenware platter of brown-crusted bread toasted with butter, garlic and grated cheese.

"Miss Chalmers' bread." The brakie took two chunks.

"And Miss Chalmers' chocolate cake to come, I hope," laughed Turner. "The three things that have made your reputation, Helen— and that have outlasted the Chile Line itself. Ponder that please."

"Indeed, indeed." Mr. Jackson glanced at his watch, a perpetual recurring gesture. "When was it you came, Miss Chalmers?"

"So many years ago!" She clapped her hands softly for Maria to bring in the meat and green chiles. How she loved the taste of the roasted green pods in late summer; their aroma in winter as she ground them into red powder; the sight of them each fall, scarlet neck-laces hung to dry from the rooftops up and down the whole valley! No wonder this little narrow-gauge which hauled them out to market had been nicknamed the Chile Line.

Uncle John wiped his hands on the red bandana knotted round his throat, and looked around the room. He did not have an eye to read the details of its beauty: the creamy adobe walls rubbed smooth with sheepskin, the fluid lines of the Indian corner fireplace, the tin reflectors behind the oil lamps. Only the effect of its gracious simplic-ity soothed him.

"By golly, you sure fixed the place up!" he declared with vehemence. "Takin' out that old counter and puttin' in a table or two makes it look real nice. You got yourself some new curtains, too!"

The memory of her early years came suddenly back to her. The appalling loneliness of an adobe lunchroom on a weedy siding of a remote baby-railroad line running from nowhere to nowhere. The strangely dressed Indians from the pueblo across river watching her with their dark inscrutable faces. The simple heart-rending fear of not making a dollar stretch to the next day. And the haunting fear of what she had left back East . . . Suddenly, unaccountably, a new premonition gripped her.

"What are you going to do now, Miss Chalmers?" the brakie asked forthrightly.

"She's going to stay right here," answered Turner calmly, "Chile Line or no Chile Line. Automobile tourists, picnickers, and visitors to the Frijoles ruins will keep her busy. I'm going to run a big ad in the paper that'll make Miss Chalmers' Tea Room known from Santa Fe to Antonito."

"I thought that little one-horse paper of yours was in worse shape than the Chile Line, Turner," said Uncle John somberly.

"It was, but it won't be long," he said sharply. "A rich Philadelphian has bought it and hired me to help spend his money on it."

"It's not that bad, Jack," Helen remonstrated. "You'll still be editor and can build it up as you've always wanted to. But anyway we're both going to get along fine. It's you we're worried about."

Uncle John opened his mouth in a wide yawn. "Time for me to retire. Albuquerque. A little house and chicken/ yard. Not too far for me and the Missus to keep an eye on you, Miss Chalmers."

"Andy and Bill are being reassigned to new runs in western Colorado," Mr. Jackson announced officially. "The System takes care of its employees."

"And you, Mr. Jackson?"

"I report back to Denver."

"Let me have the details on all of you. It's news, you know." Turner scribbled his notes on a piece of scratchpaper. "Tell me, Jackson, is it true the rails are being shipped to Burma? With war spreading—"

He was interrupted by a prolonged and impatient automobile horn sounding below at the narrow suspension bridge. A moment later the light of the car swung in upon the window. There sounded another impatient horning.

"Hey!" Turner shouted angrily.

"I'll go!" Helen walked to the door and opened it to a noisy pounding.

"This is Otowi Crossing, isn't it? Where's the sign?"

"What sign?"

"I was told there was a sign at the crossing pointing the road to the Los Alamos Ranch School For Boys."

The questioner was surveying the room over Helen's shoulder. He was in Army uniform, with shined boots, and wearing an eagle on his collar. She noticed that the two officers with him had stepped back respectfully in the dusk outside.

"There's never been a sign," she answered quietly, "but the road goes due west up the canyon. Keep to the right at the fork. The one to the left leads to the Frijoles cliff-dwellings."

"Thank you." He turned quickly and let his aides close the door behind him.

When Helen re-entered the dining room, Turner was still standing at the window, peering out between cupped hands. "A Colonel and a limousine Cadillac. What's the U. S. Army doing way up here in these Godforsaken mountains? Have the schoolboys up at Los Alamos revolted against learning Greek and Latin? Maybe I ought to run up there."

Everybody laughed. "The Colonel probably has a son up there," said Helen lightly. "It's a very exclusive and expensive school, you know."

An uneasy silence moved into the room. Uncle John gathered up from the cloth the last crumbs of his chocolate cake. Mr. Jackson glanced at his watch. The moment which she had dreaded had come. She stood up to meet it.

"It's time for you to go, boys. Let's say good-bye."

Each member of the crew said it in his awkward way, none quite believing it, as they moved to the door. Long ago she had first stood there to confirm the rumors of a woman at Otowi Crossing—a scrawny young woman with hair skinned back over her ears, scared as a rabbit, offering coffee, sandwiches and cake. In the lamplight now she seemed a different woman: full-formed and mature, with a gracious ease and quiet assurance. Yet strangely it was the younger woman they remembered and would always remember. It seemed impossible that they would never be back, that the very tracks they came on were being torn from the earth to which they were rooted.

Maria shuffled out from the kitchen in her high, white deerskin boots, offering a jocular escape.

"We're giving the land back to the Indians, Maria. Be sure and get your share." . . . "Good-by Maria! Take good care of Miss Chalmers" . . . "So long, Jack." . . .

They were gone . . . A whole era was gone. She stood in the doorway, watching the last sparks fly into the darkness from the blur of the receding train. There was a single last whistle—the voice of one of America's last baby railroads confiding its history to memory.

"That's that!" She felt Turner's arm around her, pulling her inside.

2.

A young Indian had come in the back door. He was standing in the kitchen, pigeon-toed in his muddy moccasins, wolfing the remains of the chocolate cake. When he finished, he ran his long, graceful fingers down his hair braids.

"Pretty good all time."

Maria shoved an empty bucket toward him from the sink.

"When you go to the well-house look at that rope, Luis," said Helen. "It's beginning to unravel."

"It good."

"No, it isn't good! It's liable to break and drop the bucket. Then you'll have to climb down a spruce pole and fish it out like you did the last time."

"I fix." Luis lit a candle and went out.

Maria continued washing dishes.

"I'll help wipe," offered Turner.

"No. Go in and smoke your pipe. Here." She poured him a cup of coffee. "We'll be through in a minute."

He went into the long room behind the kitchen, put some piñon on the fire, and settled down with his coffee. Helen had a knack of fixing up a room, he thought restfully. A Navajo rug or two on the bare floor, a Chimayo blanket flung on the bed, a few doodads set around, and the place somehow seemed home. Well, it had and it hadn't been for him, he thought, but he ought to be used to it by now. Why wasn't he? A little perturbed without knowing why, he rose and stood warming his back at the fire.

Luis came in, taking a package of Wheatstraws out of his Levis. Turner offered him tobacco and watched him deftly roll a cigarette.

"Did you splice that rope for Miss Chalmers?"

"I fix."

They smoked in silence. Then Luis asked quietly, "That train gone. She no come again?"

"No, Luis. War is coming to the world, and our train is going away to meet it."

"Miss Chalmer, she go too?"

"No, she's staying here."

"I take care of him same."

"I know you will, Luis. And so will I, same as always."

The Indian flipped the edge of his flimsy cotton blanket over his shoulder with what seemed a gesture of finality and stood staring out the window. Years ago, as a small boy, he had started doing chores for the incomprehensible white woman who had obtained permission to build this adobe at the Crossing on the edge of the Reservation. At periodic intervals he left to do his ceremonial duties, to plant and harvest his corn, to fish in the river or hunt in the mountains above. But eventually he showed up again with a wagonload of piñon and resumed his chores as if nothing had intervened. Only once had he explained his absence—the morning that he had brought a girl with him.

"My wife, this Maria. She do the dishes good."

Helen had shrugged a helpless and inevitable welcome. "What was I to do?" she had asked Jack later. "You know what they are—just plain fixtures!"

Fixtures she could never have done without, he thought now, watching Helen come in. What a strange woman, really! Dressed in a soft flowered print but wearing a pair of moccasins. A close-knit bundle of contradictions he had never tried to unravel.

Maria appeared in the doorway behind her. She had taken off her showy, clay-whitened boots and put on a pair of Luis' sloppy moccasins. A blue rebozo was wrapped about her head and shoulders. She was carrying a brown paper bag.

Luis turned around as if he had sensed her appearance without hearing her noiseless shuffle.

"Did you lock up, Maria?" asked Helen.

"No lock. You here," stated Luis flatly, looking at Turner with his black expressionless eyes.

If his remark carried an insinuation, neither the man nor the woman noticed nor resented it. "Tomorrow," said Helen, dropping into the big chair by the fireplace.

The couple vanished as quietly as if blotted out by night.

"Now what's the trouble?" asked Turner, sitting down crosslegged on the floor beside the big chair.

A tiny frown creased Helen's forehead as if the reason for her vague uneasiness was an enigmatic puzzle. "This terrible war that keeps spreading over the world like a horrible disease—"

"I know."

"And the Chile Line. It's the end of everything we know, and have lived with, and—"

"And you'll keep right on here just like Luis and Maria. Change doesn't come overnight, you know."

She jumped up, determined to unearth that secret, invisible root of premonition. From the mantel she took down a letter that had come two weeks ago and reread it to him aloud again. When he did not answer she exclaimed irritably, "Can't you understand what it means? A daughter coming whom I haven't seen since she was less than a year old! Why, she must be over twenty now! What does she look like? What does she think of me—a mother who abandoned her? What is she coming here for—if she ever does come!"

"Come, come, Helen," Turner said kindly, knocking out his pipe. "You're trying to work yourself up into a literary dilemma. There isn't any real problem. You walked out on your husband because he was a hopeless, shiftless drunk. His family was glad to grab and pamper the child. They never liked you anyway. All that was over twenty years ago. You've established your own life. The girl has grown up without you. Mark my words, Helen. There is no problem. She's just coming as a tourist on a short vacation."

"You think I have no feeling for my own daughter?"

He looked at her quizzically from a rugged, homely face that suddenly grew almost beautiful with a smile. "Not a bit or you wouldn't have stayed here for all these years! Now stop worrying. She'll show up eventually."

Helen folded the letter back into its worn envelope, and let her hands drop loosely into her lap. She looked so prim, like an old lady in a sentimental print dress, he thought, that he reached up and grasped her hands.

"Trouble, trouble. On the double. We've all got enough without imagining more. Well, you should have married me long ago."

"Oh, Jack! I'm forty years old!" she cried plaintively and illogically.

He reached up quietly and pulled her down upon him in a heap. The action was impelled by a loose and relaxed mood of tenderness and intimate comradeship. But the result was born, in an electrifying instant, from his first touch of her warm and pliant body. It always came like that to them, instantaneously and without warning. A quick surge of passion that enveloped them like a sheet of flame. He felt an odd flurry in the pit of his stomach, a tremor rippling up his legs and arms. Almost instantly it was gone, and he felt solidified by a strong but curiously patient desire.

The woman relaxed at once, stretching out across his lap, her face turned toward the darkness to escape the heat of the fireplace. He ran his hands lightly and possessively over her breasts. Without haste he bent down to kiss her opened lips, aware as if for the first time of the distinctive, intimate fragrance of her breath. For minutes they lay quietly together.

"And I just pressed my dress," she murmured without protest.

He got up, kicked the crumbling logs back into the fireplace, and threw the iron catches on both doors. When he turned back she was already in the bed, her clothes flung limply over an arm of the big chair.

He undressed and got in beside her. Neither of them was under the compulsion of nervous haste; they had been lovers for several years. She turned on her side to face him, and again he felt the miracle of holding so intimately close all the ripeness of her rich maturity.

"Listen to the leaves fall," she murmured haltingly. And then again, "The wind must be coming up."

The remarks meant nothing. They seemed to come not so much from her fading awareness of their factual location in space and time, but from a heightened consciousness of every sensory perception—the rasp of a brittle cottonwood leaf settling upon a flagstone outside, the faint odor of the pine slopes above, the flicker of the dying flames.

He was holding her now in a stronger, more demanding embrace that forced her breath in short gasps. It was she who broke the mounting tension with an uncontrollable surrender that was impelled not only by a natural and intense desire, but by the strange nervous tension she had suffered all day.

The man was dimly aware of this supplemental force to her passion. A quick moment of personal tenderness, of the considerate love he felt for her, halted his instant response. But with this imperative summons which could not be denied, he too plunged into the fulfillment of that desire which so long had cemented the intangible bond between them.

For minutes after consummation they still lay locked in arms before parting. Then she turned on her side away from him, drawing his hand across to her moist, limp breast. "Maybe this is the best moment of all—maybe," she murmured. "Don't go too soon, Jack."

It was the first time he felt her nervousness gone. He brushed back the damp hair from her forehead, kissed her lightly on the cheek. "Go to sleep now. I won't leave."

The wind was still up. The brittle cottonwood leaves were still rasping across the flagstones outside. The coals were still red . . .

Suddenly he was aware that daybreak was near, and that he must go. He got up quietly so as not to disturb her, dressing stealthily in the dark. But as he tiptoed across the room he heard her quiet voice. "Wait, Jack! You can't start out without a cup of coffee."

She jumped up, and ran into the kitchen to stir up the coals banked in the stove. Finding her old blue robe, he went out to join her. She was bent over the stove, her bare body full and pliant in the lamplight. His glance curved lightly and lovingly around it, then came suddenly to rest on the sun-browned, collar-like ring around her neck showing underneath her brown hair. With a shock he noticed the wrinkles for the first time. Like cuneiform characters of a language made suddenly comprehensible, they revealed to him the story of her lonely years. Abruptly he flung the robe about her, kissed the flesh-writing below her ear.

"The floor's cold. What did you do with your slippers? Don't you ever take care of yourself?"

She looked up and smiled. "Don't you want some bacon and eggs before that long ride, Jack?"

He shook his head, poured his coffee.

"Don't let that new publisher get you down," she said. "And if Emily does show up there first"—

"She will and I will. Leave it to me. Now jump back into bed."

He kissed her again and went out the door.

3.

Helen watched the lights of his car fade northward, then turned back to bed.

The coals still glowed. She stretched out relaxed and comfortable. But once again there returned to plague her all the interwoven ramifications of that vague uneasiness she could not long escape.

Day after day for years she had regulated her life by the whistle of the Chile Line. Now there was nothing to get up for, she realized suddenly. For a naturally active woman the prospect of indolence was frightening, to say nothing of her meager finances. The enforced alternative of relying upon casual picnickers and stray tourists was not encouraging. With war coming on, she might be forced to give up. After all these years? Unthinkable! Whatever happened, she had cast the die of her existence upon this remote New Mexican shore.

Why didn't she marry Turner after all? Why hadn't she long ago? She recalled his small, book-cluttered adobe on the outskirts of La Oreja, his perpetual struggle with a small country weekly whose dilapidated machinery kept putting him in debt for repairs. Yet now it wasn't because his house wasn't more than adequate, nor his income to keep them. Perhaps it was the town, she thought. La Oreja was essentially little different from all the other old towns throughout the Rio Grande valley which constituted the *tierra madre* to which she owed her allegiance. But for some reason or other, probably its scenery, perhaps its aristocratic heritage, La Oreja had drawn a colony of artists and pseudo-artists, escapists, and screw-pots that secretly offended her fastidious shyness.

"I'm just not comfortable up here, Jack," she had told him during one of her visits. "I feel I'd never really belong. These people just aren't real."

"They're just one small group of many. And people are people wherever you go. Why try to escape them?"

"I don't try to escape. I just want to be left alone."

He shrugged and dropped the subject. But just the same she was glad to get back to the lonely mouth of her remote canyon. And not until now had she questioned the craving for solitude that had become so fixed in her character.

Places, houses, people! What did they matter to a woman who loved a man? She flung over on one side, acutely conscious of the absence of his sturdy body beside her. With an intense physical ache, she could imaginatively reconstruct every curve and hollow of his body and how her own fitted them. That was what had happened the first time they slept together.

She remembered the picnic supper along the river they had had soon after their first meeting. They had built a fire on a narrow, sandy spit close to a clump of old cottonwoods. It was a warm night in early June. She remembered how palely silver the moon looked as it rose over the black rock wall, how tepid the river felt to her fingers when she knelt to splash him with water. He did not stir, not even to shake the water from his face. He kept grinning like a broad-shouldered, lazy boy.

At that instant the feeling swept over her that she could trust him as she had never trusted a man before in her life. "It's warm, Jack! Warm enough to go swimming!" Without hesitation she stripped off her blouse and pants and moccasins.

"Too shallow. You'll snag yourself on a rock," he answered without stirring.

She waded offshore to where the water rushed over her knees, then stretched out, head upstream, belly down, and let the river run ripplingly, caressingly, over her back. A river silvered by moonlight, thick as quicksilver, warm with June, and washing her with a strange contentment, a quickening and sweetening of life. She ducked her head as if in baptism, and when she raised it Turner lay stretched out beside her.

They had waded farther out then, hand in hand, to deeper, swifter water which carried them downstream. Still hand in hand, they walked back to stand drying their backs before the fire. The breeze felt chill, but it was not that which made her turn around and step within his embrace. She had no thought of his nakedness save for the comforting warmth and smoothness of his big chest and the strength of his arms around her. It was something within him, perhaps the solidity of his character and his essential goodness, to which her loneliness and aching for intimacy responded.

"I'm cold and hungry, and we're naked as jaybirds!" he shouted suddenly, releasing her.

She let out a peal of laughter. "Well, go get my clothes!"

When had she laughed like that—before or since?

So they had dressed and broiled their steaks on the coals, and sat talking while the white June light of the rising moon quenched the warm red flicker of the fire. She could not let him go!—and that night she had kept him with her. That miraculous sense of their utter unity, and even more mysterious, the feeling of her own physical completeness for the first time. How wonderful it was, even after all this time, that magic illusion which comes but once to every woman, which may be broken, betrayed or outgrown, but can never be forgotten in the depths where the spirit dwells.

Concomitant with the physical was the intimacy of their casual companionship. A simple woman, she detected in him a sharper mind than he liked to show. Practical, down-to-earth as the small-town newspaper publisher he was, he was without pretensions, sensitive to people, and ruthlessly honest. Yet at the same time he could be flagrantly idealistic as a hopeless daydreamer. It was this irrational streak in him which he seldom indulged that she liked best.

"Why haven't you gone to New York or California where you'd be appreciated?" she asked him once.

"Why didn't you become a Fred Harvey waitress? By now you'd be the hostess of El Alvarado's dining room!"

So she had come to accept him as a friend and a lover in a relationship that permitted a close intimacy while still preserving their separate independence. Yet it was a relationship that allowed her to escape her ultimate responsibility to him, and with it the annoying daily friction of constant companionship. A solitary woman by nature, Helen was not consciously aware of these deeper limits to their relationship. But she felt a lack, and knew now that through outward circumstance things might have to change. How? She was not selfish enough to marry him simply because her livelihood was threatened. Yet neither was she unselfish enough, nor aware enough of her deeper need, to enter marriage without misgivings.

So she continued to roll and toss in bed in an agony of indecision. The faint light of a car swung and held upon the west window. Jack! she thought instantly, jumping out of bed and rushing across the floor. Or Emily! But even as she peered out the window, the car rolled past. It was the big Cadillac with the Army colonel who had inquired the way up the canyon. She watched its headlights turn slowly upon the struts of the suspension bridge, then light up the big cottonwoods across river. A queer nocturnal visit! But her momentary conjectures were instantly replaced by the growing doubts of what she would have done or said if it had been Emily.

The whole problem of her daughter's impending arrival was upsetting. What was she coming for? How would she accept her own mother? What would she think of Jack? All these pent-up questions not only connected Helen's present and the impending future, but they dredged up events and issues she had submerged long ago.

It had never been a marriage, really. Merely a youthful infatuation with a Yale sweater, a coonskin coat, and a cardinal-red Marmon runabout. And then a bride's repugnance to bathtub gin and noisy dinner parties. All these combined in her one predominating memory of Gerald Chalmers: a tall, handsome young man stepping into his car with a bottle of gin protruding from the pocket of his coat. She could see herself, pregnant and sulking, watching him from the window.

The birth of Emily did not help matters. It intensified them. For now came "Pater" and "Mater" Chalmers. Pater signing checks and proudly harrumphing, "Boys will be boys!" Mater dominatingly spoiling the child, step by step, with a restraining pat on Helen's shoulder. "But Helen, darling, you're so inexperienced!"

It all happened with the smoothness of the inevitable. Gerald absent from home for days, then weeks at a time. Pater calling home from his brokerage office with patent excuses of out-of-town clients Gerald had to see. Mater insisting that Helen and Emily move into her own home.

"It's so huge, darling. A barn, really. Why, we have a whole separate apartment already prepared for you. A surprise! Now we'll just have Nurse take Baby, and you grab your hat. No! Don't embarrass us. After all, you're both Chalmers, too, especially Baby!"

Within a month after moving, Helen felt like a second maid. Mater dominated the household with an implacable sweetness. Nurse monopolized Baby. Pater and Gerald faded away into the nebulous remoteness of the brokerage office.

For a few weeks Helen sat with folded hands, staring in desperation at the specter of an impossible future. One afternoon she unfolded her hands, got up and put on her hat. It was a beaver toque lined with brown satin. As she walked through the hall, Mater called out from the living room where she was having tea. "Are you really going out, dear—this time of day?"

"To send a telegram," she replied tersely, slamming the door.

At the railroad station she sent her telegram. It was to her older sister, and it read simply, "Arriving tonight. Helen."

She never went back. Nor did she ever write, even when a divorce waiver finally reached her for signature.

Now, some twenty years later, it all came back with a vividness of feeling which she thought had been completely obliterated—as if anything truly felt could ever be erased from man's undying memory. No! Everything—past, present, future—could not heap itself upon her now, all at once! It wasn't fair! She flung over in bed and buried her face in the pillow. Unable to weep, she wearily dragged out of bed. Perhaps a hot bath would help. Putting on her old blue robe, Helen trudged out for an armful of kindling. By the time the water was hot, the first flush of sunrise colored the sky above the Sangre de Cristos.

Helen loved these early mornings when the world emerged with a pristine clarity and freshness that was ever new. She poured the hot water into a big wash basin set on the floor in front of the stove. Over a small cane chair drawn up beside it she draped a large yellow Turkish towel, laid out a bar of perfumed soap. Waiting for the water to cool off a bit, she stood staring out the window. The night wind had died. The huge cottonwoods, not yet stripped of leaves, puffed out like yellow balloons. Across the river winged a large black-and-white magpie screaming raucously. Listening intently, she imagined she heard the *cacique* at the pueblo yelling his morning announcements from the roof-top.

Leisurely she sipped a cup of coffee, disrobed, and sat down to her bath. Long ago these makeshift sponge baths had irked her. Every week she drove to town and indulged in the luxury of a tub in the scrubby hotel. But it became too much of a chore, and she had come to enjoy the peaceful procedure of scrubbing a leg and an arm at a time in her own big kitchen before Luis and Maria came.

The water was hot enough to turn her skin pink. The scented soap—one of her few extravagances—smelled rich and spicy. She stood up, wrapping herself in one of the huge towels Turner had given her for Christmas, and looked at herself in the tin-framed mirror with some assurance. The puffiness under her sleepless eyes was gone. A faint flush filled out her cheeks.

But as she patted her neck and breasts dry, her hand was suddenly arrested by a faint swelling in the hollow between her left breast and shoulder. Almost concurrently, so swift was her mindless reaction, she felt as if something had struck her in the pit of the stomach. The towel dropped to her feet. Petrified by a swift obsessing fear, she stood staring into the mirror. It gave back the image of her wide, horror-struck eyes, her half-opened mouth with its faintly trembling lips, her smooth paling cheeks. The woman saw nothing of these. Her stare was transfixed to that fatal spot on which was written the ineluctable dictate of a destiny beyond her comprehension.

She stumbled on trembling legs back to bed. Lying on her back, both hands protectively folded over her breast as if to hide it from a world of health and life, she gave in completely to its meaning.

This was what her body had been trying to tell her for days through a vague uneasiness and an inescapable premonition. Beside it nothing else mattered—the removal of the Chile Line, the coming of Emily, nothing! It was as if, in one instant, she had been moved to a plane upon which all the activities and values of life had no substance nor meaning at all.

In a new and terrible loneliness she cried soundlessly for the one link she treasured most. Jack! Oh, Jack! But now it was too late. Too late to drive to town and telephone him. Too late to give their life the deepest meaning of love.

She was aroused by a faint noise. An old Indian was standing outside, tossing pebbles against the pane: old Facundo, Luis' ceremonial "uncle" who had obtained the Council's permission for her to build her home on the edge of pueblo land, and who for years had tended her vegetable garden. In the wan light she could distinguish the red headband around his straggly, graying hair; his dark seamed face, carven by all the passion and the patience of the elements into the timeless visage of his race; the sharp steady stare of his fathomless black eyes. His look steadied her for an instant. She waved at him; he went on.

She lay back down again, staring fixedly at the spruce *vigas* overhead like a woman who had received a summons that could not remain unanswered.

4.

All that day and night she stayed in the shut up house, withdrawn from life. Then anaesthetized by fear, she rose at sunup, drank a cup of tea, and drove her battered old Ford to Espanola. Dr. Arnold's office was not yet open. She slumped down on the doorstep like a lump of clay.

Eventually he came walking toward her briskly, a little man squinting through bifocals, his thin black overcoat flapping above his worn-down heels. "Not under the weather on a day like this, Miss Chalmers? Well, come in."

He unlocked the door, opened a window, switched on the light. Once in his office, Helen was calm and resolute. Without hesitation she unbuttoned her blouse. "That's it there," she pointed. "I thought you'd better have a look."

Dr. Arnold was a little too old, and practicing in too small a country town, to keep his interest ahead of the great demands made upon him. But he had been reliable enough for years to sew up fiesta knife wounds, deliver babies against the threats and wails of native midwives in nearby villages, and cure all ordinary ills that resisted the effects of native herbs. Also he was honest enough, on difficult cases, to send his patients to specialists in Santa Fe or Albuquerque. All these courageous, commonplace ministrations paraded through Helen's mind as he began his examination.

"All right. Both arms over your head now. Let's see if there's any relative fixation of that left breast . . . Now, hands on hips . . ." He held her right hand, placed his left in her armpit. . . . Then he went behind her, placing his hands on her neck to examine the supraclavicular lymph node areas. "Any other members of your family have mammary carcinomas?"

She shrugged without answering and he continued his examination. Finally he straightened and wiped his glasses. "I don't believe there's anything to worry about, Miss Chalmers. I really don't. I've known several women to have similar swellings that disappeared in a short time. Let's give this one a few days."

Helen stared at him with a long, level look of almost indignant disbelief as she put on her blouse. How could she believe him against that secret intuitive self which had soundlessly foretold her fate with incontrovertible conviction?

Dr. Arnold had known her a long time. "Look here, Miss Chalmers," he said quietly. "You've had quite a scare. I can see that. But you're too sensible a woman to panic at a slightly swollen gland that'll probably go down in a few days. If it doesn't, go see a top man. Here." He scribbled out the name and address of a diagnostician specializing in carcinomas and thrust the paper into her pocket. "It could be a small, benign lesion of no significance whatever. But even if it does happen to be malignant there's nothing to be frightened about at this early stage. For goodness sake!"

Without a word, she put down a five-dollar bill on the table and walked out to her jalopy. It wouldn't start. Without annoyance or hurry she went to the garage for a new battery and a Spanish boy to install it. Sitting on the curb while he worked, she took out from her pocket the slip of paper Dr. Arnold had given her, stared at it a long time, then tore it up. It was almost noon when she reached home.

A strange feeling possessed her. It was as if she had gone a long, long distance away, and had been gone a long, long time. Only to come back and find that the calendar pages had not turned, and that everything appeared outwardly as before. The house . . . The ripples breaking against the sand bar . . . The raucous cries of the magpies, and the silent sweep of a hawk. Yet she seemed somehow disassociated from them. As if she had gone so far and stayed so long from the world she lived in that she was no longer attuned to its meanings.

Listlessly she sat down in a rocker by the window, and thumbed through a stack of newspapers and magazines that seemingly had accumulated during her long absence. Every newspaper screeched the war news in big, black heads. Blood and guts and whining steel. . . . She leafed through the slick-paper, fashionable magazines that came from New York. Their over-ripe, ultra-sophisticated advertisements whispered seductively to her with blasé clichés and aphrodisiacal suggestiveness of a worse death-in-life; whispered of diamond and sapphire pendants, matched furs, lace negligees, and creative headgear for the five o'clock hour . . . Still she sat rocking, unable to escape the mounting pressure of a frantic world being driven to a verge.

Nor could she escape the pressure of her own immediate worries and behind these, still more anxieties: guilt about the Chalmers she had forsaken, the betrayal of her love for Turner, worries about old friends ignored and forgotten till now, and the secret foibles of a youth and childhood she had long repressed. Everything she had done and said and neglected to do or say—her whole life pressed in upon her with an overwhelming conviction of its utter uselessness.

This was the meaning, she felt now, of that swelling over her breast. What did it matter whether it was a malignant growth or merely a swollen gland? It had thrown her life into true perspective. She did not fear death. It was that nullity of not being, of having never really been. That waste of time, of life, that horrible futility. It kept squeezing her. Her breasts ached from the pressure, her back and ribs hurt. She thought she'd choke.

Then suddenly it happened.

A cataclysmic explosion that burst asunder the shell of the world around her, revealing its inner reality with its brilliant flash. In its blinding brightness all mortal appearances dissolved into eternal meanings, great shimmering waves of pure feeling which had no other expression than this, and these were so closely entwined and harmonized they formed one indivisible unity. A selfhood that embraced her, the totality of the universe, and all space and all time in one immortal existence that had never had a beginning nor would ever have an end.

Her instantaneous perception of it was at once terrifying and ecstatic, for it was as if she had always known it and yet was comprehending it for the first time. Like a mote of earthly dust becalmed in the still, dead center of an actual explosion, she continued to sit there long after the blinding glare broke into gradations of color too infinite and subtle to define, and slowly faded and died. Within her now she could feel a strange fusion of body, mind and spirit into a new and integrated entity that seemed apart from the gross elements from which it sprang. Slowly she came to herself enough to realize that it all had happened within her.

Had she died? Suffered an epileptic seizure? A paralytic stroke? Gingerly she moved a hand, a foot. Sensations rushed back into her as into a vacuum. The hammering beat of a clock was deafening. She went into the kitchen and stopped it. A pan of cold tortillas sat on top of the stove; mechanically she broke off a piece. The taste evoked the whole shape, texture and life-cycle of the corn. It was that way with everything she saw and touched: it set off a chain of associations whose ramifications had no end.

Dazedly she wandered outside. The sun was setting in a glow that made her dizzy. Face down, she lay on the little bluff above the river only to feel herself merging into the earth. Like a piece of decomposed granite, whose every grain and particle was separate but which still maintained a curious entity, she sank through the porous, wet sand into the river. Now she knew how a drop of water felt when it dashed against a stone with a queer, cushioned shock and rubbery bounce. How it bubbled up on top; the fun of tossing on the surface; of being lifted up and riding in a cloud! There seemed nothing she did not know and feel—the slow pulse in a stone, the song of the river, the wisdom of the mountains. For the first time she glimpsed the complete pattern of the universe, and knew that everything within it, to a blade of grass, was significant and alive.

It was too much for her. She returned to the house and lay down on the couch without undressing. But she could not sleep for the joy that seemed now to bubble up within her and burst into a fountain at the top of her head, flooding every crack and cranny in the mortal body that held her. All her fears, worries and anxieties were gone. She felt freed of the past: not only from her personal, remembered life, but detached from that pattern of repetitive human passion which long before her time had begot at last her own faulty personal self. It was as if she had just been reborn with all the freshness, purity and innocence of one entering the world for the first time. But one so different—so wonderful and frightening, so joyous and overwhelming—she could hardly comprehend it. A world that was a complete and rounded moment in which she would never die. She was content to lie at its core, watching it revolve about her.

She was still lying there next morning when old Facundo came and tossed his gravel against the window pane. Helen was too engrossed to notice him. In a little while he came back; she saw him standing outside the window with a grave look of compassionate concern on his weathered face. She looked up, and something passed between them. It was as if all that she had experienced was absorbed, understood, and reflected back from the pupils of his dark eyes. Facundo knew. He knew!

"Sun good. Dark no good!"

Helen obeyed him and went out to sit on the ground. In a little while he brought her a cup of tea. It had too much sugar in it, but it gave her a surge of strength.

"*Vegetáble* gone. Berries come now. Pretty soon we catch them pine cones for fire, no?" The old Indian moved off, slowly raking the garden.

The sense of his presence, and of his complete awareness of the moment and all the things that composed it, brought her back to the familiar. She felt the warmth of the sunshine, caught the smell of pine needles, heard the wind in the cottonwoods. Facundo was right. There would be a bumper crop of juniper berries; the grosbeaks were moving in. A pair of blue herons stood motionless in the shallow lagoon at the curve of the river, reflected in the water . . . A huge pattern that kept spreading illimitably.

She was still not quite herself and kept wondering what had happened to her. It was something strange, indescribable and yet familiar; something that Facundo seemed to understand without being told.

5.

Early that morning after leaving Otowi Crossing, Turner drove home to La Oreja. It lay about fifty miles north, on a high wind-swept plateau that stretched almost unbroken from the deep gorge of the Rio Grande to the curving wall of the Sangre de Cristos. The horizontal plane of sage-gray desert structurally counterbalanced by the vertical mass of spruce-blue mountains rising abruptly into the turquoise sky, the constant subtle shifting of light and color, the miraculous clarity of the air—all these composed a landscape incomparably beautiful and justly famous. The only break in the vast expanse of sagebrush was a solitary mesa shaped into the crude semblance of a human ear. It was this that gave the name of La Oreja to the adobe town squatting at its foot.

For centuries it had kept attuned to the three races which now comprised its small population: the Indians who still lived in a prehistoric pueblo not far away, the preponderant Spanish villagers tilling their little corn *milpas,* and a thin scatter of newer Anglos who seemed to live on mere scenery. The town's last vestiges of almost Biblical serenity, however, were beginning to be erased by a long delayed commercialism. This Turner fought with his little weekly, *El Porvenir.* It dispensed the local news—its admitted function. Yet Turner was more concerned with the feature articles reflecting his interest in history and folklore. Printed in both English and Spanish, with fiesta-issue splurges into phonetic Tiwa Indian, its homely and yet poetic flavor was undeniable. *El Porvenir,* in short, was a country weekly for a retired journalist, a novelist, or a pseudo-literary effete to play with as a hobby. Its subscribers could not understand how Turner kept it alive year after year, and were sorry to learn that he now had agreed to sell it.

Everyone in town suspected the reason: Helen Chalmers. They knew he was sleeping with her and expected the affair to blow over any day. Both of them were too mature and set in their ways to be harnessed as a working team. Helen Chalmers had spent a couple of weekends with him in La Oreja, but hadn't come back. Obviously she didn't like the cozy familiarity of the town where everyone knew everyone else's business, the perpetual gossip, the squabbles, the cliques. Compared to bluff and out-going Turner, she was too withdrawn, too introverted. But Turner was hooked, really in love with her and dead set on marrying her, Hell or High Water.

He had never been married and his neighbors could not envision him as a house-broken husband; but his impasioned intensity of purpose impressed them with its maturity. They did not detect in it the same romantic streak that ran through his pursuit of Western Americana. Anyway he had sold *El Porvenir* to gain money and freedom to start a new life with Helen Chalmers. Where and when? The whole town awaited the outcome.

Eating breakfast on the plaza, Turner went directly to *El Porvenir*. It was housed in a dilapidated adobe divided into halves by a rickety wooden partition. The back shop, which he entered, was crammed with an old flat-bed press, Linotype, type cases, and a casting outfit. The floor was littered with last week's page and gallery proofs, the grimy walls hung with pin-up calendar girls. Turner went into the front office. It too was a hodge-podge of old furniture, files, and a broken glass case full of stationery supplies. His own battered roll-top desk was in back, set against the partition where he could hear the frequent breaking down of machinery in the back shop. Here in the early morning calm he settled down to lay out the week's issue.

A farewell editorial to the readers who had supported him claimed precedence over everything else. It had to be worded carefully, for Turner had not yet met the new owner, and *El Porvenir's* readers would have to draw their own conclusions about him when they read his biographical sketch. Pecking away at his typewriter, Turner tried to add up the facts into a presentable whole. But Cyril Throckmorton III didn't jell. Age forty-four, scion of the well-known and wealthy Throckmorton family of Philadelphia, Main Line, he had nothing that could be pinned on him except a Dun and Bradstreet rating. No high school graduation year, no college degree, no political positions, no jobs identified him. No hobbies to indicate a leaning to art, sports, wine, women, or song. My God! thought Turner, he couldn't be a vacuum. Or could he?

At eight o'clock the editor of the Spanish section came in and sat down primly at his desk up front. No one in town ever dreamed of addressing him other than Don Jorge. Small and impeccably dressed in a black serge suit with white facing on the vest, he seemed to have just stepped from the pages of Becquer. For years he had written birth and death notices, rosarios and requiem masses, with a Castillian flourish that made him locally famous; he was a fixture as old-fashioned and necessary as his own roll-top desk.

Jimmie came in, standing patiently at his desk until Turner's gaze climbed from his red socks to his tousled hair. Just graduated from high school, he served somewhat inadequately as reporter and more adequately as errand boy. "Hi, Mr. Turner!" he said blithely. "Can you loan me a dime for a cup of coffee?"

"There's a dime in the cash register. Be sure and leave an I.O.U. But before you go, listen. I've two assignments for you. Go to the library and get everything you can on Cyril Throckmorton I, II, and III. Where they came from and why. One of them must have rung the Liberty Bell or left his footprints on Plymouth Rock. What was his shoe size? Savvy? And get back here by four o'clock to meet your new publisher."

Jimmie grinned. "What's the other one? You said they was two."

"There were two," Turner answered patiently without looking up. "Your memory is improving, but not your grammar. Well, the second one I've mentioned before. For God's sake learn to spell—by this after-noon at four. If you misspell a branch on the Throckmorton tree, you're going to be hanged from it."

When Mrs. Weston came in, Turner put her to work on the morgue. "We're losing our Chile Line at last, Mrs. Weston. One of the most famous narrow-gauge lines in American railroading. I want to give it a fine obituary. Remember, up until a few years ago every person who came to La Oreja rode her to the junction and was hauled from there in Jenkin's stagecoach. And don't forget to add any amusing details."

Mrs. Weston's plain face lighted up with a smile. Quiet as a mouse, she kept books and posted subscriptions. But her main value lay in her extensive knowledge of people—not the Spanish people whom Don Jorge knew, nor the small elite group of artists and name-visitors, but the most important of all to any newspaper—the average, small-town, working people who comprised La Oreja's growing population.

By this time the boys in the back shop were yelling for copy, demanding mats and a dummy. Absorbed in the homely, trying duties of a job that to most men would have been too nerve-wracking and ill-paid, Turner forgot himself until almost four o'clock. Then, with a start, he came to. It was a momentous day and hour for *El Porvenir.* For promptly on the hour walked in the new publisher and his wife.

What first struck Turner was that the man strode in ahead of his wife. For a Philadelphia socialite, the incident seemed unusual. The second thing that caught Turner's attention as Cyril Throckmorton III entered the room was the extreme pallor of his face. Even through the moments when Turner got up and introduced the couple to the members of the staff in the front office, he was fascinated by that pallid skin. It was not that of a man who was or had been ill. Indeed, Throckmorton's small plumpish body showed him to be in the best of condition. The pallor of his face was like that of unpainted porcelain; it seemed to penetrate far into the fine-grained flesh; and to have been bred into him by a lifetime or even generations of indoor life. One could not imagine it ever momentarily infused with a flash of anger, embarrassment or excitement. For to balance the pallor of his complexion was the dead-pan expression of his fine, regular features. They were set like concrete in an immobile look of disinterested pleasantry; a perfect expression of the frigid, inhibited, Puritan inheritance of his controlled breeding.

Only in Throckmorton's delicate, long-fingered and nervous hands did Turner detect his unstable character. But the pleasant, aimless greetings to Don Jorge, Jimmie, and Mrs. Weston were over.

"Now come out and meet your boys in the back shop," said Turner, opening the door.

"Do I shake hands with these—employees?" asked Mrs. Throckmorton, a stout, toothy woman hiding under a large and elaborate hat.

"Certainly," answered Throckmorton. "Shake hands when you meet them. Once and never again. The same as house servants." He smiled at Turner.

The "boys" were all Spanish, likewise imbued with a tradition of courtesy, but embarrassed by their ink-stained hands. To cut short their fumbling and fustian welcomes, Turner paraded the new owners around the littered room, showing them the Linotype and flat-bed press.

"But a new press is on the way," announced Mrs. Throckmorton. "We ordered it in New York from the nicest person."

"What kind is it?" asked Turner.

"Ah, the best," said Throckmorton. "We must have the best for expansion of facilities."

"Yes, he was the nicest person!" added Mrs. Throckmorton. "A traveling representative of a well-known firm specializing in just such machinery. But very intelligent, really. He told us that a newspaper was the best outlet for releasing one's creative ability."

Turner was annoyed by Throckmorton's exhorbitant foolishness in buying a new press before he knew if one were needed, and shipping such a heavy item all the way from the East when a second-hand one could have been bought in Albuquerque or Denver. He began to wonder if Mrs. Throckmorton had been responsible.

"Why did you ever decide to buy a little paper way out here?" he asked.

"Precedent, Mr. Turner!" she answered quickly.

"Ahem! Precedent. Yes indeed," said Mr. Throckmorton.

"You see, Mr. Turner," she explained, "we have friends in Washington with eyes toward the future who are negotiating the purchase of an influential newspaper Out West. We shall share with them the great responsibility of dispensing proper news of world affairs and advising the people in this far frontier region where their best interests are. Our dear little weekly, small as it is, will give us an equal opportunity to expand our own interests."

"It is not a family habit to spend money for nothing. Not at all, sir!" said Throckmorton. "Is it, Josephine?"

"The odor in here is trying," she said quickly. "Besides, it's growing late and we all need a cocktail. You'll join us, of course, Mr. Turner, and stay for dinner?"

"Of course, of course," echoed Throckmorton.

The Throckmortons had taken a suite in the hotel, pending the purchase of a house suitable for their needs. Drinks and dinner were ordered served in their sitting room, which allowed them some privacy in which to get acquainted. When they arrived, Throckmorton excused himself to wash his hands again.

"His hands are so delicate and sensitive!" commented Mrs. Throckmorton. "I've seen him thread a needle instantly, after the maid had been struggling with it for half an hour. He loves to sew, you know." Downing her cocktail with a gulp and pouring herself another, she said abruptly, "Mr. Turner, you don't know what it means to be Mrs. Cyril Throckmorton III! The terrible, overwhelming responsibility. The feel of the world's eyes upon one—"

"You haven't been married long?"

"Two years. But the responsibility grows heavier each year. Why, the mere pensioning of the family's old butler was a task itself, to say nothing of selecting and shipping five van loads of furniture for our eventual use here. Two grand pianos. I love duets!"

"You have given up the house in Philadelphia?"

"Yes. Not the one in Washington. You see, we don't need too many houses, especially since we're establishing ourselves in a new milieu— the spacious freedom of the West!"

"Exactly!" Throckmorton entered the room and sat down stiffly in a corner chair.

"Cyril, I have been telling Mr. Turner we must all be friends as well as business associates in this tremendous undertaking."

"Precisely."

"A newspaper. A vehicle for self-expression and guidance of the people! Why, when I think of the power in our hands . . . The power we have to form public opinion . . . To make or break careers . . . The absolute power we have over everyone frightens me!"

Turner frowned. "A small, remote, weekly newspaper doesn't give anyone quite so much power as all that, Mrs. Throckmorton. People out West are pretty independent. And right here in La Oreja are three diverse groups—Anglo, Spanish and Indian—with different traditions and languages, and a good many cliques. We don't try to knock their heads together and force our opinions down their throats. *El Porvenir* simply gives them the news, from which they can make up their own minds."

"We don't want to change a thing! Do we, Cyril?"

"No indeed, no indeed," he assented.

Dinner was brought in at last. When they had finished, Throckmorton took out from his pocket two folded pieces of paper, handing them to Turner. "For this week's paper perhaps," he said stiffly.

"But you must sit down in this comfortable chair by the light to read it!" ordered Mrs. Throckmorton, rising. "I'll have the table cleared and coffee brought."

Turner unfolded the two sheets of paper. They were written in a tortuous penciled scrawl like that of a ten-year-old child. A poem, he decided. Bending closer, he read its title:

Thoughts While Treading the Trail That Kit Carson
Trod in Previous Days Long Gone By and other
Famous Pioneers.

A queer uneasiness gripped Turner.

"You like it, you think it will do?" asked Mrs. Throckmorton with a pitiless smile. "Cyril hasn't let me read it yet. He's given it to his editor first!"

Turner hesitated, then handed the poem to Mrs. Throckmorton without looking at the author. "It's obviously a quick, first draft that needs considerable editorial revision. Don't you think so?"

She skimmed through it rapidly. "A little polishing, of course, and I shall be glad to do it . . . Cyril! Your first published poem, under your own name, in the first issue of your own press! Mr. Turner, you don't realize how tremendous—tremendous," she repeated in her high nasal voice, "a thing like this is! It calls for a drink. A Napoleon brandy. Nothing else will do!"

As Turner reached out to take his small glass off the silver tray, he glanced at Throckmorton. His delicate hand was also outstretched; it was trembling slightly. But his pallid face was immobile save that his thin, unfriendly lips were pressed together in a short, straight line.

"Ahem! I instructed my lawyers to send your bank a draft for the sales price agreed upon."

"I was informed that it had been deposited to my account," answered Turner calmly. It was the greatest amount of money he had ever owned in his life; and deposited in an account that was always threadbare and often overdrawn, it had provoked considerable joshing at the small bank. He said abruptly, "According to the terms of the sale, I was to remain as editor until you could assume full management. But wouldn't you rather that I abdicate now?"

"Not at all, not at all," answered Throckmorton hastily.

"I only mentioned it because an editor has got to edit the paper. Everybody can't do it. Someone has to take the responsibility, and with it he has to have the authority. I'll stay on that condition."

"Of course, of course!" echoed Throckmorton.

Mrs. Throckmorton tucked back a few wisps of her frowsy hair. Her eyes shone with the glassy hardness of obsidian. "But you have no objections, I presume, to the publisher publishing his own views in his own paper?"

Turner braced himself against the prospect of an unending barrage of poems. "Certainly not. But all copy, whoever turns it in, should be edited thoroughly, don't you think?"

"We shall naturally cooperate in every manner possible to insure the success of our venture," she snapped, rising.

"Indeed, indeed!" Throckmorton stood up, rubbing his hands together.

Turner walked out into the chill fall night feeling he had met only the caricature rather than the living image of a man.

From *Part Two*

9.

She was aroused by a shrill, metallic squeaking outside. Peeking out the window, Helen saw that it came from an ungreased axle on Facundo's old box wagon approaching the narrow suspension bridge. By the time he had arrived at the door, she had hurriedly washed her face in cold well water and regained some measure of composure. Facundo seemed not to notice her wet hair and swollen eyes.

"Maria have that baby," he said casually. "Man-child. Big!"

"That's fine, Facundo. I'll go right over."

"Mebbe don't go," he said softly but positively. "She sleepin' all day. That the way it is." He looked quietly and unhurriedly at the cold, smoking fireplace and around the disordered room, then turned toward the door. "That noisy wheel. I grease him now. Then we go. Good day to get wood in the mountains!" He closed the door behind him.

"Why not?" she thought, dressing quickly in Levis and stout shoes, laying out mittens and a heavy coat. She was making some sandwiches when Facundo came in the kitchen door.

"Them cold sandwiches white peoples eat! No good! Fire and meat. They better in the mountains."

She found some chops, put bread and fruit in a paper sack, filled the coffee bag. Then they started up the canyon. The plodding broomtails in patched harness with ridiculous eye blinders. The springless Studebaker, with an axe bumping around in the empty wagon box. And Facundo and herself sitting on a plank seat covered with a tattered Navajo blanket against splinters.

The old Indian sat comfortably erect, the reins held loosely but without too much slack in his lap. There was a rent in the knee of his trousers, she noticed, and one ripped moccasin was held together with a greased string. Around his coarse graying hair he wore, Santo

Domingo style, a brilliant red silk rag. His dark, wrinkled face looked solid as weathered mahogany. He did not talk. Soon she forgot him.

They were plodding steadily uphill now, the horses keeping the traces taut, their breaths spurting out like smoke. The canyon wall to the left was sheer, black basalt. To the right rose a steep slope thickly forested with spruce and pine. Over them both the mist still hung, silver-gray, wispy and tenuous as a cobweb. Suddenly she felt its cooling dampness, and smelled the moist fragrance of sage and pine. Summer had been so hot and dry, with dust over everything and swarms of grasshoppers, that Helen now welcomed the mist as a promise of winter snow. It was so good on her face, so fresh to breathe!

But it was chilling too. Facundo unfolded his shoulder blanket; she moved closer to him so he could wrap it around both their shoulders. In this enclosed proximity she became aware of his peculiar, spicy, Indian smell, so different from the rather sweetish odor of her own race. It was strong but not disagreeable, and soon she did not notice it.

When the canyon widened out, Facundo turned to follow the faint, rutted track of wagon wheels. These rough, almost indistinguishable "wood roads," long used only by those going after firewood, crept through the whole area. Soon Facundo stopped in a clearing in the forest. He unhitched, unharnessed and hobbled the horses to graze. The yellow gramma or bunch grass was short and dry, but Helen knew it was nutritious; down below in years gone by it had nourished immense herds of buffalo, and stock could still keep fat on it all year if it were not overgrazed.

Without a word, Facundo took his axe into the woods with Helen at his heels. He was not idly gathering dry sticks for a picnic fire now. He wanted stout logs that would throw up a bulwark of heat against a long winter's night. Helen watched him select a high pine, dead but still sound, and measure its length with a sharp eye. Then he set to work. It was amazing how much strength his thin, aging body still held, as his axe bit into the trunk. Perhaps it was life-long skill, rather than strength, for he wasted no strokes. Each bite of his blade deepened the previous cut; the scarf was smooth as if cut into butter. With a last stroke he stepped back; the lofty pine crashed neatly into an opening in the brush where there was room for him to trim off its branches. And now, without pause, he began to cut the trunk into wagon-lengths. A strange feeling crept over Helen as she watched him. For how many generations had a woman followed her man here, watching him gathering their winter's wood?

She wandered deeper into the forest to fill gunnysacks with pine cones. How dark and cold it was under these great pines whose lofty tops soughed with the wind! Years of fallen needles had built up underfoot a soft and springy mat upon which lay the cones. Each one, it seemed to her, was the skeleton tree in miniature; and deep in the heart of its seed she was sure there must be another microscopic pattern of a future tree to complete, in a century perhaps, the ceaseless cycle. Occasionally she froze to watch a bird flutter to a nearby branch, fluffing its feathers with a sharp beak, its tiny black eyes shining like glass. How many there were, if she held still: grosbeaks, towhees, juncos, even a bluebird.

Back in the clearing she built a small fire at which she could stand, her coat spread out like a blanket to catch the heat. "These white people's fires," she remembered Facundo complaining once. "They so big, people stand far away and freeze. Little fire under the blanket, Indian way. It warm."

When he came, they cooked their chops, ate bread-and-butter sandwiches and fruit, and sat drinking coffee. The food gave Helen strength; with the hot black coffee she felt life rising within her. Trouble and weather were never so bad when you got out into them. It was always fun to be out here gathering one's own wood. Once she had been taken down a coal mine near Raton. Never thereafter could she abide the thought of burning coal; the very smell of it reminded her of those black, sweating bodies toiling underground like slaves.

Facundo was too busy to talk. The minute he finished lunch, he began sharpening his axe with a rusty file. Helen was content to sit watching the precise movements of his delicate, dark hands. Finally he stood up and smiled.

"Now I cut piñon! Burn good, smell good, too!"

"I'll help!" she offered cheerfully.

His face quieted; he nodded vaguely toward the flat top of the forested mesa behind her.

"Mebbe you climb up there, find something."

"A pueblo ruin, Facundo? Oh, why haven't you told me about it before!"

"Mebbe *pueblito*," he corrected her. "Mebbe some old houses, mebbe all gone." But he could not diminish her quick excitement.

"Yes! What's it called, Facundo?"

"Mebbe no name. Mebbe forgot. Mebbe not tell." As always he shut off her direct questioning. Nor would he point out its location and thus draw off its power. He merely nodded sideways at a rocky point, without looking at it. "Old spring by that rock. Mebbe you find trail close. Then walkin' easy."

She hurried off to the foot of the rocky point. A landslide had covered the spring, but she found where it oozed up through the brush and matted pine needles. The trail was too old to be clearly visible; with difficulty she traced its course up and across the steep slope. Soon she was above the pine tips; the canyon below, filled with mist, looked like a gray and turbulent sea. She kept climbing.

Near the top she could have let out a squeal of delight had she had a spare breath. To the right, a trail led up to the top of the mesa. Straight ahead she saw a wide, sandy passage overhung by the basaltic cap. And here at the fork she saw stuck in the rocks a weathered clump of prayersticks—the little feathered plumes, bound with colored yarn to a carved stick, that men had planted here for centuries when their hearts were right.

Without touching them, she hurried ahead on the sandy passage. There she saw it. A small group of cliff-houses clustered protectively under the overhanging ledge which had served as its roof. The front wall had fallen, its stones washing down the steep precipice. But the side walls still stood firm and smooth, like two outstretched arms holding between them the crumbling stone partitions of the tiny rooms. Inside, she dropped to her knees and let the ancient, talcum-like dust dribble through her fingers. As she had hoped, it contained a small piece of charcoal. It was then, suddenly, she felt her "radio" tuned in.

Years ago someone had asked her, "Why is it, Helen, that almost anyplace you go you can find sherds—edges, handles, all kinds of pieces of pottery? I go to the same place and hunt hours, and I can't even turn up an arrowhead!"

Helen had laughed a little self-consciously. "Why, I guess it's just my radio, or something like it in me, that seems to turn on. The farther I go in a certain direction, the more excited I get. Pretty soon I'm just so tingly all over I don't know where to turn or anything. Then I just stick out my hand—in a rock crevice, among a heap of stones, oh anyplace!—and whatever it is, it just seems to come right into my hand!"

That's the way it was now. A continually mounting excitement that led her like a radar beam to prod among the tumbled stone partitions, in the debris at the back of the ledge, and finally against the dark back wall. Feverishly now, conscious only of the excitement impelling her, Helen stuck her hand down into the choked mouth of a hollow in the floor.

It leapt to her fingers: a smooth round edge which carefully scooped out became the rim of a large perfectly formed bowl. Helen carried it out to the light with a sob of triumph hovering between laughter and tears. Brushed free of dirt, the bowl glowed reddish-brown in color, with a glazed black symbol of the plumed serpent moving in his sky-path around the rim, its smooth texture unblemished save for a thick blob of clay stuck to the rim. In this Helen now saw the clear imprint of a woman's thumb.

She was still standing on the ledge, tremblingly clutching her discovery, when she heard the faint, familiar honk of wild geese flying south. In a moment she could detect the undulating V sweeping toward her, high in the mist. Always she had believed the flocks followed the course of the river below. Now she knew that some of them used the plateau to mark their high road. That ancient Navawi'i woman, thumb pressing into the wet clay stuck to her cooking pot, must have watched their passage, too, as she prepared for winter.

A muffled report from Los Alamos sounded over the ridge. The wild geese swerved, dipped toward her. Helen could see the sharp point of the V, the two trailing lines separating into distinguishable projectiles of lightning speed. Instinctively she braced herself against the airway shock of their hurtling passage.

At that instant it happened again: the strange sensation as of a cataclysmic faulting of her body, a fissioning of her spirit, and with it the instantaneous fusion of everything about her into one undivided, living whole. In unbroken continuity the microscopic life-patterns in the seeds of fallen cones unfolded into great pines. Her fingers closed over the splotch of clay on the bowl in her arms just as the Navawi'i woman released her own, without their separation of centuries. She could feel the enduring mist cooling and moistening a thousand dry summers. The mountain peaks stood firm against time. Eternity flowed in the river below . . . And all this jelling of life and time into a composite *now* took place in that single instant when the wedge of wild geese hurtled past her—hurtled so swiftly that centuries of southward migrations, generations of flocks, were condensed into a single plumed serpent with its flat reptilian head outstretched, feet drawn back up, and a solitary body feather displaced by the wind, which seemed to be hanging immobile above her against the gray palimpsest of the sky.

Nothing, she knew, could ever alter this immemorial and rhythmic order. Not the mysterious explosions on the Hill, nor the ever-increasing mechanism and materialism of successive civilizations. This was the unchanging essence to which the life of mankind was ultimately pitched. With this reassuring conviction, the fierce proudness and humble richness of her life at Otowi Crossing rushed back at her with new significance and challenge. A woman and a cooking pot! They could defy time, bring civilization to heel!

As if a switch had been turned on again, life resumed its movement. The wild geese swept past. The wind soughed through the pines. Her heart took up its beat. But as it had before, the wonder and the mystery and the beauty remained.

When she reached the wagon, Facundo had filled it with wood and lashed the load fast with rope. What could she say? It was all in her shining eyes, in the vibratory aura about her, in the pot in her arms. Facundo stepped back as she held it forth. He was no longer a ragged old man out cutting wood on a cold Saturday. He seemed again a living receptacle into which had been ceremonially instilled the esoteric wisdom of a tribal entity, handed down from a remote past in which mankind had survived only through its direct intuition of the living powers of earth and sky.

"That got the power," he said quietly. "I no touch!"

No. He would neither touch the old bowl nor sit in contact with her all the way home. Helen shivered without a blanket on the plank beside him. She felt too happy, a little too lightheaded, to care. Nor did she mind lighting lamps and fires in the cold, dark adobe while Facundo unloaded his wagon. He showed up quietly with a solemn face at the kitchen door.

"Come in, Facundo! I'll have some supper ready in just a few minutes."

"I go."

"All right. But wait till I fix a little package of nice things for you to take to Maria."

"I wait," he answered patiently.

When the package was tied and stuffed into a brown paper bag, Helen turned around to see him steadily staring at her with a look of grave concern.

"That Luis. No come no more," he said without preamble. "Workin' on that new road. Get rich, he say."

The information struck Helen queerly. Not that Luis had gone to work on the new road being blacktopped between Espanola and the Hill; the high wages were drawing many Indians as well as Spanish men from all the valley. Nor that after all these years of service to her, he had left her without so much as a word. But that Facundo had waited all day to tell her. Why?

"Mebbe that Maria no come too. That baby mebbe make too much work here. Mebbe she go work up there too."

Why hadn't she suspected that long ago? Helen had heard that due to the shortage of help and the makeshift living quarters, almost every woman up on the Hill was working at something on the Project. Maids were at a premium. Every morning busloads of Indian women were transported from San Ildefonso and Santa Clara, and taken home again at night without cost. "A free ride for nothing, and lots of money besides!" Maria had grumbled, watching the crowded buses rumble over the bridge. And now she was going too. Helen had no doubt of it.

"You no got man to chop wood, get water. You no got woman to cook, carry them plates to people. You got nobody mebbe." Facundo's voice was flat and expressionless.

If she had received the dire news this morning, Helen knew she would have been completely stricken; it was a blow even now. Where could she ever get competent, loyal help now, at the modest wages she could afford? But she felt instilled with a new courage.

"No, I haven't," she answered forthrightly. "But I know I'll make it somehow. Just like long ago."

Facundo looked at her a long time, then stated in the same flat voice, "I come. Livin' in that little house mebbe."

"That old adobe out in back? Why, you'll freeze to death!"

"Get new door. Mebbe stove. Me fix!"

"Move here from the pueblo, Facundo? Won't Maria and Luis miss you? And—"

"They goin', I say."

It was all talk to gain time to catch her breath. For his suggestion had broken upon her immediately with the incontrovertible truth of something long written in invisible ink that she had suddenly learned to read.

"All right, Facundo. Tomorrow we'll talk about getting a little stove from Montgomery Ward. I'm going to buy you some new clothes, too. You must be neat and clean to help me with lots of people around. You won't mind that, Facundo?" she finished anxiously.

He smiled with a warmth that enveloped her wholly. "I goin' now."

Alone again, Helen felt reclaimed by a destiny that somehow always overpowered her. She dropped off to sleep without questioning it.

From *Part Three*

4.

The summer began to prove too much for her. The heat, the unrelenting task of feeding the X's [Los Alamos scientists] every night, her loss of weight, and the pain in her shoulder and arm—these worried her only as physical tribulations. It was simply that her nervous, slender body, like a candle, was burning with too intense a flame. Impulsively she closed the Tea Room for a week.

Turner had just returned. Helen insisted that he and Facundo take her on a camping trip. They didn't go too far, for they travelled behind Facundo's scrawny team in the old box wagon filled with equipment and supplies. But it was lovely, just as she had known it would be. A quiet spot downriver. A small valley threaded by a narrow stream rushing down from the mountains. The still, rapid, brown Rio Grande below. The cool, blue pine forest above.

The first night Helen slept in a little pup tent before a fire to keep away stray mosquitos. Turner slept silently outside in his bedroll. On the other side of the fire snored Facundo. The next night Helen moved outside with them so she could see the stars and the new moon shining over the pine tips.

"Facundo!" she protested almost as soon as she was settled. "Stop that awful snoring!"

The old Indian, tightly wrapped in his blanket as a tamale, went on snoring. Helen moved her bedroll to the other side of the fire near Turner. "I just can't stand the screech of that rusty buck-saw cutting through a pine knot," she said goodnaturedly. "Besides, it's scared away the rabbit."

Turner rolled over. "Rabbit? This time of night?"

"The rabbit standing on the new moon, I mean! Remember the decorative motif of the old Fred Harvey demitasse saucers? Emily says it came from the fifth sign of the Aztec calendar. She saw it in the Codex Borgia. So every new moon I always look for the rabbit and I never see one. What do you think's happened to it?"

"I don't think anything!" Turner zipped out of his bedroll and yanked it farther away. "All this crazy talk keeps me from sleeping more than Facundo's snoring!"

Turner's bark was worse than his bite; he was just trying to show his independence of her. He had come back looking a little older, with some new lines in his face and splotches of gray on his temples. He'd had a difficult time, she knew, since they had parted. But he had won through. He was so gentle, so kind; his whole manner showed not a touch of the bitterness that would have tinged the character of a lesser man. She was proud of him.

From then on they all slept apart, three spokes of a wheel evenly radiating from a glowing hub. Facundo kept busy all day long—cutting wood, trailing his hobbled horses, splicing their old harness with buckskin thongs, picking whiskers from his chin with a rusty pair of pliers. When he fished it was in the little stream above, in the cold still trout pool where the deer drank deep at dawn. Indian fashion: lying down on the bank above a still pool, and lowering into it a loop of fine horse-hair. Then, after an hour's wait perhaps, dexterously flipping up a snared trout. Only Facundo could have such patience.

Turner fished in the river below. A broad-shouldered dwarf cut off at the thighs by the brown flood; casting his Royal Coachman or Rio Grande Special, reeling his line back, casting again. His inexhaustible energy tired her to watch him.

With delicious abandon, Helen gave herself to every mood. Early mornings she climbed into the pine slopes hunting columbines and mariposa lilies. At high noon she bathed in a quiet pool, dried shiveringly on a flat rock. The afternoons were no good, really; they never were in New Mexico. The white, glaring light removed all color from the land; shapes were sharply outlined without perspective; everything went stale. Helen felt her mind and emotions go dead; life coagulated within her. There was nothing to do but give in to the sun. She stretched out naked, with closed eyes. Little by little now she could feel the radiant power penetrating and diffusing within her. Facundo was right. The Sun-Father was the noumenal source of all the earth's energy; nothing could exist without his invisible radiation. Day by day as her skin grew brown, she could feel the ache ebbing from her shoulder and arm, and a new strength and life rising within her. But the sun made her drowsy; she knew when she had enough, and crawled into the shade to sleep.

Late afternoon she awoke a different woman. It had been so good to be alone and lazy all day; now she wanted company and talk. One of the horses had broken its hobble. She helped Facundo to catch it. Then she went down to the river. Color had come back to the bold escarpment in glowing red and glossy black. The river was tawny silk. Turner, through fishing for the day, had stripped and was noisily splashing in the rapids. She slid down the bank just as he came wading out, ludicrously holding his right hand in front of his crotch.

"Jack Turner!" she accused him with laughing eyes. "I can't believe it! *You* ashamed of having *me* see you naked! Of all things!"

He laughed low and easily without self-consciousness as he pulled on his shorts. "Well, I'll tell you," he said. "When I was a kid and first started to go swimming with the boys from the pueblo, I noticed that when they came out of the water every blasted one of them held his hand in front of his penis. I thought it was the funniest thing I ever saw! Indian kids being shy and ashamed when we were out there all alone!" He paused to dry his mop of hair.

"Then one day when we all came romping out of the water, I saw an old fellow like Facundo sitting on the bank. Just as wrinkled and dark, maybe even older. Fact is, he was the *cacique.* He called me over. 'White boy better learn purty quick,' he said. 'Him cover up himself so Sun don't see. That power it come from Sun. Boy better learn not to brag of his power or Sun take it back!'" Turner grinned. "Funny how a kid picks up little things like that. I reckon I just got into the habit without noticin' it."

The quick warmth of a truth reaffirmed shot through her. "It's true! These Indians know!" She stopped and looked at him squarely. "We can talk about things now, can't we, about us?"

"Why sure, Helen. What's troubling you?" His clear eyes showed no hurt nor resentment.

"Nothing's troubling me. Something just popped into my mind I want to say. You remember that moonlight night when we first went swimming together—and went to bed together afterward for the first time, too? And how wonderful it was, the evening and the night and the next morning!" She knelt and slowly took off her shoes and stockings. When she stood up again her eyes were wet and shiny. "I just wanted you to know that having sex and going swimming were the best things we had together. Oh, we're here on this little earth of ours such a short time! Things happen, there's no planning, and the time flies and then we're gone. . . . That's what I mean!"

She stood quietly facing him, her hand resting lightly on his wet brown arm. "Someday I'll write you all I want to say. But promise me something now, will you?"

He nodded.

"That when I die, no matter what you think of me then, you'll remember that I didn't want to be different!"

"Hell, this talk of dying is morbid! Come on!"

It was over—this sudden gust of deathly seriousness that chilled both their hearts. She hitched up her skirt to the thighs and stepped into the river. "Oh, I want so much to go swimming, but I just don't feel up to it," she called plaintively. "Come on, I'll go wading with you instead. Is the current strong?"

He looked somberly at her thin, emaciated legs, then waded out and took her firmly by the hand. The water foamed around their legs, splashed back from a rock in a fine mist; the strong current sucked the sand from under their feet so fast Helen could hardly stand. Abruptly Turner picked her up and carried her back to the bank.

It had been so long since she had seen him! There was so much to talk about: Emily, Gaylord, Facundo, friends in town and at the pueblo, his work, where he had been and why. . . . The late afternoons were not long enough. Wound up like a clock after the day's restful aloneness, she talked while cooking Facundo's and Turner's hearty supper, and seldom ran down till they were in their bedrolls. How wonderful every day was! She had forgotten the Tea Room, the X's, the chores of everyday life, even the war. Even Facundo's persistent snoring echoed in sleep the inaudible and invincible pulse of the earth beneath her.

Early on the morning of the day they returned home, Helen took Turner on her walk. At the entrance to a narrow box canyon they came upon a growth of tiny wild mushrooms in a tangle of rotting logs. She knelt before them with a little cry of delight.

"Don't pick any," cautioned Turner. "They might be toadstools instead of mushrooms."

"There's no difference! It's just an old wives' belief that the edible ones are mushrooms and the poisonous ones are toadstools, and that mushrooms are converted into toadstools when a venomous snake breathes upon them. Almost all of them are good to eat—horse mushrooms, meadow mushrooms, all kinds." Helen picked one and held it up. "But if you ever see one with a little frill around the upper part of the stem—about here—and a bag at the bottom of the stem, look out! It's a Destroying Angel—the *Amanita Virosa*—the most poisonous mushroom known. But so beautiful! Tall and stately, with the satiny whiteness of absolute innocence."

"Amanita Virosa," muttered Turner. "The devil with them all! To me they're all putrid excrescences! Parasites living on other plants and

dead matter, manure! They're abnormal! They give me the creeps!"

His vehement abhorrence amazed Helen. She suddenly realized that he, as whole races of people throughout the world, was a mycophobe—one who instinctively feared these fungal growths. Helen herself was a mycophile who had always known and loved them, as had all Indian America. There was really something strange about them to have caused this great cleavage between peoples. So many of her rational Anglo neighbors hated them. Yet something about their naked, pale, curious shapes, their earthy smell and musty charred taste, made the Spanish folk and Indians about her ascribe to them an attribute of the mysterious, as had the Aztecs and Mayas long before them. "They got power," Facundo had told her once, but would say no more.

Whatever their strange properties, thought Helen as she walked along in silence, their shapes were repeated by tall rocky buttes and mesas everywhere. Soft sandstone stems eroded away from their hard basaltic caps and softly rounded mesa tops, they stood against the sky like huge mushrooms of bare rock, a primordial motif of this weird and ancient America.

Helen paused suddenly near the upper end of the canyon where the walls narrowed. Before her on the meadow was a large circle of mushrooms. Begun years ago when the spores of a fungus had started the growth of a spawn mycelium, it had spread outward year after year until it now embraced the width of the little valley.

"A Fairy Ring! Jack, look! Have you ever seen one this big before?"

Utterly charmed, Helen jumped into the magic circle and was skipping across the meadow when she was brought up sharply with repulsion and amazement. At the far edge of the ring stood the most monstrous mushroom she had ever seen. The fungus stood nearly two feet high, its cap more than a foot in diameter. Its coarse skin was turning a putrid yellow, splotched with brown; withered gills hung down from the underside of the cap. Bloated, aged, and repulsive, the thing gave Helen a feeling of such overwhelming malignancy that that she stood staring at it as if hypnotized.

Turner, a few steps behind her, let out a snort of disgust. He passed her in a flash, running toward it with measured strides. She saw him reach the edge of the clearing, all his weight and momentum thrust forward as he pivoted on his left leg like a football player about to make a drop kick. She saw his right leg go back, his heavy boot swing forward in an arc—and hang there as if fixed in a time whose movement had suddenly ceased.

"Don't Jack! Oh no!" she screamed, clenching both hands at her breast.

At that instant it happened. With all the minutely registered detail of a slow-motion camera, and in a preternatural silence, she saw the huge and ugly mushroom cap rise slowly in the air. Unfolding gently apart, its torn and crumpled blades opening like the gills of a fish, the fragmented pieces revolved as if in a slow boil revealing a glimpse of chlorine yellow, a splotch of brown and delicate pink. Deliberately it rose straight into the air above the walls of the canyon, its amorphous parts ballooning into a huge mass of porous gray. The stem below seemed to rise to rejoin it; then, shattered and splintered, it settled slowly back to earth.

Not until then, strangely enough, did Helen's sensory consciousness record the impact of Turner's boot tip when he had kicked it apart. She felt rather than heard the slight thud; the slushy rent of senile, decayed tissue; the sharp, suction-like plop when the cap was torn from its stem. The sudden disturbance, still in slow-motion, travelled toward her in a vibratory wave through the earth, shot up her legs and seemed to tap her sharply behind her knees.

When she straightened, the cancerous gray cap was still rising and expanding like a mushroom-shaped cloud in the sky. As she watched, an upper current of air pulled it slightly apart.

Now again she screamed. Crouching down in terror, she vainly covered her head with her arms against the rain of its malignant spores. Countless millions, billions of spores invisibly small as bacteria radiated down around her. They whitened the blades of grass, shrivelled the pine needles, contaminated the clear stream, sank into the earth. Nor was this the end of the destruction and death they spread. For this malignant downpour of spores was also a rain of venomous sperm which rooted itself in still living seed cells to distort and pervert their natural, inherent life forms. There was no escape, now nor ever, save by the miracle of a touch.

Abruptly she felt it upon her. It was Turner, lifting her to her feet.

"Helen! For God's sake! What's happened?"

It was over. The meadow, the far pines, the canyon walls and clear blue sky rushed back into focus. Time released the natural flow of movement. The chirp of a bird broke the preternatural silence.

Helen shuddered, wiping her damp face. "I—I don't know exactly what happened. It was just like a bad dream, a nightmare, that hit me suddenly for a few seconds. That's all. It's gone."

"Are you sure you're all right!"

"Quite, Jack. But just go off for a half-hour. Take a dip in the stream or something. I want to stretch out and relax."

He looked at her with a worried frown. "I don't want to be nosey, Helen. But I don't want to worry about you."

"Don't!" she said as lightly as she could, and with a smile. "There is nothing wrong with me. Really!"

No! Stretched out in the sun, feeling its radiant warmth and life, she kept telling herself there was nothing wrong with her, with mushrooms, the whole world.

EPILOGUE

He was an old, old man with a hairless brown head and a piercing stare. High in a New York skyscraper, he sat at a desk in an otherwise empty room whose door was lettered simply "M. Meru." The desk was bare save for a cheap household ledger labelled "Secret Journal."

For forty-three years he had been investigating psychic phenomena, and as an authority in his peculiar field he was consulted by large foundations, universities, the courts, theatrical agencies, doctors, psychiatrists, and an increasing number of persons compelled to learn of his existence.

"Most of the cases called to my attention are quickly detectable as conscious or unconscious deceptions—outright frauds, professional tricks, spurious age regressions, psychopathic disorders," he began in a gentle voice. "Those remaining take most of my time; they are of growing concern to a large number of my clients. The Throckmorton Endowment Fund, as you know, has supported some of my research. The time is coming when we shall have a National Institute of Parapsychology to take over what some people call my curious hobby. Telepathy, clairvoyance, fragmentary memories of prenatal existence, precognition—such things are no longer rare nor unusual. Even authenticated instances of the experience of creative totality commonly known as 'enlightenment' are occurring at an ever-increasing rate. It is a component of our nature derided and repressed so long, I suppose, that under the increasing stresses and strains of our materialistic age it is suddenly breaking forth . . . Or perhaps man is indeed reaching a new phase in his development."

He opened his folded, withered brown hands and gently tapped the household ledger before him.

"To get back to Helen Chalmers . . . Mr. Turner brought me her Secret Journal here; he was thinking of destroying it as the product of an unbalanced mind. I found it, on the contrary, to be the most complete and courageous record of a valid mystical experience in modern times ever called to my attention. I urged him to publish it. Mr. Turner was unable to comply with my request. How could he reverse his beliefs of a lifetime and admit that his view of Miss Chalmers had been wrong? No; we must understand these things, too. But he placed it in my care, with the understanding it would be published after my death."

Mr. Meru paused. "Mr. Turner also kindly persuaded Dr. Emily Chalmers to allow me to peruse her mother's notes on her *Inquiry* [Emily's anthropological treatise]. They complement the Journal in an extraordinary way, restating Helen Chalmers' own personal experience in the ritual terms of a primitive people. I was not surprised although I know nothing of the latter. Granting the universality of such an experience, it can be stated in any media of expression, ancient or modern. I was, however, unable to secure the Doctor's assent to make them public. For a woman so established in her field, she could hardly be blamed for refusing . . . No, one must accept both the static and dynamic points of view."

Mr. Meru's gentle voice broke off as he glanced at his watch. He pulled out a desk drawer, removed a little tin whistle and a bulky paper sack, and strolled to the open window. A thin whistle sounded, followed by a sudden whir of wings. In an instant the air was filled with pigeons fluttering around the grain he spread on the sill and flying inside to perch on his bald head and shoulders. A little man in blue serge enhaloed by white birds, Mr. Meru smiled quietly.

"Suppose that Helen Chalmers' Journal and her notes to her daughter's *Inquiry* are never released. Does it matter, really? Do they tell us anything more than the existing literature of many centuries? The myth of the Woman at Otowi Crossing, preposterous as it seems to many, is an ageless myth of deep import."

He erased his winged halo with a slight wave of his arm and sat down at the desk again. Reaching into a drawer once more, he brought out a thermos of hot tea, a cup, and a packet of brown wheat crackers. "My lunch time now. You and my inadequate teeth must permit me to dunk."

Chewing the end of a wet cracker, he went on. "In this day of over-rationalization we are inclined to disparage myths. We depend on science, which is a record of observable facts. We treat even theology as a body of historical facts which outweighs its essential metaphysical meaning. Yet myth expresses as no other medium the deepest truths of life. No one consciously creates a myth. It wells up spontaneously within us in the same involuntary processes which shape the mind, the foetus within the womb, the atomic structure of the elements. So it is with the myth of the Woman at Otowi Crossing. We ourselves created it—we of a new age, desperately crying for a new faith or merely a new form that will model old truths to useful purpose. Helen Chalmers affirms our mistrust of the neuter and negative materialism of our time. In the image of a warm and pulsing human being, she embodies the everlasting Beauty combating the Beast, the spirit versus the flesh, the conscience of man opposed to the will of man. Helen Chalmers is dead and will be forgotten, but the myth of the Woman at Otowi Crossing is woven of a texture impervious to time. We ourselves, each one of us in turn, simply tailor it anew for successive generations."

He opened the journal and pushed it across the desk. A stray pigeon flew in, lighting on his shoulder. Mr. Meru began feeding it crumbs from his cracker, some of them falling on the excerpt he had pointed out:

> *So all these scribbled pages, Jack, are to help you understand that an awakening or Emergence, as the Indians call it, is more than a single momentary experience. It requires a slow painful process of realization and orientation. Just like a newborn child, you get it all and instantaneously in the blinding flash of that first breakthrough —the shattering impact of light after darkness, of freedom after confinement. Then the rub comes. The learning how to live in this vast new world of awareness. The old rules of our cramped little world of appearances won't work. You have to learn the new ones. The hard way, too, because everything you've known takes on new dimensions and meanings. This process of awakening with new awareness, a new perspective on everything about you, of perceiving the "spherical geometry of the complete rounded moment" as Gaylord once called it—this is the wonderful experience I've been going through.*

> *How many thousands of obscure people like me all the world over are having the same experience*

right now? And for no apparent reason, like me. Keeping quiet about it, too, because they can't quite understand it at first or their friends might believe them mentally unbalanced. That's why some day you'll get this Dime-Store ledger. To reassure you it's a normal, natural experience that eventually comes to every one of us. So when your turn comes, Jack, don't be afraid. Be glad! It's our greatest experience, our mysterious voyage of discovery into the last unknown, man's only true adventure . . .

CHAPTER 13

Pumpkin Seed Point: Being Within the Hopi (1969)

With the support of the Charles Ulrick and Josephine Bay Foundation of New York, Waters embarked in 1959 on an unprecedented effort to bring Hopi thought, mythology, ritual, and history before the public. Literally "unprecedented," because the Hopis, isolated on their Arizona mesas, had up to that time held their beliefs almost absolutely secret. (Their ceremonies, for example, could not even be photographed.) Between 1959 and 1962, Waters spent a great deal of time with willing Hopi informants and his Hopi co-worker, Oswald White Bear Fredericks, making and transcribing tape recordings, researching the tribe's history, and putting together a cohesive account of their life and thought under the title *Book of the Hopi* (1963). To accomplish this, Waters had to navigate bitter factionalism and residue secrecy within the Hopi, occasional miscommunication with his co-worker, and academic opposition from orthodox anthropologists associated with his administering agency, the Southwest Museum of Los Angeles. The unity and depth of the final product, probably Waters's most widely distributed book, testify to its author's perseverance. *Pumpkin Seed Point* describes the inner dimensions of the years with the Hopi, revealing the sources of Waters's own commitment, and then extrapolates the tribe's story to the domain of universal humanity.

Foreword

Not long ago, after a lifelong association with American Indians, I spent the greater part of three years living among the Hopis in northern Arizona, the strangest, most secretive and obdurate tribe left in the United States. The purpose of my stay was to record from a number of wrinkled old spokesmen their traditional religious beliefs and instinctive perception of life processes which our rationally extroverted white observers still ignore to the impoverishment of our mechanistic-materialistic civilization. During this time I also made two trips down among the Tarahumaras in the Sierra Madre of Chihuahua, the most remote, primitive, and least-known tribe in Mexico.

The present book is a personal narrative of my inner and outer experiences in this subterranean world of Indian America. Its surface extent remains unchanged from ancient times—that vast motherland stretching southward from the mesas of New Mexico and Arizona through the plateaus of Mexico to the jungles of Yucatan, dotted by prehistoric ruins such as those of Chaco Canyon, Casas Grandes, majestic Teotihuacan, and the sublime Mayan pyramid-temple cities; and still populated by dozens of tribes once embraced within the Toltec-Aztec-Mayan complex. Over it now, since the Conquest, has spread the veneer of Spanish and Anglo-European dominance with its proud superstructures of rational thought. Underground it remains the same. An immense tract of indigenous people—of Tarahumaras hiding in the abysmal depths of their mighty barrancas and of Hopis isolating themselves on the island tips of their lofty desert mesas, in countless pueblos and Reservations on sunstruck plains and desolate deserts, and in barrios of impoverished people in the slum districts of all large cities—all still attuned to the instinctual and intuitional polarity of their primeval, uniquely American past.

Little wonder that we whites, with our desperate reliance upon surface physical reality, seldom perceive that in this Indian substream lies an America we have never known, yet embodying the truths of our own unconscious, the repressed elements of our darker, deeper selves. It was not enough for us here in the United States to almost exterminate the red race in our sweep across the continent. Its ghosts still walk the land, and in our unconscious the Indian is a potent symbol.

During my work, a number of strange things happened that revealed the hidden, obverse side of the picture. In the depths of the Indian soul there lie a mistrust and a hatred of whites unresolved by his expanding consciousness. Current government aid, tourist pampering, and false sentimentality reflect how heavy Indians lie on our conscience, but they also project on us the darker aspect of their own dual nature. Against the evil which we represent, they erect the bulwark of the exclusive divinity of their own literally believed myths whose transcendent meaning has never risen to conscious recognition. They are a people driven to secrecy and aloofness by their sense of inferiority as an impoverished minority, by a messianic compulsion that compensates for their loss of land and birthright.

So we find ourselves at this great verge, the red and the white, two brothers of a common humanity held apart by two opposite complementary principles which neither of us has reconciled.

It is so easy to generalize, to talk in terms of races and nations. But we cannot ignore the cracks in the volcanic floor of Mexico through which are re-emerging in art and architecture, music and social reforms, the Indian values of the ancient past. Yet reconciliation of the opposites, the assimilation of the contents of the unconscious into consciousness, cannot be achieved by the mass. The mass is made up of individuals and it is in the individual, both red and white, where the conflict must be resolved.

This book is an account of the conflict at close quarters, within myself and within my Hopi associates, and between us, on a level far below our surface covenants and quarrels. It is a rereading of old myths, old dreams in universal terms. Indeed, as I look back to those tortuous, lonely years spent beneath the craggy cliffs of Pumpkin Seed Point, it seems that we were re-enacting again those spiritual myth-dramas of ancient America whose meanings must some day be plain to us all.

1. The House at Pumpkin Seed Point

It was a long walk home to the little house just below Pumpkin Seed Point. The distance wasn't far, scarcely a half mile. What made it seem long was the cold and the snow, darkness and silence. The acrid cold ate like a corrosive through the woolen scarf wrapped around my ears. The snow covering the rutted dirt road was frozen hard. Every step squeaked shrilly in the silence. Under the gritty winter stars the earth spread out flat and bare, save for the jagged, rocky mesa jutting forth at Pumpkin Seed Point.

In the faint luminous starlight a small stone building emerged in empty space. The post office. Farther off, the white clapboard Mennonite mission church loomed up, a pale ghost shunned even on Sunday by all but a few converts. To its right squatted the low, sprawling trading post. It was an island in a sea of frozen mud covered with snow. A naked electric light bulb glared through its iron-barred windows, and there sounded the putt-putt-putt of the coughing gasoline engine that generated its juice. They were the only light and sound in this modern Hopi village of Kiakochomovi, which we know as New Oraibi.

Beyond and behind the trading post I trudged past most of the houses in town. Sturdy little buildings of stone hewn from the rocky mesas, a few plastered over with adobe. Others mere hovels set into the side of the hill rising below Pumpkin Seed Point. They all had been dark and lifeless since eight o'clock. Even the gaunt Indian dogs lay quiet and shivering in front of the doors barred against witches.

The hill was not high, but it was a problem in all weathers. During spring and summer rains it was slippery with thick mud. It was worse when covered with winter's snow and ice. Most of the time you abandoned your car at the bottom and walked up. There mine stood now, securely locked against stray Navajos, its windshield covered with ice.

Slipping and panting now, I reached the top of the hill. To the left, backed against the rocky slope of Pumpkin Seed Point, huddled a cluster of houses. In front of it to the right lay a huge pile of firewood that supplied many of the families. This was desert country and the great logs had been brought from mountains as far away as a hundred miles. Most of them were cedar or juniper, for cedar splits easily and burns fast. It is no good for fireplaces: it throws out too many sparks. But the Hopis couldn't afford fireplaces, and they conserved every splinter to burn in their cooking stoves. So all day long, every day, you would see men hacking away at these great, twisted tree trunks, and women and children patiently gathering up chips and splinters.

This hilltop was a focal point of life for more than the woodpile. It was also Crier's Point, for here the Village Crier stood to cry out important news and announcements. Somehow he always chose early morning for the chore. You were blasted out of bed by his guttural, singsong voice. Rushing to the window, you saw this devil's advocate, one foot propped up on the woodpile, shouting into space. Hopi is a voluble language; it took him five minutes or more to inform the waiting world of momentous news. What it had been this morning, paradoxically, was the announcement that the Independent of Gallup, New Mexico, was now starting to deliver newspapers to the Reservation for the first time. This step in progress, it is unnecessary to prophecy, would go unheeded. It was easier to listen to the Crier Chief.

How lonely it was to stand here in the freezing cold, seeing only the reflection of that one light and listening to that putt-putt below, the only light and sound. There wasn't much else to notice. Only the high spur of Third Mesa to the west, on which lay the original Old Oraibi. The oldest continually inhabited settlement in the United States, it was an archaeological ruin of falling walls still populated by less than a hundred people. Below it a dimly marked dirt road crawled south to Winslow, a hundred miles away, the closest town. Nobody took it. It was easier to cross the desert to the west, then drive south to Flagstaff, 125 miles away. Or to drive east, past Second and First Mesa, to Gallup, New Mexico, 130 miles away. How desolate and empty! The snowy sage-plain spread out as far as one could see. Here from a tiny hilltop on the high plateau of northern Arizona, here in the ancient, wilderness heartland of an America we have never known.

Man must have much of the wild animal in him yet. Or perhaps I am one who had slept out too much, and for too many years, to crawl into his lair without a look around. Nor can I enter a strange house for the first time without peeking out all windows to orient myself to the directions. So I stood here every night for a moment before going inside.

Perhaps for a look at the stars. Nowhere else do they glitter so nakedly bright, nor seem so intimately close to their faint reflection in the crystalline snow. There was the great, immortal pattern of Orion with Hotomkan, the highest star in his belt, sparkling clear. Above it the cluster of the Pleiades, which the Hopis call Choochhokam, the Harmonious Ones, the Stars That Cling Together. And below it Ponochona, the One Who Sucks From the Belly, the star that controls the lives of all beings in the animal kingdom. These and millions more in constellations and galactic clusters were spread lavishly as snow across the plain of the sky above.

White Bear and I were particularly interested in these stars, for their winter patterns and movements guided the timing of the sacred songs and rituals for the Hopi priests who watched them through the roof openings of their underground kivas. These great ceremonies were now in progress. At that very moment naked, painted men in a dozen kivas in nine mesa-top villages nearby were watching and praying to these stars for guidance. Tawdry villages they were, their crooked streets and cramped plazas littered with refuse and ordure. But villages still consecrated to their ancient faith. The thought somehow lent life to the darkness and silence, the desolate emptiness of the starlit landscape.

Our own people, our own white race, have long used these same stars to guide our physical selves across illimitable plains and seas. We are still using them in our first crude voyages into space. But few among us ever deign now to use them for guidance of our inner selves. We've proudly outgrown that nonsense, thank you. How sad! How dreary really to so stifle the whispers of our intuitive selves.

But then I, like many others, owe allegiance not to one race and people, but to two. One part of me is inherently attuned to that masculine, mental, Euro-American world whose monuments of rational materialism rise higher and higher every year. The other part of me is forever polarized to the feminine realm of instinct, the dark unconscious. Thus, every so often I find myself helplessly drawn back into still-living, ancient America; into the sub-world of continental Indian America; into the Hopi village of New Oraibi, immune, as it always has been, to change and progress.

My little house, its stone walls freshly plastered with adobe, was one of several in the group. Between the houses ran a zaguan, a narrow alley, to the lower rocky slope of Pumpkin Seed Point. Here, upright among great boulders, stood the decrepit wooden outhouses. Formerly here, as at all Hopi villages, a little ledge of rock was reserved for each family's use. Now with progress had come a rash of privies on the rocky slopes. The trail to these was deep with snow and it was unbroken. It was easier and more customary to dash outside and squat in the blue shadows of the house walls. The custom did not add to the imagined picturesqueness of the Hopi villages, so choked with refuse and human offal. But it drove home a jutting fact of life: that out of a garbage heap, a pile of manure, often grows the most beautiful flower. And this flower grown from Hopi poverty and dirt was the kachina, an art form unequalled anywhere else in the world; a flower of faith such as we have not been able to grow out of our antiseptic culture pot.

The kachina was a masked human figure, an anthropomorphic image of the spirit of life. There were as many kachinas as there were forms of life—vegetable, animal, man, and star. You could see them all, a hundred and more, during the Páchavu ceremony, when from all directions they came dancing into the plaza; each one differently masked in his own unearthly shape, each uttering his own strange cry. How strangely compelling and wonderful they were!

Where they all came from, God only knew. They seemed to come from distant stars, or to spring from myth and the earth itself. One of them manifested herself at high noon here on Pumpkin Seed Point before going to the plaza. She was Héhewúti, the Warrior Mother. On her black mask were painted two great yellow eyes with black pupils, and a rectangular mouth edged with red and showing her bared teeth. From it protruded her long red tongue. Her hair was done up in a whorl on one side and hung full length on the other. She wore a black loomed dress secured at the waist with a long fringed sash, over which was draped a black cape. Over her shoulder was hung a buckskin quiver full of arrows. In her left hand she carried a bow, in her right a rattle.

Héhewúti was a mythical figure who lived far to the south, maybe in Central or South America, in the mysterious red city of Palátkwapi. On the morning when it was attacked and destroyed by enemies, Héhewúti was putting up her hair. That is why her hair was done up on one side but still hung loose on the other. Immediately she threw on her clothes, which is why she still looks so untidy, and grabbed up her bow and quiver to help defend the city. Now on the day of Páchavu she stood on Pumpkin Seed Point, singing a song which echoed the cries of her people in their distress. The same song still sung by natives in Central America, according to some visiting missionaries. Whatever her meaning, Héhewúti, frightening, strange, and untidy, somehow expressed the feeling of Pumpkin Seed Point.

How damnable cold it was!

But the key to my little house was waiting under the stone beside the door, and the beam of a flashlight guided it into the lock.

The first spurt of the gaslight illuminated the room. In one corner was a small butane gas stove. From this ran a small pipe to a gaslight fixture mounted on the wall above the bed in the opposite corner. Its location was awkward. The light was not bright enough to work by at the table against the window. Nor was the kerosene lamp I brought with me when I moved in. So by necessity I worked at the table by daylight, and wrote up my notes in bed at night. There were two other pieces of furniture in the room: a dresser in the far dark corner and a spare chair.

There were two other smaller rooms in the house, both unlighted and unused, and closed off by blankets hung over the doorways to keep out the cold. The room at the far end contained an unmade bed, a sagging Montgomery-Ward's clothes closet, a jumbled disarray of boxes and suitcases, and a bag of golf clubs. "Pneumonia's Boudoir," the Professor called it when he came for a visit.

The room at the other end was just as dark and dreary. It contained an old iron cooking stove whose stovepipe was unconnected, and a table on which were set a bucket of water and a washbasin. On the floor beneath it was a white enamel chamber pot, as well as all the glass bottles and thermos jugs in which I brought water from the spring at Hotevilla, ten miles away.

Here in the cold darkness I washed hurriedly and came back to stand shivering for a moment beside the gas stove before jumping into bed. How pleasant it was to lie here, knees propped up, notebooks and cigarettes on the chair beside me, in this room which was my home over a period of nearly three years. What makes a room congenial is an intangible quality that cannot be planned for in advance. You can't prescribe its correct proportions, nor can you build in congeniality with interior decoration and furnishings.

Up in Taos, New Mexico, where my own home was, Indians and Mexicans achieved charm with simplicity. The clay-washed adobe walls were never laid with a plumb-line. The floors were of hard-beaten earth. A conical Indian fireplace was built into the corner, and the roof beams were great honey-smooth spruce logs interlaced with small, straight aspen poles.

The simplicity of this Hopi room lacked such elements of charm. The walls were bare and whitewashed. There were cracks between the floor boards. The roof beams were crooked, ill-matched, and white-washed too. One of them was a large knotted joint tapering off at both ends. It looked like a broken knee in a plaster cast. Over them were laced willow branches which supported a thick roof of mud to keep out rain and snow. There was no fireplace to give life to the room. And there were no pictures. Only a few kachina dolls hanging on the wall, and several clumps of small eagle feathers dangling from the ceiling. These were prayer-feathers or pahos made for me, each a prayer.

Still this bare little room gave forth an atmosphere of comfort and peace and contentment to which I was always glad to return after every absence. Despite its cozy atmosphere one always noticed its faint odor immediately upon entering. A rather acrid smell that permeated not only this house, but all the houses of every Hopi village, the earth itself.

The Professor when he came detected it at once. It bothered him because he could not ascertain what caused it. He decided it could not come from the water, for the springs on all three mesas were free of the smell. Perhaps, he conjectured, it came from the refuse and ordure that littered the ground. This I rejected. The faint odor of urine-soaked earth was Mexico's distinctive smell; every little village was permeated with it. Nor was this smell a typical Indian smell, for I had never noticed it in any of the other Indian pueblos in Arizona and New Mexico.

The Professor went away still perplexed, charging me to run down its cause. I have not yet been able to oblige him. For quite possibly this was uniquely Hopi, a tribal or racial odor that for nine centuries or more had charged every building, every village, the earth itself, with the olfactory vibration of their mysterious uniqueness. At any rate, it was not disagreeable and one soon accepted it with everything else Hopi—with the tranquility of this little house itself that nothing seemed to disturb.

It seemed strange to me, the night I first moved in, to be warned to lock the door at night.

"I don't mind the neighbors peeking in the windows. They'll soon get use to me," I answered. "Stray Navajos won't break in, either. They steal only what's left outside."

White Bear shook his head.

"You don't think any Hopis will object so much to what we're doing that they'll come to make a fuss, do you?"

White Bear shook his head more solemnly. "I have been warned to tell you that if you are in earnest, you will have a manifestation of some kind to prove your sincerity. That might frighten you. So lock the door."

It seemed odd to me then that a mere locked door would keep out either a witch or a good spirit if it chose to enter, but White Bear refused to say more. But that night, long after midnight, I was suddenly awakened by a noise that sounded like gravel being thrown against the window pane. I lay stiffly in bed until there sounded another loud splatter against the glass. Then I jumped up and flung open the door. No one, nothing was there. The hilltop, all the village, was dark and silent. There was only the reflection of that bare globe in the trading post and the putt-putt-putt of its coughing engine.

After that, nothing of the sort seemed strange at all. Other things occurred, over and over, inexplicable perhaps but not frightening. Even then, that first night, I somehow felt that here I was confronting what might be an added dimension to the life we normally lead in our highly mental and materialistic civilization so far removed in time and space from this still-living, ancient, heartland of a dwindling remnant of another race. I do not mean to imply that the Hopis had a monopoly on witches and spirits; our overcrowded mental institutions attest to the invisible forces that plague us also. Rather that their beneficent and inimical images assumed different forms, for they all are created alike by our own minds to manifest our secret fears and desires.

So I lay here in bed, knees up, scrawling in a stenographer's notebook with a blunt copy pencil my nightly notes. If they seemed to accentuate the differences between the Hopis and us, it is only because we are two sides of the same coin. I kept reminding myself that it was a room in New York which launched me to this room in New Oraibi.

I recalled it vividly and pleasantly. It was in the Wall Street skyscraper that housed the New York Stock Exchange. Nowhere in the world save on the lower tip of Manhattan Island—not even in postcard Arizona—rises such a fantastic growth of lofty buttes, dizzy stone pillars, and needlepoint crags from a maze of dark canyons and sunless gorges swarming with toiling ants. This directors' room on the eighteenth floor seemed comfortably isolated from all signs of labor. You could, if you wished, be quickly conducted to the Pit for a peep at the saturnalia of shouting men and streamers of ticker tape that controlled the national industry, international trade, and the price of a bag of flour in the trading post at New Oraibi. But it was more pleasant to sit on the long couch in front of the massive directors' table and look at the view.

There were two views in the room.

The magnificent wallpaper gave a nostalgic view of sailing ships docking at the wharves below, long before other white-sheeted schooners rolled westward over the pelagic plain to find the remote and isolated Hopis obstructing the course of empire. The window gave a contemporary view of the same scene: the great liner Queen Mary being tugged upriver to her dock.

These two views were separated in space only by the width of a window frame, but in time by a century and a half. During that long span the rolling sweep of conquest had caught up with the Hopis, engulfing them in riptides of military domination, government control, and racial discrimination. Then it had spewed them out again—a rejected handful of people clinging to nine crumbling villages on the high summits of three mesas a hundred miles or more from the nearest transcontinental highway.

There were several persons in the room, all dominated by a single woman wearing a long mink coat and sitting in the director's seat at the table. "The First Lady of Wall Street," as reporters often called her, was middle-aged, with a commanding presence and sharp eyes; a woman of considerable importance whose business acumen was respected in many fields. Yet this only threw into sharper relief the kindness and understanding that infused her whole personality.

The spokesman of the group was a tall, lanky man who knew what he was talking about. He put it briefly. The group wanted to help the Hopis. Not by making an academic study of them and their present difficulties—neither an ethnological or economic report, nor a sociological or psychological paper, to be filed away in museums and libraries—but by persuading them to relate freely, for the first time, the complete history and religious beliefs of their people. This, it was hoped, would provide both a basis for understanding their current problems and a permanent record of their traditions for their children and their children's children.

"We ourselves desire to remain anonymous, although charitable funds made possible by this Foundation will provide financial support for the effort," he concluded. "Does this summarize our discussion and correctly state our position?" he asked the other directors.

It was that fabulous, that simple, really. A manifestation of national conscience in a Wall Street brokerage office? An Angel with a seat on the New York Stock Exchange unfolding wings over the forgotten Hopis?

The project appealed to me from the start. All my life I had known Indians and had written much about them, and I felt I now owed them some constructive help in return for all they had given me. Perhaps this was merely a rational excuse for doing still another book on those neglected people who, despite my efforts to break away from the mold of their thought, had always drawn me back with an incomprehensible fascination. This was an unusual challenge. It involved obtaining from the Hopis, secretive as they were, their complete Creation myth, the legends of their prehistoric migrations over this continent, the esoteric meanings of their religious ceremonies, and their own view of historical events since the coming of the white man—the first full record, to my knowledge, of an Indian tribe from its own uncontested viewpoint.

As my work progressed, it kept throwing into focus many incompletely realized things I had felt about other Indians. The Hopis, unique as they were, seemed to be speaking not only for their race but for all primitive peoples who still preserved the ancestral myths and archetypal images which linked them with the nurturing unconscious. At the same time, it kept throwing into new perspective a strange Euro-America perversely strangling itself with its excessive rationality and materialism, the specter of modern civilization.

Yet, enriching as this was, I found myself ever so often rebelling against the Hopis' obdurate aloofness, their needless squalor, lack of initiative, and illogical prejudices—everything that characterized them as Indian. An overpowering compulsion urged me to get away for awhile. There is always a great danger in developing too great an empathy with a primitive people. For consciousness evolves out of the unconscious just as the physical body evolves from primeval anatomical forms; and despite the exhortations of D. H. Lawrence and his cult, we can't go back.

But we whites, I felt, were succumbing to the greater danger of closing off, with the rationalizations of our limited conscious minds, the images and urges of the boundless unconscious which fed life itself. So again I returned to New Oraibi to feel the Hopis' archaic closeness to the wonder and the mystery and the sense of wholeness that stemmed from it.

This polarity of opposite dualities I found was the basic difference between Indian America and Euro-America, between the Hopis and ourselves. It was also the schism that divided each one of us internally. I discovered that every Hopi in some measure, like myself, was two persons: an outer man consciously confronted with the problems of existence in a swiftly changing, material world; and an inner man attuned to the greater realm of the unconscious, the matrix of all creation.

Over and over again, as my work developed surface differences between the United States and the Hopi Empire, as this staunchly independent little tribe pathetically called itself, I saw the same differences reflected on a vaster scale by rival world powers. These differences would not be reconciled on the expedient level of politics, economics, and the threat of war. They could only be resolved by tearing down the Iron Curtain that divided our inner selves.

So here at Pumpkin Seed Point I lay in bed after work each night scribbling notes about the two peoples who objectified the conflicting forces of my own nature and illumined my quest of self-discovery. Personal notes and anecdotes about the Hopis who projected their fears and prejudices on the whites who for so long have projected their own fears and prejudices on all Indians. Two invisible projections clashing in the air. Which one had thrown gravel against my window pane? Perhaps, after all, I had better get up and throw the catch on the door.

4. *The Plaza*

The longer I stayed in New Oraibi the more restless and uninte-grated it seemed. I could not at first quite understand why; it is always the obvious that escapes notice.

The post office, isolated in a patch of sand, was always compara-tively deserted. One waited through the morning until the mail truck rumbled in from Winslow, then walked down for the day's mail, a nec-essary chore accomplished as quickly as possible. The lawn of the gov-ernment school, so inviting on hot afternoons, was always just as deserted. Nor did people stand gossiping outside the church on Sunday mornings.

In one sense, the trading post seemed to be the focal point of town. A gasoline pump stood in front of it, and the town's only available tele-phone was mounted on a shelf on the outside wall. Here, freezing in winter cold or standing unprotected in pouring rain, one jiggled the hook for an hour before the operator in Holbrook answered. There was no one to answer an incoming call. The trading post had been a famous one years ago when it was operated by the beloved Lorenzo Hubbell. Then it had been bought by a large mercantile company which operated it as one of many. During recent years it had been run by a succession of managers, none of whom had been liked by the Hopis. They claimed, for one thing, that the prices were far too high. For another, they insisted that the post showed preference to the many Navajos who drove in from the desert with turquoise and silver jewelry to pawn. Whatever the reasons for their dislike of the post, the Hopis, though obliged to trade in it, never lingered around it. Like the post office, school, and church, it was a utility building that served its purpose and nothing more.

As a government town, New Oraibi boasted a community hall. Standing just below Pumpkin Seed Point, it was a long, low cellar whose walls and roof protruded above ground just high enough to let light in through the windows. What it was used for I could not imagine until I was awakened one morning by the Village Crier announcing a public meeting there of the Tribal Council at nine o'clock.

Watching out the window of my house, I could see a few people beginning to arrive at ten o'clock. By eleven there was a sizable group standing outside. At noon I walked down to join some fifty people who were finally let inside. A hearty lunch had been prepared by women of the village, and when it was silently eaten the meeting began.

At a table up front sat the agent from Keams Canyon, a thin, sallow, sick man courageously enduring his tenure of government office until time for retirement; the tribal lawyer, an affluent Mormon from Utah; and the Tribal Council, comprised of representatives from all the villages except Hotevilla. The Tribal Council was sponsored by the government as a Hopi self-governing body entrusted with the management of all secular affairs. It and its supporters comprised the faction of Americanized Hopis known in Yukioma's time as the Friendlies. As such it was opposed by the Traditionalists who insisted on the right to govern their own affairs through the Village Chief. Hence the Traditional stronghold of Hotevilla refused to name a representative to the Tribal Council and to be bound by its decisions. It regarded the Council, as did many Hopis, as a concept of foreign white democracy, not representative of all the people, and without real authority as it was merely a puppet government controlled by the agency at Keams Canyon.

Talk got under way on several issues confronting all Hopis.

The Hopi Reservation comprised about 4,000 square miles located in the middle of the immense Navajo Reservation of nearly 25,000 square miles. The government had established it some eighty years ago with the solemn promise to protect it from Navajo encroachment. Yet now the swiftly growing tribe of 80,000 Navajos had so encroached on Hopi land that the 5,000 Hopis were confined to less than a fourth of their own Reservation. Hence a Hopi suit against the Navajo tribe was being drawn up. The outcome of the case would rest on proof that the Hopis owned and occupied the land prior to the coming of the Navajos. This occupancy could easily be proved, it was believed, by the existence of ancient ruins, rock writings, and secret shrines established long before the Navajos had migrated into the Southwest. Help was needed, for only the Hopi Traditionalists knew their locations and meanings.

The Traditionalists, however, stubbornly refused to impart the information. "Why hasn't the government kept the Navajos out as it promised? Why doesn't it now?" they asked.

Moreover, they opposed filing such a suit. The land had been given to the Hopis by their spiritual guardian long before the arrival of either the Navajos or the white man. They would never assent to having a white man's court decide whether their land belonged to them. As a matter of fact, they already had written to the Navajo Tribal Council saying that they would never authorize or recognize such a suit.

The subject was tabled for future discussion.

Another matter came up. An electric company had requested a

franchise to build a line into the Reservation. Should the right-of-way be granted? There was a long, dreary silence. The Tribal Council members looked at each other's simple, puzzled faces in despair.

"Our land is not for leasing or for sale," a voice from the audience reminded them. "This is our sacred soil."

The agent rapped on the table with his gavel; the interjection was obviously out of order. The franchise was granted.

Approval was now requested of a new hospital being built by the Public Health Service at the Hopi agency headquarters, Keams Canyon, thirty miles east. The hospital had long been a contentious subject among Hopis. Why was it being built so far away from all Hopi villages? The answer was obvious: to accommodate encroaching Navajos who would admittedly fill ninety percent of its beds. Approval was duly voted.

The meeting dragged on, so boring that most of the few people in the audience got up and left. What could they do about the confused welter of secular affairs? They did not gather outside to discuss the issues, nor to gossip.

No, the community hall was not a community center. Nor was New Oraibi a Hopi village. It had no Village Chief; simply a governor elected by the Tribal Council. New Oraibi was merely a government town, a straggle of utility buildings without tradition, without meaning. There was no place to loaf, to gossip, to enjoy life. It had no center, no plaza. This, I finally realized, was what was wrong with New Oraibi.

Life on this continent from earliest times has revolved about a central plaza. The ruins of almost every prehistoric pueblo show it to have been a walled city or great terraced apartment house built around an inner court or plaza. Often rising five stories high and containing as many as 800 rooms, they were immense communal dwelling places, great fortresses breasting the solitude of earth and sky. There were few doors and windows. The entrance to each family's quarters was an opening cut in the roof. To reach it the people climbed up an outside

ladder which they could pull up after them in case of attack by
marauding tribes of nomads.

Defensively practical as the shapes of these great pueblos were, they
also reflected the people's primary concern with the inner values of
their lives. They were great mandalas. A mandala, the Sanskrit word
for circle, is a geometrical design expressive of the unity and wholeness
of all Creation, a design which produces an effect upon its maker. Its
basic form is that of a four-petalled lotus with infinite variations in the
shape of a cross, a square, or a circle divided by four, but always with
four as the basis of the structure. Mandalas have been found everywhere, in all ages. Christian mandalas show Christ in the center, with
the four evangelists at the cardinal points, as in Egypt where Horus
was represented in the same way with his four sons. Jung considered
the mandalas of Tibetan Buddhism the most beautiful, and those
found in the sandpaintings of the Pueblo Indians notable examples.
The Hopi concept of a four-world universe, each world designated by
a directional color, is itself a symbol of the soul-form of all Creation—
a mandala. The superlative sandpaintings of the Navajos are undoubtedly the finest examples today. Made of natural colored sands
sprinkled on the floor of a medicine hogan, they are an essential part
of every healing ceremony. The patient is seated upon them, and at the
conclusion of the songs, prayers, and rituals the medicine man sprinkles
the sand upon him.

The ancient pueblos, whose terraced walls enclosed an inner court
with circular or rectangular kivas in the center, were in effect great
structural mandalas; and the subterranean kivas themselves—so dia-
metrically opposite to the Christian church with its phallic spire—
further symbolized the depths of the unconscious which held its
meaning. The plaza, then, was the center of the people's outward
communal life and the focus of their religious thought and ceremonies.

The contemporary Hopi villages—small, one-story, and tawdry as
they were—deviated little from this ancient pattern. Each genuine

Hopi village enclosed a quadrangular inner court or plaza, the kisonvi or "center of the village," dominated by one or more kivas. The kiva, like the kisonvi, was rectangular in shape, both repeating the four-world universe, the four-square pattern of psychic wholeness. There was never any doubt as to the supreme significance of this mandala form. During the Niman Kachina ceremony when the kachinas emerged from the underground kiva into the open kisonvi, their dance was patterned and their song was built on its four-square shape, urging man to conform his life to this sacred pattern too.

The withdrawal of [Hopi elder] Old Dan's support had worked to our advantage. White Bear and I were forced out to all the villages where we found other spokesmen, all well informed, loyal, and eager to contribute to our effort. Winter and summer, day or night, we attended nearly every ceremony in every village, learning how every aspect of village life—family, communal, and religious—centered in the plaza.

We went often to Shongopovi. It was the largest village on Second Mesa and its ceremonies were the most colorful. The village had two plazas and looked out over the vast expanse of desert to the snow-capped mountains nearly a hundred miles southwest. Earl and Evelyn and their children always made us welcome. They lived in one large room opposite one of the kivas. The door was usually left open and we could see and hear everything that went on: the old men squatting against sunny walls, the constant parade of naked children, the circuits of kachinas, women shouting or gossiping from their own doorways, the braying of a burro. This was what New Oraibi lacked—life springing from a center.

Earl was a slightly built, neatly dressed man who was always tuning in a battery-run radio to cowboy songs. Evelyn, his wife, seemed his direct antithesis: a big, sturdy-framed woman with sharp black eyes and an unbounded capacity for work. Her hospitality lived up to Hopi tradition. A pot of coffee was always warming on the wood stove and usually a big pot of knukwivi, a stew of lamb and hominy, the customary meal. With this set on the table, we all gathered around, picking out chunks of meat with our fingers and spooning out hominy and juice with piki, the distinctive Hopi bread, made of finely ground cornmeal baked to a paper-thin cake on a piece of tin, then rolled up to the size of a large sausage. Crisp and delicately flavored, it came in all the colors of Hopi corn: white, yellow, red, and blue. Stacked like cordwood on a woven plaque, it made a wonderful sight. Evelyn always carried a huge plaque of it to the kiva when a ceremonial was under way, reserving another huge plaque for gifts to visitors. Preparation of it was an art and it required hours of work. She was no less adept at weaving plaques: stripping fiber from yucca leaves, staining it different colors, then coiling it into plaques that bore distinctive designs. Like a woman at a sewing bee, she seemed to do her best work when a group of neighbors came to sit on the floor and work with her.

The two smaller villages on Second Mesa, Mishongnovi and Shipaulovi, lay across the valley to the east on the end of another spur of Second Mesa. Both were spectacularly perched, like eagle eyries, on the tops of the two high, pyramidal buttes separated by a sloping hogback. One could drive past them in the valley below without distinguishing them from their rocky escarpments.

Shipaulovi was my favorite village. How tiny it was! Merely a cluster of rock houses surrounding a square plaza whose floor was solid rock. It gave an air of compactness, unity, and completeness that was reflected in the soft voices, gentle manners, and pleasant faces of its people. This feeling of confinement was artistically alleviated, as in the composition of a painting, by a passageway at the northwest corner. Like a Spanish zaguan, it was a deep and narrow hall roofed with cedar poles and brush that gave a view of the tremendous sweep of sky and desert. This was the entrance to the plaza used by dancers on the day of a ceremony. Standing here, you could see them winding up the rocky slope single file from the hidden shrine below like figures emerging from the earth.

Hotevilla on Third Mesa lay about ten miles north of New Oraibi.

It could well have been built in the middle of the Sahara rather than on top of a mesa. Its main plaza was choked with drifting sand, and all around it stretched dunes of fine white sand out of which grew fields of corn and tiny peach orchards. Standing at the steep edge of the mesa, you could see more dunes rolling away in waves toward the desert beyond. Despite its dominant aridity, Hotevilla boasted several good springs. The village itself was named from a spring that gushed out of a cavern on the side of the cliff, so small that the roof scraped a man's back as he stooped to gather water. Hence the name of Hotevilla from hote (back) and villa (scratch). The water from another underground spring had been piped to the surface close to the road, and here the two Bears and I drove every few days to fill our water bottles and thermos jugs.

Our best friends in Hotevilla were Paul Sewemaenewa, Corn That Has Been Rooted, and his wife, Jeanette, who with their two small children lived in one big room. Paul stood more than six feet tall: big boned, heavy muscled, strong as a horse; but gentle and kind as a child, and humbly devout in his traditional belief. Jeanette was small and meek, forever feeding splinters into the little iron cooking stove, seemingly unmindful of their poverty. Between them existed a faith that had endured years of hardship, and a courtesy that was inspiring to observe.

Paul was a leader of the Eagle Clan. After being immured in the kiva for a long ceremony, he would return to the house to be greeted quietly by his wife. "I thank you for the long concentration and prayers you have made for us, for our people, for everybody throughout the world. May our life be blessed and grow richer for your work. Now I welcome you back to your home."

More than any man I know, Paul was a true Hopi, a dedicated man of peace. When the United States entered World War II, Paul and five other Hopis refused to register for selective service in the Armed Forces and were arrested by the county sheriff who had come from Holbrook at the summons of the agent at Keams Canyon. They were jailed in Holbrook for several days, imprisoned in Prescott for three months, and finally taken to Phoenix to stand trial. Here Paul reaffirmed his Hopi faith.

"With us is our Guardian Spirit whom we promised not to kill any white man that would come to our shores. For we knew our lost white brother, Pahana, would come. If we fought any white man we would fight our own brother, and we do not want our own brother's blood shed on our sacred soil. If we did sign our name and go to war, we might not have a chance to live in the next world. This is our main purpose for not wanting to fight. We are doing this for the Hopi people, not for ourselves."

Paul and his companions were adjudged guilty, evidently on the grounds that they could not be exempted as conscientious objectors because their Hopi belief was not a recognized church or religion. They were sentenced to three years hard labor and taken to the prison camp at Tucson to work in a gang blasting a road up Mount Lemmon.

Reinforced by a vision from their Guardian Spirit, the Hopis worked so hard that they were taken off the rock pile to work on farms. This was work they loved, and Paul found time at night to weave belts and sashes which he presented to the men in charge of the prisoners. When he was finally sent home, he found that his sheep had increased to more than a hundred. Then a government agent came, demanding that his flock be reduced. Paul refused to comply. Again he was arrested, stood trial, and was sent back to the prison camp for another year for refusing to give up the sheep that the Creator had given him in answer to his prayers.

While he was away, the Hopi stock reduction was enforced. Half of his flock was taken away. His old mother and his wife, heavy with child, were forced to drive the rest nine miles back home across the desert. On the way Jeanette lost her child. That winter all the remaining sheep had to be killed, for the women were too old and weak to take care of them. So when Paul was finally released, it was to come home to an impoverished family and a wife who had lost her child.

Still he could say, "I am glad we have suffered these things, because we were working not only for ourselves, but for all the people in the world; and we are going to follow our life plan and religious teachings."

Now, twenty years later, Paul had another small flock of sheep and an old pickup truck in which he hauled things for other Hopis. It was always breaking down and he had difficulty finding money to pay for repairs. A few months after I met him he lost the sight of one eye because of an infection that was not treated promptly enough at the hospital in Keams Canyon. Despite this, he still wove belts and sashes on a small loom in the corner during the winter.

Paul and Jeanette's two small children, a boy and a girl, loved to visit us in New Oraibi. Everything in the Bears' apartment seemed so new and wonderful!—the clean white dishes, shiny forks and knives, the gas stove, and the refrigerator. Most of all they liked to thumb through magazines to look at the full-color advertisements. Every so often one of them would stop, point at an article, and say proudly in English, "apple," "chair," "car." Sharp and avid to learn, they were not permitted to go to school. They faced the prospect of growing up uneducated in this Space Age, fortified against the Tribal Council, the government, and the white people who had betrayed their father. Paul and Jeanette's point of view was easy to understand.

Although we also had friends and spokesmen on First Mesa, we visited its three villages less often. Hano, Sichomovi, and Walpi especially, were spectacular on their high clifftop and the best known to tourists. Yet to me they seemed the least "typically Hopi." They had always been the first point of contact for whites throughout history, and they were closest to the agency in Keams Canyon which made them susceptible to government influence. Hano itself was not Hopi; it had been settled by refugees from the Rio Grande and the Tewa tongue was still spoken, along with Hopi. Aside from these rational excuses for prejudice, I felt a miasma of defeat and decay clinging about them all. It seemed to permeate every villager, every building. Even the ceremonies seemed imbued with an air of careless abandon. Old Oraibi was frankly dead, an archaeological ruin. This was worse. Here on First Mesa one felt the disease and corruption setting in as the tide of life ebbed away. The survivors lived, like zombies, a meaningless life-in-death. Only in the pottery, for which it was famous, did the last effulgence of life burst into flame—into deep yellow and burnt-orange bowls and vases of exquisite shape, design, and texture. All the women made pottery and one of the best of them was Faye Avachoya, a cheerful little wraith I had met years ago when she was visiting the Rio Grande pueblos. I visited her often.

The fatal blight that had struck First Mesa comprised all the innovations and advantages offered by our own culture. They were condensed in Polacca, a complex of missionary, school, and government buildings at the foot of the mesa. Like New Oraibi which had drained the life out of Old Oraibi, Polacca was draining the life out of Sichomovi, Hano, and Walpi by negating their own inherent center. It was inevitable, of course. But I often wondered if the process of deterioration could have been halted, and the transition to new values made easier by the simple provision of a plaza in these centerless, utility complexes.

6. *Two Views of Nature*

Contemporary Hopi, Zuni, and many other Indian tribes, as well as the prehistoric Toltecs and Aztecs, believe in the myth that they lived successively in three previous worlds before coming to this one. What root race of mankind these Indians of Mesoamerica belonged to, what vanished or still-existent continent they came from, when, and how, no one knows. Their origin is lost in a time that is being continually pushed back to the edge of the one great mystery of life. Yet these documentary questions need not trouble us. The great myth of their Emergence, as the Hopis most aptly call their arrival upon this continent, is the dramatized story of the emergence of consciousness from the great pool of the unconscious—the evolution of that consciousness of object and self which has enabled man alone to distinguish himself from the rest of nature. It is one of the great awakenings along the Road of Life. By it man gives the world its objective existence and so partakes himself in the process of Creation.

How wonderful it must have been, this ancient and unknown America, this new and promising Fourth World, when man first saw it through Indian eyes! So glistening fresh with the dawn's dew on it. So pristinely pure, so virginly naked in its beauty. How enchantingly diverse the land was with range upon range of snowcapped mountains, shimmering deserts lying below the level of the seas that gnawed at its shores, arctic tundras merging into illimitable plains of waving grass, rising into high-level plateaus, and sinking again into fetid tropical jungles. All teeming with life in every form, tiny plants and dense forests, birds, reptiles and insects, and countless animals of many unique species now extinct, like the buffalo whose vast herds blackened the tawny plains. A land with its own great spirit of place, its own brooding destiny hovering over it with invisible wings.

The Hopis, like other branches of their race, knew themselves as privileged newcomers to this great new world. So upon their arrival they first asked permission to live upon it from its guardian spirit and protector. The spirit gave his permission, telling them, however, that they were not free to wander over it rampantly, using it as they wished. They were to make ordered migrations, north, south, east, and west, to the four pasos where the land met the sea, before settling in the place prescribed for their permanent home. There they were to establish those annual ceremonies which would recapitulate their wanderings and reclaim the land for its Creator.

The meaning of the myth is clear. The emergence of consciousness does not set man entirely free. He is still obligated to the dictates of the unconscious which embodies all his primordial past. He may travel to the limits of his mind and will, but he must always observe those thaumaturgical rites which acknowledge his arising from the one great origin of all life and which keep him whole.

Such a tradition, like many other versions of its kind, marked the relationship of the Hopis to the land. If the directional peaks and boundary rivers to their tribal homeland were stained with the blood of a virginal youth and maiden, the memory of their sacrifices was perpetuated through uncounted generations by male-and-female prayer-feathers planted on ceremonial altars to remind all men of the sacred foundation of their tenure. The land was not tangible property to be owned, divided, and alienated at will. It was their Mother Earth from which they were born, on whose breast they were suckled, and to whose womb they were returned in a prenatal posture at death.

The earth-mother had many children other than man: the stem of long wild grass that developed into a stalk of maize, the lofty spruce, all the birds of the air, the beasts of plain and forest, the insect and the ant. They too had equal rights to life. They supplied the needs of man, but they were not sacrificed ruthlessly and wantonly. A deer was killed only after obtaining his ceremonial assent to the killing that enabled all life to endure in its ordered pattern. Eagles were needed for their down and feathers. But first their heads were washed to signify their adoption into the tribe. Then their lives were snuffed out (bloodlessly) with a blanket and their stripped bodies were carried to an eagle burying ground. The tall and stately spruce furnished its trunk, branches, and tufts of needles. The tree was asked also to consent to its necessary sacrifice, and it was given a special drink so that it would not feel pain from the axe. How remarkably similar these still-observed rituals were among widely separated tribes throughout the Southwest and Mexico.

They may seem curiously sentimental to those of us who are accustomed to think of matter and spirit as antithetical. Yet they conform to the common belief, held by all American Indian tribes, in a mysterious force or dynamic energy, an impersonal spirit of life, pervading and uniting every entity in nature—the living stone, the great breathing mountain, plant, bird, animal, and man. It was the orenda of the Iroquois, the maxpe of the Crows, the Sioux mahopa, the Algonquin manito. And their belief is validated by the mystery teachings of the

East which assert that everything is alive to the degree in which its consciousness is dormant, sleeping, or awakened. Hence the Indians did not set themselves apart from all other physical forms of life. They regarded themselves as a part of one living whole.

Each entity in nature, then, possessed not only an outer physical form but an inner spiritual force. Man was free to utilize the fleshly form for his own bodily needs. But he was ever aware that its spiritual component remained alive as a source of psychical energy which could be invoked to manifest its benign powers for his need.

These spiritual components the Hopis called kachinas, "respected spirits," and they are invoked each year still. Spirits of plant, bird, animal, and human beings who have died; of all the invisible forces of life, they manifest themselves in the physical forms of men wearing masks imbued with the powers of the spirits they represent. So they come dancing into the plazas, uttering their own strange cries, singing from dawn to sunset.

Such a ceremony is a profound mystery play which if produced in Europe would draw thousands of Americans in an annual and fashionable pilgrimage. Still there are pitfully few people here who appreciate it as a superlative, indigenous art form whose anthropomorphic masks, stylistic dancing, and subtle rhythms of song have no equal throughout the world. This superficial artistic consideration, however, is validated by the basic truth and meaning of the kachina. However unique and complex it may seem, the Hopis have created with it a form for the everlasting formless; a living symbol for that universal spirit which embodies all matter; and which speaks to us, as only the spirit can speak, through the intuitive perception of our own faith in the one enduring mystery of life.

This primitive, animistic view of nature, as we are accustomed to regard it, emerges in true perspective only when we compare it to our own Euro-American view of nature.

It too, like the Indians', springs from a long religious tradition. One reads in the first chapter of Genesis, in our Judaic-Christian Bible, that man was created in God's own image and divinely commanded to subdue the earth. The connotations of the word "subdue" cannot be lightly disregarded. For in this view of the dualism of man and nature perhaps lies the real beginning of human tragedy in the Western Hemisphere.

The Christian-European white race, from its first discovery of this pristine New World of the red race, regarded it as one vast new treasure house of inanimate nature that existed solely to be exploited for the material welfare of man. So one sees the Spanish spearheads of conquest thrusting into Peru under Pizarro and into Mexico under Cortés. And one watches closer home the Anglo course of empire sweeping like an engulfing tide across our own America from sea to sea. How little time it took to subdue the continent! It was a rapacious achievement whose scope and speed have not been equalled in all history. Year by year, and mile by mile westward, the white conquerors leveled whole forests under the axe, plowed under the grasslands, dammed and drained the rivers, gutted the mountains for gold and silver, and divided and sold and resold the land itself. Accompanying all this destruction was the extermination of birds and beasts, another aspect of nature inimical to man. Not for sport or profit alone, but to indulge a wanton lust for killing that wiped out vast herds of buffalo at a time, leaving tens of thousands of carcasses piled in a heap to rot in the sun.

The results of our savage onslaught against nature are now all too evident. We have so denuded the grasslands and forested mountains that the topsoil is washing down the drain into the sea. The underground water level is lowering so rapidly that we are being forced to develop means for purifying sea water for our use. The very air we breathe is becoming dangerously toxic in all our large cities, and radioactive fallout from our latest technological triumph is laying to waste wide swaths around the whole planet.

Yet it is not enough to have subdued a continent and exhausted its natural resources. There still remains a vast domain of untouched nature in the universe—the other planets in outer space; and to reach them we have already committed ourselves to exploratory voyages. Is it naive to ask if the purpose of our national space effort is to subdue, colonize, and exploit them also for our material ends? Or is it simply because we are caught in the maelstrom of a technology that cannot be stopped?

In the field of inquiry which these questions pose lies the human tragedy of America, both ours and the Indians'. For accompanying the rapacious destruction of nature from the very start was the virtual extermination of all Indians. These savages, as often viewed by the whites, were not human beings. Like wild beasts which possessed neither souls nor reason, they too were an inalienable part of that vast body of nature inimical to man and hence an embodiment of evil.

History has documented the tragic massacre of tribe after tribe across the continent throughout our "Century of Dishonor" far beyond the need to comment on it here. But when at last the holocaust was over, there were left throughout all the land scarcely 200,000 Indians penned up in ever-dwindling Reservations.

Chief Seattle, for whom one of our cities was named, spoke the epitaph of his race:

"We are two distinct races with separate origins
and separate destinies. To us the ashes of our ancestors
are sacred and their resting place is hallowed ground.
You wander far from the graves of your ancestors and
seemingly without regret. . . .

"But why should I mourn at the untimely fate of
my people? Tribe follows tribe, and nation follows
nation, and regret is useless. . . .

"But when the last red man shall have become a
myth among the white men . . . when your children's
children think themselves alone in the field, the store,
upon the highway, or in the silence of the pathless
woods, they will not be alone. In all the earth there is
no place dedicated to solitude. At night when the

streets of your cities are silent and you think them
deserted, they will throng with the returning hosts that
once filled them and still love this beautiful land. The
white man will never be alone.

"Let him be just and deal kindly with my people,
for the dead are not powerless. Dead?—I say. There is
no death. Only a change of worlds."

These noble sentiments did not mitigate the cumulative effects of
this fateful disaster upon us all. They perceptively forewarned us of the
ghosts that now stalk our streets, the burden of guilt under which our
national conscience is beginning to stagger, and the racial prejudice
against people of all colored skins engendered in us. Yet when we view
the decimation of the red race within the context of white belief, our
retrospective compassion loses much of its emotional intensity. For the
tragedy was not only the Indian's, but the white man's too.

Man was not created apart from nature, as he thought, but out of
nature whose unconscious forces and instinctual drives still swayed
him. So we, the whites, while subduing nature, also tried to subdue
the aspects of nature within ourselves—the secret and shameful desires
of "natural" man, the appetites of the flesh, all the instincts so incompatible and hostile to the mores of rational man. Our own minds and
bodies became the battleground of man against nature, man against
God, and man against himself, divided into two warring selves: reason
and instinct, the conscious and the unconscious.

The outcome was never in doubt, for the white newcomers had
committed the one sin against which the great spirit, Masaw, had
warned the arriving Hopis. They had cut themselves off from the roots
of life.

With the phenomenal rise and spread of Western civilization we
have now become the richest materialistic nation that ever existed on
this planet. The monstrous paradox is that while we have created
untold benefits for all mankind, we have impoverished ourselves

spiritually in the process. In achieving what seems to be a complete triumph over nature, we have established a machine-made society so utterly devitalized that it is anticipating the synthetic creation of life within a laboratory test tube. What could be more reasonable, then, than to enthrone the machine as its deity?

The refutation is expressed by nature itself—that one great unity of all Creation, imbued with one consciousness and infused with one power, of which everything in the universe is an embodied part. Everything is alive, differentiated not in kind but only in the degree of sentiency with which it reflects this all-pervading life in the ascent from mineral to man. The life of the whole is an unconscious process illuminated by consciousness. But pragmatic consciousness is limited. It lights up not the whole, but only a fact-section of it. Hence man's viewpoint is partial. He selects only that part which seems useful to him, ignoring and disowning the rest.

That part, to rational Western man, has been constantly decreasing. It has been successively reduced to that small segment of humanity comprising the white race, to Western Europeans, and now with excessive nationalism largely to American-dominated political entities. The trend is against the evolutionary tide of nature, by which he must constantly extend his frontiers of consciousness. Not only to include all the races of humanity, primitive as they may be; but to establish a living relationship with the animal kingdom, the plant kingdom, that of the living earth itself, and finally the whole of the universe of which he is in reality an enfranchised citizen.

These then are the two pictures broadly outlined by our opposite views of nature. The extrovert view generally held by white Europeans and the introvert view traditional to the colored races of the Far East as well as to Indian America are complementary sides of the same coin. If rational man came from nature in order to stand apart and see nature objectively, nature came to itself in man in order to see itself subjectively. The comprehensive view, it would seem, must come from a perspective that includes both instinct and reason. How are we to reach it?

This problem of means and ends seems strangely acute to a man not too well informed of current events by the Village Crier here in New Oraibi. Like many undeveloped countries it stands on the perimeters of two worlds, owing full allegiance to neither. Which way is New Oraibi to turn? It cannot remain in the primitive Hopi past. Nor can it go forward into a technological future so threateningly sterile. Western civilization also stands at a major crossroads. Its hard-won consciousness cannot sink into the unconscious. Nor can it persist in its rational, willful alienation from life. We both have reached an impasse that the H-bomb may well solve for us.

The Village Crier does not, of course, keep us posted every morning on the steadily rising fallout rate. But almost daily we are informed of the widespread trend of Hopi prophecy. It suggests a way out of our present tragic dilemma. Long, long ago when the Third World became evil and sterile, preparations were made for mankind's Emergence to a new Fourth World. The people were told simply to keep open the kopavi at the crown of the head.

Through this "open door" to the Creator they would receive guidance to the shore of their new world and then to their homeland during their fourfold, continental migrations. So it was they were led by the voice of their guardian spirit, by kachinas, by a star—by all the voices, shapes, and symbols through which intuition speaks to our inner selves.

Today, says Hopi prophecy, mankind is ready for an Emergence to a new Fifth World. Once again we must strive to keep open the door. Through it we will hear a new voice, glimpse a new star to follow. It will be Sasquasohuh, the Blue Star, far off and invisible yet, but to appear soon. We will know when it appears, for Sasquasohuh, the Blue Star Kachina, its manifested spirit, will dance in the kisonvi for the first time.

We whites also stand on the threshold of a new epoch in the evolution of mankind. Nearly 2,000 years ago a new star appeared to the wisest of our kind also. It led them to the manifested spirit of a new urge within man, to a new faith that for century after century embodied all our needs. The meaning of Christianity is not antiquated today, but it has been distorted into moral precepts by a church community which has deteriorated into a social-political institution. Excessively rational man now reads its mythical parables as mere historical events, substituting knowledge for faith, forgetting that the seat of faith is not consciousness but the unconscious. It is from this only source of religious experience that we too must look for the appearance of a new star, a new symbol to rejuvenate our faith in life itself.

By it we must chart our course through the great, unknown interstellar spaces within us, the new world of the future. Even modern science, in its reduction of material units to smaller and smaller size, recognizes that matter does not exist. It consists only of electrical fields unified by the attraction of their opposite polarities—the invisible kachina forces envisaged by our generally ignored Hopis. Is it impossible to concede that beneficent psychical energy may be evoked from them as well as the destructive physical energy released by the hydrogen bomb?

So it seems to me as I lie here in the little house below Pumpkin Seed Point that our two views, ours and the Hopis', are not too divergent after all. Extravagantly pessimistic and suspicious of each other as we are, we are both curiously imbued with the same unfounded belief in the mysterious continuity of life that will raise us to a level on which we will see reconciled in fuller perspective the opposite and complementary sides of our common coin. Already we have come a long way from the speck of green scum in that fetid pool beside the dinosaur tracks imprinted on the rocky floor of Shalako Canyon. But the journey ahead, like that behind us, lies through the subjective realm of time and love; there is no short cut through outer space by mechanical travel.

CHAPTER 14

Mountain Dialogues (1981)

When he finished the essays making up *Mountain Dialogues* in early 1979, Waters wasn't sure he had a marketable book in hand. He wrote to his publisher with characteristic directness, "Objectively, I think such a book will not be popular and easy to sell. It will undoubtedly appeal to a small minority of readers vitally interested in such subjects." He could not have anticipated the rush of place-oriented memoirs that would flood bookstores in the 1980s and '90s. Once again, as with his advancement of serious thought about Indians, his remarkable insights on consciousness-altering drugs as early as 1942, and his critique of Western religion and philosophy through his long career, Waters was quietly ahead of his time. *Mountain Dialogues* came without fanfare, but its essential energy (in Waters's account) derived from a polarity as profound and heavyweight as the two mountains dominating the author's *tierra*. These peaks, *El Cuchillo del Medio* to the north and the Sacred Mountain of Taos to the south, marked the literal, eastern outlines of his days in Arroyo Seco, and for Waters held also another power, sponsoring in the tension between them insight and continuing reflection. They helped keep his life work vivid into the final chapter.

From *Part One*

I. THE LIVING LAND

A small girl in a group of other neighboring children came to see me some time ago with an enigma clutched in her somewhat scrubby hand. The visits of these Spanish-American children to the first Anglo-American living on our mountain road were not unusual. They enjoyed prowling through the house, asking questions about its unfamiliar gadgets. This little girl brought me instead a fistful of earth. "How does this dirt make our garden grow?" she asked simply.

Her question struck a responsive chord in me. In these days we seem to know everything about the planet Earth itself. But for some strange reason we know nothing about a mere handful of dirt whose miraculous fecundity makes our gardens, fields, and pastures grow.

My neighbors and I, more fortunate than big-city dwellers, see a great deal of earth from our homes along the steeply rising road from the small village of Arroyo Seco in northern New Mexico. Vast landscapes of it in every direction. Above us towers the Sangre de Cristo range in an enclosing semi-circle of forested mountains and snowy peaks. Below us, the land slopes westward through a sage plateau to the desert beyond, and extends far beyond that to the faint blue rise of the Rockies.

One would think that my young visitor would know better than to ask how the earth gives life to this immense plant kingdom of pine and sage, corn and wheat, and vegetable gardens. She comes from an earthy, hardy group of Spanish-Colonial ancestors who settled this remote mountain valley on a land grant made in 1716 by the will of His Majesty, the King of Spain. For more than two centuries they have lived solely from this earth, most of them on the same family ranchitos. They have lived within it, too, for their very homes are adobes fashioned from the earth.

Still her question demanded an answer. We spread out her handful of dirt on a newspaper laid across the coffee table. How variegated were its tiny particles, of all sizes, shapes, and colors. One thing we didn't see: whatever held them together in an invisible, creative unity that makes our vegetables grow. We wisely decided that it was the same mystery that somehow gave life to the colts, calves, and lambs in our pastures, all different but reflecting the creative powers of what we call Nature. Thank goodness, she was content with this. But I was left to seek a more conclusive answer.

Another visitor who used to come was Juan Concha, who had served several terms as the governor of Taos Pueblo, a horseback ride of an hour or so across the Indian Reservation extending south from the road. He was a little man, old, dark, and wrinkled. He would sit on the portál with me, waiting for supper, and watching the flanks of the Sangre de Cristos turn blood-red as their name in the flare of the sinking sun. For this range, the birthplace of his people, Old Juan held special reverence.

"Our Mother Earth. It borns us. Everything! Rocks, trees, grasses, corn. All them animals and birds. Us too."

How often, from so many Indians of other tribes, have I heard expressed this devout belief. To the Mayas, two thousand years ago in Yucatan, the earth was not dead, inorganic matter, but a living entity to which they were as intimately related as is it to the stellar universe.

The living land.

But we don't need for the moment to depend solely upon the ages-long belief of all Indian America. The earth itself assures us it is a living entity. Deep below surface one can hear its slow pulse, feel its vibrant rhythm. The great breathing mountains expand and contract. The vast sage desert undulates with almost imperceptible tides like the oceans. From the very beginning, throughout all its cataclysmic upthrusts and deep sea submergences, the planet Earth seems to have maintained an ordered rhythm.

Just how it was created no one knows. There have been many versions; the Planetesimal, Gaseous Tidal, and Gaseous Nebular hypotheses, and the Big Bang theory. All are variations of the modern belief that the planet was created by the Sun, the mysterious primal power, through the primary elements of fire, air, water, and earth. Our scientific myth of creation, uncertain of mechanistic details as it is, does not conflict in principle with the creation myths of Indian America which also assert in their own terminology the patrimony of our Father Sun.

What our earth, the planet, was like when born we don't know either, considering that the blessed event happened, according to current guess, about 4,700 million years ago. (Quite a good way back from the world creation date of October 26, 4004 B.C. at 9:00 a.m. exactly, the moment set by Archbishop Usher of Ireland in 1654. This date was then inserted as a marginal note in the King James version of the Bible, and adopted into scripture.) Whatever it was, this newborn child took its place in a family of nine revolving around the Father Sun of our solar system, one of many such systems in our galaxy, which is but one of many such galaxies in the illimitable universe. A tiny mote in cosmic space, but still to us a sizeable global speck. A great natal rock mysteriously imbued with life from its birth and which had a function to perform in the universe as it slowly matured through constant movement and change.

What this functional purpose was we can't define. Modern historical geology records only the slow physical evolution of Earth into the form we now know by reading the age and composition of successive layers of rock—a chronology of deep sea submergences, continental uplifts, colossal volcanic eruptions, glaciation, and erosion. One can view the static record of these changes in the paleographical maps of any standard textbook—an autobiography of the earth neatly divided into chapters entitled eras and epochs. What a pity we can't see the dramatic story of these mighty changes in a TV special, condensing the history of millions, billions of years into a dynamic moving picture of one hour, with time out for commercials.

Beginning perhaps 500 million years ago, there appeared the earliest forms of what we call life—the trilobites and brachipods, the first spokesmen of the evolving earth. Then came the succession of those great time-spans, the Age of Fishes, the Age of Amphibians, and the Age of Reptiles, which marked the rise to dominance of gigantic land creatures. Monstrous dinosaurs of many tons, standing twenty feet high and as long as sixty-five feet, with scientific names just as long and frightening. And yet some power beyond our comprehension obliterated forever the entire species of these lords of the earth, in order to clear the stage for the Age of Mammals and the appearance of that puny, cringing, and defenseless creature which would endure as man.

If, as Eastern sages assert, a mere stone possesses an unmanifest consciousness, we must believe that the living earth itself was endowed with a basic threshold of consciousness by the universal consciousness that gave it birth. The earliest trilobites and brachipods, too, must have possessed a dormant consciousness, and human life represented rises of consciousness to ever higher levels, being necessary accompaniments to the geological stages of the earth.

Undoubtedly the purely physical or geological record of the earth's long primordial past must be paralleled by a psychical record. The undying memory of man's own short and relatively recent primeval past is still preserved, according to C. G. Jung, as primeval images or archetypes in his collective unconscious. The psychical record of the life-forms that preceded him still lies in unplumbed depths beyond our present cognizance, but which eventually will be read as our expanding consciousness is gradually attuned to its spectrum.

As the archetypes of man's collective unconscious rise into consciousness which gives them form and meaning, so must the inherent consciousness of the earth itself have risen through the life-forms of its plant, animal, and human entities to give ever clearer voice and meaning to the universal consciousness informing from birth this great natal rock. Do we dare to suppose, then, that the human consciousness formulating these thoughts must also have derived from this living planetary rock?

Certainly the physical structure of man is akin to that of the earth. His body is composed of the same four living elements of our great global entity—earth, air, water, and fire. All are interrelated in one living whole. The earth pulsates in an almost imperceptible but ordered rhythm. Water in man and on earth moves in tune with the phases of the moon, as reflected by the tides of the sea, the rises of sap in trees, the female menstrual periods. Air circulates through both bodies, ascending over warm land areas and descending over cool areas, constituting the "breathing of the continents." And our common life energy of light and heat relates us to the sun.

How appallingly simple and complete it seems for a moment! A wholeness in which every part is interrelated in one vast body of universal Creation. How dependent we are upon each—the lofty pine and blade of grass at its foot, the deer and the eagle wheeling above it, mountain and man—all spokesmen who contribute their voices to the chorus of the living land. The topsoil layer of the earth's crust owes its fecundity to the worm. Still, I hesitate to move a pebble at my foot for fear of disturbing the equilibrium of the planet. Yet movement, constant cyclic change, is the immutable law of the whole. Only by it can the earth and its many forms of life fulfill their own functions and interact with every other planet, themselves evolving toward a common destiny.

What this might be has been conjectured by the sages of many time-honored religions, including those Native American philosophers in hairbraids living across the Reservation from me. What makes the question significant is that its answer may lie beyond the context of life on this planet, even beyond our comprehension. If so, our earth is but striving through mankind, its highest level of consciousness yet developed, to comprehend the purpose of its role in a universal order of creation. The earth is as dependent upon us as we are upon it.

Still the fecundity of a handful of dirt is as amazing to me as it was to my childish visitor. It seems to draw its life-giving power from the depths of the earth. The residents of an anthill metropolis subsist on the energy derived from a tiny area around it. Deer restrict themselves for generations to a small browsing area in the mountains. An elk herd migrates but a few miles back and forth between its summer and winter feeding grounds. My horses have subsisted for years on their small homeland of open pasture and tiny wilderness of chokecherry trees, wild rose bushes, and a variety of weeds and herbs. This is their world, small but self-sufficient, as our neighborhood has been for my Spanish-American neighbors.

Despite a common fecundity, every place on earth bespeaks its own rhythm of life. Each continent has its own spirit of place which it imparts to its distinctive species of plants and animals, its human races. So does every country, every locality. Even great cities impart their own special essence, apart from their architectural and cultural backgrounds. And within them, one runs into a barrio, a neighborhood, that seems to exude a sense of peace or evil without apparent cause. There is no accounting for the mysterious magnetism that draws and holds us to that one locality we know as our heart's home, whose karmic propensities or simple vibratory quality may coincide with our own.

Thus have I often wondered how I happened to choose this slope of the Sangre de Cristo Mountains for my own home. There was little to recommend it thirty years ago. Eight thousand feet high, the spot lay nine miles from the small, backward town of Taos and one mile above the tiny, old Spanish village of Arroyo Seco. The rutted dirt road was almost impassable several months of the year, deep in snow during the winter, and in sticky adobe all spring. My house was a deserted adobe whose roof was falling in and whose foundations needed bolstering. But the first time I saw it on a walk up into the mountains, something about it claimed me.

The ruined adobe and the land behind it I finally bought from a lifelong resident of the valley, Josephine M. Córdova, whose husband was a rancher and a part-time gambler. With the purchase price she built in El Prado, a settlement on the road to Taos, an adobe building of two or three one-room living units whose rental supplemented her income as a schoolteacher. She became and remained the principal of the small El Prado school for thirteen years. Upon her retirement she wrote a small book, *No Lloro Pero Me Acuerdo*, "I Don't Cry, But I Remember," recounting the old Spanish way of life here, and nearly three hundred Spanish proverbs. A dear friend and a great lady.

Making my small new adobe liveable was a task. I put on a new roof and bolstered the foundations of the walls with the help of Indian and Spanish-American neighbors. There was no heating save the fireplaces in each of the three rooms, which required hours of cutting wood for them and the iron cookstove. Nor was there running water in the house. We dipped water from the stream in front, the Arroyo Seco, and used an outdoor backhouse. Under these conditions, we could live in the house only during the summer.

The land in back was overgrown with chokecherry and wild plum thickets, and wild rose bushes. It had to be cleared and seeded for pasturage and hay for our few horses. The fences had to be repaired. Eventually an electric cooperative ran a line up this way, enabling us to drill a well and install running water and plumbing fixtures.

But I do not wish to emphasize our small effort. When my wife Janey and I first moved into our small adobe, Salomé Duran, a sheepherder in Wyoming, had not yet settled permanently in his small house just above us. But farther above, where the rock-strewn road ended at the base of the mountain wall, Emilio Fernandez was establishing a home for his tiny wife and children. He was a big, wide-shouldered man with an open heart and gentle manner, who spoke little English. Alone and unaided, he built his adobe house, bridging the Arroyo Seco stream, and clearing a road to it. He constructed barns and corral of stout logs, then cleared a mountain slope of huge pines for his pastures and fields. It sounds so romantic when we read of pioneers "clearing the land" for homesites. But the phrase assumes new significance for one watching Mr. Fernandez felling tall pines, burning the stripped branches and undergrowth, and pulling out the huge stumps with a team. Then plowing, planting by hand, and irrigating with water drawn from a mountain stream. Often on a fall night I could glimpse the glow of the tiny campfire beside which he squatted to protect his ripening corn from deer, raccoons, an occasional bear. The corn and squash he dried in the sun for winter use, unable to afford sugar for canning. For the purchase of staples, he sold pine logs for use as vigas, or roof beams, and a few head of cattle or sheep.

Only seldom did he have time to go down into the village, riding a pinto horse, although the family walked down each Sunday to attend Mass. As the road was impassable during the deep snows of winter, he moved his family into the village in order to put his children into school. Through all these years of lonely, backbreaking toil, he built up his ranch, reared his children. He still passes by on foot, his muscular frame beginning to shrink, his favorite pinto gone. For him I have great admiration, respect, and affection. He is a true man of the earth.

If I had been unaccountably drawn here, it took me some time to become accustomed to its spirit of place. Not that it seemed as strangely alien and foreign to me as to many friends who called it "Little Mexico." There was some truth in their assertions, for the little village of Arroyo Seco with its mud-brown adobes reminded me of remote pueblos in Mexico. But still the area had a distinctive aura, a rhythm, a flavor of its own. There were so many intangible influences, vibrations, seismic oscillations of feelings between opposite poles! All these invisible forces helped to mold me into their pattern, whatever that is. Gradually they began to speak to me with the voice of the living land, and its chief spokesmen were the two great peaks that rose from the mountains above.

2. EL CUCHILLO DEL MEDIO

The high mountain wall rises steeply to the east, not far from the house. From it lift two near peaks. To the southeast is Pueblo Peak, the Sacred Mountain of Taos Pueblo which lies at its foot on the opposite side, a horseback ride around it. It is softly rounded in shape, thickly forested with pine and spruce, a benign, motherly mountain. The Indian reverence for it and the exquisitely beautiful blue lake that lies like a turquoise beyond it is quite special. For from this sacred lake, according to tradition, the tribe had made its Emergence to the surface of the earth, and to it the tribe still makes annual pilgrimage to conduct ceremonies no white man ever has witnessed.

Not far north, separated from it by lower ridges cut by two canyons, rises another great peak—this one a malign, masculine mountain. Protruding toward us is a rounded shoulder whose sheer, bare granite side on the south looks as if it had been sliced down the middle with a knife. From this comes its appropriate name of El Cuchillo del Medio.

The peak offers testimony to its negative character. Legend relates that in the long ago two Indian maidens were in love with the same man. Their rivalry came to a tragic climax upon the summit of the sheer cliffside one day when they fought and both fell to their deaths from this falling-off place, El Salto. This name is given more specifically to a narrow rocky cleft on its western side, in which lies a great cave believed to have been used during human sacrifices in prehistoric times. Over the top of the cave cascades a waterfall—un salto de agua—which freezes into stalactites and stalagmites covering its opening with a curtain of ice. The phenomenon occurs only in early spring when weather conditions are right. I have seen it but a few times, when from my back pasture the ice sheet reflecting the setting sun looked like a plate glass window.

The cave is fictionally famous. D. H. Lawrence used it and its alleged human sacrifices as a setting for his novelette *The Woman Who Rode Away*, transporting it to the Sierra Madre of Mexico. The rocky back walls of the cave used to be inscribed with prehistoric pictographs and petroglyphs. These have been pried out by tourists and replaced with the usual backhouse inscriptions; but the place now is generally shunned by Indians.

The trail to it is difficult to follow, leading through a dense forest of huge pines flanked by high cliff walls believed to hold the dens of small brown bears and a few large black bears. Every fall the bears come down into my back pasture to eat chokecherries, spooking the horses. Harmless as they seemed to me, all Arroyo Seco viewed them with alarm. One afternoon shortly after I moved here, I heard the bells of church and school wildly ringing, and glimpsed men coming up the road armed with guns, pitchforks, and clubs. What had happened? A small brown bear had strayed down into the village at three-thirty in the afternoon when school had let out, giving rise to the general alarm, I suppose, that the bears of El Salto were attacking the village. Pursued by the mob, the frightened animal fled safely back into the mountains. Since then large black bears occasionally have come down, posing actual problems. Their presence adds another negative aspect to the character of El Cuchillo.

If our immense global rock, the Earth, embodied the principles of cosmic opposites from the beginning, as does perhaps even the power of all Creation, it is not strange that the complementary polarities are manifested in all parts of the whole—even in the malign, masculine Cuchillo and the benign, motherly Sacred Mountain. An interesting parallel to them was called to my attention recently when I was visited here by Professor Robert Gustafson, head of the Department of Philosophy and Religion at Pembroke State University in North Carolina. He referred to Mt. Ebal and Mt. Gerizim mentioned in the Old Testament as the mount of blessing and the mount of cursing, and added that during his recent trip to Jordan he found that the natives of the region still regarded these mountains as good and evil.

That the two bipolar mountains here imprint their forces both on the physical and inorganic world, and on organic life—without the Biblical tradition of Moses' commandments—is borne out in many ways.

The dichotomy is marked by the Arroyo Seco River which flows out of the steep canyon on the south side of El Cuchillo and down through the little Spanish village of Arroyo Seco, a mile below my house. It is paralleled by our rutted dirt road. Along the north side live all the members of the Spanish community. On the south side extends the Indian Reservation of Taos Pueblo, a vast sage plateau whose sparse fields are watered by the Rio Lucero which flows out of the deep canyon on the north side of the Sacred Mountain. Hence our mountain slope is sharply divided into two realms, Indian and Spanish, with different racial backgrounds, culture, and language.

A major dispute has been over the boundary of the land ever since Charles V of Spain in 1551 awarded a large land grant to the pueblo, now comprising its Reservation, followed two centuries later by smaller land grants to Spanish settlers and the founding of the village of Arroyo Seco in 1745. The ramifications of the land dispute are too complicated to detail here, and are still continuing.

Another grievous quarrel has been over water rights. For the Rio Arroyo Seco is no river at all; it is but a small stream without enough water to provide irrigation for the Spanish fields. It has been necessary to divert a proportion of the flow of the Rio Lucero to the Spanish domain. The allocation for a century or more has resulted in violent quarrels. In my early years here when the irrigating water was insufficient for our drying fields and it was obvious that the Indians were stealing our rightful share, my neighbors enlisted me to accompany a group of them to the "division of the waters" on the Reservation. They were all armed with shovels and pickhandles.

Fortunately we encountered no Indians. But at the division, just below the mouth of the Lucero, they had diverted our flow of water into their own irrigation ditch with a dam of stones and mud. Destroying this, we returned home. This crude separation of waters has now been replaced by a cement, headwater partition structure, allocating the proper percentage of the flow to both Indian and Spanish domains.

Ostensibly, the centuries-long antipathy between the two segments of our upland community has been based upon differences of racial and cultural backgrounds supported by government-imposed geographical limitations. Fundamentally, I'm inclined to believe it reflects the opposite polarities of the two mountains.

I do not want to intimate in any way that the Indian segment, polarized to the Sacred Mountain, is "good," and that the Spanish segment within the sphere of influence of El Cuchillo is "bad." I am a resident of the Spanish community, yet my belief in Indian values has been rooted in me since childhood.

When I first bought this crumbling adobe and the land behind it, Ralph Meyers, the noted old Indian trader in Taos, was vociferous in his denouncement of it. "The damned location is no good. It lies too close to El Salto. The place has an Indian jinx on it and it's full of Spanish brujas. You won't last a month. And how the hell are you going to get up there, eight thousand feet high, in winter anyway?"

I reminded him that I already had bought it. Whereupon he offered his sage advice. "You've got to take the jinx off it. Propitiate the evil spirits. A charm will do it. Piss and a prayer. Just the thing!"

A few days later he came up to execute the powers of the charm. A copious urination was followed by the sprinkling of sacred cornmeal from a small buckskin sack hung around his neck. Apparently that did it. I have never been troubled by evil spirits.

Nevertheless, the aura of El Cuchillo and a bad reputation hovered around Arroyo Seco. In its early days, when its huddle of mud-brown adobes was practically isolated by the tortuous wagon road, the village was believed to be a refuge for horse-thieves and other tough characters nibbling at the fringes of the law. Occasionally Indians rode over for bootleg whiskey. Later, in my own time, the place was regarded as the toughest settlement in the Rio Arriba because of the many knifings that took place among its rowdy youths.

When my neighbor got married, I was invited to the house of his mother for the great wedding feast given for the host of neighbors. I was then asked to attend the customary wedding dance that evening. But the young man drew me aside and suggested that I not come, as there might be a knifing. So just as delicately, I did not accept the invitation.

Next morning I learned that the affair had erupted into a knifing, just as he had predicted. Other incidents of the kind were constantly taking place. I must add that I was never involved in a fracas even though I was an Anglo, and that I was always accorded courtesy and friendship. One could not blame the youths for their sometimes bloody quarrels. Not only were they possessed by a hot-blooded temperament, but they were all poor, without cars to drive into Taos or for pleasure, without amusements of any kind. They sat dejectedly along the road, waiting vainly for something stimulating to turn up. In recent years a succession of enterprising parish priests have had their hands full initiating sports and games.

And of course the area was reputedly full of brujas, witches, whose midnight rendezvous was the cave in El Salto. Almost anyone could tell a hair-raising story about them. One verified story comes readily to mind. An aging woman who had been given a pair of new shoes wore them to church one winter evening, and afterwards left to walk home. She was never seen again. When her neighbors tried to track her through the deep snow, they followed her footprints up the steep road toward El Salto, where they ended. There was no other trace of her; she had vanished completely. A couple of years later a woodcutter climbing La Ceja, "the Eyebrow" curve of the mountain slope far to the north, found her decomposed body, which was identified by her shoes. How it got there was inexplicable. An aging woman in new, stiff shoes could not possibly, in bitter cold and deep snow, have walked up the rising road to its end, through several miles of forest, and climbed up the slope of the mountain. The consensus was that brujas had transported her there.

Who the brujas were, no one knew, of course. But I heard gossip when I was moving into my house that one of my neighbors was one of them. The rumor would have horrified her. She was a descendant of an old family that had been awarded this immense land grant. Her husband had been a schoolteacher, then a sheepherder pasturing his flock during the winter in the lower and warmer valleys along the Rio

Grande, and driving it up into the mountains for the summer. They had many sons and daughters, over whom she ruled with assured authority.

She was a sturdily built woman with an iron constitution. I once saw her watching two of her sons trying to lift a seasoned log. Finally, with a snort of disgust, she walked over, hoisted the log to her shoulder, and strode off with it. While the old man was away with his sheep, she assumed management of the farm—supervising the planting and harvesting of the fields, nursing the vegetable garden, tending the stock, and mending the fences. She was up at daybreak—rousing out of bed all the rest of the family. She adhered to the old traditions. Periodically, she made soup, for which I gave her all my bacon grease, in a large cast-iron kettle set on an open fire in front of the house. I observed her once insisting, when her sons were castrating a colt, that the cut be made, not by cold steel but by the teeth. In addition to all this work, she assumed the task of personally caring for the village priest and providing fresh flowers for the church. One of the most remarkable women I have ever known, she was a true matriarch in the old Spanish tradition. It was little wonder that all Arroyo Seco regarded her as a powerful figure.

Soon after I met her, I had a dream about her. I was standing one night in the kitchen of my small adobe. Beside me was standing an Anglo youth with auburn hair. The woman was sitting in a chair in the corner. In the candlelight she looked like a spirit. The house too gave off the feeling of eeriness and evil. The Anglo youth beside me was frightened. He cringed against the wall, hands over his face. "You're not used to it," I told him. I too felt the somber, eerie atmosphere, but at the same time I felt cheerful and unafraid. I walked toward her . . .

In retrospect, I see this dream as constellating the two aspects of my own dual nature. The fearful Anglo youth representing my white, Puritanical component, contrasted with my other shadow self drawn to darkness and evil.

Some time later I had another dream. I was in the house when my

sister Naomi, a fey soul with intuitive promptings, came in to tell me
of a discovery she'd made. I went out with her to look at it. Along the
back fence of the orchard, and hidden under brush, we found an old
log carved into the semblance of a queer animal—short-legged as a
dog, but big-bodied, with the protruding snout of a pig. It reminded
me of a South Sea or Central America effigy. I knew immediately it
was for our protection; and hunting around, I found another close to
the house. In its front was carved a symbol which I have forgotten.

I related to Naomi the gossip that the woman might be a bruja, a
witch, but that lately I had been told she was an arboleria. The word
derived from arbol de la vida, the "tree of life," or arbol de la ciencia
del bien y del mal, the "tree of the knowledge of good and evil." In
other words, she was not only able to cast spells like any run-of-the-
mill bruja, but to take them off.

What changed my first dream impression of her to a more favorable
one was an amusing incident. All Arroyo Seco must have regarded
with some suspicion the first incursion of an Anglo into the region.
Our boundary fence was broken time after time so that stock could
graze at will in our fields and orchard. The dramatic climax came after
I had laboriously hauled stones from the river to lay for the floor of
our front portál. Upon returning home after a short absence, I found
that they had been uprooted by a pig. That afternoon the pig returned
to continue its destruction. Never in my life have I seen such a monstrous animal. It looked exactly like the queer animal effigy in my
dream, short-legged as a dog, big-bodied and with the protruding snout
of a pig. But monstrous beyond belief, looking like a huge hippopotamus.

At the sight of it, Janey's small and fierce Chow dog, descended
from the war-dogs of ancient China, hurled himself against it, tearing
out from its flank a chunk of flesh but being stunned by the impact.
The monster merely turned around in mild annoyance. At this
moment the woman strode through a broken gap in the fence exclaim-
ing, "Madre de Mio! I hope your little dog has not hurt himself?"

Whereupon Janey, with her excitable nature, loosed upon her a violent tirade in French and Italian, not a word of which my neighbor

understood, but whose meaning she comprehended fully. It is quite likely that she had never been so addressed. She immediately had the monstrous pig confined in the corral.

A week or two later, her oldest son trucked the pig to offer for sale in the public stock auction in Alamosa, Colorado. He reported that he was quite embarrassed by the whole proceeding, shrinking down in the back row. "What am I offered for this gigantic animal?" shouted the auctioneer. "They call it a pig. But it looks like a hippopotamus. Who will make me an offer?"

Thereafter the two women were the closest of friends. The boundary fences were patched up. And when we had to leave in the winter, I simply turned over the keys of the house to our neighbor. During the many years I lived alone here after Janey's death, she and her daughter looked after me with boundless solicitude, coming over almost every day and bringing fresh vegetables.

Her husband was a character himself. He was a short, sturdy man, with a peculiar growth of huge warts on his head prevented him from wearing a hat. In due time, the warts were removed at the hospital, only to return. A man of the earth, he had spent much of his life outdoors. When he had to give up herding sheep, due to both his age and the Forest Service restrictions on grazing in the mountains, he felt lost. Growing a few head on his own pastures, he helped to shovel snow off my roof in the winter, and while I was away, hayed the horses, and watched the house like a hawk. Until he died at the age of eighty-two, he made a daily inspection tour of my fields and came to visit me every morning.

All the children and grandchildren familiarly called me "Frank." But the parents always addressed me as "Mr. Waters," a formal courtesy I also extended to them. Little wonder that I with Naomi, Carl, and my niece Susie who came periodically from California, looked upon these people as members of our own family. Of them all, of course, the mother was the dominating spirit. The beauty in her face grew daily.

Yet in her I sensed a peculiar streak that seemed to welcome misfortune. All the members of this family, persons and animals, were accident-prone. Whenever someone was hurt or became seriously ill, or a horse died of a punctured bowel or broke its leg, it was reported with an air of positive cheerfulness. The old woman developed an unremitting burning pain in one leg for which none of the local doctors could find the cause or the cure. The last doctor she tried gave up the effort, saying, "So it still burns like fire, eh? Well, it'll keep you warm all winter!" Thereafter, every freezing day when she came over to see me, her face pinched with cold, she would slap her ailing leg and exclaim with a joyful chuckle, "Ai. Ai. But this is keeping me warm!"

My turn came one Saturday afternoon when the local dentist extracted all my teeth, slapped in two new plates, and gave me a pill the size of a large marble to stop the pain when I went to bed. In the middle of the night I awakened with blood filling my mouth and nostrils. Sleepily, I stuffed cotton in my mouth and wrapped a towel around my head. Early next morning, my neighbor walked in the house without knocking, as usual. I could well imagine what she saw from the doorway of my bedroom: a still figure in bed whose face, head, pajamas, pillow cases, and bed sheets were covered with blood. At her first start of shocked surprise, I moved and spoke. Whereupon she let out a small scream of relief that somehow, at least in my imagination, contained that strange element of ironic humor.

"No! I haven't been murdered!" I shouted crossly. "I've just got a bloody toothache!"

She laughed uproariously. "So no one has killed you with an axe, Mr. Waters! But perhaps you will die anyway, losing all your blood, God willing!"

Then, of course, came her deep compassion and helpful hands as she bathed my face, replaced the towel and pajamas with fresh ones, brought more cotton to stuff in my mouth. This went on all day Sunday. For the dentist, a Spanish friend of mine, had forgotten to stitch up my torn gums in his haste to leave town for a weekend vacation, and I could not see him until Monday morning.

What engendered this curious streak in her may have been a healthy ironic humor, or a philosophical acceptance of all misfortunes as the will of God; but it certainly reflected the mood of the locality, the influence of El Cuchillo which lay upon us all its dark shadow.

I never discussed spirits with her, knowing her staunch Catholic faith. Still, one incident led me to feel she at least believed in spirits. A young couple in Los Angeles were told of the sacrificial cave at El Salto by my sister and brother-in-law, and resolved to see it during their vacation trip to New Mexico. I was away when their car appeared in my driveway. My neighbor immediately came over to inquire what they wanted. Upon being told, she offered to guide them to the cave despite the arduous long walk and her fear of bears. Upon their return, and after she had gone home to rest, the young couple asked me why she had stopped periodically along the trail to ring a small brass bell before proceeding.

This, I knew, was not to frighten away the bears. It immediately recalled a trip I had made with a Hopi priest, John Lansa, to a sacred shrine in a remote area north of Black Mesa in Arizona. The shrine was known as Kisiwu, the Spring in the Shadows, a mysterious place and the home of several important spirits sacred to the Hopis. The spring itself lay in a cave high on a rocky escarpment rising out of the sandy plain. John preceded me as we climbed up the narrow trail. Four times he stopped, taking off his shirt, pants, and moccasins. Then from a little buckskin medicine-bag suspended from a thong looped around his throat, he sprinkled a pinch of cornmeal on the ground, and gave a loud call. Finally reaching the cave, he offered his prayers and motioned for me to join him. He had of course been notifying the spirits of Kisiwu of our approach, just as had my neighbor on her approach to the cave of El Salto.

The parallel illustrates how deeply rooted and widespread among Indian and Spanish alike in all this harsh and naked land is the belief in spirits which may be invoked for good or evil. Their invocation for evil is known worldwide as witchcraft. Throughout the Rio Arriba, this region of the upper Rio Grande in northern New Mexico, witch-craft has been perhaps the most prevalent. Documented records for three centuries amply attest that the belief in witchcraft here equalled that in Europe between the thirteenth and seventeenth centuries. The literature on these tragic case histories of trial and torture of accused victims is voluminous, but there is no need to summarize it.

Still, we are told that the word "witch" is derived from the Anglo-Saxon word "wicca," meaning craft of the wise. Hence the craft is not necessarily directed towards evil ends; it may be employed to lift spells cast by lesser brujas, and to cure mental and physical illnesses.

If we don't doubt the possibility that demonic powers can be invoked by witchcraft, neither can we doubt that divine powers can be invoked by prayer and religious rites. They seem to be complementary, reflecting the dual forces of all life. The Navajos maintain the tradition of two opposing ritual practices, the religious ceremonial of Blessing Way among others, and the Witchcraft Way. Among the Hopis there emerged in early days a ceremony based on the power of the animal kingdom, tuvósi, which became extinct when its members used the power for selfish ends. Nevertheless, its beliefs and practices still exist as witchcraft. Pósi (Eye) is the name for a medicine man who uses the eye of the animal kingdom which can see in the dark. The Hopi name for a witch or sorcerer is powága (eye, walking, doing), because he uses the eye of the animal kingdom for evil purposes—destroying crops of his neighbors, bringing winds, driving away snow and rain, shooting ants, insects, and glass into his victims, and causing the deaths of even his own relatives in order to prolong his own life. Who these alleged powága are, no one knows. Yet fear of them is spreading at the same rate as ceremonialism is breaking down.

Evil itself seems to have originated in man with the creation of Adam and Eve in the Garden of Eden, according to Christian doctrine: or, as the Tewas believe, it was brought up by the First People during their Emergence from the underworld. Despite modern psychological belief that evil is a component of man's own nature, it is commonly believed that evil is projected upon us by other persons or forces outside ourselves.

Among the Spanish people here the Church has been the equivalent of Indian ceremonialism as a bulwark against evil. In testimony, perhaps, is the holy power invoked by Mrs. Elizaida Duran, another close neighbor. Salomé Duran, her husband, has long been a sheepherder. When sheep-raising was given up here due to Forest Service grazing restrictions, he began the custom of herding sheep in Wyoming all summer, returning home to live during the winter. A few years ago, he settled here permanently to graze his own small flock of fifty or sixty sheep and goats on his ample pastures. A big, muscular man, he spent all day outside, according to custom: mending fences, irrigating, cutting wood, doing chores, or simply watching his flock. His neighborliness has been of immense benefit to me. For when my own fields, converted into permanent pasture for my remaining horses, became overgrown with wild roses, he turned his flock into them. As goats are browsers, not grazers like sheep, they soon cleared my fields completely. In return, my horses wandered through the open gates to graze on his own pasture. More important, his residence at home lifted from Mrs. Duran the heartbreaking tasks required of a lone woman to keep up the place. It permitted her to spend her time on work in the house and tending to her garden. She is an excellent cook, sometimes working during the winter in a gourmet restaurant, and her flower garden is the best in Arroyo Seco.

An Anglo woman visitor once remarked to me that she couldn't understand why our small homesites in such a comparatively wild area should seem so peaceful and protected. And then, glancing out my window, she pointed to Mrs. Duran's front lawn. "Ah! Of course. I see now. No wonder!"

What she saw was a shrine built of cement blocks upholding a statuette of Our Lady on top, with an array of flowers at her feet, and surmounted by an American flag.

Aside from the conjectural existence of brujas evoking evil, I can affirm the presence everywhere of celestial influences imbuing localities, even the small group of aspen trees in my back courtyard. A large grove of much older and higher aspens stands outside, flanking the driveway, but there is something special about this small group. There are seven of them. One of them grew so close to the wall of the house I was afraid the jutting eaves would either stunt its growth or kill it, so I had a hole cut through the protruding roof to allow space for its upward climb. As I lie in bed, their tall, slim, white trunks, ghostly pale in dawnlight or moonlight, are the first things I see in the morning and the last at night.

If aspens long have been my favorite trees, since childhood the Pleiades have been my most intimate constellation. The relationship between them appeared in a curious fantasy. One winter night I seemed to see these seven, white, slim aspens, now stripped of leaves, rising like tall tapers higher and higher toward the seven principal stars in the Pleiades. At the moment of contact their tips were ignited as by a burst of energy, and a glow of soft light was diffused from every bare branch and twig. The fantasy lasted only a moment or two, but it assured me they were intimately related.

The interrelationship of stars, earth, and man posits, of course, an exchange of influences. Yet this area—despite its natural beauty, its often joyful moods, my good neighbors, and the connection between my seven aspens and the Pleiades—is nevertheless curiously impacted with the negative spirit of bare-faced El Cuchillo.

I still ask myself what drew me here to spend such a considerable span of my earthly existence. Undoubtedly, our karmic propensities were much the same, and El Cuchillo and I are kindred spirits in some way. It has affected me profoundly, of course. But has my presence here affected it? Am I exerting in some small manner an influence upon that stark bare peak, or am I projecting upon it the negative aspects of my own being, or do I merely maintain with it a polite and guarded speaking acquaintance, as it were? At least we jibe without conflict, even at night when the October wind shrieks at the eaves and I feel pressing down upon me the heaviness of its dark power.

3. THE SACRED MOUNTAIN

How different seems the benevolent, maternal Sacred Mountain! You feel its full force when you cross the road, lead a horse through a gate, and ride south around the base of the peak.

This is Indian land, the Taos Pueblo reservation. A great upland expanse of waist-high sagebrush sloping west from the foot of the mountains. The sage glints silver-green in early sunlight, interspersed with yellow-flowered chamisa, tall sunflowers, and clumps of juniper and piñon trees. It is an unspoiled land overlooking the desert below cut by the narrow slit of the Rio Grande, and the upturned blue horizon far to the west. To the left, the Sacred Mountain looms bigger, softer, and greener. And from the mouth of Lucero Canyon there extends a road and the narrow, government-built cement irrigation ditch.

My mare, Cry Baby, knows the overgrown wagon road well. It leads through a thick growth of piñon trees. In the fall, one can dismount here and gather up from the ground a sack of piñones, the small sweet nuts which are roasted and sold throughout the Southwest. The road peters out into a trail that dips down into a glorietta, a marvellous glade hidden in great cottonwoods and pines, and cut by a clear stream that widens into a deep pool. The grassy, isolate meadow is a favorite camping place for Indians, especially for newlywed couples. Janey and I often used to strip and bathe in the pool and then dry out on its grassy banks.

From here there are trails in several directions through groves of cottonwoods and pines. Cry Baby drinks from the pool, gingerly fords its rocky bottom, and waits for further direction by a pressure of the reins.

One of them, after climbing out of the sequestered glorietta, leads across an open meadow toward the dark lower slope of the Sacred Mountain. She takes it in an unreined, furious gallop, heading straight for a lone cottonwood. Here, I slow her winded pace. For we now climb a trail beside an irrigation ditch, past flanking pines, spruces, and the first aspens, through carpets of bluebells, lupine, crimson paintbrush, white onion, and purple asters, to the cliff-walled mouth of the Lucero—to the division of its waters.

It is one of the wild spots we seldom see. The water pours down, white and foaming, from the snowcaps above. Many are the picnics we have had here with Indian neighbors. One of them included "Grandma" Concha, nearly eighty years old and blind. She wanted only to be set at the foot of the falls where she could listen to the voice of the water.

The Lucero in the past has been a good trout-fishing stream. It is a tortuous stream to follow, swift, narrow, obstructed with fallen trees and boulders, necessitating one to cross it from side to side. Up above, the canyon seems filled with one solid forest of towering aspens through which the light is filtered, in a greenish haze in summer, or a deep yellow glow when the leaves turn in the fall. There sounds the chattering of squirrels, then the explosive burst of a mountain grouse from darkness into silence.

From the mouth of the Lucero Cry Baby knows the way home. The short way is impassable by horseback, leading through a tangled jungle of scrub oak directly to the road past my house. So we must ride the longer way: down the road and back across the sagebrush.

Beautiful as it is, the mouth of the Lucero has about it an aura of mysterious, eerie wilderness in which a strange thing happened that my sister Naomi and I once experienced. I say "aura" advisedly, because the strange occurrence apparently was not caused by a material incident.

It was late afternoon. My brother-in-law Carl had gone fishing and had not yet returned. While waiting for him, Naomi and I went for a walk up the road toward the base of the mountains. When the road ended, we cut south toward the mouth of the Lucero across an open, high meadow. It was a lovely spot whose peace and silence were enhanced by the wild flowers underfoot, the mellow glow of the sinking sun. Ahead of us lay the thick growth of scrub oak I have mentioned.

Suddenly Naomi, with her acute perceptions and fey intuition, stopped short, and I noticed on her face a look of trepidation. At almost the same time, I was halted by what seemed an invisible and intangible barrier. For a moment, I believed that she had instinctively sensed the presence of a bear, which had come down to feed on the acorns. Previously, I had been warned not to ride in this vicinity, as Cry Baby would be spooked by the smell of bear. Yet as I tried to step forward anyway, I was held in check by that mounting, intangible wave that had no sound nor smell, but was more impassable than any physical barrier.

At this instant, the cloying silence was broken by a shrill cry that seemed to come from the cliff walls at the mouth of the Lucero. It was so loud and clear that it filled the meadow. Wild and frightening, it came from a human voice imploring help, but in words I could not understand. Surely someone over there, perhaps an Indian, had been attacked, fallen from a cliff, or met with another serious accident. Unable to ignore its wild plea, I gave a loud shout, although that intangible barrier prevented me from moving forward.

As we stood there rooted to the spot, another shrill cry sounded. Now years later, I cannot describe it though it is etched indelibly in my memory. It was as if it were uttered by someone who had been pushed or jumped to his death from the cliffs; and now, too late, gave one last despairing, agonizing death-cry. An earthly cry, but unearthly, too, as if it had been filtered through an abnormal or supernormal medium. It filled our small world with a horror that destroyed completely all serenity, and broke against the benevolent Sacred Mountain its soul-torturing anguish.

Naomi, her face pale and drawn, and I turned about and trudged home without a word. In the house, we still sat wordless and shaken. We could not ignore those two heartrending cries. I proposed saddling Cry Baby and riding the long way around to the mouth of the Lucero.

But by the time I caught, saddled, and rode her there, it would be too dark to see anything. Still we had to do something. So leaving a note for Carl who had not yet returned from fishing, we got in the car and drove down to the pueblo.

Albert and Clara and one of their sons were eating supper by the light of a lamp. I explained what we had heard, suggesting that I drive Albert and some other Indians up there to find out if someone from the pueblo had met with an accident. Albert's son quietly rose from the table and went out. In a little while, he came back. Apparently, he had reported the incident either to the Governor or to the War Chief, the "Outside Chief" who is responsible for all happenings outside the pueblo itself. No Indians had gone up the Lucero that day, no trouble had been reported, nor were any Indians reported missing. Albert seemed disturbed, but said to us simply, "Come back tomorrow."

Early next morning, we drove back to see him, still disturbed ourselves. Albert gave us coffee at his kitchen table. He affirmed that further inquiry had revealed no accidents at the mouth of the Lucero, no Indians missing from the pueblo. The door was open. The morning sun shone in, bright and clear. Out in the plaza, people were serenely going about their daily chores. Yet all this only accentuated the frightening cries we had heard the previous evening, the intangible barrier we had encountered.

Albert was a man of few words. He finally said simply, "Long time ago that happen. You just hear it now."

Nothing puts into such few words the belief—not only Indian—that time is not a linear flow, as we think it is, into past, present, and future. Time is an indivisible whole, a great pool in which all events are eternally embodied and still have their meaningful being. Into it we may dip by chance, or by a meaningful flash of supernormal or extrasensory perception, and glimpse something that happened long ago in our linear time. And this, I believe, is what happened that late afternoon. We did not break completely through the time barrier—that intangible, mysterious wall—to glimpse what had happened. But the cries had penetrated it, and we were momentarily, psychically attuned enough to hear their audible vibrations.

To return to the glorietta . . .

The alternate route of Cry Baby and myself from here is a wagon road curving around the base of the Sacred Mountain to the pueblo at its foot, directly opposite the northern side of the peak from my house. The road opens up a new perspective of the Sangre de Cristo range. One sees between and behind the Sacred Mountain and El Cuchillo the majestic snow-covered Vallecito, hidden from sight at Arroyo Seco because we are too close to see it. It in turn obscures, at our still relatively close range, the mighty mass of Wheeler Peak, more than thirteen thousand feet high and the highest mountain in New Mexico. This is the peak below which lies the sacred Blue Lake of the pueblo, from whose drainage of snow waters come Pueblo Creek and the Rio Lucero. The summit of Vallecito contains a depression which appears to have been scooped out by a spoon, and from this it is locally called La Cuchara, the Spoon. One asks a neighbor if he thinks there has been enough snow in the winter to provide irrigation water all summer. He points with his chin to Vallecito and answers simply, "The Spoon is full."

This view of the snowy Vallecito between and behind the Sacred Mountain and El Cuchillo throws into larger perspective not only their geographic but their psychical relationship. It is as if they are cupped within the enclosing Sangre de Cristos as the Yin-Yang symbols are circumscribed by the circle of cosmic unity. For if most local storms seem to originate from the dialogue between them, their result is a unifying snowpack which provides life-giving water for all of us, Spanish and Indian alike.

The road now winds through outlying fields and solitary adobes. For while all Indians are required to occupy their pueblo apartments during a portion of the winter—"The Time of Staying Still"—they are permitted to live out on the Reservation in their "summer homes" in order to farm their individually owned land. Their small fields of corn, squash, beans, and wheat delight the eye. They are not mathematically laid out as if by a ruler in rectangles and squares, as are those of the Anglo and Spanish. They conform to the flowing, natural boundaries of the land, its hillsides, streams and arroyos.

Through them, the road curves on its way past thickets of wild plum. In the spring, these beaches of white blossoms perfuming the air give the landscape a decidedly Chinese look that only Lao Tsu and Chuang Tsu could describe. And then—in high time, for Cry Baby is sweating—we ride into one of the most perfect architectural forms in America. The two halves of the five-storied, adobe pueblo are separated by a large open plaza through which flows Pueblo Creek. The whole was originally surrounded by a wall, battered down last century by American howitzers. It still preserves the feeling of a self-enclosed unity isolated from the encroaching influences of Spanish and Anglo invaders. It owes its allegiance only to the maternal mountain mass that rises above it, whose outline it architecturally reflects in its tiered, pyramidal form.

I loved to come here simply to enjoy its peace and the slow tenor of life. Women walking down to the creek to fill their pottery jars or tin pails with water. Men herding their horses in the corrals. Children running up with pleas for a "nickle-penny." The fragrant smell of piñon from cooking fires. There were always friends who had a pot of chile warming on the stove, an armful of hay for Cry Baby. And then, after a rest, we would ride back home.

This was the long horseback ride which Albert took each day to Arroyo Seco and back when he helped with the work on my small adobe. Often, he brought his small son Red Bird for company. Becoming bored with watching us work, the boy would beat a small drum, sing in his childish voice, and dance. Later, I depended upon Frank to help break our colt Star, to shoe our horses, and to build another room. He, too, rode horseback from the pueblo and back again after his hard day's work. The work was backbreaking labor indeed. Every adobe was of mud dug from the back pasture, mixed with water and straw, molded in wooden forms, dried in the sun, and then laid in the walls. Each huge viga or roof beam was a lofty pine felled in the mountains above, stripped of branches, and snaked down by a team of horses. Preparation of it followed Indian tradition. The tree had to be cut in the phase of the waning moon, when the sap was low. Once brought down, the trunk was carefully covered by chips of the bark stripped from it, and, thus protected from the sun, allowed to dry out gradually. Only then was it hoisted into place to support the heavy roof. Otherwise, the viga developed the long cracks often seen in those supplied by less careful Anglo building contractors.

My nearest Indian neighbor, old Juan Concha who had been a Pueblo governor for several terms, lived in a summer home scarcely a mile away. He visited me often—always at mealtimes. When entering the house, he always exclaimed, "This Indian house!" And upon this theme he launched into its history. Evidently, in previous times, the Rio Arroyo Seco had followed a course in back of my house, still marked by a shallow arroyo between the house and the barn. The stream then, as now, had been established as the boundary between Indian and Spanish land, but the Spanish had diverted the stream to flow in its present channel a hundred yards south. Hence, Old Juan called my house "La Isla," for it stood on an island, as it were, between the former and present channels of the stream. It was his contention, of course, that the land between them still rightfully belonged to the pueblo, and he prophesied that the Indians would eventually get it back.

The prospect is improbable but not impossible. At this late stage, after having enjoyed it for many years, I would be discomfitted at losing it, but would make no rumpus about it; for I have always upheld the efforts of all Indian tribes to regain the land unjustly taken from them by the federal government. And from recent developments, it seems that the Indian cause is gaining ground, literally and ideologically.

The long and obdurate flight of Taos Pueblo for restoration of the mountain wilderness around its sacred Blue Lake is a heartwarming example. I have detailed it in books, articles, and essays, but a few pertinent facts may highlight it.

In 1551, when King Charles V of Spain established claim to New Mexico as a Spanish province, he gave to Taos Pueblo a land grant of 130,000 acres. The grant was confirmed by Mexico in 1821 when she gained independence from Spain, and by the United States in 1848 when it acquired sovereignty over New Mexico. Meanwhile, much of the land had been preempted by Spanish and Anglo settlers who founded upon it the modern town of Taos, a few miles from the pueblo. Then in 1906, President Theodore Roosevelt established the Taos National Forest (now Carson National Forest), taking for it 50,000 acres of pueblo land, without compensation to the Indians. Then began the fight for restoration of their land.

In 1926, a Pueblo Lands Board found that the United States had unlawfully extinguished Indian title to the very land on which stood the modern town of Taos, and offered to pay the pueblo the 1906 valuation of the land, $297,684.67. The pueblo waived payment in consideration that it be given clear title to its sacred Blue Lake area of 50,000 acres. Instead, after a delay of seven years, a Congressional act was passed, authorizing only a fifty-year use permit to Taos Pueblo for only 32,450 acres.

Hampered by lack of funds to pay lawyers' fees, the pueblo continued its agonizing legal fight to gain complete restoration of its land. It was a stormy period during which I wrote innumerable letters for the Pueblo Council and attended meetings with its members and its friends, including Oliver La Farge and John Collier. Adverse publicity was generated on all levels. By the senior United States Senator from New Mexico, who introduced his own bill proposing that the pueblo be given only 3,150 acres. By the Forest Service, eager to appropriate and cash in on the sale of the area's virgin timber, and to open it to recreational development. And even by the Town Council of Taos itself, which supported the unfounded allegation of the editor of the town's weekly newspaper that the Indians were attempting to steal land in the public domain, thus obtaining title to the watershed, blocking off the rivers and streams and depriving the Spanish communities of water for their fields. A petition condemning this outrageous Indian theft was signed by members of all Spanish communities, including my own Arroyo Seco neighbors. My own refusal to sign was an unfavorable exception.

The mounting national controversy was highlighted by the appearance at a Congressional hearing of ninety-year-old Juan de Jesus Romero, the cacique, or religious leader, of the pueblo, who testified to the religious significance of the Blue Lake area with its many sacred shrines and sanctuaries. He was supported by other Indian tribes throughout the country, by church groups, civic organizations, and thousands of individuals, all acclaiming the constitutional right of Taos Pueblo to religious freedom and preservation of their wilderness "church." Finally, on December 15, 1970, Congress passed a bill providing that the area would be kept in wilderness status under Pueblo ownership, with the federal government acting as trustee.

We may view this Congressional action in perhaps not too exaggerated perspective as a significant victory of the Sacred Mountain and the wilderness area it imbues with its benign blue spirit. I say "blue" advisedly. For not only the sacred Blue Lake reflects its ineffable clear color. The whole region vibrates to this one section of the spectrum—the entire landscape of mountains, sagebrush, and desert; and in times past both Indian and Spanish villagers painted their doors with that shade which came to be called "Taos Blue." One notices it immediately upon climbing out of the brown rocky gorge of the Rio Grande, when all the visible world seems permeated by an invisible, mystic blue spirit. It is little wonder that Indians, Anglos, and Spanish alike have developed a mystique about the Sacred Mountain with its living blue spirit. I don't doubt its existence after experiencing it myself in this curious dream:

I was alone in my living room in the dead of winter. It was dark and bitterly cold. The electric power was off again, and my only dim light was an old coal-light lamp with a dusty, fly-specked chimney. The butane tank had not been refilled, so there was no heat from the gas stove; and there was no wood in the fireplace. I sat shivering in darkness, rubbing my cold hands together.

Then, I noticed through the front window a peculiar blue glow on the Sacred Mountain, which I first thought might be a forest fire. Getting up and walking to the window, I saw then that it was deep inside the peak, diffusing its light through the rocky cliffs and forested canyons. The glow was round in shape, vivid blue in color, and radiant with warmth. I felt immediately that it was the energy-giving blue spirit of the mountain. So I spread my cold hands, knowing that it would keep me warm. . . .

5. SILENCE

It is my habit, weather permitting, to observe a moment of meditative stillness each morning when the sun first tips the rimrock of the mountain range behind my adobe. The place for it is always the same. An unprepossessing spot on a slight rise in the waist-high sagebrush, flanked by a clump of huge gnarled junipers—cedars, as we call them. There are many more beautiful, if not more striking "scenic" spots within the half-moon curve of mountains, and I did not choose this one. It simply drew me years ago by some curious magnetism, until I have now worn a barely discernible trail to it through sage and chamisa, around clumps of piñon and cedar, and across dry arroyos.

Here I stand, sniffing the early morning breeze and spying out the vast landscape like an old coyote, as if to assure myself I am in the center flow of its invisible, magnetic currents. To the sun, and to the two oppositely polarized peaks, El Cuchillo and the Sacred Mountain, I offer my morning prayers. Then, letting the bright warming rays of the sun engulf me, I give myself up to a thoughtless silence.

One, I suppose, could call it meditation. I don't, for I'm not sure how one is supposed to meditate. Once, I attended an hour's talk on meditation given by a noted esotericist from England. He carefully explained the best hours of the day to observe it; how to choose a corner of the room; what kind of a religious painting or photograph to hang on the wall with a burning candle beneath it; the choice of the proper incense to burn; the posture to assume. By then his hour was up. I left the hall, thinking of a question that Dr. Evans-Wentz once had asked Sri Ramana Maharshi, the famous sage of India.

"Is it helpful to sit on a tiger's skin?" he asked. "Should one sit in the lotus position, or may the legs be kept straight? What posture is best?"

"All of this is unnecessary," the Maharshi answered. "Let the mind assume the right posture. That is all."

Meditation may mean prayerful contemplation to some; to others, concentration on one form or object; or to still others, the fixation of the mind on one thought in order to empty the mind of all other thoughts, often aided by controlled breathing. None of these techniques or yoga disciplines have I followed. Nor have I had a specific goal to achieve. It is enough for me, as a prelude to a busy day, to attain for a moment at sunrise a measure of unbroken silence, of profound stillness within.

It doesn't come immediately, the crisp morning is so invigorating. There isn't a cloud in the sky. The earth emerges pristinely pure, virginly naked in its beauty. The snow-tipped peaks of Jicarita and the Truchas to the south, down toward Santa Fe, rise sharply into the blue. Beyond the slit of the Rio Grande to the west, the upland desert rises to the southern thrust of the Colorado Rockies. And to the east and north, directly behind me, the Sangre de Cristos curve in their great semi-circle. From down in Arroyo Seco, a mile below, sounds the clear pealing of the church bell. Reluctant wisps of smoke rise from the adobe village. Around me, the magpies are stirring awake. How cleanly beautiful these Rocky Mountain peacocks are, with their snowy wing patches and long, blue-black tails. A chipmunk scurries out from a rock. So much to see and hear and smell, as if one had never noticed it all before! And with all these appeals to the senses, the mind like an alarm clock jangles out a discordant medley of thoughts. "Are there any eggs left for breakfast, or must I have another bowl of atole? . . ." "What became of that coyote I heard last night? . . ." "Don't forget to put air in that tire when you drive to town. . . ." The tyranny of thought. When will it ever end?

But end it does. Abruptly, without warning, just as sleep overtakes you. As if one had suddenly broken through an invisible barrier, to be becalmed in an immeasurable, profound quietude, broken only by the voice of silence itself.

Silence. One would think, as I do now, that it is incongruous to break it with these random remarks. Still, there is much to be said for it. For silence has many gradations of its own, and comparative degrees depending upon where and how we experience it. Occasionally, out-of-town guests spend a night or two in my spare bedroom, like a recent couple from New York. In the morning I casually asked the lady how she had slept.

"I couldn't sleep at all!" she replied, rushing to the coffee pot. "Not a single wink, it was so ominously quiet!"

Her remark momentarily amazed me; I thought she might be deaf. For all night long could be heard the ripple of the stream, the thin clatter of leaves in the aspen grove, the deeper rustle of the cottonwoods in every breeze. At dawn one could hear the clip-clop of a horse's hooves as the Major-Domo, the Master of the Ditch, rode by to make his daily round of inspection. The constant tinkle of a bell from Salomé Duran's flock of goats and sheep was musical and reassuring. And at sunrise bird calls and the bell of the village church ushered in the new day. Still I could understand why a woman from New York, accustomed to all the noises of city streets and the ever-present roar of the city, had not heard these sounds. She was not attuned to their spectrum in the wide range of sound.

Living here alone for so long, I still do not have a phonograph, a recording machine, a TV set. My little portable radio I turn on only for a newscast at breakfast, interrupted by wordy and singing commercials. Not until a few years ago did I have a telephone. The comparative silence, I have grown used to.

But this is only an upper layer of silence; its lower layers I experienced when I was snowed in for several days. I began to feel it in the still, warm hush that always precedes a heavy snow. It was like a blanket muffling all sound. Then as the big, soft flakes fell steadily through the late afternoon, all night, and next day, covering flields and mountains, this whole little world seemed smothered in snow and silence.

Salomé I could see occasionally clearing a path to his immense woodpile or throwing hay to his flock, but they seemed like moving figures on a movie screen not wired for sound. Occasionally, to get out, I plodded through the drifts up to the mouth of the canyon. The absence of all movement seemed to contribute to the quality of stillness, for it is movement that creates sound. The branches of pine and spruce hung motionless and heavy with snow. No birds stirred among them. No animals moved through the weighted sage, although I could see the hieroglyphic marks of their tracks—rabbit, deer, a fox or coyote. What I noticed most was the stillness of the stream that usually rippled noisily in its swift flow, booming at the waterfalls, gurgling in the trout pools, singing through the small glades. It, too, was iced over and covered with a heavy blanket of snow, moving in its subterranean course without betraying a sound of its serpentine passage.

But gradually at night, my hearing opened up to a new spectrum of sound. It was curious how faint yet how distinct these sounds were. The house had something to say. Every room spoke with its infinitesimal creaks and groans. I could tell when the cold was increasing by the faint changes in whine of the water pump. One midnight, I was awakened by a loud, sharp explosion outside. Next morning, I saw the smooth white trunk of one of the aspen trees split open in a long vertical crack. Many other aspens in the grove bore such cracks. No one knew what caused them. The most prevalent conjecture was that they had been struck by lightning—which seemed improbable, considering that there were so many. Now I thought I knew the cause; the bark had been split by the expansion of its sap frozen by extreme cold. For sap rises in trees, not in the heart of their trunks but in their bark—which is the reason one can kill a tree simply by ringing its bark.

How still it was! I could even hear a rabbit munching at the alfalfa I had spread out in the snow. A small plop of snow, whenever a half-frozen, puffed-up bird moved on a twig outside my window, was just as distinct. One dawn, I heard a faint twinkle of ice in the stream out front, so unusual I wondered what caused it. In the morning, I found tracks there at an airhole. A deer smelling water had come to drink, breaking through the rim of ice. Long before sunup I could hear the muffled sound of my two horses' feet, padded with snow, as they came up to the rail of the corral to stand waiting for their morning feeding. And when I didn't rouse out of bed promptly, their low, throaty neighing would have awakened a saint out of his contemplation. At the same time, there came a bombardment of wings and feathers on the portál, as dozens of large, crested bluejays launched themselves to the table on which I spread their breakfast of birdseed. What a racket they made! With them came, of course, the Duran's cat, crouching under the table for the opportunity of springing upon one of them. The large magpies were more wary. They waited for the suet I hung in the trees. And then came the multitudinous common people of the bird tribe, the little birds, to feed on the table leavings of the rich.

Eventually, a little boy came over to help me shovel snow off the roof, and Celestino to clear my driveway with his tractor and blade. Next day, the road was cleared and I drove into town. Seeing people and hearing sounds and voices suddenly made me realize the quality of silence I had experienced, a quality not measured by the few days of its duration.

Could it be that silence expresses itself visually as well as audibly, having the same gradations as the color spectrum? The silence of a forested mountain often seems dark blue or violet, while that of the desert at high noon takes on the quality of yellow. These colors may be imaginatively evoked, of course, by the predominant colors of their landscapes. White silence is the most profound; but curiously enough, its evocation is not restricted to a snowy mountain valley, for example. It may be felt among brilliantly colored surroundings and in the darkness of the night. Its complete absence of sound, its deep profundity, seems confirmed by the fact that white is the composite of all colors in the spectrum.

Many years ago, a Buddhist friend of mine from Bombay, India, Dr. Sakhârâm Ganesh Pandit, gave me a bit of advice just before I was inducted into the army at the outbreak of the Second World War. He recommended that whenever I was emotionally upset I remain absolutely quiet until I could hear the constant ringing in my ears. This advice I have tried to follow. Whenever I was called to speak to a large audience—a chore for which I am temperamentally unfit, which I have always dreaded, and which made me extremely nervous—I stood silent at the podium until I could hear the deep sound in my ears. This practice I have passed on to other speakers, to singers and the like, who have found it helpful.

And so it is this deep silence, this white silence, that I experience during my moment of meditative stillness in the sagebrush at sunrise. All the sensual morning sounds seem to merge into one sound, the steady ringing in my own ears which merges into the steady hum of silence itself, the voice of the living land, or perhaps the sound of the moving universe itself. Quien sabe? I myself have never questioned it.

It seems odd that Western science, in breaking the so-called sound barrier with fast jet planes and exploring the perimeters of outer space with manned capsules propelled by rockets, has never investigated the unknown element of silence. Perhaps because it has never remained still enough to listen to the ringing in its own ears. Eastern religious-philosophy on the contrary, which we envisage in the image of a "naked fakir" perpetually sitting still, has reported many properties it possesses.

The Hindu sage Sri Ramana Maharshi asserts that mouna, silence, is eternal speech. It is achieved by meditation without mental activity, and practiced by most sages. "How does speech arise?" he asks us. There is unmanifest abstract knowledge. From it rises the ego, which gives rise to thoughts and then to words. Words are therefore the great-grandson of the original source. If they can produce an effect, how much more powerful can the effect be through silence? Take preaching for an example. Compare a man haranguing a crowd for an hour without effect with one who sits silently sending forth intuitive forces to play upon the world to its great benefit.

If this is true, we must question the word-conscious premise of Western civilization with its ever-mounting flood of books, magazines, and newspapers, its unremitting barrage of wordy radio and TV commercials. To a bar of soap they impute emotional properties, and project on it our physical desires, sexual imagery. And our diplomatic gobbledygook seems dedicated to expanding our foreign markets for it. Benjamin Lee Whorf, formerly regarded as a great linguist but who is now out of fashion, pointed out that our manner of thinking depends on the language we use, the shaper of our ideas. We are not only saying what we are; we are what we are saying.

If I have not been wholly receptive to these wordy harangues, I have been more susceptible to the silent exhortations of the spirits of the living land. Our communion with these nonverbal spirits is achieved in that strange element of silence in which our inner selves are as much at home as our outer selves in the world of multitudinous sound. For in it, the human spirit discovers its own identity and its kinship with the spirits of distant stars.

CHAPTER 15

Flight from Fiesta (1986)

Toward the end of his long life, Herman Melville consolidated his great themes, and his intense wonderment at the universe, into the marvelously distilled novella, *Billy Budd*. *Flight from Fiesta* is Frank Waters's "Billy Budd." A willful young white girl, Elsie, whose upbringing has taught her how to get what she wants without fail, but nothing about what happiness might look like, has run away from home, commandeering the accompaniment of an old Pueblo Indian, Inocencio. Inocencio has problems of his own, but he accepts this strange assignment stoically, and then finds himself drawn into unexpected but seemingly inevitable complications, including the killing of a Navajo man who had attacked Elsie, and then a chase by the police. It would be hard to imagine two companions more unlike, but they stick together, increasingly bound in a strange, compelling polarity.

➤➤

All afternoon the old murderer and the delinquent child had been rolling steadily eastward in the Apache's creaking wagon. The team of broomtails, small and scrawny as they looked, was tough and tireless; they maintained a slow trot that kept the traces taut.

The Apache sat tall on the plank seat in a black sateen shirt and his new black hat whose high, round crown, not yet creased, stuck up like a length of stovepipe. Inocencio sat beside him, soft and shapeless in his faded red blanket. Behind in the empty wagon box jolted Elsie. Each time the wagon clattered down the slope of a rocky arroyo she clutched at the sideboards. When it leveled off again, she lay flat on a worn Navajo blanket to escape the dust. Her little bottom was sore, her thin back ached. She was hungry, tired and thirsty. The men in front never spoke nor looked back, and she suffered without complaint.

Sometime in the afternoon she dropped off to sleep. Awakening, she looked out with an anticipation that immediately changed to childish disappointment. The wagon seemed not to have moved at all. As far as she could see, the sunlit plain spread out empty and illimitable as before. There were the same deep arroyos slashed through the sage. The same red-rock buttes weirdly carved by wind and weather into lofty pinnacles and spires, great cathedrals, ships and sea shells. Far behind her two flat-topped mesas still rose pale lilac on the horizon. This was Indian Country. But where were they? A solitary horseman crossing a wash a mile away. A woman forlornly shepherding a tiny flock of sheep. That was all.

The little girl in her cowboy suit lay down again on her back to escape the dust and played with the toy pistol in her holster. Tiring of this, she folded her hands on her breast and lay staring up at the changing shapes of the white clouds gathering in the turquoise sky. "Now would be a good time to chew some bubble gum if I had any," she said aloud. "My mother isn't here." Neither of the Indians on the front seat spoke. The wagon kept moving on.

Late that afternoon the sweating broomtails puffed up the gradual slope of the foothills. The road forked: two wheel tracks continuing on, two more turning north. The Apache pulled up his team.

Inocencio clambered down from his seat. "We gettin' out," he said.

Elsie climbed out stiffly. The Apache slapped out his reins. As the team swung north, he flung up one arm in silent farewell. In a few minutes the wagon vanished over the rise.

"Where's he going, Inocencio?" the girl asked.

"Him Jicarilla."

"What's that?"

"Jicarilla Apache. This country belongin' to them Navajos."

Elsie looked around her with dismay. "But it looks all the same. I don't see any fences."

The old Indian strode off with his blanket roll without answering. The little girl trudged behind. Still the low hills sparsely covered with sage and piñon kept spreading out into an immense and rugged heartland that seemed to have no end at all. Scrambling to keep up with his long legs, the girl cried out, "Are we lost, Inocencio?"

"Not lost," he called back. "We gettin' there."

An hour later he lowered his roll and stopped to let her rest. Elsie dropped to the ground, taking off her new boots so she could wriggle her bare, tired feet in the sand.

Inocencio waited patiently. Then he shouldered his blanket roll again. "We goin' now."

"But where, Inocencio?" the girl cried plaintively.

"Indian pueblo," he said shortly.

Envisioning a hot dinner and a comfortable bed with people like Pilar and Inocencio's old mother, Elsie scrambled to her feet and tucked her boots under one arm. They straggled on.

The sun was setting in a mass of darkening storm clouds when they reached the top of a low ridge and looked down into a desolate valley cut by a dry arroyo and flanked on one side by a wall of cliffs. There was no sign of life: no house, no man nor bird nor beast, not even a tree. There loomed only the spectral shape of a vast pile of crumbling masonry.

Tired, hungry, lonely and a little frightened, Elsie cried out in disappointment. "You said we were going to an Indian pueblo!"

"Cómo no? This Indian pueblo. Long time lots of peoples." He took her hand, and limping in her bare feet beside him, the girl trudged down toward the ruins.

Slowly it took shape before them under the scudding clouds: an immense walled city semi-circular in shape, its back wall once four stories high; a gigantic single building containing hundreds of rooms in the terraces surrounding its inner court.

"Muy grande! Qué bonito!" Inocencio said in a subdued voice, oppressed with veneration for the Old Ones.

"I don't think there's anything pretty about it!" said Elsie. "It's all fallen down! I'll bet nobody's lived here for a dozen years!"

"Long time," agreed Inocencio somberly.

Long before Marco Polo had journeyed to the court of Kublai Khan, five hundred years before Columbus had sailed to this old New World, it had stood here swarming with people at the crossroads of an ancient civilization. Looming out of the dark, prehistoric past, it still stood here, the first great building and the first great city in America, a metropolis deep in the desert heartland of a yet unknown continent. The storms of ten centuries had crumbled its walls, yet above it still hovered the dark wings of its high destiny.

Elsie shivered in the wan light. "It's kind of spooky, isn't it?"

The storm clouds were piling up now and the wind was whipping dust down the wash. Inocencio found some protection in a corner of two high walls; lowering his blanket roll, he went off to hunt for wood. Elsie wrapped up in one of the blankets, imitating him as she flipped it over her shoulders. She huddled down against the wall, idly trying to pry out one of the stones. The stones of Westminster Abbey had not yet been hewn when the stones in this strange old wall had been smoothed and set like mosaic, so perfectly fitted that they still held tight without mortar. Inocencio came back, built a fire, and put on meat and coffee.

Elsie watched him with a thoughtful face. Finally she asked, "Why did that man back there want to hurt me? I never did anything to him."

Inocencio stirred the fire without answering.

In a little while she asked haltingly, "Is he—he's dead, isn't he, Inocencio?"

"He dead."

The little girl shivered. "It's going to rain. I felt a drop right on my head. There's not even a roof on this old place."

Inocencio calmly turned over the meat.

Once again the girl broke out with a troubled question. "It isn't right, is it, Inocencio? Killing somebody, I mean."

"No good. Policemens don't like it."

"Well . . ."

The old Indian turned and looked at her with a dark and fathomless face. "I do it! What I has to do! I don't say nothin' more!" It was the voice of a man who had done what he had done and abided by it without regrets or excuses.

Elsie, however, still struggled childishly to link the past with the future. "Does that mean we can't EVER go home again? That I'll NEVER see my mother again?" Pathetically huddling against the wall from the drops of rain, she looked little like the arrogant child who had boasted proudly she would never go home. "But what will we do, Inocencio?"

Inocencio spoke firmly like a man who had long learned to live only in the existing moment. "We doin' what we do when we has to do it!" He got to his knees, lifted up the dripping mutton ribs. "Good meat! We eat him now!"

It was dark now, and they ate quickly under the spatter of raindrops. Inocencio stowed away his gear, slung the roll over his shoulder, and picked up a brand from the fire for a torch. Tripping over her dragging blanket, Elsie followed him into the dark, deserted city.

How weird it all was now—this vast honeycomb of empty cells through which she stumbled, following the flare of Inocencio's torch. He turned a corner far ahead of her and she was left in sudden, pitch blackness. Frantically trying to keep up, she tripped and fell headlong. She could not see his torch when she scrambled to her feet, but off to one side she glimpsed a length of wall lit by its pinkish flare. Across it moved the shadow of a cloaked monster. Soon there was another, smaller one running after it. They kept winding through a labyrinth of narrow passageways. Zaguans, plazas and rooms periodically outlined by flashes of sheet lightning.

The sky was suddenly rent by a jagged whiplash of fire. An instant later came the sharp crack of thunder followed by a roar reverberating with an ominous rumble. It was as if the gates of the storm had been cracked open—through them rushed a torrent of stinging rain. Inocencio stopped. Elsie had caught up with him and was jerking at the tail of his blanket.

"It rainin'," he said, looking down at her.

Elsie, too frightened to speak, pointed off to her right.

Inocencio raised his torch higher. From an open stretch of plaza protruded the top of a ladder. They walked toward it and stopped. Then testing its rungs, Inocencio slowly climbed down, followed by Elsie.

They found themselves now in a circular, subterranean room that looked to the girl at first glimpse like the inside of a big well. The hard-beaten earth floor was dry. The top—except for the ladder opening—was covered with logs and dirt. Inocencio, holding up the torch, was staring at the walls. They were covered with layers of colored pigment peeling away, each revealing queer symbols and figures of dancing men, birds and feathers painted in rich, faded colors.

"This old well's dry and it's got a roof," said Elsie, huddling down with relief.

"No well. It kiva."

Obviously it was one of the ancient, ceremonial kivas unearthed and partially restored by the archeological party mentioned by the trader back at the post. Inocencio remained standing with one hand on the ladder, uneasy and anxious to climb back out of the sacred ceremonial chamber of the Old Ones.

"Mebbe go somewheres else," he said uneasily.

"Not me. I'm staying here where it's dry."

Elsie remained staring at the trickle of water coming through the roof opening and listening to the lash of the storm overhead. Reluctantly, Inocencio propped up his torch in the ancient fire-pit and unwrapped the blanket roll. Elsie took one of the dry blankets and wrapped it around her in imitation of Inocencio as he squatted down.

"What's a kiva?" she asked.

Inocencio looked at her with a curious expression on his dark, wrinkled face. It was the seed-pattern of the whole multiworld universe itself. In the floor at the girl's feet was a little hole: the sipapu, leading down into the first underworld, the Place of Beginning whence came man. The floor level, circular as the earth when glimpsed from a midpoint, was the second world into which man emerged. Around the wall still stood remnants of a seating ledge, representing the third world which opened through the roof to the fourth world of man's successive existences. Overhead stretched the great hand-hewn viga or roof-beam; the Beam-Above-the-Earth, the immortal Galaxy in the sky above, leading toward the world existences yet to come. Through them all, from the fire-pit to the altar place, ran mankind's Road of Life upon which centuries ago men had danced here the ceremonial recapitulation of their long evolutionary journey . . . And yet if the kiva was the symbol of the macrocosmic vastness of the universe, it also symbolized the microcosmic womb in which man had developed. For to these men of a new race on a new and unknown continent, the whole universe was contained within the Mother of Creation, within man himself . . . Inocencio and the wordless forefathers of his race had no way nor need to explain all this. They had only to look about them here to see the architectural form of their vast cosmological universe; and to know that it was duplicated within their own bodies, each a fleshly kiva, a living universe, as the psychical soul form of all creation. It was all here, form and faith, expressed simply as an abstract and archetypal symbol.

"I said what's a kiva?" Elsie repeated in a petulant voice.

"It Indian church."

"But it doesn't look like a church to me!" persisted the child.

"White people's church stick up in sky pointin' at White people's Heaven. Indian church go down deep in belly of Our Mother Earth. We no forget she borns us. She give us ever'thing good we got!"

The old Indian's voice was curt. He drew his blanket up over his face. Plainly he did not want to talk about such matters.

Elsie sat staring at the mural designs in the flickering flare of the torch. The queer-looking men reminded her of the masked dancers she had seen in the plaza of the pueblo. There were lots of birds, too. All in a soft, muted patina. But so strange, everything.

"Well, anyway, it's got some pretty pictures." She twisted her head around to follow a queer figure that ran like a motif around the room. "What's that funny snake with wings on like a bird? There isn't any such thing!"

"You keepin' quiet!" warned Inocencio darkly. "Him got the power of the earth and the sky, too. Long time the Old Ones paint him on them big rocks at home. Pilar put him on her potteries, too. He got the power all right. Awanyu. That his name. You be polite!"

The torch was beginning to burn out. Its red flare barely lighted their faces. Both that of the child and the old Indian showed that they were deeply conscious in their own ways of the other-dimensional functions for which this ancient, sacred chamber was built. The rain kept trickling down the pole ladder.

Elsie, like any inquisitive child, could not forbear asking forthrightly, "But I saw you kneeling in church that morning, Inocencio. You say your prayers, too. I thought you believed in God, not idols."

The old Indian looked annoyed. This matter of why he believed in the power of Awanyu, and of God, too, was too complex for his simple mind. "It everywhere, in earth and sky and trees and rocks—everything. White peoples think they close him up in church like jail."

The torch suddenly burned out, leaving them in darkness. Still, a moment later, Elsie's voice sounded again. "But Inocencio . . ."

"No!" The old Indian's voice was stubborn. "I not talkin' about them things! I sleepin'!"

Above them, like the disembodied kachina forces of generations of storms, the wind and the rain prowled through the ruins of the ancient city.

BOOKS BY FRANK WATERS

Fever Pitch. New York: Liveright, 1930. (Rpt. as *The Lizard Woman.* Austin: Thorp Springs Press, 1984, and Athens: Swallow Press/Ohio University Press, 1995.)

The Wild Earth's Nobility. New York: Liveright, 1935.

Below Grass Roots. New York: Liveright, 1937.

Midas of the Rockies: The Story of Stratton and Cripple Creek. New York: Covici-Friede, 1937. (3d ed. 1972, rpt. Athens: Swallow Press/Ohio University Press, 1989.)

The Dust within the Rock. New York: Liveright, 1940.

People of the Valley. New York: Farrar and Rinehart, 1941. (Rpt. Athens: Swallow Press/Ohio University Press, 1984.)

The Man Who Killed the Deer. New York: Farrar and Rinehart, 1942. (Rpt. Athens: Swallow Press/Ohio University Press, 1989.)

River Lady (with Houston Branch). New York: Farrar and Rinehart, 1942.

The Colorado. The Rivers of America series, ed. Hervey Allen and Carl Carmer. New York: Farrar and Rinehart, 1946. (Rpt. Athens: Swallow Press/Ohio University Press, 1984.)

The Yogi of Cockroach Court. New York: Rinehart, 1947. (Rpt. Chicago: Swallow Press, 1972.)

Diamond Head (with Houston Branch). New York: Farrar and Rinehart, 1948.

Masked Gods: Navaho and Pueblo Ceremonialism. Albuquerque: University of New Mexico Press, 1950. (Rpt. Athens: Swallow Press/Ohio University Press, 1984.)

The Earp Brothers of Tombstone. New York: Clarkson Potter, 1960.

Book of the Hopi. New York: Viking, 1963. (Rpt. New York: Ballantine, 1969.)

Engineering Space Exploration: Robert Gilruth. Chicago: Encyclopedia Britannica Press, 1963.

Leon Gaspard. Flagstaff: Northland Press, 1964.

The Woman at Otowi Crossing. Denver: Swallow Press, 1966. (Rpt. [Rev. Ed.] Athens: Swallow Press/Ohio University Press, 1987, 1998.)

Pumpkin Seed Point: Being within the Hopi. Chicago: Swallow Press, 1969, 1973.

Pike's Peak: A Mining Saga. Chicago: Swallow Press, 1971. [Note: Waters usually used an apostrophe in his home mountain's name, departing from standard atlas practice.]

Conversations with Frank Waters. Ed. John R. Milton. Chicago: Swallow Press, 1971.

To Possess the Land: A Biography of Arthur Rochford Manby. Chicago: Swallow Press, 1973.

Mexico Mystique: The Coming Sixth World of Consciousness. Chicago: Swallow Press, 1975.

Mountain Dialogues. Athens: Swallow Press/Ohio University Press, 1981, 1999.

[Edited, with Charles L. Adams] *Cuchama and Sacred Mountains,* by

W. Y. Evans-Wentz. Athens: Swallow Press/Ohio University Press, 1981.

Flight from Fiesta. Santa Fe: The Rydal Press, 1986. (Rpt. Athens: Swallow Press/Ohio University Press, 1987.)

Brave Are My People: Indian Heroes Not Forgotten. Santa Fe: Clear Light, 1993. (Rpt. Athens: Swallow Press/Ohio University Press, 1998.)

Of Time and Change: A Memoir. Denver: MacMurray and Beck, 1998.

Note: The above list, limited to original publications and currently available reprints, is far from comprehensive. See the entries for Tanner, Terence A. and Luther, T. N. under Further Reading.

FURTHER READING

Adams, Charles L., ed. *Frank Waters: A Retrospective Anthology.* Athens: Swallow Press/Ohio University Press, 1985.
Well-chosen selections, introduced by knowledgeable commentary. Adams is one of the leading Waters scholars, and editor of the important series, Studies in Frank Waters (Las Vegas, Nev.: The Frank Waters Society).

Blackburn, Alexander. *A Sunrise Brighter Still: The Visionary Novels of Frank Waters.* Athens: Swallow Press/Ohio University Press, 1991.
A penetrating analysis, combining scholarship and apperception. Blackburn deals originally with Waters's major fiction.

Deloria, Vine, Jr., ed. *Frank Waters, Man and Mystic.* Athens: Swallow Press/Ohio University Press, 1993.
A gathering of tributes, studious readings, and memoirs, creating a many-sided view. Included are essays by Rudolfo Anaya, Alvin Josephy, and Larry Evers, among other writers. Barbara Waters's "The Final Task" offers a most interesting, close-up, Jungian analysis.

Luther, T. N. *Collecting Taos Authors.* Albuquerque: New Mexico Book League, 1993.
A good overall survey of Waters's work, updating Tanner's bibliography. Includes commentary on Waters's literary standing as reflected in the demand for first editions.

Tanner, Terence A. *Frank Waters: A Bibliography*. Glenwood, Il.:
  Meyerbooks, 1983.
  A thorough compilation that includes several letters to and
  from Waters. Indispensable for perspective on both the composition and editing of several of Waters's books.

Waters, Barbara. *Celebrating the Coyote*. Denver: MacMurray and Beck,
  1999.
  As close to Frank Waters as we are likely to come. Anyone
  interested in Waters, or more generally in the process of grief
  and retrospect, should consult this no-holds-barred book by
  his widow.